Jenny twisted in her seat and studied the pavilion anxiously, half-expecting a swarm of people to suddenly emerge from it and charge them down, hell-bent on pulling them out of the car and ripping their throats out.

My God, doesn't this feel just like that ... Like one of those crazy zombie movies?

This whole situation was like some post-apocalyptic scenario; the glimmering firelight from the bonfire, the debris and detritus strewn across the tarmac, the flickering torchlight and the frantically scrabbling crowd inside the building, the noise, the chaos.

Paul drove across the car-park towards the exit leading on to the slip-road that led out to the motorway and headed south once more.

She watched the service station in the wing mirror until it disappeared from view.

My God, this is how it is after only four days.

Alex Scarrow lives a nomadic existence with his wife Frances and his son Jacob, their current home being Norwich. He spent the first 10 years out of college in the music industry chasing record deals and the next 12 years in the computer games business. His previous novel – *A Thousand Suns* – is also available from Orion paperbacks. Visit his website at www.scarrow.co.uk.

By Alex Scarrow

A Thousand Suns
Last Light

LAST LIGHT

Alex Scarrow

An Orion paperback

First published in Great Britain in 2007
by Orion
This paperback edition published in 2008
by Orion Books Ltd,
Orion House, 5 Upper Saint Martin's Lane
London WC2H 9EA

An Hachette Livre UK company

1 3 5 7 9 10 8 6 4 2

A CIP catalogue record for this book
is available from the British Library.

ISBN 978-0-7528-9327-3

Typeset by Deltatype Ltd,
Birkenhead, Merseyside

Printed and bound in Great Britain by
Mackays of Chatham plc, Chatham, Kent

www.orionbooks.co.uk

For my son Jacob, smart, imaginative …
and maybe one day, competition. I love you man.

For Jacob's eyes only:
VQ BMJJN RJXB GR ZWB BDWCB RNBADC
FADNSRMPR
OQXL CGN JRMP NO RWZTDUZWC

Acknowledgements

There's a small list of people that deserve a mention for the help they gave me in putting together this book. There's no particular order in which I want to do this, so I'll dive right on in.

Robin Carter for extensive proofing and valuable comments. Yes … his name does appear in the book as you, dear reader, will soon see. Obviously for legal reasons, I need to say something about this being utterly coincidental and any resemblance … blah, blah, blah. A damn good character name that. I also want to thank Andy Canty for his proof reading and comments as well, and again … that's another Christian name that has turned up in the book! Funny old world.

My thanks also go out to someone I can't name for security reasons, who gave me some useful 'on the streets' details of life in Iraq. He knows I'm thanking him anonymously like this, and that's how it needs to be.

I want to thank my wife, Frances, for reading the first draft. I must extend my apologies for making her cry with the second draft. Her comments were many and varied; you'll never truly know how valuable her feedback is. Dad, Tony, and brother, Simon, thanks you two for your encouragement. Additional thanks go to Jerry Stutters for some background military details.

Finally, a thank you to my editor, Jon Wood, and agent, Eugenie Furniss, for working with me on this and helping me to finesse the story and take it up to the next level.

December 1999

Room 204

She stared at the door of room 204.

Like every other door along the corridor, it was a rich dark wood with the room number and handle in gold plate.

A *bloody* expensive hotel, that's what Dad had said.

'*Enjoy it guys … we'll probably never stay in another as expensive as this one.*'

He'd made a joke to Mum about sneaking out the bathrobes and selling them at some place called 'eee-bay'.

The corridor was silent; leaving the lift her footsteps were hushed by the thick carpet – not even the muted noise of quiet conversations or a TV on low, coming from any of the rooms, the doors were so thick and heavy.

Now it was decision time … and she *knew* this would happen on the way up from the foyer, where she'd left Mum waiting impatiently. She knew she was going to forget the number in the lift going up – way too busy thinking about what she was going to buy with the spends Dad had given her for the trip.

204? It is 204 isn't it? … Or was it 202?

Leona wondered if Dad's business was all done now, or if he was still waiting for his mystery visitor. He'd been a little nervous and jumpy when he had shoo-ed her and Mum out to go window-shopping; snappy, tense, just like Leona remembered being on her first day at big school earlier that year.

Nervous – *exactly* like that.

Mum was pretty sure he must have finished his meeting by now. Since he'd bundled them out a couple of hours ago, they'd both visited a big department store glistening with Christmas displays, and grabbed a coffee and a Danish in a bustling coffee shop that overlooked the busy streets surrounding Times Square. And Dad had assured them his *very important* business meeting would be over quickly.

Leona hoped maybe he would be able to join them; to come back down with her now that the 'work' part of their family trip to New York was over. It wasn't the same without him. But either way she *really* needed to pick up that beanie-bag of hers with all her spends in. There were just too many things she'd seen in the last two hours that she desperately *needed* to buy.

She decided it was room 204 they were staying in, not 202, after all. She placed her hand on the old-fashioned brass door-handle. She noticed a flicker of light through the keyhole beneath.

Dad nervously pacing the room? Or maybe his meeting had started already? She was about to hunker down and spy through the keyhole to be sure she wasn't going to interrupt his business, but her grasp of the door-handle was heavy enough that, with a click, the latch disengaged and the door swung in heavily.

The three men stared at her, their conversation frozen in time. They stood at the end of the emperor-sized bed; three men, old men, very smart men, looking down at her. She noticed a fourth, younger, dark-haired man standing to one side, a deferential distance away from the others. He broke the moment, starting to move swiftly towards her, his hand reaching into a pocket.

'No,' whispered one of the three. That stopped him dead, although his hand remained inside his smart jacket.

The one who spoke turned towards Leona, stooping down slightly. 'I think you've come into the wrong room my dear,' he said, his voice pleasant and disarming, like a doting grandfather.

He smiled warmly at her, 'I think your room is next door.'

'I'm really s-sorry,' Leona replied awkwardly, taking a contrite step backwards out of the room and into the corridor, pulling the door after her.

*

The door closed gently with a click of the latch and there was a long silence before one of the two older men who had remained silent, turned to the others.

'She saw all three of us. We were seen together.'

A pause.

'Is this going to pose a problem?'

'Don't worry. She doesn't know who we are. She doesn't know why we're here.'

'Our anonymity is everything … as it has always been, since—'

'She's a little girl. A few years from now, the only thing she'll remember will be whatever she got for Christmas and the Millennium Eve fireworks. Not three boring old men in a room.'

The Present

Monday

CHAPTER 1

8.05 a.m. GMT

BBC, Shepherd's Bush, London

'He's lost some weight,' said Cameron.

'Really? I think he's put some on.'

Cameron studied the monitors lined above the mixing desk. On them, Sean Tillman and his co-anchor, Nanette Madeley, were exchanging a few improvised witticisms between items.

'No, you can see it in Sean's face. It's less jowly.'

His assistant producer, Sally, wrinkled her nose in judgement. 'I don't think he's lost any weight. Do you suppose he's feeling threatened by the younger news team over on Sky?'

'Christ, yes. Can't blame him though,' Cameron replied. 'Let's be honest, if you've just woken up and you're channel-hopping first thing in the morning, whose face would you want yapping the news at you? Flabby old Sean Tillman, or someone who looks like Robbie Williams' younger, sexier brother?'

'Hmmm, tough call,' said Sally casting a casual glance across to their news-feed screen.

The domestic feed, a horizontal news text bar, was scrolling some dull story on a farmers' dispute in Norfolk whilst the Reuters' feed was streaming results on an election in Indonesia. Pretty uninteresting stuff all round.

Cameron cast a glance up at the monitor to see Sean Tillman checking himself in a small hand-mirror. 'I know Sean's also worried about the *chin* factor.'

Sally snorted with amusement.

'Yuh, that's what he calls it. He's really pissed off about the studio floor being re-covered last month with a lighter linoleum.

I heard him having a good old moan to Karl in make-up that the floor's deflecting the studio lights. That he's getting lit from underneath.'

Cameron leant forward and studied the monitor, watching both Sean and Nanette preparing for the hand-back from Diarmid. 'He's got a point though. He's really coming off worse there. Nanette actually looks better, more radiant since they changed the—'

'Cameron,' muttered Sally.

'—floor covering. Poor Sean though. It sort of makes the flesh under his chin glow. And there is a fair bit of it wobbling away under his—'

'Cam!' Sally said, this time more insistently.

'What?'

She pointed to the Reuters' news feed.

As the words scrolled slowly across the display bar, he read them one after the other, gradually making sense of the text he was reading.

'Shit!' he said, turning to Sally. 'We're going to need a whole bunch of graphics. This is going to hog the news all day.'

'It's not *that* big a deal, is it?'

'You're kidding me, right?'

Sally shrugged. 'Another bomb. I mean we get a dozen of those every day in Ira—?'

'But it's *not* Iraq, is it?' Cameron snapped at her. She flinched at the tone of his voice, and despite the sensation of growing urgency and the first prickling of a migraine, he felt she deserved a word or two more from him. 'Trust me, this story's going to grow very quickly, and we don't want to be left chasing it. Let's get ahead of the game and get all the assets we're going to need. Okay?'

Sally nodded. 'Sure, I'll get on to it.'

'Thanks,' he muttered as he watched her disappear out of the control room. He shot another glance at the Reuters' feed, more detail on the story was already coming in.

There were a couple of other control-room staff in there with him and they stared silently at him, waiting for orders. Normally he fed his input through Sally to them. But with her gone and chasing down the things they were going to need, it was just them.

'Okay Tim, patch me through to Sean and Nanette. I suppose I'd better let them in on this.'

CHAPTER 2

8.19 a.m. GMT

Shepherd's Bush, London

Jennifer Sutherland hopped awkwardly across the cold tiles of the kitchen floor, whilst she struggled to zip up the back of her skirt and tame her hair with the straighteners, all at the same time. Too many things to do, too few hands, too little time. That bloody little travel alarm clock had let her down again.

Jenny checked her watch; she had ten minutes until the cab was due; time enough for a gulped coffee. She slapped the kettle's switch on.

Today, if all things went well, was going to be the beginning of a new chapter; the beginning of a *brand new* chapter to follow the last one, a long and heartachingly sad one – twenty years long. She had a train to catch from Euston station taking her up to Manchester, and an interview for a job she dearly wanted; needed, in fact.

So this was it.

If they offered her the job, she could be on her way out of what had become a painful mess for her and Andy. This whole situation was hurting him a lot more than it was her. She was the one who was leaving and she knew when the dust settled, and both his and her parents performed a post-mortem on this marriage, the blame would fall squarely on her shoulders.

'*Jenny got bored of him. She put herself before their kids, put herself before Andy.*'

And the rest …

'*You know she had an affair, don't you? A little fling at work.*

He found out, and he forgave her, and this is how she repays him.'

The kettle boiled and she reached into the cupboard above it pulling out the last mug. The rest were packed away in one of the many cardboard boxes littered throughout the house, each box marked either with 'Jenny' or 'Andy'. Jennifer had been busy over the last week, since Andy had gone off on his latest job, sorting out two decades of stuff into *his* and *hers* piles.

The house was now on the market, something they both agreed they might as well get on and do now that they were going to go their separate ways. Living together under the same roof, after both tearfully conceding it was all over, had been horrible: passing each other wordlessly in the hallway, waiting for the other to leave a room before feeling comfortable enough to enter it, cooking meals for one and then eating alone.

Not a lot of fun.

Dr Andy Sutherland, the geeky geology student from New Zealand she had met twenty years ago, who had loved The Smiths and The Cure, who could quote from virtually every original episode of *Star Trek*, who could do a brilliant Ben Elton impersonation, whom she had once loved, whom she had married at just nineteen years of age; that same Andy had somehow become an awkward and unwanted stranger in her life.

She tipped in a spoon of decaf granules and poured some boiling water into her mug.

But it wasn't all her fault. Andy was partly to blame.

His work, his work ... always his bloody work.

Only it wasn't *work*, as such, was it? It was something else. It was an obsession he'd fallen into, an obsession that had begun with the report he'd been contracted to write, the special one he couldn't talk about, the big earner that had bought this house and paid for a lot more besides. And of course, the rather nice family trip to New York to hand it over in person. He'd earned a lot of money for that, but ultimately, it had cost them their marriage.

The walls of his study were filled with diagrams, charts, geological maps. He had become one-dimensional over that damned fixation of his. It had eroded the funny, complex, charming person that he had once been, and now it seemed that anything that he could be bothered to say to her, in some oblique way, linked back to this self-destructive, doom-laden fascination of his with the end of the world.

And she remembered, it had all started with a report he'd been commissioned to write.

When he'd first stumbled upon ... *it* ... and breathlessly talked her through it – what they should do to prepare, should it happen – she had been terrified and so worried for their children. They had taken a long hard look at their urban lifestyle and realised they'd be thoroughly screwed, just like everyone else, if they didn't prepare. In the early days they had looked together for remote properties hidden away in acres of woodland or tucked away in the valleys of Wales. He had even nearly talked her into moving to New Zealand; anything to get away from the centres of population, anything to get away from people. But, inevitably, life – earning a crust, paying the bills, getting the kids into the *right* school – all those things had got in the way. For Jenny, the spectre of this impending disaster had faded after a while.

For Andy, it had grown like a tumour.

Jenny gulped her coffee as she finished fighting with her coarse tawny hair and turned the straighteners off.

Sod it. Good enough for now. She could do her make-up on the train.

The interview was at one o'clock. She was surprised at the shudder of nerves she felt at the prospect of sitting before a couple of strangers and selling herself to them in just a few hours' time. If they gave that job to her she would have to pull Jacob out of his prep school; the very same school she had fought hard to get him into in the first place. Jake would be going up north to Manchester with her. Leona on the other hand, had just started at the University of East Anglia; home for her was a campus now, as it would be for another two years.

Jenny hated the fact that she was being instrumental in breaking her family up, but she couldn't go on like this with Andy.

She was going to make a new home for herself and Jake, and there would always be a bed for Leona – wherever it was that Jenny eventually found for them to live.

The worst task lay ahead of course. Neither of the kids knew how far things had gone, and that she and Andy had made the decision to go their separate ways. Leona perhaps had an inkling of what was on the cards, but for young Jake, only seven, whose focus was on much more important matters such as his next major Yu-Gi-Oh deck-trade, this was going to be coming right out of nowhere.

Outside she heard a car horn, the taxi. She drained the rest of the coffee and grabbed her handbag, heading out into the hallway. She opened the front door, but then hesitated, looking back inside the house as the taxi waited outside.

Although she planned to be back in a couple of days to begin tidying up all the ends that were left for now flapping loosely, it felt like she was walking out for the last time; it felt like this was the moment that she was actually saying goodbye to their family home.

And goodbye to Andy.

CHAPTER 3

8.31 a.m. GMT

University of East Anglia (UEA), Norwich

Leona stirred, slowly waking by inches. And then still half-asleep, she remembered who was sharing her bed. She shuddered with a smug, secret pleasure, as if she were holding a million pound prize-winning lottery ticket but had yet to tell anyone.

Danny moved sleepily in the bed next to her. She sat up and looked down at him. He was breathing evenly and deeply, still very much lost in the land of slumber, a content half-smile spread across his lips.

Daniel Boynan.

He looked even more lovely with his eyes closed, his lips pursed, and not pulling any stupid faces to make her laugh. Totally angelic. His mop of dark hair was piled around him on the pillow, and his dark eyebrows momentarily knit as his mind randomly skipped through a dream. Leona had spotted him on the first day, registration day, queuing like her to get his Student Union card and his campus ID.

Donnie Darko, she thought. That's who he had reminded her of.

And throughout most of the first term Leona had pursued him, discreetly of course. Never appearing too interested, though, just enough that he got the message, eventually.

God, boys can be so flippin' blind – he hadn't noticed Leona had been eyeing him up for the last eight weeks.

And then it sort of happened last night. What should have been Step Five of her Ten Step Plan to conquer the heart of Dan

Boynan, had turned into a rapid tiptoe through Six, Seven, Eight, Nine …

And Step Ten had been just about perfect.

She watched him breathe easily, and pushed a lock of hair away from his porcelain face. Here he was, Daniel, gorgeous normally – doubly-so asleep. A brass ankh pendant, dangled down from his neck, the fine leather thong draped over his collar-bone, the small looped cross nestled in a hollow at the base of his throat. That's what she liked about him – with any other lad, that would have been a big chunk of *bling* on a thick silver chain.

Outside her room, she could hear the others stirring in the kitchen. The dinky little portable TV was on, and she could hear the tinkle of spoons on mugs as someone was making a brew.

Beside her, the radio alarm clock switched on quietly and she heard the nattering, way-too-cheerful voice of Larry Ferdinand bantering with one of his studio sidekicks. Leona smiled, Mum listened to him too. If you asked Mum, she would swear blind that it was *her* who turned on to him first, and then got Leona listening to him, which was, of course, rubbish.

She turned the volume down slightly, not wanting Daniel to be woken up, well, not yet anyway, and then slid gently out of bed. She picked up Daniel's burgundy coloured FCUK hoodie, discarded by the side of the bed, and slipped it on. It was so big on her, it hung down almost to her knees.

Daniel said he loved her Kiwi accent. Leona didn't think she had even a trace of Dad's clipped vowels. For the most part she thought she sounded like everyone else: same ol' Home Counties' blandness. But there you go.

It was odd though, it's not like she had been particularly close to Dad, not for the last four or five years, anyway. In fact, she hardly ever saw him. He was always either off on some contract abroad, or distracted with some freelance work in his study. But perhaps from earlier years, when he'd had the time for her and Mum and Jake, that's where the faint echo of his New Zealand accent had been picked up.

Still who cares, Danny loves it. Bonus.

On the radio she heard Larry Ferdinand hand over to the newsreader.

Daniel stirred in his sleep, mumbling something that sounded like 'take my other d-d-dog …'

He had the slightest stutter, just very slight. Leona found it charming. It made him seem just a little vulnerable, and when he was cracking a joke, somehow that little hitch in his delivery seemed to make the punch line that much more amusing.

She smiled as she looked down at him. *Love* seemed too strong a word right now – way too early to be throwing around a word like that. But she certainly felt she was more than just *in lust* with him. And sure as hell she wasn't going to let Daniel in on that little secret.

Play it cool, Lee.

Yup, that was what she was going to do, especially after she had let him get his cookies last night.

'… now this could mean a very serious shortfall in oil supplies …'

Leona cocked her head and listened to the faint voice coming from the radio.

'… if the situation is allowed to get much worse. As it is, it's early days, and it's unclear exactly what has happened over there. But this much is certain: it will have an immediate knock-on effect on oil prices …'

She sighed. Oil … terrorists … bombs – that's all news seemed to be these days; angry mobs, guns being fired into the sky, faces full of hatred. The news reminded her of the tired old doom 'n' gloom Dad tended to spout after a glass or two of red wine.

'*It'll happen quickly when it happens … one thing after another, going down like dominoes. And no one will be ready for it, not even us, and Christ, we're in the minority that know about it …*'

Shit. Dad could be really wearing when he got going on his pet hobby-horse; rattling on about stuff like Hubbert's Peak, petro-dollars, hydrocarbon footprints ... it was his special party piece, the thing he talked about when he couldn't think of anything else interesting to say. Which, to be honest, was most of the time. God, he just wouldn't shut up about it when he got going, especially when he thought he had an interested audience.

Leona reached over and snapped the radio off.

She knew Mum was getting to the point where she'd had enough, to put it bluntly; she wondered if Mum was getting bored of Dad. She could feel something brewing at home, there was an atmosphere. Leona was just glad to be away at uni, and glad her little brother, Jacob, was at his prep school. It gave her parents some room and an opportunity to sort out whatever they needed to sort out.

She padded lightly across the floor of her room, stepping over the trail of clothes both she and Daniel had shed behind them as they'd worked their way briskly from first base to last, the night before.

She opened the door of her room and headed into the kitchen where a pile of pots, plates and pans encrusted with beans and ravioli were waiting in vain to be washed up, and a couple of her campus floor-mates were watching *Big Brother Live* through a haze of cigarette smoke on the TV nestled in the space above the fridge.

CHAPTER 4

11.44 a.m. local time

Pump station IT-1B

Ninety-five miles north-east of Al-Bayji, Iraq

Andy Sutherland reached into the back seat of the Toyota Land Cruiser and grabbed hold of a large bottle of water. It had been sitting in the sun back there, and although he had pulled it out of the freezer that morning a solid bottle-shaped block of ice, it was now almost as hot as a freshly brewed cup of tea. He gulped a few mouthfuls and then poured a little across his face, washing away the dust and the mild salt-sting of his own sweat.

He turned around to look at Farid, standing a few feet away from him.

'You want some?'

Farid smiled and nodded, 'Thank you.'

He held out the bottle to him and then shot another glance at the burned-out remains of pump station IT-1B.

There was nothing worth salvaging, just a shell of breeze blocks and twisted piping that would need to be pulled down before a replacement could be built. IT-1B, along with three other sibling stations, serviced the north-south pipeline leading to Turkey. The whole thing, pipeline, connection nodes, pretty much everything, was screwed-up beyond belief in so many places.

Utterly fubar.

Farid handed the bottle of water back. Andy noticed the old man had only taken a small amount of water, just a few sips.

'Have some more if you want,' he said, miming washing his face. After all, the old translator was just as covered with dust and dried-on sweat as anyone else.

Farid shook his head. 'Not know when you will need the water only for drink,' he replied in the weak, cracked, high-pitched voice of an elderly man. His command of English was pretty good, better than the last translator, who had just decided to vanish without warning a few days ago.

'Okay,' Andy nodded. That was a fair point. Finding regular clean water was still an ongoing concern for many Iraqis. Water scarcity was what they had grown accustomed to over the last few years.

Parked up nearby, in a rough approximation of a defensive laager, was another Land Cruiser, used by the other civilian contractors, and three modified Nissan pick-up trucks manned by a dozen men from the Iraqi Police Service, who were warily scanning the irregular horizon of building carcasses around them.

The caution was well placed; the militia had been this way only a few days ago – not to destroy the pumping station, that was old damage – but instead to make an example of some of the men at the local police station. Four men had been taken from outside the police building the day before yesterday, friends and colleagues of the men standing guard. Their bodies had yet to be discovered, but undoubtedly right now, they were lying out in the afternoon sun at some roadside waiting to be found.

According to Farid, for now, they were relatively safe. The militia had been, done their work and moved on. They'd be back again of course, but not for a while. There were so many other places that needed their special attention.

Andy picked up his hat; a well-worn, sun-bleached turquoise fishing cap, that he wouldn't dare don in public back in England, but over here it cast merciful shade over his head, face and neck. His pale scalp, inadequately protected by a sandy-coloured mop of hair, was beginning to burn as he pulled on his cap and tugged it firmly down.

He wandered across the densely packed, sun-baked clay ground towards the other engineers surveying the remains of IT-1B. He approached the engineer he had shared the Land Cruiser with on the way up, a big, round-shouldered American with a dense black beard called Mike. He reminded Andy of a bigger, less cuddlier version of Bob Hoskins.

'It's totally fucked,' Mike offered analytically as Andy drew up beside him.

Andy nodded. 'I don't see anyone getting much out of the Kirkuk fields until this mess is sorted out.'

Mike shrugged. 'That isn't going to happen for a while.'

Too true.

As they all well knew, it really didn't take much to trash an overland pipeline; hundreds of miles of thin metal casing riding across the ground. It only took one small improvised explosive device placed anywhere along its length, and that would be a done deal until the damage could be repaired. In a country like Iraq, you could forget about using overland pipelines, especially up here in the Salah Ad Din region where every single mile of pipeline would need to be guarded day-in, day-out. Of course it had been a different story thirty or forty years ago when most of the pipelines were laid down. Iraq had been an ordered, prosperous country back then.

'Who're you working for?' asked Mike.

'A small risk assessment consultancy in the UK. But it's Chevroil-Exxo who's paying them. What about you?'

'I'm freelancing for Texana-Amocon.'

Andy smiled. They all seemed to be hyphenated now, the oil companies. It was a sign of the times; struggling companies merging their dwindling reserves, all of them desperately consolidating their assets for the end-game.

'They want to know how long it's going to be before we can get something out of this damned country,' the American added. 'I mean, what the hell do you tell them?'

Andy half-smiled and cast a glance at the darkened shell of the building in front of them.

'Not for years.'

Mike nodded. 'It's sure looking that way. So,' he turned to look at Andy, 'we haven't done full names yet. I'm Mike Kenrick.'

They'd spoken only briefly this morning as the convoy of vehicles had taken several hours picking their way north-east along the road out of Al-Hadithah. They had talked about the crappy hotel they were both staying in, a dark maze of cold empty rooms, tall ceilings sprouting loose electrical cables, and sporadic power and running water.

'Dr Sutherland, call me Andy though,' he replied offering the American a hand.

'So Andy, where you from anyway?'

'Originally a Kiwi. But I guess home is England now. I've been living there on and off for nineteen years,' replied Andy. 'It doesn't much feel like a home right now,' he added as an afterthought.

'Problems?'

'Yeah … problems.'

The American seemed to understand that Andy wasn't in the mood to elaborate. 'Shit, this kind of job does that,' he added gruffly after a moment's reflection. 'Time away from home can bust up even the strongest of marriages.'

'What about you?'

'Austin, Texas.'

Andy fleetingly recalled seeing this bloke strutting around the hotel the day before yesterday wearing his 'Nobody Fucks with Texas' T-shirt and some white Y-fronts.

Nice.

There were two other civilian contractors currently poking through the remains of the building and photographing it with digital camcorders. Andy had seen them around the compound, but not spoken to them yet. One was Dutch or French, the other Ukrainian, or so he'd been told. They had kept themselves to themselves, as had Andy.

In fact, the only person he'd really spoken to since coming out earlier this week was Farid, their new translator. The four-man field party had been assigned a translator along with the two Toyota Land Cruisers and the two drivers. They didn't get to choose them or vet them, they just inherited them.

'You been out here before?' asked Mike.

'Yeah, a couple of times, but down south – Majnun, Halfaya. Different story down there.'

The American nodded. 'But that's changing as well.'

They heard a disturbance coming from one of the Iraqi police trucks. Andy turned to look. One of the policemen was talking on his cell phone, and then turning to the others, relaying something to them. The others initially looked sceptical, but then within a moment, there were half-a-dozen raised voices, all speaking at the same time. The policeman on the phone quickly raised his hand to hush them, and they quietened down.

Andy turned to Farid and beckoned him over.

'What's all that about?' asked Mike.

'I find out,' the translator replied and went directly over to the policemen to inquire. Andy watched the older man as he spoke calmly to them, and in turn listened to the policeman holding the mobile phone. And then Farid said something, gesturing towards the driver's cabin. One of the policemen rapped his knuckles loudly on the roof and shouted something to the man dozing inside. He lurched in his seat and craned his neck out the driver-side, presumably to ask who the fuck had woken him up.

The guy holding the mobile phone repeated what he'd heard, Farid contributed something, and the driver's expression changed. He pulled back inside, reached to the dashboard and flipped on the radio. There was music which he quickly spun away from, through a wall of crackles and bad signals, finally landing on a clear station and the sound of an authoritative voice; a newsreader.

'Something's happened,' muttered Andy.

The policemen were all silent now, as was Farid. All of them listening intently to the radio. Then out of the blue the American's Immarsat satellite phone bleeped. Mike jumped a little and looked at Andy, one of his dark eyebrows arched in surprise as he opened up the little hip-case it came in. He walked a few steps away to answer it privately.

Andy instinctively checked to see if his mobile phone was on – it was, but no one was calling him.

Andy, growing impatient, caught Farid's eye and spread out his palms, *what's going on?*

The translator nodded and held up a finger, asking him to wait a moment longer, as he craned his neck to listen to the news crackling out of the radio.

He turned back to Mike, who was frowning as he listened to what he was being told over his phone.

'For fuck's sake, what is it?' asked Andy, exasperated that he seemed to be the only person left in the dark.

A moment later, Farid stepped away from the police truck and wandered over to Andy, his face a puzzle … as if he was trying to work out exactly what he'd just heard.

'Farid?'

Mike snapped the case on his Sat phone shut just as the Iraqi translator came to a halt before them. The American and the Arab looked at each other for a moment.

Andy cracked. 'Is somebody going to tell me what the fuck's going on?'

CHAPTER 5

8.45 a.m. GMT

He took off from JFK at just after ten at night. Not a popular time to take a flight so there were plenty of seats in business class. He had checked in effortlessly using his Mr Ash identity. The passport paperwork was good, impeccable. It always was.

Ash.

A good enough name for this particular errand. It was fun anyway, assuming a stolen identity, trying to imagine what the real *Mr G. J. Ash* was like, to get a feel for the person who had lived in this particular skin for the last thirty-seven years. Not that it mattered greatly.

For the duration of this task, *he* was Mr Ash, no one else was, not even the real Mr G. J. Ash, whose identity had been temporarily cloned for the job. *Ash* was the name he imprinted on himself in his mind. Until this job was done, *Ash* was the only name he'd answer to.

There was a sense of urgency to this job. Time was going to work against him this time round. Things were going to start happening very soon, if they hadn't already. When law and order began to unravel, and it would do so rapidly, it would get theoretically very difficult for him to find his given target. So he was going to have to work as quickly as possible.

Ash looked out of the window at the grey Atlantic below.

Leona Sutherland. Eighteen. Occupation: student. Current residence: University of East Anglia campus.

He had no problem with this target. She was a girl, just a child still. But far more important than that, she was a security risk. A very big risk, certainly right now, with what was going on.

Quickly in and quickly out.

He'd make sure she died quickly and painlessly, he could at least do that; after all it wasn't her fault she was a security risk. Leona Sutherland had made a simple mistake, adding a 'PS' to an email, that's all – half-a-dozen words tagged on to a chatty email to her father … words it seemed, she hadn't set out to write but had popped into her head at the last moment.

Unfortunately, those few words were going to be her death sentence.

Ash sighed.

How careless people are with what they say, blurting out things – intentionally, unintentionally – that are best left unsaid. He often thought most of the pain and death and misery in the world was caused by people unable to keep inside them what should rightly stay there.

This wasn't going to be his finest hour though, killing an innocent child, but it was necessary. It was a lesser evil for a greater good.

He was clearing up a few loose ends which to be honest, he should have been allowed to do years ago. Those foolish old men had let the little girl walk out of that hotel room alive.

That's why they needed people like him; to tidy up after them.

CHAPTER 6

12.35 p.m. GMT
Manchester

Jenny stepped out of the swing-doors on to Deansgate and took a deep, deep breath.

'I've got it!' she whispered to herself, clutching her hand into a fist and discreetly punching the air when she was sure no one was looking.

The interview had been so much easier than she expected it would be. She had made them laugh a couple of times, everyone's body language seemed to be relaxed and open. Jenny felt she had been on to a winning ticket from the moment she walked into the interview room. It was just one of those things, they all *clicked.*

The give-away, or so she felt, was towards the end when one of the lads asked her how much notice she would need to serve out with her current employer.

'I've got it,' she muttered to herself again, as she walked down Deansgate towards a café bar she'd spotted on the way to the interview.

Of course they couldn't say to her 'you've got it'. There were several more applicants they had to see that afternoon. It would be improper, unprofessional even, to do that. But in every other way – how they had said goodbye, the way they shook hands, nodded and made eye-contact screamed to her *we'll be in touch.*

She grinned in a way she hadn't for a long time. It felt like one giant leap away from the mess in London. There was much to do of course, and the very first thing on the list would be sorting Jake out. Her poor little boy was going to be bewildered by all of this, but once they got settled in Manchester, Jenny was going to spoil him rotten for a bit. Make a real fuss of him. And most importantly, get him into various activity groups and clubs. She knew he liked those little Games Workshop characters. He spent ages painting them and then playing with them. Well, they had one of those shops up here, and they did Saturday and Sunday clubs which she'd take him along to, positive that he'd make a few friends there in no time at all.

Jenny arrived outside the café bar, pulled the door open and stepped inside.

She ordered a hot chocolate with a small mountain of cream – the type Andy referred to as shaving foam – and a Danish pastry and went and picked a seat in the window. The combined plate and mug count was probably close to a thousand calories, but stuff it, she'd played a blinder back there, and put one in the back of the net, so to speak.

She deserved a 'well done' present from herself.

She sat down at a window seat, her mind still running through the mental tick-list of things she needed to do. In the background a TV behind the counter babbled away to itself.

'... spreading chaos over there. News has just come in that senior members of the Saudi royal family have been flown out from the King Khalid International airport in Riyadh. Although no official confirmation has been given on this, it's clear that unrest has spread to the capital and there was a perceived threat to them ...'

She'd have to give them a month's notice down in London. But then Jenny knew they owed her a couple of weeks' leave, so she could work out two of those weeks, and take the last two off. Andy would have to take charge of selling the house though. Mind you, there's not a lot he'd have to do, just make sure he was around to let in the estate agent.

'... it's clear now that the rapid escalation of events in Saudi Arabia was triggered this morning by the bombing of the Sunni holy mosques in Mecca and Medina. Although nobody has come forward claiming responsibility for the bomb, Shi'a Muslims and mosques across the country have been targeted by the majority Sunnis and Wahhabis in what appears to be the beginning of a very bloody and dangerous civil war in the country …'

And there's all that furniture, the bric-à-brac of twenty years to get rid of. Jenny really didn't want to cart all of that stuff up with her. They could probably shift a lot of it on eBay, or maybe try something like a garage sale. She drew the line though at taking herself down to a whole load of car-boot sales as a vendor; their stuff was worth more than the penny prices they could expect to get.

'… on Wall Street this morning, share prices took a major tumble as oil prices rocketed to over $100 a barrel. There are some murmurings that the worsening Saudi situation will trigger what is known in some obscure corners of the oil and gas industry as an artificial Peak Oil scenario …'

Jenny turned towards the TV.

The phrase cut through her meandering this-and-that planning, like a hot knife through butter.

'Peak Oil'.

That was one of Andy's pet phrases; a pair of words that had become conjoined together like Siamese twins in their household. It was a phrase that she had grown utterly sick of hearing over the last few years. And now on the TV, on daytime news, for the first time, she'd heard *someone else* use that term. The words sounded odd and a little disconcerting coming from someone other than Andy. But not just some fellow petro-geologist, or some other frothy-mouthed conspiracy-nut that Andy had struck up a relationship with courtesy of his website; no … a newsreader, on the BBC, on the lunchtime news had used the phrase.

The barman behind the counter finished serving a customer, picked up the remote control and deftly flicked through a few channels before settling on one showing a football match; Manchester City versus someone or other.

Jenny almost called out for him to turn it back. She looked

around, half expecting several other customers to join her in calling out for the news to be put back on, but none of the little packs of students, nor any of the other customers hurrying in for a hasty lunch-break sandwich, had taken any notice of the news. Everyone seemed too busy to care.

Just like her, too busy with the minutiae of life: earning a crust, paying the bills, getting the kids off to school … getting a new job.

Her mind went back to the news. Someone else, other than Andy, had just muttered the phrase 'Peak Oil'.

All of a sudden, the sense of euphoria she'd felt walking out of that interview began to evaporate.

CHAPTER 7

3.37 p.m. local time

Desert, Salah Ad Din Region, Iraq

'Where the hell are they going?' yelled Mike.

The Iraqi police vehicle ahead of them had suddenly lurched to the right off the bumpy road heading south-west back to Al-Bayji.

Andy watched the vehicle rattle away across the rough terrain and then on to a small tributary road. The other two police trucks followed suit, pulling out of their convoy and heading off after the lead truck, away from them.

'Shit. What do we do? Do we follow them?' asked Mike.

Andy shrugged, 'I don't know, that's taking us in the wrong direction.' He watched the three vehicles recede amidst a plume of dust.

'They have other business,' Farid offered from the front seat. The old man pointed to the radio recessed into the dashboard, 'Al-Tariq, the radio station, say Sunni–Shi'a unrest in Saudi has spreading over here. They have much explosions, a lot of fighting in Baghdad.'

Mike looked at Andy, 'That's just great.'

Farid frowned uncertainly, not getting the irony. 'The police now go and fight for their side,' he added.

'Sunnis?'

The old man nodded.

Andy bit his lip and took a deep breath. They were dangerously exposed now. With no escort they were going to be a very tempting soft target. There was, of course, their driver, a young man called Amal, and in the other Land Cruiser there was another driver called Salim. Both drivers had on them AK47 assault rifles. How prepared they were to use them in a stand-up fight, he wasn't so sure. The truth was he couldn't expect Farid, Amal or Salim to lay down their lives to protect him or the other three westerners. Shit, if the roles were reversed and they came across an American patrol looking for some likely looking ragheads to play around with, it's not like he, Mike and the other two contractors would level those same guns at the Americans to protect them.

They just had to hope the road back into town was open, and everyone with a gun and a chip on his shoulder would be too busy laying into each other to worry about jacking them.

He looked out of the window at the passing scrub and dusty ground, the occasional cluster of date palm trees, and wondered just what was going on this morning. Mike said his phone call had been from his head office in Austin, Texas, to tell him what they were hearing from Reuters; that all hell had broken loose in Saudi Arabia after some mosques had been blown up, with hundreds killed. That country was ripe for this; a tinderbox waiting to go up. Understandably, with the situation so volatile in Iraq, things were predictably going to flare up in sympathy, and the same was probably going to happen in other vulnerable Arabic nations: Kuwait, United Arab Emirates, Oman.

Andy could imagine the focus of world news right now was on events in Riyadh as they unfolded hour by hour, and he guessed that experts on Arabic culture and Islamic affairs were being rushed into television studios across the globe to pontificate on what was going on. But he wondered who was taking a look at the bigger picture.

As of this morning, with the troubles rapidly destabilising Saudi Arabia, the world had just lost the regular supply of somewhere between a quarter and a third of its daily oil needs.

He reached into a pocket and pulled out his mobile.

'Who're you calling?' asked Mike.

'I'm phoning home,' Andy replied, flipping it open and hitting the quick-dial button. There was a long pause before he finally heard a flat tone. 'Shit, can't get a signal.'

'It's hit and miss, some cells work better than others,' said Mike. 'We're on the move, so try again in a minute.'

Farid turned round in his seat to talk to them. 'Maybe bad driving into Al-Bayji. Riots, fighting.'

'Shit, well what else do you suggest we do?' snapped Mike. 'We can't stay out here.'

Andy looked up. 'I think we could skirt the town, and head on for K-2. It's another hour or so.'

K-2 was an airstrip extensively upgraded by the Americans and a pivotal supply and extraction point for forces deployed in the north of the country.

'You want to leave Iraq?' asked Mike.

'Yeah, I want to leave Iraq. I see this getting a lot worse.'

Andy tried the home number again, and this time he got a tone. Several rings later he got their answerphone, his own voice coming back at him. 'Shit.'

Do I try her mobile?

She was likely to hang up on him. He wanted the kids back at home, not at school or university, and he wanted Jenny to go down to their local Tesco and buy up enough food and water for a few weeks.

Christ, am I being paranoid?

Maybe. But then if he was over-reacting, so what? It's only food, it would get eaten, eventually. But right now he suspected Jenny would just tell him to piss off, and that she wasn't going to mess the kids around just because he was having some sort of panic attack.

Or maybe she would just be more concerned about him, being over here whilst this was all kicking off. Not thinking for one moment that what was happening in Saudi Arabia would have the slightest effect on her cosy life in Shepherd's Bush, London.

He tried Jenny's number anyway, and got a 'this phone may be switched off' message.

'No luck?' asked Mike.

'Nope.'

Andy wondered whether he should just bypass her for now. He could see this getting a lot worse. If he was right about things, they were going to know about it in two, three or maybe four days. That's how quickly he suspected the impact of a sudden oil strangulation would be felt. Even now he suspected emergency oil conservation measures were being discussed in Downing Street, and would be announced by the Prime Minister sometime before the end of the day. And when that happened, the penny would drop for everyone else and all hell would break loose.

Sod Jenny.

Andy called the only other mobile number he had on quick-dial.

CHAPTER 8

12.38 p.m. GMT

UEA, Norwich

Leona was walking out of the lecture theatre and heading towards the student union bar across a courtyard busy with students criss-crossing it to use the various on-campus shops, when the phone trembled in her breast pocket.

She reached in and pulled it out, expecting it to be Daniel wondering where the hell she was. Things had overrun somewhat, which was fine with her. She didn't want to turn up before him, or worse still, exactly on time. Leona was still firmly in the let's-appear-to-be-cool-about-things phase.

She quickly read the display to see who was calling her. At first glance the number was unfamiliar, but she answered anyway.

'Yuh?'

'Leona? It's Dad.'

'Dad!' she replied, the pitch of her voice shooting up with surprise.

He rarely called her. If it was a call from home, it was Mum, and Dad might pick up the other handset and say 'hi', ask how things were going, and if she needed anything. But that was it. Mum was the one who got all the gory details. She wondered if something bad had happened to her.

'Is Mum okay?'

'What? Oh yeah, she's fine.'

The signal was awful, crackling and dropping.

'Are you okay Dad?' she asked.

There was a momentary delay suggesting the call was from abroad.

'Yeah, yeah I'm fine, love.'

'Are you still out of the country?' she asked.

'Yeah, I'm still over here. I'm coming back very soon though.'

'Oh, okay. Cool. So is that why you rang?'

'No. Listen Leona, did you watch the news this morning?'

'No, not really.'

'There are serious problems over here. There was a bomb in Saudi—'

'Oh yeah, I heard about that on the radio. Riots or something.'

A pause, or maybe it was the signal dropping, it was hard to tell.

'I'm worried about this, Leona. I think it's going to affect everyone.'

Oh not this. Not the big oil lecture. Why now?

'Dad, look, if it was serious there'd be an announcement on the campus of some sort. Don't worry about us,' she replied with a weary sigh. Then it occurred to her that *he* might be in some danger. 'How are things over there for you?'

'I'm okay right now. But I'm planning to get a plane out tonight if I can, honey. I think it's going to get very nasty here. But listen, this is really important, Leona.'

She reached the student union bar and pulled the door open. Inside she could see Daniel sitting in a window seat, watching for her. He waved.

'Dad, I've got to go.'

'No! Listen. Leona …?'

She halted, nodded at Daniel and put a finger up to indicate she'd be with him in a minute. And then let the door swing to, shutting out the noise coming from inside.

'What is it?'

'Where's Mum?'

'She said something about going up to Manchester for something … to visit some friends, I think. She's up there until the end of the week.'

Leona heard him curse under his breath.

'Listen sweetheart, I'd like you to go home to London, right now.'

'What?'

'I'd like you to pick up Jake from his school, go to the supermarket and spend as much as you can on food, water and—'

'Dad! I can't do that!'

'Leona … I'm asking you!' he replied, his voice beginning to develop *that* tone; the one that ultimately led to a bollocking if you pushed him hard enough.

'No, you can't ask me to do that. I can't bail out of uni before the end of term—'

He surprised her when his voice softened, 'Please, Leona. I know you're all fed up hearing about crap like this. I'm not stupid. I know I've bored you with all those oil things. But I think this situation is going to get bad enough that you need to be prepared for it. I have to know you're all okay.'

'We're fine! Okay? We're absolutely fine.'

'Leona, you know I'm not go—'

The call disconnected suddenly and left her with the soft purr of a dial tone. She pulled the phone away from her ear and looked down at it as if it was some kind of alien life form.

My God, that was strange. Really strange.

She waited a moment for the phone to tremble again, and after hanging on patiently for a minute, she tucked it away into her jacket pocket, pulled the door open and entered the bar. Daniel was still sitting in his seat, same posture, but with a quizzical look on his face.

As she sat down beside him she said, 'Don't ask. It was my dad being really weird.'

'What's wrong with him?'

'Oh God, it would take too long.'

He smiled and shrugged. 'Fair enough. What do you want?'

'Half a lager.'

Daniel got up and squeezed past her, placing a hand on her thigh and pinching gently – a little gesture that he was thinking about last night – and then wandered over to the bar.

But her mind was elsewhere. On the call from Dad, and also on those short soundbites she'd heard on the radio that morning, only what … four or five hours ago? Surely things hadn't changed that much in such a short time.

CHAPTER 9

6.42 p.m. local time

Road leading to Al-Bayji, Iraq

'I don't know for sure. They look like ours.'

Andy squinted at the line of vehicles in the weakening light of the early evening. They were motionless, none of them with their lights on. The only light was a muted, flickering torch coming from beneath the bonnet of the front vehicle. They looked like Land Rovers to him, at least the silhouettes did.

'British,' muttered Farid.

'Brits?' echoed Mike. 'Yeah, probably. Those definitely aren't Hummers.'

Andy watched as the torchlight flickered around, catching the movement of several men standing outside the front vehicle.

So why are they sitting around like that, lights off?

'Bloody suspicious,' Andy offered after a while.

'What? Like us?'

As the light had begun to fail, they had elected to drive on with the lights of their two vehicles off. With the police escort's sudden departure earlier in the day, they had felt dangerously exposed, and as the shadows of the late afternoon had lengthened and given way to twilight, they had decided not to advertise their presence any more than they had to.

The engine of their Land Cruiser idled with a steady rumble as Andy took a couple of steps away from the open door and studied the short column of vehicles, three – four hundred yards away.

Mike climbed out and followed him. 'You know, if we can see them—'

'They can see us. I know.'

And we're sitting here with our lights off.

Andy found himself hoping they were British, and not a trigger-happy US patrol. Over the last year, it had been the American troops that had policed the worst of the growing chaos the Iraqi government still refused to call a 'civil war'. There were a lot of battle-weary and frightened young US ground troops out there carrying some very powerful weapons and ready to fire at any vehicle that moved, especially at night, especially if its lights were off.

'I think you're right,' said Mike, clearly guessing what Andy was thinking. He nodded towards them, 'I know our boys are pretty strung out right now, and liable to loose off first, and apologise after. Maybe we should stick our lights on and hope they're British.'

Andy nodded. 'Yeah.' He turned to Farid. 'Let's put 'em on.'

And hope for the best.

Farid nodded silently, and spoke in whispered Arabic to Amal. A moment later their headlights flicked on and cast twin fans of light along the pitted tarmac road towards the parked convoy of vehicles.

Immediately Andy could see they were army vehicles. Not American, not the fledgling Iraqi army, but were, as they suspected, British troops.

They watched as a section was issued a barked order, and began to approach them warily in two flanking groups of four – spreading out as they closed the distance, their weapons raised and aimed.

Andy cupped his hands and called out, 'We're civilian contractors!'

A reply came out of the gloom from one of them. 'Don't bloody care! Everyone out of the vehicles where we can see you!'

Andy turned to nod at Farid, Amal and to the second car where the other two contractors had already begun to climb out.

He wanted to assure their old translator that the worst of the day was over and they were now safe. But watching the eight young lads approach, caught in the glare of their headlights, meeting their eyes along the barrels of their weapons and through their weapon sights, Andy wondered how much trigger weight was already being applied to their SA80s.

'That's it. Outside, all of you!' one of them shouted.

Andy kept his eyes on the nearest of the soldiers. The lad closed the last few yards alone, whilst the rest of his section held their position in a spread-out semi-circle. The young soldier – a lance corporal, Andy noticed by the chevron and scrawled name and rank on the front of his combat body armour – lowered his gun slightly, and after a moment spent silently studying them, offered a relieved grin.

'Sorry about that gents, we've had one fucking shit day today.'

'It's gone absolutely bloody crazy out there,' said Lieutenant Robin Carter shaking his head. 'I woke up this morning ready for another *normal* day in this place, and ... well, since then things have gone a bit haywire.'

Erich, the French contractor, spoke for the first time today with heavily accented English. 'What is going on?'

Lieutenant Carter looked surprised. 'You don't know?'

'We heard a little about some bombs in Saudi, and some riots,' added Mike.

'Oh boy, are there riots. It started with bombs in Mecca, Medina and Riyadh this morning. Someone blew up the Ka'bah, or at least detonated somewhere near it. If you wanted to start a holy war, that's the way to do it. It's spread right across Saudi Arabia, a full-scale civil war; Wahhabis, Sunnis and Shi'as. And it's spreading like bloody bird flu. There are riots in Kuwait, Oman, the Emirates.'

'All this over one bombing?' asked Mike.

Carter shook his head. 'The Holy Mosque in Mecca? You couldn't pick a worse place in the world to target. It's the centre of the Muslim universe. It seems like some radical group of Shi'as immediately announced they were behind it.' The officer shook his head. 'If you want to trigger a global Sunni versus Shi'a civil war ... I guess that's how you'd go about doing it. From what I've heard, Riyadh is a slaughterhouse, Saudi's a mess, there are explosions, pitched battles, riots everywhere, and it's spreading like wildfire right across the Middle East.'

Andy nodded. This was one of the things he'd written about eight years ago, in that report. A brief chapter on how easily religious sensibilities could be used as a tool to destabilise the region; a small act of leverage ... damaging or destroying somewhere sacred, like the Holy Mosque, the Ka'bah, yielding maximum impact – civil war.

'Jesus,' muttered Mike.

'Yup. And of course Iraq was one of the first countries to get into the spirit of things. It's seriously screwed up out here,' the lieutenant replied. 'There have been multiple contacts going on all day in virtually every town and city. The Iraqi police and the army are joining in the bloodletting, of course. God knows how many casualties we've had in the battalion. Our boys have been caught out all over the place.'

Andy nodded towards the Rover at the head of the six-vehicle convoy. 'You got a problem?'

Carter nodded. 'Yup. It's looking like we've got a sheared drive-shaft.' The officer cast a glance out at the flat arid plain, dotted with the darker shapes of date palms, clustered in twos and threes. 'We put out a call a few hours ago for a vehicle recovery team to pick us up. No bloody sign of it yet.' He looked at Andy. 'To be honest, I don't think they'll send out a recce-mech tonight. Not into the shit that's going on out there.'

Lieutenant Robin Carter looked to be in his mid-twenties.

Christ, he's only half-a-dozen years older than Leona.

'Take a look over there.' The Lieutenant pointed to the horizon in a south-westerly direction. The sky, finally robbed of the last afterglow of the sun, was showing the faintest orange-red stain.

'Al-Bayji. I guess there's some buildings on fire over there.

I'm sure the locals right now are tearing into each other. Our boys are all hunkered down in battalion HQ, the other side of the Tigris. The only way to us by road is via the bridge at Al-Bayji. So I'm guessing nobody's coming out for us tonight.'

Mike looked at Andy. 'Great.'

'You're staying out here tonight?' Andy asked. He studied the officer, biting his bottom lip for a moment, weighing up God knows how many factors.

'That Rover's going nowhere without a lift. And frankly, I don't fancy driving through Al-Bayji, or any other town, this evening. I think we'll be better holding up here until first light, and then make a go of it in the early hours. Hopefully things will have died down by then, and we can sneak back home whilst they're all fast asleep.'

'Do you mind if we hook up with you?' asked Mike. 'Our goddamned IPS escort bailed on us.'

'You'd be stupid not to.' Lieutenant Carter offered a lopsided grin. 'Anyway, the more pairs of eyes and hands the better.' He cast a glance at Farid and the two young Iraqis. 'Do I need to spend men watching them?'

Andy shook his head. He didn't think so. After all, they had stayed on course when the police had decided to casually break off and abandon them. But the gesture was lost in the gloom. It was Mike who answered aloud.

'You probably want to relieve them of their guns, Lieutenant. They're carrying AKs in the drivers' compartments.'

Carter considered that for a moment and then nodded. 'Yes, maybe that's a prudent measure, for now.'

Andy turned round to look at Farid, who shook his head almost imperceptibly, before turning to the two young drivers and explaining to them in Arabic that they were going to have to surrender their weapons.

Lieutenant Carter summoned over a lance corporal and instructed him to retrieve the assault rifles from the drivers of the two Land Cruisers.

Andy studied the reactions of the three Iraqis. The drivers, both much younger men, answered Farid in an animated, yet wary tone. Clearly they were unhappy at having to hand over their guns, casting frequent and anxious glances at the British soldiers gathered at the roadside beside the stationary convoy of vehicles. Farid carried an expression of caution in his manner, speaking softly, seemingly offering them some kind of reassurance.

'All right,' said Lieutenant Carter, clearing his throat and raising his voice for the benefit of the platoon as well as the four internationals before him, 'let's pull these Rovers round into a defensive circle – those two Cruisers as well. Sergeant Bolton?'

A hoarse voice – with a northern accent Andy couldn't quite place – barked a reply out of the darkness.

'Sir?'

'See to that will you? Post some men to stand watch and establish a vehicle control point down the road. Everyone else can stand down and get some rest. We'll be moving out again at 05.00. There's another two hours' drive ahead of us. We should get back to battalion HQ just in time to catch the first trays of scrambled egg.'

None of the men laughed, Andy noticed.

He's new to these men. He sensed the jury was still out amongst Carter's platoon.

CHAPTER 10

9.21 p.m. local time

Road leading to Al-Bayji, Iraq

Andy squeezed the last of the meal around in its flexible foil pouch. After a dozen or so mouthfuls of tepid chicken and mushroom pasta he decided his hunger had been more than sated. In the same way of the all-too-common roadside burger van, the smell of the field rations stewing in boiling water over their small hexamine field stoves had been about a hundred times more appetising than the actual taste.

In the dark interior of their Land Cruiser, Andy, Mike and the French engineer, Erich, ate in silence; the only noise the rustling of their foil food pouches. Outside, the full moon cast a worryingly bright light down on the quiet road and the surrounding flat terrain. In the last three hours they had seen no more than a dozen vehicles pass by. Each one had been stopped by the hastily established vehicle control point, and then waved on after a cursory inspection by flashlight. All of the vehicles passing were heavily laden with possessions and people on the move, presumably away from the growing unrest in the larger towns. Out here, with only the moon and the stars and the gentle hiss of a light breeze for company, Andy conceded you could be excused for thinking it was a quiet and uneventful night for all of the country. Except for the distant and disturbing orange glow of Al-Bayji on the horizon, you could think that.

From the snippets they were picking up from the BBC World Service and the more detailed reports coming from local stations, and translated for them by Farid, it seemed as if the unrest that had started first thing this morning in Riyadh had spread right across the Arabian peninsula like a tidal wave.

'They've gone insane,' said Mike, breaking the silence.

In the darkness Andy nodded in agreement, although the American wouldn't have been able to see the gesture. 'I just can't believe how quickly this seems to be spreading,' he replied after a moment.

'There's no working these crazy assholes out. First they're turning on us because we kicked out their tinpot dictator, now all of a sudden they're turning on each other. Do you think they just got bored with blowing up foreigners?'

Andy sucked in a breath and let it go. He had sat through so many conversations that started like this back in London, around the dinner table in the company of Jenny's friends and their husbands. Invariably the hubbies rarely strayed beyond talking about *Top Gear*, football, property prices and very occasionally, politics, and even then only in a superficial 'that's how I'd sort things' kind of way.

Erich sat in silence for a moment before murmuring something in French that suggested he agreed with the Texan. He ended his sentence with a solitary English word, 'savages'.

The driver-side door opened and a cool flurry of wind blew in a cloud of grit and dust. Farid climbed in, his *shemagh* fluttering around his face. He quickly pulled the door closed.

'The others okay?' asked Andy.

Farid nodded. 'Amal and Salim sleeping. The other engineer, U-u ...'

'Ustov,' said Erich.

Farid nodded politely, 'Ustov sleeping too.'

The silence was uncomfortable until Mike decided to break it in his own blundering way.

'So why are all you people fucking well ripping the crap out of each other?'

The old Iraqi man turned to Mike, 'Is not *all* of us. Many, like me, we want just peace.'

'Yeah? Well every time another roadside mine blows a hole

in one of our convoys, there's one hell of a lot of you out there celebrating on the streets jumping up and down and firing your guns in the air.'

'That is not *everyone.*'

'And now you're doing it to each other,' Mike said, almost laughing with exasperation, 'I mean … I don't get it … why?'

'I do not expect you to understand.'

'But you're all brothers aren't you? … All Muslims? *We're* supposed to be the *big bad guys* aren't we?'

'Would you ask me to try understand why so many Christian brothers died in your American Civil War?'

There was a lull in the car that Andy suspected might precede an enraged outburst from Mike. But to his credit he replied in a measured manner. 'No, I suppose you wouldn't understand if you're not from a southern state. Shit, of course you wouldn't.'

Andy turned in his seat to face both Mike and Farid. 'Why don't we leave off politics for now, huh?'

'I just want to understand what makes these people tick,' said Mike. 'We came in and kicked out Saddam, we've tried rebuilding this country, fixing the power stations, the sewage systems, the water supplies, the hospitals. Rebuilding the schools so all the little boys and girls—'

'You rebuild our country, yes … but in *your* image!' Farid replied, his soft voice raised ever so slightly in pitch. It was the first time Andy had seen the normally placid old man raise his voice in anger. Under the stress, his very good English began to fracture a little.

'We not wanting our girls go to school, to learn how to become business lady, to dance around undressed in exercise gym before other men, to do power lunch, make big business deals. We do not want to buy McDonald burgers, or Coke, or Pepsi, or cowboy boots.'

Farid came to an abrupt halt, ground his teeth in silence and stared out of the window at the moonlit desert. 'It still our country. Only Iraqi people can know how to make fixed again, like a puzzle. We know what all the pieces is … are, and how they going together. You Americans don't even know what picture is on the jigsaw!'

Mike laughed. 'Oh Jesus, what a load of crap. I tell you this – I know you ain't got your goddamned *pieces* right when you have women and children blown to bloody shreds in the market-places every day. The best chance you had of rebuilding this shit-pit piece of desert you call a country, was when we rolled in and knocked over Saddam's statue. And you threw that chance right back in our faces. And frankly all we've *ever* wanted to do since, is get the fuck out again.'

Farid shook his head. 'Everyone know why America comes here.'

'Let's just leave it there,' said Andy addressing both men. 'We don't need—'

'Shit! Who are you? My mom?' snapped Mike.

'I'm just saying we can do without this right now.'

'Yeah right, this is bullshit,' his deep voice rumbled. He opened the back door and stepped out, slamming the door behind him.

They watched his large frame, a dark silhouette against the glowing, pale blue moonlit ground, fade quickly into the night. A moment later they saw the flare of a match, and then a glowing orange tip move up and down every so often.

'He just like every American,' Farid muttered.

'Farid, enough of this for one night, okay?' said Andy quietly looking sternly at the old man. 'They,' he said nodding towards Mike, 'want to get out of here just as much as you want them out. It's not your oil they're here for.'

The translator looked less than convinced by that assurance, but he offered no reply. After a moment's silence listening to the gritty dust tinkle against the windows, blown across by a lively breeze, he stirred.

'I get rest now,' he said before bidding goodnight to Andy and Erich and leaving their Land Cruiser for the other one.

Andy shook his head at those words.

It's not your oil they're here for.

If only it were that simple. Anyone who had a fair understanding of Iraq's complete incapacity to pump and export oil knew that. Anyone who'd taken the time to look at the much bigger picture knew that. Anyone who took the time to research the long-term game-plan knew that. If Andy was asked *why* the Americans were over here and was only allowed to give one straight and clear reason, just to make this complex scenario simple and digestible, he knew what answer he would give.

They're here to keep the Saudis in line.

The Gulf War, the second one at least, wasn't about hunting down Al-Qaeda, it hadn't been about finding weapons of mass destruction, nor about removing a dictator. It had been about placing a permanent and very visible military presence right in the middle of all of these oil-producing nations. A crystal clear warning to all of them, particularly the Saudis, that they better just keep on playing ball with America.

And now it looked like things had all gone wrong.

He suspected the focus for US forces would be damage limitation, a desperate attempt to guard and preserve the oil facilities in Saudi, and for that matter in Kuwait, Oman and the other big producers. He wondered, however, if they'd be able to put a lid on this thing before every other refinery and pump station in this part of the world ended up looking like IT-1B, the burned-out shell they'd been picking over this morning.

Christ, if all of the Arabian oil producers head that way ...?

This was a scenario, one of many, he had imagined *could* happen. And that's all it would take to start things tumbling down, a few months, shit ... a few weeks, maybe even a single week without a regular flow of the stuff, would do it.

He had imagined something like this might eventually happen. In fact he had actually *predicted* it.

Andy pulled out his mobile phone once again, checked for a signal and cursed.

CHAPTER 11

8.33 p.m. GMT

UEA, Norwich

Ash looked around the room. It was as messy as he would have imagined; discarded clothes lay in a pile on the end of the bed, a small mountain of shoes lay at the foot of it. Beneath the small sash window, there was a modest desk, cluttered with cheap cosmetics and text books and folders. From the look of them she was studying something to do with movies.

However, it looked like good news. Leona Sutherland may have decided to go out tonight, but her study books and papers were all here. She'd be back, if not tonight, then first thing tomorrow morning, to collect them before going in to study.

He spotted a packet of photos on the table and leafed through them. A collection of fresh-faced kids squished together into a tent, pulling faces at the camera. He spotted Leona in only one of them; she would have been taking the pictures.

Her hair was darker in this picture, darker than in the picture he'd been given, and a little longer. She also looked somewhat older. The picture they had secured of her was not as recent as they had assured him it was. No matter, he would recognise her easily. Ash was particularly good with faces.

He smiled – *as good as young Leona here.*

She had been so silly with that email of hers. But then that was perhaps a harsh judgement; she had no reason to think that was a foolish thing to do. And hers wasn't a life lived in shadows and under pseudonyms. Her mind wasn't, by default, switched to checking every room she entered for bugs, checking windows for line-of-sight trajectories with some building across the street.

She wasn't to blame for attracting her death sentence.

There was nothing else here that was going to help him track down where she was right now; no phone books, no hastily scribbled notes or 'don't forget' memos to herself. He decided it was time to go talk to her flat-mate.

He stepped out of her room into the communal kitchen and squatted down beside the girl, taped up to one of the kitchen stools, and gagged with a strip of tape across her mouth.

'I'm going to remove the tape,' he said gently. 'Don't tense your lips when I do it, or it'll rip some of the skin off. Ready?'

She nodded.

Ash grabbed one corner and pulled it quickly. The girl flinched.

'Right then, to work,' he said with a tired shrug. 'Let's start with an easy one. What's your name?'

'A-Alison … Alison Derby.'

He nodded. 'Alison's good enough for now. Thank you. You can call me Ash. So then, here's another easy one for you. Do you know where Leona has gone this evening?'

Alison shook her head. 'No … n-no, I d-don't. She-she never told m-me,' she replied, her voice trembling uncontrollably.

Ash placed a hand lightly on her shoulder. 'Okay,' he laughed gently, 'okay, I believe you. I know what you kids are like. Spur of the moment and so on.'

Alison nodded again.

He looked around the kitchen, it adjoined the lounge – clearly the one main communal space for them. 'How many of you share this place?'

'S-six of us.'

'And where's everyone else?'

'Th-they've gone, f-for a reading week.'

'Skiving?' smiled Ash.

She nodded.

'So you're telling me, it's just you and Leona here this week.'

She nodded.

'Well that's good. No one's going to come barging in on us then. Very good.'

Alison looked up at him – direct eye contact for the first time. 'P-please d-don't rape me … I—'

'Rape you?' his eyebrows knotted with a look of incredulity. 'I'm not going to rape you, Alison. What kind of animal do you think I am?'

'I … I'm sorry, I … but … I just—'

'Don't worry,' he said in little more than a soothing paternal whisper, 'no raping, Alison. Just some questions is all.'

'O-okay.'

'So then, let me see, who is she with?'

'Dan. Th-that's her boyfriend.'

'Dan huh? You know where he lives?' he asked.

She shook her head.

'Hummm … do you think they'll come back here tonight?'

She shook her head again. 'I don't th-think so.'

'Why's that?'

'She said she was s-staying at h-his tonight.'

Ash stroked his chin. 'Hmmm. I'd dearly like her to come back here tonight. Call her.'

She shook her head. 'I c-can't.'

'And why's that?'

'I d-don't know her number.'

'You live together, but you don't know her number? That's not a very good lie, Alison.'

'I'm not lying!' she whimpered. 'She replaced her phone a couple of weeks ago.'

'But you would know her number by now.'

'I d-don't! Honest! I just … I hardly ever call her, I don't need to, we see each other all the time.'

He looked down at her, placed a finger under her chin and lifted her face up so that she met his eyes again. That seemed to be the truth. There were no deceitful micro-tics in her expression; no involuntary looking upwards as her mind hastily constructed a piece of fiction.

'Tell me, what do you think would make her come back here tonight?'

Alison shook her head, 'I-I don't … kn-know.'

He smiled cheerfully, 'You know what? I think I've got an idea. And you can help.'

CHAPTER 12

11.55 p.m. GMT

Whitehall, London

'Those figures have to be incorrect, surely?' he said looking around at the men and women sitting at the table with him. 'Surely?' he asked again.

'I'm sorry, those are the figures, that's our best approximation.'

The Prime Minister looked down at his legal pad. He had scribbled only a few hasty notes, but the last three words he had written down were the ones he found most disturbing.

Two weeks' reserves.

'Two weeks? That's *all* we have in our strategic reserves?'

'Our *strategic* reserves actually only contain about a week's worth of oil at normal everyday consumption rates,' replied Malcolm Jones, the Prime Minister's Strategic Advisor, and confidant.

'However, within the distribution chain throughout the country, terminals, depots, petrol stations, there's perhaps another week's worth of supply at the normal consumption rate. If we locked down any further selling of petrol, right across the country, right now we would have a reserve that might last our armed forces and key government installations six to nine months.'

The Prime Minister stared silently at him for a moment before finally responding.

'You're telling me that in order to supply the army and the government with the oil it needs to keep operating for the next few months, we'd have to suck every corner petrol station dry?'

Malcolm nodded, 'Until, of course, normality returns and shipments of crude from the Gulf resume.'

'And the week's worth of oil in our strategic reserves?'

'If restricted only to the armed forces and government agencies,' the civil servant replied, 'we could perhaps make it last three or four months.'

The Prime Minister jotted that down on his pad and then looked up at the assembled members of his personal staff. He had his Principal Private Secretary, his Director of Communications, Malcolm, his Chief Advisor on Strategy and Malcolm's assistant. These were the people he worked with daily, these were the small band of colleagues he trusted. None of them were party members, none of them politicians, none of them secretly jostling for his job. He'd long ago learned that his smartest and most effective decision-making was done here, in this office, with these people, and not around the long mahogany table with his cabinet. The cabinet meetings were where policy was *announced*, not *decided*.

'So,' he began calmly, 'how the hell did we let ourselves get so bloody exposed?'

He directed that towards Malcolm. 'How did we let this happen?'

Malcolm stirred uneasily, but retained that dignified calm that seemed to stay with him always. 'We've not been able to buy in enough surplus oil to maintain, let alone build up, our reserves. In fact, we've not been able to do that for the last few years,' he replied. 'It's been a gradual process of attrition, Charles. It's not that we let it happen, we've had no choice.'

The Prime Minister nodded.

'And we're not the only ones,' added Malcolm. 'The increasing demand for oil from China and India, combined with Iraq being a damned basket-case and Iran's continued oil embargo; all of that has made it difficult for *anyone* to build up a surplus. We're all over a barrel.'

'What about the Americans? Can they help us out?'

Malcolm shrugged. 'They have significant reserves, but

whether they'll share it with us, I'm not sure.'

The Prime Minister cast a glance across the table towards his Private Secretary. 'Well then let's ask. It's the least they can do after all the support we've been giving them since … well, since 9/11.'

His secretary scribbled that action point down.

'So, what do we do right now?'

Malcolm nodded to his assistant, Jane. She consulted some papers she had brought along to the meeting. 'There's a trickle of oil coming in from other smaller oil producers; Nigeria, Qatar, Mexico, Norway …'

'What about Venezuela?' asked the Prime Minister. 'I know their preferred client is China, but surely during this temporary crisis they'll negotiate some short arrangement with us? I mean they'll screw us on price, but surely …'

'Prime Minister, this came in an hour ago,' said Jane. She read from an intelligence bulletin. 'An explosion at the Paraguaná refinery, Venezuela. Fires still burning, damage yet to be assessed, casualties unknown.'

'Venezuela has loads of crude,' Malcolm cut in, 'loads of it. And yeah … they might well have been happy to cover our short-term problems, but it's heavy. It's not fit for purpose until it's been through a refinery specifically configured to deal with that particular blend. And Paraguaná was it.'

'How long will this Paraguaná refinery be out of action then?'

Malcolm shrugged. 'Who knows? This is all we have on this so far.'

'Well then what about the Tengiz oilfields in the Caspian? There's a lot of oil coming out of that area, isn't there?'

Jane nodded. 'Yes Prime Minister, we can hope to share some of what's coming through Georgia, but then so will every other country in Europe. With all the major Gulf producers out of the loop, that's sixty to seventy per cent of the supply chain gone. We're all now feeding on the last thirty per cent. With regard to Tengiz oil, we're right at the end of the supply chain.'

'You can be sure that our European cousins, along the way, will all want their share,' added Malcolm.

The Prime Minister looked around the people assembled in the conference room. 'Then what? What are you telling me? We're screwed? That we've only got the oil that's sitting in our reserves, depots and petrol stations around the country, and that's it?'

Jane looked down at her crib sheet again, 'There's also a residual drip-feed of oil still coming in from the North Sea.'

'But not enough to bail us out of this … right?'

'Not even close.'

He looked down again at his legal pad. He'd written nothing there that was going to help him. The only information that stood out on the legal pad were those three words: *two weeks' reserves*.

'Okay so we've got a big problem with oil. That means for the next couple of weeks no one's going to be driving. What about power generation? We're okay on that front, aren't we?'

'The good news, Charles, is that we don't make much power from oil. It's mostly gas and coal as you know. The bad news is, we import most of our gas and coal,' said Malcolm.

Jane consulted some notes. 'Thirty-six per cent of capacity from gas, thirty-eight from coal.'

Charles looked from one to the other, he could see where they were going. 'And our usual suppliers, Russia, for the gas …?'

'Australia, Colombia, South Africa, Indonesia for the coal,' responded Jane.

Malcolm looked at him. 'I imagine they'll want to hold up on exporting to cover their energy gap.'

'Shit. What about nuclear?'

'We produce less than five per cent of our needs from that, right now. You know this yourself, the old stations are mostly being mothballed, and the new ones … well they've only just started building them. If this had happened in a couple of years' time—'

Malcolm gestured at Jane to be silent. 'Charles, this has really caught us on the hop.'

'So what, if our regular gas and coal suppliers decide to get twitchy, we're down to five per cent of our normal capacity?'

'Eight per cent if we count renewables,' said Jane.

'Christ.' Charles loosened his tie. It was getting stuffy in the conference room.

'We will have to put into place some kind of immediate rationing of power. Whether we share it out on a rota basis, or whether we concentrate it on some nominated areas.'

'Fan-fucking-tastic,' he grunted and looked down silently at his legal pad.

'Charles?' said Malcolm quietly.

'What is it?'

'We have another time-critical decision to make. Our boys in Iraq.'

He was right.

The Americans were pulling most, if not all, of their men out of Iraq and deploying them in Saudi, Kuwait, Oman, overnight. It was already happening. During the day, a lot of damage had been done to the Saudi pipeline network, and many installations had been damaged and destroyed in the rioting. There were still significant oil assets that could be protected if they moved quickly. But that meant a drastically reduced military presence left behind in Iraq; soldiers who would be dangerously exposed.

'We have to decide what to do with our forces out there,' prompted Malcolm. 'And quickly.'

'And your suggestion?'

'We have to pull them out. We can't leave them on their own in Iraq. As soon as the insurgents there realise the Americans have gone …'

It didn't need saying. With US military might focused elsewhere, the seven or eight thousand troops they had committed to regions in the north and the south of Iraq, some of them in small battalion-sized garrisons, would be overrun within days.

'The decision is whether we help the Americans to guard

what's still intact over there. Or, we pull them out and bring them home,' said Malcolm. 'If we leave them there and this crisis lasts much longer ...'

They could be stranded there.

Charles looked at them. 'We're going to want them to come home, aren't we?'

Malcolm and Jane shot a glance at each other and nodded.

'This is going to be a tough one to ride out. Before this week's finished, I think we're going to need to have troops on the streets, Prime Minister,' Jane added.

'My God, this has happened so quickly,' Charles muttered, reaching up unconsciously to undo the top button of his shirt. 'I got up this morning with nothing more serious to worry about than looking good at an informal sixth form college Q and A.'

The small trusted band before him offered a muted nervous chuckle.

'And now I'm facing some kind of end-of-days scenario. Shit.'

Malcolm leaned over and patted his shoulder, 'We'll get through this.'

He then turned to Jane and nodded. The young woman pulled out a slim folder from beneath her crib sheet. 'Prime Minister, if I may, we do have some emergency protocols drawn up within the Cassandra Report for this kind of situation,' she said, opening the folder and flipping forward through pages of text and charts.

Charles nodded. He vaguely recalled an approval being passed during the previous government's tenure for a committee of experts to discreetly go away and worry about all manner of oil and energy emergency scenarios, and then to write up their findings.

'This report was compiled three years ago, after the road hauliers' strike back in 2004. If you recall it was a handful of depots blockaded by less than a hundred or so truck drivers that nearly brought this country to a standstill after only three days.'

'I know, go on.'

'There were some recommendations for dealing with an intermediate oil shut-off scenario.'

'Intermediate?'

'Intermediate ... defined as between two and eight weeks.' Jane cleared her throat before continuing. 'I'll cut to the recommendations.'

Jane continued. 'Action point one: sale of any oil fuel products should cease immediately. Petrol and diesel will then be rationed to key civilian personnel such as doctors or technicians. Point two: food supplies should be rationed. Vendors and distributors of food products should be forced to limit the sales of food products to customers to minimum sustenance levels until a proper rationing card or book system can be put in place—'

'Christ! Rationing food? At this stage?'

'Yes sir,' Jane looked up from the report. 'The earlier we do that, the better.'

'I can understand telling people they can't fill up their cars ... but—'

'Charles, think about it,' Malcolm interrupted. 'The vast majority of the food we eat in this country comes from abroad. As a matter of fact, we produce only a tiny fraction of what we consume, and even then it tends to be niche food items like ... I don't know ... crap like Marmite, mayonnaise. Your basic food stocks like wheat, grains, root crops, meat – most of those things come from overseas suppliers. We don't grow that kind of stuff over here any more. With a suspension of oil supplies across the world, one of the very first things to be affected is going to be the transportation of goods ... food.'

The Prime Minister buried his face in his hands for a moment, trying to massage away the stress-induced migraine he knew was well on its way.

'So now we also have to worry about a strategic food reserve?'

'Which we don't have, Prime Minister. We have only the food that exists in the domestic distribution chain.'

'In other words, what's currently sitting on the shelf in my local supermarket down the road?'

Jane shrugged apologetically, 'In a manner of speaking … yes.'

Malcolm gestured towards the report, 'Carry on, Jane.'

'Point three: immediate application of martial law, and a curfew, enforced by armed police and military units deployed in every major city. Point four: cessation of all inter-city travel services—'

Charles raised a hand to stop her. 'This is over the top. If I get on breakfast TV tomorrow morning and announce measures like these, they'll be rioting in the streets by lunchtime!'

He got up from the table and walked towards the bay window, pulling it up a few inches to allow a gentle breeze into the room. The window overlooked the modest rear garden of Number 10.

'This is day one of the crisis … *day one*! I can't dive in with measures like this. It'll cause more harm than good. And this thing in the Gulf may blow itself out in a few weeks. Okay, so we'll need to tighten our belts until then, of course, but these action points will come across as a panic reaction.'

Malcolm got up and walked over to the Prime Minister standing by the window staring out at the garden, illuminated by half-a-dozen security floodlights.

'What if it doesn't blow itself out in a few weeks? What if this situation escalates? What if we have China and Russia fighting over the Tengiz oil reserves?' Malcolm gestured towards the report.

'Charles, you need to read that thing. I've been reading through it this afternoon. There's an analogy they use in it to describe what's happening,' Malcolm closed his eyes for a moment, trying to remember the wording.

'The world is an old man with a weak heart, and oil is the blood supply.'

He opened his eyes again and gazed down at the garden as he continued. 'It needs only a single blocked artery to throw him into a seizure, and if it lasts long enough, the organs start dying, Charles, one by one.'

Malcolm turned to look the Prime Minister in the eye. 'Even if the blockage clears and blood starts flowing again – once those organs start failing, there's really no way back.'

He looked out at the garden. 'It's a very fragile world Charles, very fragile, built on very vulnerable interdependencies. And something like this ... what's been happening today, really could bring the whole lot down.'

Tuesday

CHAPTER 13

5 a.m. local time

Road leading to Al-Bayji, Iraq

Andy was aware he was dreaming, no, not dreaming – replaying that memory, as he dozed on the front seat.

A gentle tap on the door. And then it opens. A man enters the hotel room. Andy can only see his silhouette. As per the instructions they sent him, the main light in the room is turned out, the thick velvet curtains are drawn. The man closes the door, and now the room is lit only by the pale ambient glow of daylight stealing in beneath the curtains.

'I advise you to look away as well, Dr Sutherland. If we are certain you can't identify us, then we shall all feel happier.'

Andy does as he's told, turning in his seat to face away from the man.

'The report's on the end of the bed,' he says.

'One copy only? Handwritten?'

'Yes.'

Andy hears the rustle of movement and paper as the man picks it up. The flicker of a pen light. A few moments of silence, as the man inspects the first pages.

'Whilst I can't tell you who commissioned this report, I can say that your work will certainly help make the world a safer place. They are grateful.'

'I wasn't aware of quite how . . . fragile the world was until I started working on that,' Andy says.

'Yes it is fragile.'

'I hope what's in there will convince somebody at the top

– whoever – that we need to come off our oil dependency before it's too late,' Andy adds. 'Something like that is going to happen one day.'

The man says nothing at first. 'Perhaps it will.'

Andy wonders about that response. Or something will convince someone? Or something like that is going to happen one day?

He hears the man moving towards the door, then, he stops before opening it.

'The balance will be transferred this morning to the account you specified.'

'Thank you.'

'A final reminder. You are not to talk about the contents of this report to anyone, ever. We will trust you on this, but also … we will be listening.'

'Don't worry,' Andy smiles nervously, 'you've spooked me enough already.'

He hears a gentle laugh. 'Good.'

A pause. The man is still there.

'You know, I did this for the money at first,' says Andy quickly. 'But having written it … you know, it's scary stuff. I really hope it makes a difference.'

'It will.'

Another silence, just a few moments.

'Please remain here for ten minutes before leaving your room. Do you understand?'

Andy nods. 'Yes.'

'Goodbye.' Andy hears the door open, and light from the corridor floods in, then it's dark, and he hears it click shut behind the man.

It's silent, except for the muted rumble of traffic and bustle outside. Several minutes pass, he wishes he'd set his stopwatch to countdown ten minutes, just to be sure.

Then he hears a knocking on the door …

The persistent knocking roused Andy from the past.

He opened his eyes and saw Sergeant Bolton rapping his

knuckles heavily on the passenger-side window. Andy lowered the window letting in a cool blast of air.

'Wakey, wakey little lambkins, we're moving out in five minutes,' muttered the NCO quietly, a small plume of steamy breath quickly dispersing in the chilly early morning air. He casually rapped once more on the roof of their Cruiser and then headed over to the second one to wake up Farid and the two drivers.

Andy blinked the sleep out of his eyes as he watched the occasional flicker of torchlight illuminate the soldiers climbing aboard five of the six Land Rovers. The army Rover that had broken down had been stripped of anything useful.

It was still dark outside, although the sky was just beginning to lighten. He wondered if Lieutenant Carter had left things just a little bit late. They still had about another two hours' drive time to get them back to the battalion headquarters beyond Al-Bayji. It would be approaching seven in the morning as they rumbled through the narrow streets of the town. It would be broad daylight, and there was no knowing if those streets were going to be obstructed with the results of last night's anarchy. He guessed Carter was banking on the people in Al-Bayji stirring later than normal after such a busy night.

Andy leaned over the back of his seat to give the others a prod. 'Wake up guys, we're on the move.'

Mike, Erich and Ustov stirred silently, as Andy opened the door and stepped out into the cool early morning to stretch his legs.

He realised for the first time how nervous he was. This wasn't the normal, ever-present always-check-over-your-shoulder wariness that one experienced as a westerner in Iraq.

This was a whole new order of scary.

Their only way back to the relative safety of a friendly camp was over a bridge and through a town that, only a few hours ago, had been tearing itself apart – a majority of Sunnis versus a minority of Shi'as. If that was still going on, any white faces turning up were going to be a viable target for both sides. He hoped to God things had died down and they were all tucked up in their homes getting some sleep as Carter's recon platoon rolled discreetly through.

What was most frustrating for him, though, was knowing so little about what was happening on a wider scale. The situation in Saudi had stirred things up in Iraq, but then to be fair, it didn't take a lot to agitate the constant state of civil war in this country. But had it spread? Or had it run its course?

Lieutenant Carter approached Andy with a friendly nod. 'A couple of my boys are going to need a lift in your vehicles. We're down one Rover as you know.'

Andy nodded. 'That's okay. We've got space enough for another two at a pinch, in each car.'

'Good. I'd like at least one armed effective in each vehicle. It might help if you and your colleagues also armed yourselves with those AKs we took off your drivers.'

'I uh … I've never held a gun. I'd probably end up shooting myself in the foot.'

Carter looked surprised. 'Didn't your employer provide you with some kind of basic firearms training?'

'No.'

'Oh great. What about the others?'

'I don't know. But I'd guess Mike probably has.'

'The American?'

Andy nodded.

'Right, well we'll issue him with one I suppose, and you can decide amongst you who'll have the other one.'

'All right.'

Andy noticed the young officer nervously balling his trembling hands into fists. 'How long have you been out here?'

Carter looked at him and smiled. 'It shows does it?'

'Just a little,' Andy lied.

'I only got commissioned this year, and they sent me out here last month. The lads lost their platoon commander a few weeks ago. I think he was caught out by a mortar attack. Those bastards are getting more and more accurate with those damned things.' The Lieutenant put his idle hands to use and tightened the straps of his webbing. 'So anyway, that sort of makes me the new boy, as it were.'

Andy offered a wan smile.

Wonderful.

The convoy rolled along the road, heading south-west. They passed through a small village in the dark without incident. Making good progress, they reached the outskirts of Al-Bayji at about ten to seven in the morning. Lieutenant Carter was in the front Rover, on top cover, standing up in the back of the vehicle between the bars of the roll cage with another soldier, both of them holding their SA80 assault rifles ready and cocked. The soldier on top cover in the following Rover had the platoon's Minimi, a belt-fed light machine-gun, mounted on a barrel-fitted bipod. Following that, were the two Toyota Land Cruisers.

Andy was in the first, with Mike, Farid, the young driver Amal, and a chatty lance corporal from Newcastle who just wouldn't shut up, called Tim Westley. Mike was holding Amal's AK. Andy noticed the young Iraqi casting a resentful glance over his shoulder at the American. Apparently, the two young drivers actually *owned* these weapons. Farid explained that possessing their own assault rifle had been one of the prerequisites for the job; as well as being able to drive, that is. Andy could understand the lad's rancour, an AK cost a month's salary.

In the following Cruiser was Erich carrying the other AK, Ustov the Ukrainian contractor, the second driver Salim, and two more men from Carter's platoon. Bringing up the rear were the other three Land Rovers, with Sergeant Bolton on top cover in the last of them.

Lance Corporal Westley was in full flow, as he had been pretty much since they set off at five that morning.

'—and the other fuckin' idiots in second platoon like, was wearin' them *shemaghs* thinkin' they was right ally with it man,' continued Tim Westley's stream-of-consciousness one-way conversation. Mike listened and nodded politely at all the right moments, but from his expression Andy could see the Texan couldn't understand a single word he was hearing.

'—an' it's right naff, man. Aye, was all right first time round, like – Desert Storm an' all, but right fuckin' daft now, mind. Only the TA scallys wear 'em now. You can spot those soft wallys a mile off . . .'

The convoy slowed down to a halt, and with that, Lance Corporal Westley finally shut up as he wound down the window and stuck his head out to take a look-see.

Up front, Andy could see Lieutenant Carter had raised his hand; a gesture to his platoon to hold up there for a moment. Beyond the leading Rover he could see a swathe of coarse grass and reeds leading down a shallow slope towards the River Tigris, and over this a single-lane bridge that led across the small fertile river valley into the town of Al-Bayji beyond. On the far side of the bridge, some 500 metres away, he could see the first dusty, low, whitewashed buildings topped with drab corrugated iron roofs. Beyond them, taller two and three-storey, flat-roofed buildings clustered and bisected randomly with the sporadic bristling of TV aerials, satellite dishes and phone masts along the rooftops.

With his bare eyes he could see no movement except for a mangy-looking, tan dog that was wandering slowly across the bridge into the town, and several goats grazing on the meagre pickings of refuse, dumped in a mouldering pile that had slewed down the far slope of the small valley into the river. He spotted several dozen pillars of smoke, dotted across the town skyline, snaking lazily up into the pallid dawn sky. The columns of smoke seemed to be more densely grouped towards the centre of the town.

'It looks like they had a lot of fun last night,' muttered Mike.

Andy could see Lieutenant Carter had pulled out some binoculars and was slowly scanning the scene ahead.

'We should just go for it,' said Mike quickly checking his watch. 'It's almost seven already.'

Andy nodded in agreement. Through the town was the only way, flanked as it was by fields lined with deep and impassable irrigation ditches.

If they put their foot down and just went full tilt, they'd be out the far side and heading down open road towards the British encampment before anyone could do anything about it.

Come on, come on.

But then, what if there was an obstruction, a burned-out vehicle, or a deliberately constructed roadblock? They'd find themselves stuck. Andy decided, on reflection, that the young officer's caution was well-placed. But time was against them, the sun was breaching the horizon now, and even from this side of the bridge, he could sense Al-Bayji was beginning to stir, perhaps readying itself to face a second day of sectarian carnage.

Lieutenant Carter raised his arm once again, balled his fist and stuck a thumb upwards.

'All clear ahead,' said Westley, translating the hand signal for them.

And then the officer patted the top of his helmet with the palm of his gloved hand.

'Follow me.'

Carter's vehicle lurched gently forward with a puff of exhaust, off down the pitted tarmac road towards the bridge, and one by one the convoy of vehicles revved up and followed on.

'Here goes,' said Mike, winding his window down and racking his AK, ready for action. The American looked comfortable with the assault rifle in both hands. But then, Andy reflected, Mike was probably the kind of guy that had a display-case back home in Texas full of interesting firearms.

Andy noticed a look of unease, perhaps anger, flashing across the face of Amal, and a subtle gesture from Farid, placing a calming hand on the lad's arm.

CHAPTER 14

6.57 a.m. local time

Al-Bayji, Iraq

Lieutenant Carter's Land Rover rolled off the end of the bridge and into the outskirts of the town, with the convoy following tightly behind.

Up close, the signs of yesterday's chaos were apparent. Splashed across the side of the road, Andy spotted a dark, almost black, pool of congealed blood and a long smear leading away from it towards the doorway of a nearby building; no doubt the body of some poor unfortunate dragged back home to be mourned in private.

The lead Rover picked up speed as it rumbled down a relatively wide, but scarred, road, flanked with a few single-storey buildings. They approached an open area that Andy recalled passing through about this time yesterday, a market square full of traders preparing their stalls for the day ahead. This morning it was deserted.

Travelling through this open and exposed part of the town, he felt they were a little less vulnerable. The doorways, the windows, the roof terraces from which an opportunistic ambush might be launched, were far enough away from them, beyond the area of the market-place, that most of the shots would go wide, and they'd have a chance to react. However, up ahead the road that they were cruising along at a fair clip, punishing the suspension of each vehicle with every pot-hole, carried on towards the centre of town, and vanilla-hued buildings, one or two storeys high, encroached on either side. To Andy's inexperienced eye, the way ahead looked dangerously constricted and overlooked.

‘Keep yer eyes peeled lads,’ said Westley, his cocky demeanour now subdued and replaced with a flinty wariness.

Mike exchanged a glance with Andy.

‘Rooftops an’ garden walls,’ Westley added. ‘They don’t like firing off from *inside* the buildings, like … it leaves ’em vulnerable to being bottled up.’

Mike seemed to understand that. ‘Gotcha,’ he replied.

Lieutenant Carter’s Rover led them into a shaded alley, and as the sun flickered and disappeared behind the rooftops overlooking them, it felt disturbingly like driving into the gaping jaws of some menacing beast.

‘Shit,’ muttered Andy.

Let’s do this quickly.

The road bent round to the right, a tight corner that had them slowing down to a crawl as they weaved their way past a van parked inconveniently on the bend.

And then Carter’s Rover came to an abrupt halt.

Amal responded quickly enough so that they slewed to a halt only a foot from the Rover in front.

‘What’s going on?’ asked Mike. The van and the corner were obscuring Carter’s vehicle from view.

Westley put a hand to the ear of his PRR – personal role radio – headset. ‘CO says the road round the corner’s blocked. We’ve got to fuckin’ well back up and find another way through.’

Andy turned in his seat, and saw the rear-most Rover, with Sergeant Bolton up top, reversing already.

And that’s when he heard the first crack of gunfire.

‘Ahh shit, someone’s firing already,’ growled Mike.

Turning to face forward again, he saw a flicker of movement from the balcony of a building directly ahead and above them. The squaddie on top cover in the Rover just in front of them spotted the same movement, and swung the Minimi machine-gun swiftly round on its mount, aiming upwards at the chipped and flaking waist-high balcony wall.

Instantly a string of white puffs of plaster powder erupted along the length of it and the man dropped down out of sight.

'Ah smeg, tha's really gonna wake 'em all up now!' shouted Westley.

Amal, meanwhile, was reversing their Cruiser following the other vehicles backing up along the narrow road.

They had passed a right-hand turn fifty yards up, just a few moments earlier, which would take them more or less in the direction they wanted to go. It was another narrow street, overlooked by tall buildings with balconies, but maybe it wasn't blocked.

Andy spotted movement now in the windows of several other buildings: the fleeting faces of some children and their mother, in another an old man wearing a white *dishdash* staring out curiously from the darkened interior of his home.

The rear of Lieutenant Carter's vehicle now appeared, reversing around the corner, the young officer and the soldier beside him double-tapping – firing two or three-round bursts – at the balcony to keep the man up there down on the ground and out of trouble.

The convoy moved backwards slowly, with no further rounds being fired at them. That single shot seemed to have been all there was; and even then, Andy wasn't sure it had been a gunshot. It could well have been a vehicle misfiring in a nearby street for all he knew.

Still, the damage was done. The Minimi burst, and the subsequent bursts from Lieutenant Carter's Land Rover must surely have roused the locals.

They pulled past the right-hand turning, going back several dozen more yards to allow the two vehicles in front to back up past it. Then, with a squeal of tyres and a shower of gravel spat out from beneath it, Carter's Rover spun right into the narrow street, and the rest of the convoy swiftly followed suit.

'Let's go!' Mike urged Amal, banging repeatedly with his fist on the back of the driver's seat.

The short exchange of gunfire had definitely stirred the townsfolk. They spotted many more faces peering from darkened windows and doorways down the narrow street and on the balconies above them. Andy, looking up, could only see a narrow strip of blue sky criss-crossed with electrical cables and dangling laundry. This street was even narrower than the one they had just backed out of.

We're going to get trapped.

To him that seemed bloody obvious; a foregone conclusion the way things seemed to be going already. They were getting tightly boxed in here. If there was an obstruction this way, things could get hairy.

Up ahead, the convoy approached another corner, this time turning left. The lead Rover spun round it quickly dislodging a cloud of dust in its wake, and the others followed swiftly.

To everyone's relief, the street widened out, and opened on to a much wider stretch of road; a dual lane, with some semblance of paving on either side and a grass-tufted island running down the middle. There were only one or two vehicles parked on either side, and along the central, weed-encrusted island, several withered old date palms were dotted, giving the street the notional appearance of a once pleasant boulevard gone to seed. Andy noticed, though, that there were quite a few pedestrians out and about, gathered in clusters. Whether they were about their normal business, or roused by the short burst of gunfire and curious, he wasn't sure.

Lieutenant Carter's Rover came to a halt, and the rest of them followed his lead.

'Why's he stopping?' asked Mike.

Andy leaned his head out to get a better look at what was happening ahead, and saw that the far end of the boulevard was packed with a gathering of men; some kind of town meeting in a building that had spilled out on to the road. The people were blocking the way ahead.

'Shit, we can't get through, the road's blocked. That's why he's stopped.'

Westley cursed under his breath. 'Shit. We could just push through, like. You know?'

Farid cast a glance over his shoulder at the soldier in the back seat. 'You want we run over them?'

'Yeah, smeg it. If they won't move out of the way.'

'I agree,' Mike said to the young squaddie, 'anyway, if we fire off some warning shots first, they'll move aside. And if they don't … well that's their look out.'

'I am thinking they will not move,' Farid countered sternly.

'So what? We just sit here and let them swarm us?' Mike snapped back at the old man.

'It is murder to just drive into them. That is *haram*. Bad.'

'Them or us?' added Westley, 'Fuck, I say us.'

Farid turned to Amal and spoke to him quickly in Arabic.

'What the fuck are you telling him?' shouted Mike angrily.

Farid turned in his seat to face him. 'I ask him if he know another way around. Amal have family in Al-Bayji. He knows the town.'

Andy, ignoring the debate, was watching the distant milling crowd. There were many faces now turned towards them, and hands pointing. The convoy of vehicles nestling discreetly in the shadow of the side-street had finally been noticed by the crowd.

'Ahh shit!' said Westley, listening in on his PRR headset. 'CO says he sees some RPGs amongst them.'

Andy nearly asked what an RPG was, but stopped himself. Even little Jacob knew what those three letters stood for: rocket-propelled grenade.

The crowd began to move slowly towards them, and as they spread out, Andy could see for himself that they had a fair distribution of weapons of various types amongst them.

Whatever we do, we better bloody do it now.

As if in answer to his thought, he noticed one of the crowd stopping, kneeling down and swinging a long tube round and up to an aiming position.

The next second he saw a momentary flash and a puff of smoke, and a small black projectile weaving up the road towards them.

'RPG! Shit!' shouted Westley.

It whistled by the convoy easily missing them by a dozen yards, but close enough that they heard the angry hum of displaced air. It thudded against the wall of a building fifty yards behind them, dislodging a large patch of plaster, but failing to explode.

Lieutenant Carter had apparently decided enough was enough and gestured to the soldier manning the Minimi in the Rover behind to lay down some suppressing fire.

The machine-gun began chattering loudly, and Andy watched with horror as half a dozen of the men leading the advancing crowd seemed to disintegrate as pink clouds of blood and tissue erupted from chests and heads. In response, every armed man in the crowd decided to open fire at pretty much the exact same moment and the hot air just outside their Land Cruiser seemed to pulsate with shots whistling past.

Carter's vehicle swung erratically to the left, and Andy could see the officer gesturing wildly with one hand towards a two-storey pink building with a high-walled compound in front of it. There was a sturdy iron gate in the middle of the wall that was closed and appeared to be padlocked. His vehicle cannoned towards it, bouncing up on to the kerb and a moment later crashing heavily into the gate. The gate rattled violently on its hinges as it swung inwards.

'Go, go, go!' shouted Westley. Amal instinctively spun the wheel round and slammed his foot down, pulling out from behind the Rover with the Minimi towards the building. The Rover in front of them remained stationary, the machine-gun still chattering suppressing fire at the crowd, keeping them from advancing any closer.

Andy realised something must have happened to it, and as they pulled past and swung left, he saw the windshield had gone and the driver was slumped forward on the dash. There were three other men in the Rover; two had climbed out of the back and were kneeling down using the rear of the car as cover, the third was still standing up through the roll bars and firing the Minimi in a series of long bursts that were rapidly eating up the belted ammo. All three were in danger of being left behind.

Amal drove towards the pink building, bumpily mounting the

kerb as the lead Rover had done, everyone inside banging their heads on the roof as they rode over it and through the now open gates into the compound beyond.

Their Cruiser slid to a halt amidst a cloud of dust, and in quick succession, the second Cruiser entered, followed by the remaining three Rovers.

Through the fog of dust Andy could see that Lieutenant Carter was already dismounted, running across the compound towards the open gate and shouting orders to his men who began piling out of their vehicles. Carter took cover behind the wall, beside the gate, leaning out quickly several times to check on his three lads trapped in the middle of the street.

CHAPTER 15

7.21 a.m. Local time

Al-Bayji, Iraq

'This is bloody mad,' Lieutenant Carter whispered breathlessly to himself.

Sergeant Bolton jogged over and joined him leaning against the wall beside the gate, catching his breath in short gasps, and tightening the straps on his Kevlar helmet.

'All right sir?' he grunted.

Carter nodded. 'I'm fine. It's those poor bastards outside I'm worried about.'

They could hear the Minimi continuing to fire in short disciplined, regular bursts. But they were becoming shorter and the pauses between them longer.

'Whatever we do sir, it's got to be quick.'

Carter nodded. 'Sergeant, I don't know their call-sign, I haven't learned yet who's—'

'Those lads are part of Yankee-two-two, sir.'

The young officer nodded. 'Okay, okay. Right.' He looked anxiously around the compound as he bit his bottom lip, thinking.

'Sir, we've got to do something now,' barked Sergeant Bolton impatiently.

Carter peeked around the wall at the three men. The man on top cover was still firing. The other two were offering sporadic double-taps from the rear of the Rover, whilst the ground around them danced with plumes of dust and sparks that sprayed off the pock-marked, bullet-dented metal of the vehicle.

He touched the push-to-talk button of his radio and did his

best to speak calmly into the throat mic. 'Yankee-two-two … this is Yankee-two-zero. You've got to make a run for it lads. We'll give you covering fire from the gate and the wall.'

'Fucking make it quick, sir!' the crackling response came back from one of the three men.

Carter turned to Bolton. 'Sergeant, get some of our boys up on the wall.' He looked around and saw there was a stacked pile of wooden pallets in the corner of the compound. 'Use those to stand on. And rally a section over here by the gate. We'll assemble some firepower here, all right?'

Sergeant Bolton nodded and began issuing voice commands on a separate channel.

'And Sergeant, I want a man watching those three Iraqi gents we have with us.'

Bolton acknowledged that, and then jogged across the compound with a confidence and an aura of invincibility that Carter would have given anything to possess.

A few moments later, eight men of his platoon, including a burly-looking Fijian, were shifting the pallets across the ground to the base of the seven-foot cinder-block and plaster wall and stacking them high enough to allow them to see over.

The chatty Geordie lance corporal – Westley – scrambled over and slumped against the wall beside Carter, followed by a section of twelve men, who all followed his lead and fell in against the rough cinder blocks. Carter turned to see a line of anxious young faces studying him intently and waiting anxiously for their CO to formulate a way out of this mess for them.

'All right lads, first thing we're doing is getting Yankee-two-two out of that fix and in here with us. Then … then we'll deal with the next thing on the list. Okay?'

Shit Robin … never bloody well ask them if an order's 'okay'.

'So, that's what we're doing,' he hastily added. 'On my command take half this section out through the gate and break right. There's a truck you and your men can use for cover. I'll take the other half, and we'll cover your move from the gateway. When you're settled in we'll come out break left, and we'll all give those lads out there covering fire. Hopefully that'll give them enough time to scarper over here. You got it?'

'Aye sir,' nodded Westley.

'All right, take up your position on the other side of this gateway. Let's get ready.'

Outside Carter could hear that the Minimi's chattering bursts were diminishing in length and frequency. The bloke firing it – damn, he wished he'd had a little more time to learn their names – was clearly doing his best to conserve the last of his ammo, yet keep firing often enough to hold the crowd back.

Westley slapped six of his comrades on the shoulder and led them in a loping dash across the open gateway to the wall on the other side of the compound's entrance, where they squatted in a row, ready to go.

No time to waste. Do it.

'Yankee-two-two,' said Carter over the radio, 'we're coming out to give you covering fire. On my command just get the fuck out of there and get over here.'

He looked over his shoulder to see that Sergeant Bolton had some men hunkered down on top of the pallets and ready to give covering fire over the top of the wall. He nodded to Bolton and then turned back to face Lance Corporal Westley on the far side of the gate.

He raised his hand so that both Bolton and Westley could see it and then counted down.

Three … two … one.

He pulled his hand into a fist as he jumped to his feet, leading his men round the iron gate and into the opening of the gateway. All seven of them dropped down to their knees and let loose a barrage of fire on the crowd that now was almost upon the stranded Rover. Meanwhile, Westley led his men out through the gate, breaking right across half-a-dozen yards of uneven paving towards a rusting truck parked with two tyres up on the kerb. There, they quickly found covered positions, and placed a withering barrage of suppressing fire down the boulevard. The advancing crowd, as one, dropped to the ground to avoid the opening salvo of gunfire.

'Yankee-two-two ... Go!' Carter shouted into his throat mic.

The squaddie who had been doing an excellent job of top cover with the Minimi, instantly ducked down through the roll cage and began to scramble towards the back of the Rover. The other two men, meanwhile, leapt out from the meagre cover provided by the rear of the vehicle and started across the thirty feet of open ground towards the pink-walled compound, weaving to and fro in the hope of throwing off anyone attempting to draw a bead on them.

The third man still in the Rover suddenly stopped, and was hesitating, like some piss-head wondering whether he'd left his wallet back in the pub. Then Carter saw him reach up through the roll cage bars to retrieve the machine-gun.

He was tempted to shout out an order to the man to forget about it. But the Minimi was such an effective support weapon, to have it would make a real difference to the platoon's chances of holding this position. They had plenty more belts of ammo for it in the other Rovers.

'Come on, come on,' he found himself muttering as he and his men continued to offer staccato bursts of covering fire, which for now was keeping most of the heads down out in the street.

The soldier in the vehicle managed to pull the awkwardly shaped weapon, with its extended bipod, down through the bars of the roll cage, and then out of the back of the Rover, tumbling out on to the ground with it in the process.

'Smeggin' hell move it, Shirley, you lazy bastard!' Carter heard the Geordie lance corporal shout over the platoon channel, completely dispensing with formal call-sign protocol.

Over the shared channel, he heard the laboured breathing of the man, as he struggled with the gun and made ready to cross the open ground towards the entrance.

'Fuck off Westley, you girl's blouse,' he heard the man reply.

'Yankee-two-two ... Dammit! ... *Shirley!*' barked Carter,

making a mental note to ask him how he got that nickname. 'Get over here now!'

The man shouldered the weapon, took a moment to steady his nerves, and then lurched out into the open, adopting the same weaving pattern as his two comrades had, but dangerously slowed down by the bulk and weight of the machine-gun.

The suppressing fire coming from Carter's men, Sergeant Bolton's position over the top of the compound wall and Lance Corporal Westley's men was breaking down as magazines began to empty. At least half the men in all three sections were now somewhere in the process of ejecting a spent magazine, pulling a new one out of their pouches and slamming it home.

The armed militia amongst the crowd were beginning to be encouraged by the faltering volley of gunfire and several of them emerged from places of cover across the boulevard. They tapped short bursts in the direction of the lone soldier, desperately scrambling across the road.

Inevitably, a shot landed home.

A puff of crimson exploded from the man's leg and he clattered to the ground still some yards from the kerb.

'Get off your fuckin' arse, you twat!' bellowed Bolton from the top of the wall, his booming voice carrying over the din of gunfire.

The intensity of the fire suddenly increased as the militia-led mob were further encouraged. The cinder-block wall beside Carter and his men began to explode with bullet impacts, showering them all with a cascade of plaster dust and stinging splinters of cement.

Carter heard a hard wet smack and glanced to his left to see that the squaddie who had been kneeling next to him had been thrown backwards by a shot dead centre to his face. There was nothing he could recognise above the chin and below his ginger eyebrows – just a crater of mangled tissue.

Shit, shit, shit.

The lad was gone, dead already, despite the drumming of his boots on the kerb.

And there was the soldier in the road with the leg wound; he was screaming in agony, rolling around on the ground clasping his thigh.

Carter knew he had to pull his men back inside before he lost any more.

'Everyone inside, now!' he screamed over the radio.

Lance Corporal Westley's men moved swiftly back towards the gate in well-practised fire-and-manoeuvre pairs. But Westley hovered by the truck he'd been using for cover.

Carter caught his eye as he gestured for his section to fall back inside. 'Get inside! NOW!' he bellowed to him. The Geordie hesitated a moment longer before reluctantly sprinting full tilt for the gateway.

Carter grimaced. *We're leaving that poor sod out there, still alive.*

He brought up the rear, emptying his clip in one long wildly sprayed burst before turning round and diving for the open gateway.

With all of them inside, the iron rail gates were closed, clattering noisily as they slammed together. Sergeant Bolton had some men ready with more wooden pallets and other detritus found in the compound and swiftly piled it against the gates.

Carter clambered up the pallets stacked against the wall and then, waiting for a slack moment in the firing, chanced a quick glance over the top.

The soldier, Shirley, with the Minimi, had taken another couple of hits, by the look of his shredded combat fatigues, darkened from the blood of several wounds, the poor young lad was on his way out. Then, mercifully, perhaps, a shot knocked his head back and dislodged his helmet.

He was dead.

Shirley ... he'd wanted to know where the fuck that daft name had come from ... but of course, he was never going to find out now.

CHAPTER 16

8 a.m. GMT
Manchester

'Oh come on!' cried Jenny impatiently.

The digital tune playing over and over as she sat on hold was very quickly driving her insane. The bleeping melody was broken periodically with a recorded announcement that she was on hold to On Track Rail Customer Services, and would be answered by an operator shortly.

Jenny was still in bed, in the Piccadilly Marriot Hotel. The plan had been to take a detour up to Leeds to see some old friends and then home again to begin sorting her life out.

But, with all these worrying things going on thousands of miles away, it didn't seem like such a good idea any more. All of a sudden, a piss-up with some old, old school friends – ones she had only recently got back in contact with courtesy of Friends Reunited – had lost its appeal. She'd probably go through the motions, buy drinks, get pissed, reminisce, but her mind would be on other things; including Andy, stuck out there, and from what she was picking up on the news, possibly in a dangerous situation.

Jenny wasn't really that news-savvy generally. She probably put more time into watching soaps and reality shows than she did keeping an eye on current affairs. But, yesterday, in that café bar, she had heard one or two phrases – no more than soundbites – that had sent a shiver down her spine.

At his most obsessive, perhaps a year ago, Andy had warned her that only those who were listening for it, the *Big Collapse*, listening for the tell-tale signs, would get the crucial head start.

The advance warning would come through on the news in phrases that were like a code, encrypted for the few that knew what to listen out for. They would be the ones who would have a chance to prepare before widespread panic kicked in.

Yesterday, watching the news, she felt she had heard something very much like that coded warning.

Peak Oil.

She felt stupid at first, of course. Walking out after her coffee, shopping in the Arndale Centre, having some dinner and coming back to the hotel, she had almost managed to dismiss the nagging notion that maybe she had better get a move on back to London and do an extra-large grocery shop.

Then this morning, having slept on it, and rehashed all those doom and gloom predictions of Andy's that had so worn her down over the last few years, she realised she'd heard the warning.

And she'd climbed out of bed.

Her friends could wait for another time.

If she was panicking, over-reacting, so what? Better to be back home sitting on more cans of food than they'd normally keep in the kitchen, than be caught out. It would eventually get eaten anyway.

What about Leona and Jacob?

At least if she was back in London and things did look like they were going to get worse, she could nip across and pick Jacob up easily enough. Heading up to Leeds for a pissed-up reunion? ... Well, she just wasn't going to enjoy herself if she was distracted with niggling concerns.

The digital tune was interrupted by the voice of a *real* person.

'On Track Rail Customer Services,' answered a man.

'Ahh, about time! I had a ticket booked to London at the end of the week. And I wondered if I can change it for one going back down from Manchester today?'

'I'm sorry, inter-city rail services have been suspended this morning.'

‘What? For how long?’

‘I’ve not been given a time. All we know is that they are currently suspended.’

‘Why?’

‘I’m sorry, that’s all we know … services are suspended until we hear otherwise.’

‘Well, how am I supposed to get back home?’ she asked angrily.

‘I … uhh … I’m sorry madam,’ the man replied awkwardly, and then disconnected the call.

‘Great,’ she hissed, ‘flipping great.’

She picked up the remote from her bedside table and turned on the small TV which was perched on a bracket in a corner of the room. Flipping across the meagre selection of five channels, all of them had a news programme of one sort or another, and every single one of them was talking over some new development of the troubles. She turned up the volume.

‘… the incident in Georgia. Early reports are that the explosions at the Baku refineries near the Tengiz oilfield may be the result of an accident caused by a sudden increase in demand and production, coupled with the ageing Soviet-era oil infrastructure and machinery. However, there are conflicting reports that the explosions may have been caused by a deliberate act of sabotage …’

Jenny flipped over to another channel.

‘… sources from the Pentagon say that additional troops may be re-deployed from the Gulf to guard the other refineries and pipelines in the Caspian region. However, it’s clear that US forces already out there are being stretched dangerously thin, to the point that command control and supply routes to the men could possibly begin to become a problem. Commentators in Washington are suggesting that the President may be forced to announce some kind of draft to cover the additional manpower needed in the immediate future. But even then, things are happening very swiftly and troops are required now to …’

And another.

'... unclear what happened to the Amoco Dahlia this morning. The explosion ripped the super-tanker's hull open just as the vessel entered the main shipping lane through the Straits of Hormuz. The Amoco Dahlia has shed many millions of gallons of oil, and is still burning. It's unknown whether the super-tanker hit a mine, or perhaps more likely, was targeted by a fast-moving terrorist boat rigged with explosives ...'

And another.

'... this morning. The Prime Minister's press secretary said that an announcement would be made later today. Traders in the City of London will, of course, be trying to anticipate what he's going to announce. The obvious thing to be looking out for would be a temporary relaxing of duty on petrol and diesel. With prices per barrel this morning rocketing past the $100 barrier and still rising, it's clear that short-term measures to counter immediate damage to the already fragile economy will be at the forefront of his mind ...'

Jenny looked down at the mobile phone, still in her hand and realised that, for the first time in a long while, she wished Andy was right there, and telling her what she needed to do.

CHAPTER 17

11 a.m. local time

Al-Bayji, Iraq

Andy ducked back inside the pink building as Sergeant Bolton bellowed a warning. A moment later the mortar shell they had heard launched from nearby dropped into the compound with a dull thump, but no explosion – another dud.

He heaved a sigh of relief. The armed insurgents amongst the gathering crowd outside had launched half-a-dozen mortars at the compound, only two had landed on target, and neither had exploded.

The sporadic gunfire was beginning to die down again.

Throughout the morning, the pattern had been consistent; sustained and intense periods of gunfire coming from nearly every rooftop along the boulevard and outside along the street itself, punctuated by interludes of peace and quiet.

The crowd outside had grown in size, presumably as word had spread across the town that a small patrol of coalition forces had been run to ground.

Andy was surprised at how bold they were. Surely the people out there had to be aware that a relief force would be combing the area looking for Carter's patrol? The battalion HQ was only thirty minutes away, they'd be sending someone, surely?

Or perhaps they know something we don't?

The comms system installed in Lieutenant Carter's Rover had taken several hits from gunfire as the vehicle had swerved across the road towards the pink building. And now they had no reliable means of getting in touch with the battalion.

The only other way they had of contacting the battalion HQ

was, believe it or not, via mobile phone. Out in the wilderness, it was down to luck. But in a place like Al-Bayji, the coverage was pretty thorough.

In the last hour, once it became apparent that there was no imminent threat of being overrun, and that for now, they could hold the compound, Lieutenant Carter had set about trying to get a call through to somebody, *anybody*, at battalion HQ. Eventually he managed to get through to a Quartermaster Sergeant, a buddy of Bolton's, and through him to Major Henmarsh.

Carter had made the call well away from where any of the lads in his platoon could hear, but for some reason, he had allowed Andy to be within earshot. Andy had heard the news, and it wasn't good.

The battalion had abandoned their permanent camp southwest of the town and pulled back to K2, the region's main airstrip, where they were holding a defensive perimeter as a steady stream of Hercules C130s were landing and evacuating the British army from this region of Iraq, one company at a time.

Carter had said that the Major was looking into putting together a relief effort of some sort to bail them out, but from the grim look on the young man's face, Andy guessed the officer had been told this was going to be a very long shot.

'You okay?' asked Andy.

'Why the hell are they leaving?'

Andy shook his head. 'This situation must have got worse.'

A lot worse if the British army was pulling out.

'I just don't get it. Surely they'd be sending more troops here to help calm this thing down.' Lieutenant Carter wiped dust, sweat and grime from his face with his *shemagh*. 'Things have just gone crazy.'

'I've got a feeling there's much more going on than we know about,' Andy said quietly. 'We know it started with a series of explosions in Saudi designed, by *someone*, to provoke widespread rage.'

'Someone? You mean like Al-Qaeda?'

Andy shrugged, 'Possibly, they're the obvious candidates.

This does feel … *orchestrated*, doesn't it?'

Carter nodded absent-mindedly, distracted with more immediate concerns.

'Listen,' he said after a while, 'I'm not sure they can spare the men to come after us. It sounded like they were stretched thin and getting a lot of contacts around K2.' He bit his lip again, and then added, 'We might have to make our own way out of this mess.'

'Oh Christ,' replied Andy.

'But don't tell anyone. Don't tell my men. Okay?'

'Sure.'

Carter squatted down on his haunches and leant against the pink wall, burying his face in his hands.

'Shit, I don't know what to do,' he muttered.

Andy looked around and noticed some of the platoon looking uncertainly at the officer from their stations around the compound wall. He kneeled down beside him.

'Your men are watching you,' he whispered quietly.

The young officer immediately straightened up and sucked in a deep breath. 'You're right,' he replied with a nod and a grim smile. 'I'll work something out.'

Andy nodded, 'Sure.' He wanted to give the lad a reassuring pat on the shoulder, but with those squaddies intently studying their CO, he knew they probably shouldn't witness that. No matter how screwed up the young Lieutenant thought the situation was, as far as the lads were concerned, this had to look like a momentary operational glitch, that things were in hand and a remedy already on its way. Lieutenant Carter had to look upbeat.

Andy didn't envy him having to brass it out like that. He stood up and made his way across the compound to where Mike, Erich and Ustov sat in the shade of the parked vehicles and, a few yards away, Farid and the two young drivers sat, watched over by a soldier.

Mike nodded in the direction of the Lieutenant. 'What's the news then?'

'We're not the only ones with problems.'

'And what the fuck is that meaning?' asked Erich.

Andy felt he had to support Carter and throw some sort of a positive spin on things, but it felt crap lying to them. 'It means it might take them a little while to get round to helping us out. But they will.'

Mike offered a wry smile. 'Sure.'

Andy's mobile phone began to ring. He looked down at it with some surprise and checked the number of the incoming call.

'It's the wife,' he muttered with a bemused look, which triggered a snort of laughter from both Mike and Erich, whilst Ustov simply looked confused.

'I told you honey, never call me at work,' quipped Mike.

Andy smiled and then answered the call. 'Jenny?'

'Andy?' she replied. The signal was astonishingly clear. 'Oh God. Are you all right over there?'

Andy was tempted to reply with some dry humourless sarcasm; after all, the last time they'd spoken, as he'd packed his bags preparing to leave for this particular job five days ago, it had been somewhat less than cordial.

'I'm okay.'

'I was worried. They're saying on the news that the whole of the Middle East is in a right mess.'

'What the hell's going on, Jenny? What do you know?'

'I don't know, it seems like things are happening everywhere. There've been bombs and explosions in … in central Asia somewhere.'

'Georgia, near the Tengiz fields?'

'Yes, that's right. They mentioned that place on the news … Tengiz. They're talking about oil shortages, Andy. Just like … you know, just like—'

'Yes,' he finished for her, 'I know.'

'And then this morning there was one of those huge oil-tankers blown up in—'

'The Straits of Hormuz?'

'Yes. You heard about it? Apparently it's blocked off the Straits to all the ships that had oil and could have delivered it.'

Andy felt something ice-cold run down his spine. 'Yes ... yes, I heard that from somewhere.'

The Tengiz refineries hit, Hormuz blocked, pan-Arabian unrest triggered by an attack on something like the Ka'bah – all these events within twenty-four hours of each other. Exactly as described.

'Andy, I'm scared. The trains aren't running. They've stopped the trains, and there's going to be some big announcement made by the Prime Minister. The radio, the TV ... they're all talking about problems right across the world.'

The only edge Jenny and the kids had right now over most of the other people around them was the few hours' advance warning he could give her. She had to sort herself out right now.

'Jenny, listen to me. If they announce the sort of measures I think they might at lunchtime, the shops will be stripped bare within hours. It's going to be fucking bedlam. You've got to get the kids home, and go and buy in as much food—'

'I can't! I'm stuck up in Manchester.'

Damn! He remembered she'd arranged some bloody job interview up there. Part of her whole *screw-you-I-can-do-just-fine-on-my-own* strategy.

'Is there no way you can get home?' he asked.

'No. No trains, no coaches. It looks like they've stopped everything.'

'Then get Leona to make her way down from Norwich, pick up Jake, take him home and buy in as much as she can!'

A pause.

'Jenny,' continued Andy, 'she won't listen to me. I spoke to her yesterday. I think she thinks I'm just being an over-anxious wimp or something. She'll listen to you. After all, you were always the big sceptic.'

He heard laboured breathing on the end of the phone; Jenny was crying. 'Yes, yes okay. Oh God, this is serious isn't it?'

'Yes, I think it will be. But listen, you need to do this now.

Do you understand? Don't take "no" for an answer from her.'

She can be so bloody wilful and stubborn.

'Of course I won't,' she replied, her voice faltering.

'And then you've got to find a way to get down to London to be with them,' Andy added.

'I know … I know.'

'Any way you can, and as quickly as possible.'

Jenny didn't respond, but he could hear her there, on the end of the line.

'Andy,' she said eventually, 'this is really it, isn't it – you know … what you've been—'

'Please, Jenny. Just get our kids safely home,' he replied.

CHAPTER 18

11.18 a.m. local time

Al-Bayji, Iraq

Sergeant Bolton joined Private Tajican standing on the stack of pallets and keeping a watch on events outside in the street.

'What is it?' he asked the Fijian.

'Movement, Sergeant. Something going on.'

Bolton looked up at the soldier who dwarfed him both in height and width. Tajican pointed towards some activity down at the far end of the boulevard. 'There, sir.'

He squinted against the dazzling mid-morning sunlight; even though the normally blue sky was veiled by a coating of featureless white cloud, the diffuse light leaking from behind made it hard not to screw up his eyes. A crowd of men were gathered around a truck parked in the entrance to a side-street, they were doing *something* with it, but it was hard to make out exactly what.

'What are you buggers up to?' Sergeant Bolton murmured to himself.

'No good?'

Bolton grinned and nodded. 'S'right lad, up to no bloody good.' He spoke quietly into his throat mic on the command channel. 'Lieutenant? I think we might need to get ready for another contact.'

Across the compound, Carter stirred to life, walking swiftly across the dirt, doing his best to look relaxed and in control. He weaved through the vehicles parked in the middle of the compound over to where Bolton and Tajican were standing on the pallets stacked against the wall.

'What is it, Sergeant?'

Bolton ducked down behind the wall and turned to face his CO. 'Well, sir, looks to me like they're rigging something up on a truck.'

'More specifically?'

Bolton shot a glance at the big Fijian. 'I think they're loading some ordnance, some sort of improvised explosive device.'

Tajican looked at the Sergeant and then nodded in agreement, 'Reckon so, chief, an IED.'

Carter sighed. He climbed up on to the stack to join them, studied the activity for a few seconds, before ducking down and turning to the two men.

'Well, it's obvious isn't it? They'll drive the bloody thing over here, probably park by the gate and then set it off.'

Sergeant Bolton nodded. 'Yup.'

'So, we've got to stop it getting over here. What have we got in the platoon that's meaty enough to disable it?'

'The Minimi might have done it,' replied Bolton. 'We've got a couple of SA80s with grenade launchers … USGs.'

'Have we got anyone good enough with their aim to drop a grenade into the back of that truck?'

'Lance Corporal Westley, the Geordie lad, he's pretty fit with it, but not at this range, sir. We'll need it to be closer. Maybe we can catch it on the approach.'

'Wait till it's a moving target? That's a pretty crap idea, Sergeant.'

'Or we can try sending some of our boys out to nobble it before they get going, sir?'

Lieutenant Carter thought about it for a moment, and then shook his head. 'No, they'd be dead before they got fifty yards – they've got guns on every damned roof.'

The options weren't great, or varied. He balled his fists and tapped them together a few times as he weighed one against the other.

'Okay, let's go with your first crappy idea, Sergeant. We'll put every gun we have on it, and the two USGs too if … when, it starts heading towards us. Maybe we'll get lucky and something will hit the explosives they've loaded in the back.'

Carter took another peek over the wall. It looked like they'd just about finished loading whatever it was, and some activity was going on amongst the crowd towards the front of the truck.

Looking for a volunteer to drive, eh? That was something they seemed to have an endless supply of over here in this land of martyrs; young men ready to die.

Andy watched Mike as he got up and wandered over to the three Iraqis huddled anxiously together in the shadow of one of the Land Cruisers, a soldier a few yards away watching them. Mike squatted down in front of them, studying them silently for a moment as he held the AK47 loosely – not aimed, but not exactly swung away either.

'What are you doing here?'

Farid shrugged, 'I'm not understand.'

'It's simple, why the hell are you in here, and not out there with your buddies? I mean, if you're such a good little brother like you said, and you think our shitty western ways stink, why aren't you out there with them, taking pot-shots at us?'

'I am a Muslim, is wrong for me to take your life, even though you are an infidel – even though you are nothing.'

Mike screwed his face up in disgust. 'Oh we're *nothing* are we? We've sacrificed several thousand young American lives so you savages can have a democracy; a chance to fucking well vote.'

'And we will replace with Shari'ah as soon as you Americans gone,' replied Farid defiantly. 'Your ways are not ours.'

Andy could see the exchange between the two men was going to escalate quickly, particularly given how strung out they all were. He pulled himself up to his feet and walked over, uneasily, wondering how he was going to calm him down.

'Mike,' he interrupted quietly. 'Take it easy. I don't think he means "nothing" in the same way we'd mean it. It's a language thing.'

'Yeah, right,' he smiled dryly. 'Tell you what, why don't I just hand over this gun to him, or one of his little buddies? You heard him … we're nothing to him, just vermin. You think that's a good idea? Think your little old friend here will stand shoulder to shoulder with you?'

'Look,' Andy replied, 'this isn't helping anyone, Mike. Like it or not, Farid and these two boys are in this mess alongside us. They're here because they're just as big a target as we are. Think about it! They're LECs – locally employed civilians. If the insurgents out there get hold of them, they'll be made an example of. You can bet on that.'

Mike looked at him. 'You trust them?'

Andy shrugged. He wasn't sure what answer he could honestly give; trust them or not, they were all in the same boat right now.

CHAPTER 19

8.21 a.m. GMT

UEA, Norwich

Leona smiled.

Two nights in a row now.

It was definitely looking very promising. She had half-expected Dan to make up some excuse yesterday, about not being able to get together again last night. Most lads his age were like that.

Break the glass, grab the goodies and run.

But it seemed not Dan. She hated leaving him this morning, dashing out whilst he was still stretched out and dozy in his messy bed. Staying over at his place hadn't exactly been planned, and now she had to scurry over to her rooms on campus to get her books before today's first lecture. It was only halfway back up the Watton Road entrance to the UEA grounds that she remembered she had left her phone switched off.

It rang as soon as she switched it on.

'Leona?'

'Dad?'

'For crying out loud, Mum and me have been trying to get hold of you all morning. Are you all right?'

'I'm fine.'

'Listen, your mum and I have talked. We both want you to go get Jake and go home.'

'You mean because of those riots?'

'Yes.' He sounded tired and stressed.

Leona ground her teeth with frustration.

Not now. Please, not now.

'Dad, I'm right in the middle of some *really* important assignments,' she replied.

And I've finally landed Daniel, don't let's forget that.

'Leona, I'm not going to argue with you, love.'

Love. Leona rolled her eyes. God that was irritating, Dad only called her that when he was about to blow off steam, like some flipping primeval volcano; annoying actually, rather than intimidating.

'Look Dad, I'm not—'

'SHUT THE FUCK UP AND LISTEN!' his voice barked furiously.

Leona recoiled. The phone nearly slipped out of her hand on to the ground.

'YOU WILL do as Mum said. Leave now, pick up Jake, go home, and get as much tinned food as you can.'

Leona was stunned into silence. Now, all of a sudden, sensing things had become serious.

'Are we going to have riots over here?' she asked. 'I heard something on the radio yesterday about—'

'Yeah, it may happen. Food shortages, power shortages, all sorts.'

His voice sounded stretched and thin, and worried – frightened even. She had heard that sort of fear in his voice once before, years ago.

'Dad, did you get my email?'

'What?'

'My email. I sent it on Friday?'

'What? Yeah … yeah I got it, but what's—'

'I saw one of those men on TV, Dad. One of those men I saw in New York.'

There was a pause, although she could hear a lot of noise in the background. Voices shouting and banging like someone hitting a nail with a hammer.

'I'm not sure we should talk about this, Leona. Not over the phone.'

'Why?'

Another long pause.

'Leona, please just get your brother, and go home. Buy as much food and water as you can.'

In the background she heard voices rising in timbre; several of them, loud, insistent.

'Dad? What's going on?'

And then she heard the staccato sound of hammering again, more of it joining in.

'Leona!' Dad shouted, his voice distorted by the noise. 'Leona! I've got to go now!'

She'd never heard him sound like that, not ever. Angry a few times, but never like that.

'Dad! What's going on?' she replied, her voice beginning to wobble, sown with the first seeds of panic. She heard a man in the background, close by, as if he was standing next to Dad. It was the sort of voice she guessed was normally very deep, but was now raised, almost shrill with panic – God, it was frightening. Something was going on.

She heard Dad one last time. 'Please! DO AS I ASK! I've got to—'

And then they were disconnected.

The call left her trembling. The voice in the background had sounded foreign, American perhaps. But if truth be told, it wasn't the shrillness of his timbre, but the words she had heard this man shout that had set the hairs on her forearms standing.

'*Here they come.*'

The memory came back to her five minutes later, as she was playing over and over the last few seconds of that bizarre phone call. It was the tone of Dad's voice though, that had brought the memory to the surface – fear, not for himself of course, fear for her …

Dad seems so on edge. He sits her down on the bed, and looks at her intently.

'You saw nothing important Leona. Do you understand? Nothing important,' he says, speaking loudly, clearly … almost

as if he's speaking to someone else, someone on the other side of the hotel room.

'But who were those men Daddy?'

'No one you need to concern yourself with. Just a bunch of boring old business men, nothing to worry about, okay?'

Leona knows that's a brush-off. Those men were the 'mystery men' Dad was meant to meet. They're the reason Dad's been so distracted, short-tempered, nervous these last few days. But she knows by the way he's staring at her, by the tremble in his voice, that she should do as he says and forget about them.

Leona smiles reassuringly at him. 'Okay.'

'It happens, sweetheart, wrong room. I've done that before. No harm done.'

Leona nods.

'Good girl. Let's just forget about this now, huh? Just a silly little secret between you and me?'

'Okay.'

'Good. Remember Leona: our secret. Come on, I'm going to buy you that Beanie Doll you're after … what's her name?'

'Sally Beanie.'

'Sally Beanie, that's right. And maybe, if you're good, we'll get the pony-riding set too?'

Leona finds herself grinning, the men in the room next door forgotten for now.

The memory, from when she was ten – that family trip to New York – had all but faded. She had almost forgotten wandering into that wrong room, then the right room, walking in on Dad, sitting in the dark. And then telling him what had just happened.

But seeing that old man's face again on the TV recently had been unsettling, and hearing that fear again in Dad's voice – the memory had come tumbling out from a dark and dusty corner, as clear as day. She wondered for a second time, if she *should* have emailed Dad about it. There'd been something so intense about him – the day he made her promise to forget.

He hadn't been frightened, he'd been terrified.

CHAPTER 20

11.22 a.m. local time
Al-Bayji, Iraq

Lieutenant Carter watched the approaching truck. It chugged up the boulevard towards them, belching a cloud of exhaust behind it, and complaining loudly as the gears crunched and it gathered speed.

'Move your fucking arses,' shouted Sergeant Bolton as he waved the last of the platoon forward into firing positions up along the wall and beside the barricade of detritus covering the iron gate.

Lance Corporal Westley waited beside Carter, the SA80 with the grenade launcher fitted beneath the barrel in his hands. He pulled the stock against his shoulder and prepared to fire.

'Easy,' he said, 'not yet, let it get closer.'

'Aye, sir.'

Following in the wake of the slowly moving truck, a respectful distance behind, he could see a large group of armed men and boys jogging to keep up. They were using the truck for cover to get closer. Carter could see their game-plan as clear as day. The truck would roll up to the compound, or crash through the iron gate, and then the explosives in the back would detonate. The armed men running behind the truck would storm through the open gateway seconds after the explosion and clean up quickly and easily.

Simple and sensible.

Westley was their best bet to set the bastard off before it hit them, but only if he could drop a grenade somewhere in the back of the flatbed truck. In their favour, the vehicle looked as if it was on its last legs and struggling to build up any significant speed. It rumbled closer, and with a shuddering clatter it bounced up on to the island running down the centre of the boulevard. The armed crowd jogging behind the truck were beginning to lag behind as the truck finally seemed to find its legs and began to pick up some speed.

'Okay,' muttered Carter, 'when you're ready.'

Westley nodded and then lined the approaching truck up through his weapon sight. He raised the barrel, calculating the drop as best he could.

With a thud and a puff of acrid smoke he launched a grenade.

It arced through the air tumbling erratically as it went, coming down and bouncing up high off the ground several yards in front of the advancing truck. It exploded, shattering the windshield and ripping the hood of the truck off, exposing a grime-encrusted and rusty engine that shuddered violently on its ancient mountings.

'Shit. Get the other USG, quick!' ordered Lieutenant Carter.

Westley picked up the second SA80 fitted with the grenade launcher, and lined up his second and final attempt.

The truck bounced off the near side of the central island on to the road, amidst a cloud of dust and flecks of rust thrown and shaken loose.

He hunkered down, aimed and then raised the gun upwards, once more allowing for the drop.

A second thud and a puff of smoke exploded from the stubby and wide barrel of the launcher. The grenade arced upwards again, a steeper angle and much higher than the first, tumbling in the air and then finally dropping down.

With only about twenty yards between the truck and the gate, Sergeant Bolton gave the order to fire. Every gun in the platoon, plus Mike and Erich both issued with the AKs, let rip. The front of the truck seemed to explode amidst a shower of sparks that reminded Carter of a Catherine wheel.

Fifteen yards ...

The truck's driver flopped back in his seat, shredded by

the volley and only vaguely recognisable as having once been a human being. Carter watched Westley's grenade continue to drop. It landed on the back of the truck and then bounced high again, off the back of the flatbed area … and then detonated.

The blast pushed both of them back off their stack of pallets down on to the floor of the compound. Carter landed heavily and lay on the ground, temporarily winded – but bizarrely, looking up at the pale sky and enjoying the slow-motion cascade of a million comets of debris trailing ribbons of black smoke.

And it was silent.

He'd expected the detonation to be loud, but the only noise he could hear was the dull rush of blood in his ears, like the roar of waves crashing on a rocky shoreline. Really quite pleasant.

He sensed movement around him, and slowly the reassuring rumble of distant ocean waves receded, to be replaced with the sound of voices screaming, impact, gunfire. He pulled himself up on to his elbows, still struggling to get his breath and looked around.

The momentum of the truck had done its job and the shattered and burning chassis had managed to smash through the gateway. The immense blast seemed to have knocked everyone to the ground, and he watched as his platoon picked themselves up. Two of the Land Rovers and one of the two Cruisers nearest the gate had caught some of the blast and were burning fiercely.

And there were some casualties; a couple of the lads who had been standing closest to the gateway were lying still – one of them in several pieces.

Through a curtain of flames in the gap that had once been occupied by an iron gate, he could see the armed insurgents gathering. They were savvy enough to know their attack needed to follow in quick succession to take advantage of the shock and disorientation of the blast. And even as he pulled himself to his feet and fumbled for his weapon, the first and most foolhardy of them were scrambling through the burning debris strewn around the compound entrance.

*

As the last fragments of the truck rained down around them, Andy stuck his head up over the bonnet of their Land Cruiser.

'Shit, they've broken through!' he shouted.

He spotted the prone forms of a couple of British soldiers, the others were scrambling for cover, ready for the insurgents to stream in through the gateway.

Mike reached for his AK. 'I'm going to help them,' he said.

Andy took a look at the situation.

Lieutenant Carter was rallying men behind some scattered pallets to the left of the gateway; he had about six or seven men with him, and Andy watched as they settled in and trained their rifles on the opening either side of the burning chassis of the truck.

Sergeant Bolton, meanwhile, had called the rest of the platoon to him. Andy counted only another half-a-dozen men. They took up position around and behind the burning vehicles in front of the gateway. He was impressed at the speed with which they had gathered their wits and found effective covering positions; Andy's head was still spinning from the noise and shock wave of the blast.

There were a couple of weapons spare, lying on the ground beside two young men caught in the blast. He could rush out and grab one, if he was quick. But Andy could see the shimmering forms of men through the blaze, and one or two un-aimed shots whistled through the flames and smoke towards them. He didn't fancy running out from behind the cover of their Cruiser to retrieve one of the guns.

Mike turned to him. 'You better stay here,' he shot a glance at Farid, and the two Iraqi lads, 'keep an eye on them.'

Andy nodded. It made sense. He didn't have a gun to fire, and if he did, he suspected he'd be more of a liability than a help.

Several rounds thudded into the side of the Land Cruiser they were cowering behind. The gathered mob outside began to grow impatient waiting for the flames to die down and fired indiscriminately through the curtain of flames at the smouldering vehicles inside.

Mike shook his head in disgust. 'No fucking way I'm dying

here in this piece-of-crap town,' he muttered to himself. 'I've got more important shit to attend to.'

It was then that young Amal made a dash away from the soldier who was meant to be watching over him, but was now distracted – focusing on the threatening press of enemy bodies beyond the diminishing flames.

'Hey!' shouted Mike. 'The bastard's making a break for it!'

The Texan raised the AK in his hands and drew a bead on the young lad as he raced two dozen yards across open space towards the gateway. As he pulled the trigger Andy knocked the rifle upwards, and three rapidly fired rounds whistled harmlessly up into the sky.

'Are you fucking crazy!'

Amal wasn't trying to escape from them.

The young man slid to the ground dislodging a cloud of dust as he reached the nearest of the two bodies, and the dead man's rifle. The ground around the body suddenly exploded with several puffs of dirt, as the insurgents zeroed in on the movement inside the compound. Amal waited, lying as flat as he could behind the body of the British soldier, using it as cover as several more bullets thudded into the side of it.

'He's going for the guns.'

Mike said nothing in reply, as he watched the Iraqi lad cowering nervously, with the rifle lying flat across his chest.

The gunfire diminished momentarily and Amal flipped himself over on to his belly, ready to leap to his feet at a moment's notice.

Mike hunkered down and aimed down the barrel towards the young man.

'Jesus! I said he's going for the guns!' shouted Andy.

'Shut up!' grunted Mike. 'I'm giving him a hand.'

He fired off half-a-dozen well-aimed rounds towards the mob on the far side of the truck. One of them threw his arms up and went down; the others ducked instinctively.

'Amal! Go! *Yallah*!' shouted Andy realising Mike was offering covering fire.

The young man sprang to his feet and lurched another dozen yards across the compound, and then hit the dirt as he arrived beside the second dismembered body and reached out for the gun there.

It was at this point that the first and most courageous of the mob outside decided to pick their way through the smoking and scattered debris, and enter the compound with their guns firing.

Lieutenant Carter's and Sergeant Bolton's men both opened up at the same time, releasing a criss-crossing lattice of bullets that quickly cut them down. Several more of them filed in from behind, dropping down behind the bodies of their comrades, using them for cover, and firing back with surprisingly cool heads.

Amal remained where he was, trapped by the incoming and outgoing gunfire zipping past only inches above his prone form. The intense exchange lasted for only about ten seconds, and then a shared lull occurred as both sides reloaded.

Amal took his chance then, pulled himself to his feet, clutching both of the SA80s in his arms and began to scramble back across the compound towards the Land Cruiser.

'Oh shit, come on!' Andy yelled. Farid had joined them and was yelling something, probably very similar, in Arabic.

Amal's luck lasted most of the way across, but a well-aimed burst coming from one of the half-dozen men that had gone to ground and established a toe-hold inside the compound, brought the lad down. He fell forward as a shot punched him squarely between the shoulders, and the two assault rifles spilled out on to the ground beside him.

Mike thrust his AK into Andy's hands, and then leapt out from behind the Rover. He loped across twenty feet of open ground towards the two valuable weapons, frustratingly close to being retrieved.

Sergeant Bolton's men were firing again, having reloaded. They were managing to keep the heads of the men inside the compound down. Even so, more of them were stepping through the steaming, smoking debris and firing towards the American, attracted by the sudden burst of movement.

Mike dropped to his knees as he reached the two weapons. He grabbed the strap of one of them, and slung the gun over his shoulder. Then, he reached down and grabbed both of Amal's hands.

The lad was light, and Mike dragged him roughly across the ground, like an empty sleeping-bag, as bullets threw divots of dirt up around him.

Sergeant Bolton spoke over his radio on the command frequency to Lieutenant Carter.

'Sir, we need to push these bastards back out – now.'

'Yes I know,' the Lieutenant's voice crackled back.

Bolton counted about half-a-dozen men that had managed to make their way into the compound and find secure, hardcover positions amidst the scattered mess of debris inside. From there, those buggers were doing a good job of holding the door open for the mob outside. He had some grudging respect for them. Those men were seasoned fighters, perhaps having cut their teeth in Afghanistan; the hardcore few that one would find at the centre of every contact that seemed to exist in the midst of every street riot. And they were prepared to die, happy to die, longed to die. In Sergeant Bolton's experience, a mindset like that, having no fear of death, was more than a match for any type of cutting-edge battlefield technology they could counter them with.

The mob outside was gaining confidence, and the first few were picking their way through the gateway, given covering fire by those hardcore bastards. Bolton decided they couldn't wait any longer. This was the moment that would swing things either way. They needed to push hard right now, and dislodge their toe-hold on the compound, before numbers overwhelmed them.

'Right lads,' he said, turning to the six men sheltering with him behind the two unharmed Rovers. 'We've got to kick those raggys out, or ...'

Or this'll be all over in the next minute.

'Or we'll be well on the way to being buggered,' he added.

One of the lads, Lamby, nodded towards the dug-in enemy gunmen. 'How do we do that? They got a fucking good position.'

'If we sit here they have,' replied Bolton grinning, 'but if we take them by surprise and charge them – they'll bolt like rabbits.'

Actually, he doubted very much that they would. He hit the press-to-talk button on his PRR. 'Sir, we're going to charge over and barrel-shoot the bastards.'

Lieutenant Carter's reply was hesitant. 'Okay, in that case we'll give you covering fire Sergeant. Give me your shout and we'll try and keep their heads down.'

'Yes sir,' he replied as he refreshed his magazine and then turned to the others. 'Check your ammo, lads. On my command we're going over there and giving those shits a good kicking. The other boys will give us covering. You ready?'

The six young men nodded in unison as they clambered to their feet, keeping low, but ready to charge on their Sergeant's command.

Bolton smiled.

Good lads, all of them.

'All right then.'

He spoke into his throat mic. 'Sir, we're ready to go.'

'We're ready to cover you.'

'On "one" then sir?'

'Understood.'

Bolton counted down loudly, 'Three … two … ONE!'

He leapt out from behind the parked Rovers, his rifle held at the hip, and without a moment's hesitation the six men with him followed suit. Simultaneously, Lieutenant Carter's men opened fire on the dug-in militia and as sparks flew around them, they all hunkered down.

Sergeant Bolton found himself laughing breathlessly as he screamed encouragement at his men. They scrambled across thirty feet of open ground with gunfire whistling past them inaccurately from the mob outside.

As they reached the smouldering tangle that had not so long ago been a truck, the men dug in there were largely caught out, looking up at the screaming, enraged faces of the British squaddies with only a scant moment to try and swing their AKs up in response.

Bolton stumbled upon an old man who looked old enough to be his grandfather; a tanned face rich with laughter lines and framed with a white-and-grey beard, and big blue eyes opened wide with surprise. As he pulled the trigger and destroyed that face, he oddly found himself thinking in the heat of the moment that the man had looked a little like Santa Claus.

His section made quick work of the other half a dozen; firing down at the prone forms quickly and ruthlessly. He saw one of them drop his gun as if it were red-hot and quickly raise his hands. But the soldier standing over him made a snap decision to ignore that and fired a dozen rounds into his chest and head.

Bolton nodded approvingly, this wasn't the kind of exchange where prisoners could be taken.

Lieutenant Carter led his men out from their position behind the stacked pallets and emerged into the open, dropping smartly into a firing stance. They unleashed a sustained volley at the mob that had begun to press forward through the wreckage to reclaim their toe-hold. As the first few of them dropped to the ground, the others quickly fell back and within little more than a dozen seconds Carter's men had pushed them back out of the compound and on to the kerb outside, where a sense of panic swept through the crowd like wildfire, and the mob began to waver, then disperse. They turned on their heels and beat a retreat back across the boulevard to the shelter and safety of the buildings and walled gardens on the far side.

The ground around the gateway was littered with the bodies of many of them. Only a couple of the prone forms were still moving.

Lieutenant Carter waved his arm. 'All right, cease firing!' he shouted. He knew the section's wind was up, but they desperately needed to conserve the ammo they had left.

He turned round to look for Sergeant Bolton, firstly to congratulate him on having the bottle to pull that charge off, and secondly to issue orders to seal that gateway somehow. They'd probably need to push one or two of the blast-damaged Rovers over to plug the gap. That would be enough of an obstruction for now.

And then he saw Bolton standing amidst the wreckage holding both hands to his pelvis and looking down at the spreading dark stain and the ragged hole in his tunic.

'Bollocks.' Bolton groaned angrily before dropping to his knees.

CHAPTER 21

8.55 a.m.

UEA, Norwich

Ash stepped silently over the stiffening corpse of Alison Derby. The blood that had gushed from her carotid artery last night was now a dry pool of dark brown gel on the linoleum floor. She was dead within two minutes of him slipping the narrow blade of his knife into the side of her neck – unconscious after only a minute. He had decided he couldn't afford to be distracted by her shuffling and whimpering.

A shame; she had been nice, courteous and helpful.

But he needed it to be quiet inside, so he'd hear when Leona Sutherland came up the stairs and approached the door. He had waited all through the night, sitting on the stool in the kitchen, in the dark, patiently waiting. It seemed likely, after midnight, that the girl was staying over with her boyfriend. But he couldn't afford to be asleep just in case she did turn up.

He'd had the dark hours alone, to sort through his thoughts.

We could have closed the door on the little girl, when she entered. I could have finished her there.

But no, that would have been needlessly reckless. Processing a body in an exclusive hotel, in the middle of Manhattan, would have been difficult. Yet, what she had seen was dangerous; three of The Twelve. Worse still, the three of them together in the same room.

He knelt down beside Alison Derby; her face was grey, her lips a bluey-purple, her eyes still open, dull and not quite focused on anything. Ash could kill a ten-year-old girl just as easily as an eighteen year old. The end always justified the means. And in any case perhaps it was a kindness. The next few weeks were going to be truly apocalyptic. A young girl like Alison, with no advance knowledge of what was coming, unprepared, no stocks of food, or water … reduced to living like a cave-dweller and at the mercy of a very brutal form of Darwinism? She'd not have lasted long. She almost certainly would have been one of those who failed to make it out the other side.

Ash passed several hours confessing to Alison everything he knew about the *plan*, and why *they* were doing it. Why it needed to be done. And then he told her all about himself. How lonely it was to live only within the shadows, to move from one pseudonym to the next.

She was a great listener. The dead usually were.

Dawn arrived early, a clear sky, a strong sun and Ash listened to the campus slowly wake up, the noises drifting in through the open kitchen window; an alarm radio snapping on, a kettle boiling, the laughter and to-and-fro from a couple of girls on the floor above, the thud of a dance track from someone's stereo.

And then he heard footsteps on the stairwell outside. It could be her, could be someone else. Either way, he should be ready to pull her in and quickly deal with her as soon as that door opened.

Leona took the stairs up to the second floor of her accommodation block fogged with worry and jumbled thoughts. In the foyer she stood with the keys jangling in her hands. Coming down the stairs from the floor above she could hear someone's stereo pumping out a bass line that made the stairwell window vibrate subtly.

Everyone seemed to be calmly going about their business.

'… it'll catch everyone by surprise, no one will know what's happened until all of a sudden there are soldiers stationed around every petrol station and food shop …'

Dad's words sent a shiver down her.

'… you don't want to be the last person to react to this …'

‘Shit, I really have to go home,’ she muttered quietly to herself.

But there were a few things she needed to get: some clothes, the house keys, her iPod; and then she’d have to see what time the first available train down to Liverpool Street station was. She shuffled through her keys and found the one for their door, hoping that Alison had the kettle on so she could grab a quick cup of tea before packing her bag to go home.

Of course, Alison was going to want to know why the hell she was going home all of a sudden, instead of sticking around for reading week like she’d promised. Leona wasn’t sure she was quite ready to come out with something like, ‘Oh I’m heading home because my Dad said the end of the world’s about to happen. He knows about that kind of stuff.’ Alison was pretty cool though. Unlike the four other girls they shared with, who spent most of their time talking *Big Brother*, she was quite switched on.

She was about to slide the key into the door lock when her phone rang.

CHAPTER 22

8.57 a.m. GMT
UEA, Norwich

It made her jump.

She looked at the number on the display, it was Dad again.

'Dad, you okay? It sounded like something was going on over th—?'

'Leona, listen to me. I haven't got much charge on my phone. I …'

'Dad, I was so worried about—'

'LISTEN!'

She shut up.

'Do *not* go to our home. It's not safe! Do you understand?'

'What? Why?'

'I haven't got time to explain. It's going crazy here, my phone could cut off at any time. Look, I might be wrong. I probably am, but just to be safe … get Jake, get some food and water, you know what kind of food. Tins. And then go to Jill's.'

Jill was a friend of Mum's, she lived alone three houses down on the opposite side of their leafy little street.

'Jill's? Why?'

'Just do that will you? Stay away from home. Go to Jill's instead.'

'But why Dad?'

'I haven't got the time. Where are you right now?'

'I'm just letting myself into my digs, I was going to pack some—'

'Oh for Christ's … Leona, get the hell away from there!'

'What?'

'Please, do me a favour and leave right now.'

'Dad? What's going on ? You're scaring me.'

'Leona, leave RIGHT NOW—'

The call disconnected.

She stared at the door in front of her for a moment, suddenly very wary of what might be inside. Her key had been poised inches from the lock when the phone rang. It was still hovering inches away now. There was no ambiguity there. Dad said to 'get the hell away' from her digs. If he'd said that in any other way; a nagging, hectoring tone, a snotty irritable voice, his softly-softly *do it for me* voice, she would probably have decided to tune him out.

But he'd said it in just the right way to scare the shit out of her.

Leona put the key back in her pocket, turned as quietly as she could on her heels and took the stairs quickly down to the front door of the building.

He was still splayed out on his bed, dead to the world, fast asleep.

She crossed the room and knelt down beside him. 'Dan. Wake up, Dan,' she said quietly.

He stirred almost immediately, stretching, squawking out a strangled yawn and then rubbed his big blue eyes with the backs of his hands.

Baby eyes.

Leona had to ask him a favour. She had to try. Walking briskly back across the centre of town she had tried the Virgin ticket line only to find out that for some unspecified reason, there were no trains down to London. She'd had the same luck with Express coaches. Oh God, she hated that she had to ask such a big favour, with them only being an item for what … no more than 24 hours? Not that they were officially an item yet. It's not like any of it was *official* – they were both sort of still finding their way through whatever it was they had going together.

'Dan?'

'Yeah,' he muttered sleepily, reaching out with one hand and cupping her small chin in it. 'Ask me anything you want, sexy babee,' he added.

'Dan, I need a favour. A really big favour.'

Oh crap, here goes. And if he says 'NO' you know you can't really blame him.

'Could you drive me to London?' she blurted, wrinkling her face in anticipation of his answer. It really was unfair to ask him like this, and she really did feel like a selfish, needy cow for—

'Sure,' he muttered sleepily.

They drove the first half an hour in silence, some music blaring from the van's cheap stereo. Leona wasn't really listening to it; instead she was wondering how she was going to explain this sudden, desperate need to head home, without sounding like a total doomsday propeller-head, like Dad.

Daniel drove on quite happily nodding his head to the music, trundling uncertainly along in the slow lane as his van, an ancient-looking rust-encrusted Ford given to him by his foster mum, struggled doggedly to achieve a steady sixty miles per hour.

As the A11 merged into the M11, they managed to overtake a surprisingly long convoy of army trucks. Daniel counted twenty of them, all of them full of soldiers, some of whom had spotted Leona in the passenger seat as they passed by and waved, grinned and made some crude and suggestive gestures towards her. She stared rigidly ahead, determined to ignore them.

It wasn't until they eventually hit the M25 and the outskirts of London that either his patience finally ran out, or the idea occurred to him to actually ask. He turned the music down.

'Why *are* we going to London anyway?'

Leona sighed. 'Dan, you're going to think I'm a bit mad.'

He smirked, 'I know you're mad.'

So, she wondered, *how do I begin?*

'Have you seen the news?'

Daniel shook his head, smiling goofily. 'Uh … no, not recently. It's all ugly old members of the government humping office staff, and losing lots of money, isn't it?'

Leona ignored his joke. 'Well, give me an idea of the last news you saw or heard?'

He was silent for a moment, giving the question serious consideration. 'Last time I was home, I guess,' he pursed his lips, counting silently, 'yeah … about five weeks ago, I saw some.'

Leona shook her head. 'My God, we could be facing the end of the world, and you wouldn't have the first idea, would you?'

Daniel thought about that for a moment, before turning to look at her, still smiling. 'Are we?' he asked.

Leona shrugged. 'I don't know. I really don't know.'

The last track on the CD came to an end, and he reached out to restart it.

'Can we put the radio on?'

'Sure,' he said, 'I s'pose I better find out if the world is ending, huh?'

As they began to negotiate the increasing traffic heading west across the north of London, Leona hopped from radio station to radio station, dialling through inner-city urban stations pumping out R&B without a care in the world. They caught several news bulletins on Radio 1, and then she tuned to Radio 4, a station she wouldn't normally touch with a barge-pole, except today. They had some experts in the studio talking with great solemnity and concern about the developing global crisis and more specifically, about the lunchtime announcement the Prime Minister was scheduled to make.

Leona's navigation left a lot to be desired and they struggled to find the correct way off the M25 to head down to North Finchley, where Jake's prep school was located, doubling back on to the ring road several times before they found the right junction to come off at.

'So, what … we're suddenly going to run out of electricity or something?' asked Daniel, after listening to a heated exchange between a couple of guests on the programme they were listening to.

'Yeah,' she replied, 'I think that's what'll happen.'

He hunched his shoulders, 'Oh, okay. Not so bad then, I suppose. I thought we were—'

She looked at him in astonishment. 'You've gotta be kidding me?'

Go easy on him, Dan's not had the five-year oil paranoia crash course, that you have.

'Uh no, I'm not kidding … am I?'

'Dan, running out of electricity is just one thing. Do you know what else it really means – running out of oil?'

He thought about that for a moment. 'Hospitals and stuff? Shit, UEA would have to close as well, right?'

She gestured towards a road sign. 'There, left at the traffic lights. That takes us south towards North Finchley. Anyway, no it means much more than the university closing. God, much more.'

'What do you mean?'

'No oil means so much more than no petrol for your car, or power for your … for your guitar amp.'

With a sudden realisation it occurred to her that she sounded so much like Dad. Even her barely detectable inherited accent was coming through more strongly.

'Dan,' she continued, 'it means no bloody food, no water—'

'Uh! No food? No water? How's that then? It's always pissing down in England, there's water everywhere! And food, shit, there's loads of it around.'

'Yeah?'

'Yeah. I mean, it's all farms and fields out there, once you get out in the countryside. That's all food isn't it?'

'*Some* of it is food. But not nearly enough.'

Daniel laughed out loud. 'What's this all about? There's some, like, riots on the other side of the world and suddenly you're telling me we're all going to be starving over here?'

Leona said nothing and looked at him.

Daniel laughed some more, and then turned to look at her. His smile slipped quickly away when he saw how intense she looked.

‘Oh come on,’ he said after a while.

‘Daniel, my dad’s an oil engineer. And for the last few years, you know what? All he’s talked to me and Mum about, is how one day the oil might suddenly be stopped from flowing. At first it was a little frightening. He’d be telling us this stuff, how easily, you know, *society* would fall apart, what could start it all happening … the warning signs. And he was so paranoid too, Dan. Talking about all this crap and then saying we should keep it to ourselves.’

Leona laughed. ‘As if I was going to spout that stuff to my mates at a party. He was so secretive about it all, he …’

‘It’s our little secret, Leona. Forget about those boring old men …’

‘Well anyway, it all started getting very boring. And for the last couple of years I started to think of Dad as a tediously paranoid dick.’

She looked out of the window at the street, clogged with cars nudging slowly forward amidst a soup of exhaust fumes shimmering in the mid-morning warmth, pedestrians passing by seemingly without a care in the world and enjoying the sun, the shop fronts on either side full of goodies at bargain-basement prices … an electronics store, with several forty-inch plasma screen TVs in the window all showing some monster trucks racing around a dirt track.

‘And this morning I discovered, after all this time … that maybe he wasn’t.’

CHAPTER 23

9.41 a.m. GMT

Manchester

The taxi-cab controller stared at her with a look of disbelief spreading across his face.

'Yes, that's right,' said Jenny, 'London. How much?'

He shook his head. 'You're taking the piss.'

Jenny sighed. 'I'm not taking the piss. I really *need* to get home. So, come on, how much?'

The controller pointed out of the window towards the road leading down from Whitworth Street to the station. 'Get a train, love.'

'I can't get a bloody train,' Jenny snapped, 'because the trains are not running for some reason.'

A customer who had been waiting in line behind Jenny stepped forward. 'Yeah, I just discovered that too,' he said leaning on the cab controller's counter beside Jenny. 'Apparently there was some terrorist threat received this morning. That's the rumour I heard, some sort of bomb threat.'

Jenny turned back to the controller. 'There, see? That's why I need a flippin' cab. Did you know the coaches are out too?'

'And the airports,' added the man standing next to her. 'There've been security alerts everywhere, it seems. There were tanks rolling up outside Heathrow I heard.'

The controller shook his head again. 'Well, whatever. We only do a local service, love.'

'Okay,' replied Jenny digging into her bag to produce her purse, 'how much then? A couple of hundred?'

'No, look sorry, sweetheart, we can't take you down to London.'

'Would five hundred cover it?' said the other man.

The controller looked at him with a sceptical frown. 'You'll pay five hundred pounds?'

He nodded. 'Yup, I've got a meeting this afternoon I can't afford to miss. I'll pay five hundred.'

The controller scratched his head. 'O-o-okay, your money. I'll see if we have a taker then,' he muttered shaking his head with bemusement. He began talking over the radio.

Jenny turned to the man behind her. 'Could we possibly share? I can pay half.'

The man, tall, slim, wearing a dark blue suit, the jacket carefully draped over one arm and the top button of his striped, office shirt unbuttoned, turned to look at her. She guessed he was in his mid-thirties, sensibly short dark hair, and glasses that looked as if they were at the cheaper end of the scale. Jenny thought he wouldn't have looked out of place holding a mug of coffee and a doughnut in either a teachers' common room, or standing, Magic Marker in hand, before a flip-pad in some ad agency's creative mush-pit.

He pursed his lips as he considered the offer. 'I need the cab to get me to Clapham. I'm not sure if—'

'That's fine,' she replied quickly, 'just as long as I can get to any tube station. I can get where I'm going from there.'

He tipped his head slightly, 'Well I suppose so then, if you're going to cover half.'

Jenny felt a small surge of relief. 'Yes, I will. Thanks, I was beginning to wonder if I'd have to walk home,' she added with a nervous chuckle.

'You're in a big hurry too?'

Jenny nodded. 'I just … well, with things the way they are, I want to be home.'

He seemed confused by that. 'The way *what* is?'

'You know? The news. The riots.'

'The riots? Do you mean that Middle East thing?'

She nodded.

'Oh right. Yes, I suppose that's a little worrying, especially if we're now getting bomb threats over here. It's really screwed up travelling today. But you know, hopefully it'll all be back to normal again tomorrow, business as usual.'

The controller thanked the driver he'd been talking to and turned to them. 'Yeah, all right I've got a driver who'll do it later on this morning. But he wants the five hundred in cash, and wants to see it in your hand before he'll take you.'

'Oh God, thank you!' Jenny sighed with relief. 'Thank you.'

The controller shrugged. 'It's your money, love. Me, I'd spend the money on a nice hotel tonight and try my luck with the trains tomorrow.'

Trains tomorrow? Anything at all running tomorrow?

She wondered if she should just come out and say something like that. But then, she didn't want to scare off the man standing beside her by sounding like some kind of nut.

'I'm just in a really big hurry, all right?' she said.

CHAPTER 24

9.45 a.m. GMT

UEA, Norwich

He listened to the call connect, then a short electronic warbling as the digital encryption filter kicked in, then a voice, masked with a pitch filter answered.

'Yes.'

'I nearly had the target. But someone warned her at the last moment.'

'Yes. We know this. She received a call from her father. He now suspects we may be after her.'

'That makes things a little more difficult.'

'Yes. The father gave her instructions to go to another location. He called it "Jill's" place.'

'Jill?'

'Possibly a member of the family or a close friend. The target can be reacquired there.'

'Were there any other details?'

'No. We just have the name "Jill".'

'There'll be something at the target's home to identify this "Jill".'

'That is what we think too.'

'Understood.'

'Proceed quickly. Things will begin to disintegrate soon, you may lose her.'

The call disconnected.

Ash pocketed his phone and cast one last glance around the room. He had been tempted to set fire to the place, so that his tracks would be covered for a while. The body of the girl would be discovered, and a good forensic pathologist might discern that she was dead before she was burned. Under normal circumstances that would be a sensible tactical move. But given how things were going to be in a few days' time, he was confident he'd not have to worry about the police following in his footsteps.

They were going to be far too busy to worry about one dead student.

As he stepped out into the stairwell, a young man passed by, casting a suspicious glance back at him as he descended the stairs.

Ash knew his appearance was incongruous. He looked completely wrong for this environment; too old, too smart, clearly not a student, and clearly with no business being here. The young man would undoubtedly tell somebody this morning, and someone would come knocking to see if everything was okay.

He let the lad go on his way.

Again, leaving a trail was of no concern to Ash. Right now his immediate priority was working out where Leona Sutherland was headed.

Next stop then, the Sutherlands' home in Shepherd's Bush. He knew the address off by heart – 25 St Stephen's Avenue. Perhaps he might even catch her there, if she was silly enough to chance a quick visit to grab a change of clothes.

CHAPTER 25

11.37 a.m. GMT

North Finchley, London

Leona instantly recognised the tree-lined gravel driveway that led up to the main school building, a stately stone structure that had, once upon a time in a previous century, been built amidst smoothly rolling green acres, but was now hedged in on all sides by suburbia. Tall, mature conifers kept the world outside from peeking in at the dozen or so acres of manicured grounds, sports fields and tennis courts.

Leona had come with her dad a few times to drop Jake off. His school tended to return a week or so before college, and Jake usually begged for Leona to come along too. She wasn't sure whether that was because he wanted to spend as much time with her as possible, or because he enjoyed showing off his older sister to the lecherous and spotty boys in the years above.

'Wow,' said Daniel, 'this is sort of like Hogwarts.'

'Yup, and very expensive,' she replied looking out of the window at the boys taking turns to volley over the net on the tennis courts to their left. The tennis coach shot a disapproving glance at the scruffy little Ford van as it coughed and crunched up the gravel drive.

'You sure it's okay for us to be here?' he asked uneasily. 'I mean school's in session, aren't we trespassing or something?'

Leona shrugged. 'Don't care. Dad asked me to get Jake out.'

Daniel parked the van in a visitor's slot beside the imposing main entrance, sheltered by a grand-looking portico supported on two stone pillars. The last time she had seen Jake was six weeks ago, helping Dad to drag his trunk up the stairs and in through that entrance. The little monkey-boy had been doing his level best to look cool in front of all the other boys arriving in their parents' lumbering Chelsea tractors. She knew he was holding the tears back and would probably blubber once Dad had placed the trunk at the end of his dormitory bed and was giving him a final goodbye hug.

Mum never came along when it was time to take Jake back; she'd be in tears, sniffling and beating herself up with self-reproach and parental guilt all the way up from Shepherd's Bush, and then embarrass the hell out of Jake when it came time for hugs and kisses. Ironic really, Mum was the one who had worked the hardest to get him into this school, and yet was totally unable to deliver him come the start of each new term.

'So what now?'

'I'll go in and see if I can find his housemaster,' she replied. She turned to look at Daniel, dressed in his ripped jeans, and his FCUK T-shirt. 'You're probably best waiting here, okay?'

Daniel smiled with some relief. 'Sure.'

After asking directions from a confounded and harried-looking young boy, who was clearly late for a class and flushed crimson as he spoke to her whilst staring, transfixed, at her pierced navel, exposed above the low waistline of her jeans, she eventually found the housemaster's study. She knocked, and hearing a muffled acknowledgement coming from within, opened the thick, heavy wooden door and stepped inside.

A man in a scruffy brown suit jacket and dark trousers that were scuffed with chalk dust was standing over an untidy desk shuffling through a tray of papers.

'Yes?' he grunted, without looking up.

'You're Mr North, the housemaster?' she asked.

Mr North looked up, and did a double take. 'I'm sorry, who are you?'

'Leona Sutherland. My brother's in your house.'

'Uhh, right well, you do know family visits are limited to specific weekends, don't you?'

Leona nodded. 'Of course. But I'm not really visiting.'

He stopped shuffling through his tray. 'So then, how can I help you?'

'I'm here to collect Jacob and take him home.'

Mr North frowned. 'I don't know anything about this. When was this arranged? Because I've not received any written approval from the Head. At least I don't think I have. Let me just check my in-tray.' He leant across his desk and started rummaging through another tray, full to overflowing with papers and envelopes yet to be opened.

Leona wondered whether she could take advantage of his apparent inability to keep abreast of his paperwork, and lie to him – make out that it had already been approved and he'd simply lost the letter.

'I mean it's possible that I just missed it,' he continued, slightly flustered as he sorted through the haphazardly piled envelopes and notes, 'and the approval's in here somewhere. When did your parents write to me about this?'

Decision time … oh shit, I'm crap at lying.

'They didn't.'

Mr North looked up, a momentary confusion written across his face.

'They decided this morning to take Jake out, and they sent me to collect him,' Leona added.

The housemaster frowned and then shook his head. 'No. I'm sorry. It doesn't work that way. We need a written request from a pupil's parents or legal guardians, and a very good reason given before we allow them to be taken out in the middle of a term.'

'They have a very good reason, Mr North,' replied Leona. 'They both think the world's about to come to an end.'

That sounded pretty bloody silly, well done.

Mr North stopped shuffling through his in-tray and looked up at her. 'The riots?'

Leona nodded.

He came around from behind the desk and took a few steps towards her. 'Your mum and dad aren't the only ones.' He lowered his voice ever so slightly. 'I've already had two other parents call me this morning to ask if their sons could be taken out.'

'And can they?'

He shook his head, 'Only with written consent, and approval from the headmaster.'

'Please, I really need to get my brother.'

The housemaster studied her silently for a moment. 'I was watching the news last night. It does look very worrying. It does seem like the world went a little mad yesterday. I do wonder if there'll be more going on today.'

'I don't know. But my dad's in the oil business, and he's the one who's panicking.'

'Why haven't your parents come for him?'

'Dad's stuck in Iraq, and Mum's stuck up in Manchester. They've stopped the trains and coaches.'

Mr North looked surprised. 'Stopped the—?'

'They didn't say why. So it's just me, and I need to get him.'

He nodded silently, deep in thought. 'Look, I have to get to my lesson, I'm already late.'

Leona took a step forward. 'Please!'

He studied her silently for a while, a long silence, punctuated by the sound of a clock ticking from the mantelpiece above a decorated Victorian fireplace. 'Maybe your father's right,' he said quietly. 'You can see the way this could possibly go.'

Leona nodded. 'My dad thinks we're going to be in really big trouble.'

'I see.'

She offered him a wan smile. 'That's why I've got to get my brother.'

Mr North nodded. 'Hmmm. It *does* seem really quite worrying.'

'Please,' she said, 'I have to get him. I'm in a hurry.'

He looked at her silently for a moment. 'I can't give you my permission to just walk in and take him without prior written consent. But,' he said, 'I can't really stop you if I don't know about it, can I?'

She understood and nodded a thank you.

'Who's your brother?'

'Sutherland. Jacob Sutherland.'

'Ahh yes, junior year two. I think you'll find his class in C block, that's the language wing.'

'Thank you Mr North.'

'You go and get him. And the first I'll know about this is when we do our afternoon assembly roll call. Which means we haven't met, all right?'

She nodded and then turned to go.

'So,' he said as she reached out and opened the door, 'what advice do you think your dad would give us here at the school?' he asked. 'What advice do you think he would give me?'

Leona turned round. 'Leave now. Get out of London before everyone else wakes up to this.'

'I see.'

'Goodbye,' she said. And then as an afterthought, 'Good luck.'

He smiled politely as she closed the door on him.

Leona looked up and down the wood-panelled corridor, and decided she might need Dan's help.

'No, see, this isn't right Leona. I'm sure this is basically illegal.'

'No it isn't, he's my brother,' she replied, craning her neck to look surreptitiously through the small window in the classroom door. Inside she could see a class of boys who looked a couple of years older than Jacob. 'Shit, not in this one either.'

Daniel cast a wary glance up and down the hallway between the classrooms. 'Look, it's abduction isn't it? Taking a minor like this?' he muttered.

'It's not, we're getting him on my mum and dad's instructions. Come on,' she waved him on, and they paced down the hallway towards the next pair of classroom doors.

'Look, even if you find him, they won't let you take him right out of the classroom.'

She stopped and looked at him, and smiled. 'Which is sort of where you come in.'

'What? How?'

'If one of the staff stands in the way …'

'What, you want me to knock 'em down?'

She nodded, 'Well maybe not punch them or anything, just sort of push them aside.'

Daniel shook his head. 'Look Leona, I think I've been pretty good so far this morning, driving you here and—'

She grabbed his wrist. 'God, please Dan, just this last favour. I have to get him home.'

He spread his palms. 'Because here … what? He's *not* safe?'

She led him up to another window, looked in briefly and saw instantly that they weren't Jake's age.

'Look in,' she said.

Dan shrugged and did as she asked. The boys inside were wearing headphones and repeating French phrases in unison.

'So?'

'So, you've been listening to the radio this morning. The trains and coaches have been quietly stopped and the army is coming home from abroad, and there's no more oil coming in. And they,' she gestured at the classroom door, 'are still doing stupid French oral.'

Which seemed to strike him as pretty dumb, once put in that context.

'Dad was right. Everyone's standing around with their heads in the sand, just like he said they would, you know, if something like this happened,' she added, trying to keep her voice down as it started to thicken with a mixture of anxiety and anger.

She jogged across the hallway to look through a door window on the far side. 'Okay,' he said following her across. 'Just this last thing, then I'm heading back to—'

'That's Jake!' she hissed, looking through the window. Without a second's hesitation, she grabbed the handle and flung open the door.

The heads of thirty seven-year-old boys and the teacher, a lady who looked a few years younger than her mum, spun round to look at them.

The silence was broken by the teacher, 'Yes?'

'Jacob,' she said ignoring her, 'you have to come with me.'

Beneath his mop of curly blond hair, and behind the milk-bottle glasses, Jacob's round eyes darted towards his teacher then back to Leona, whilst his jaw slowly dropped.

'I'm sorry,' said the teacher, 'you can't just burst in here and take one of my students.'

Leona continued to ignore her. She flashed a warning glance at Jake. 'Now!' she barked.

Jacob obediently began to rise from his seat.

'It's all right Jacob,' said the teacher gesturing for him to take his seat again, 'sit back down, there's a good boy.'

'JAKE!' Leona barked as she smacked her fist on the corner of the desk next to her, it hurt – but it also got everyone's attention. 'Mum and Dad want you home, RIGHT NOW!'

He rose uncertainly out of his seat again.

The woman advanced toward Leona. 'You're his sister?'

Leona nodded.

'Well, look, you'll have to leave. I'm in the middle of a lesson. If his parents need him home then you need to tell them that they should contact the headmaster.'

Leona turned to her, acknowledging the teacher for the first time. 'He's coming with me right now,' she said calmly and then nodded her head at Daniel standing just behind her, 'and you better not get in our way, all right?'

Daniel puffed himself up slightly and attempted a menacing frown.

'Jake, get over here now!' shouted Leona taking a few steps across the classroom towards her brother. Daniel filed in behind keeping a wary eye on the teacher and balling his fists in what he hoped was a vaguely intimidating way.

Jake did as he was told, standing up and starting to pack his exercise books and stationery back into his shoulder bag.

'Oh for God's sake, leave that Jake! We've got to go right now!'

He looked confused, placing his things back down on the desk. 'Why am I going?'

'Questions later, okay? We're in a hurry.'

The woman stirred. 'Yes, why? Can you at least tell me that? I can't let him go without knowing why—'

'Because the world's about to end,' Daniel offered uncertainly with a shrug.

'What?' the woman replied, frowning with disbelief.

Leona reached out for Jacob's small hand, and led him towards the classroom door before turning back towards the teacher. 'He's right. In a few days' time, we're all going to be hungry, and people are going to get mad, and fight. And these boys,' she gestured with her free hand at the pupils who had watched in silent and rigid disbelief at the surprise intrusion, 'should all be sent home to their families, before it's too late.'

Leona led Jacob out of the classroom and Daniel backed out after them.

'You know I'll have to notify the school security guard,' the teacher called out. 'And the police!'

In the hallway outside Leona turned to Daniel. She was trembling.

'Oh my God, we're going to be in so much trouble if Dad's wrong,' she said.

Jacob looked up at Daniel and pointed a finger at him. 'Who is he? Is he your boyfriend? Where are we going?'

She knelt down in front of him. He was tiny for his age. 'Jake, I'll explain everything later. Right now, we just need to get home, okay?'

He thought about it for about three seconds, then nodded and saluted like a trooper. 'Roger, roger.'

All of a sudden, they heard the deafening ring of what sounded very much like a fire-alarm bell.

Daniel cupped his mouth, 'I think we should run!' he shouted.

CHAPTER 26

12.30 p.m. GMT

Whitehall, London

He stared at his reflection in the mirror above the basin as he washed his hands. Caught in the downward glare of the little recessed spotlight above him, every bump, groove and crevice on his face stood out with merciless clarity. He looked ten years older standing here – fifty-five instead of forty-five.

It occurred to him that what he was doing was a job much better suited to a younger man. It was the arrogance and confidence of youth that carried you through this kind of undertaking. Doubting, second-guessing, checking the dark corners ... those debilitating habits came with *maturity* ... shit, who was he kidding ... *old age*.

His passport might say he was forty-five, but the tread-marks on his face spoke of a man much older. The wear and tear of staying at the top of the game had made its indelible mark on him. And now there was *this*.

He heard knuckles rapping against the wooden door to the gentlemen's wash-room.

'They're ready in the press room, Prime Minister.'

Charles nodded. 'Just give me a few minutes.'

His press secretary was still outside, Charles could see the twin shadows of his legs punctuating the strip of light coming through under the door.

'Sir, we are running short of time. Your broadcast is rescheduled for 1.30, and the TV people need you down in the press room to put some make-up on and do their lighting.'

For Christ's sake ...

‘I said I’ll be along in a minute!’ he shouted irritably.

The twin shadows shuffled beneath the door for a moment, and then vanished.

He splashed some water on his face and let out a ragged sigh. With only an hour to go, he had yet to fully decide what exactly he was going to announce.

How honest should I be?

That was the question.

During the night most of the Cassandra recommendations had been discreetly put into action. Internal travel arteries had been locked down. The terror threat cover story was being pushed hard, and all airports, sea ports and rail stations had been successfully closed. But the cover story wasn’t going to last for long.

Throughout the morning the process of blocking the main motorways had begun. Each blockage explained as either a severe traffic accident, or some truck losing its load across all four lanes. Again, those cover stories were only going to last a few hours at best; if they were lucky, until tomorrow morning.

Most of the main oil storage depots had, by now, been garrisoned with soldiers. The oil out there in the wider distribution system; the tankers, the bigger petrol stations – all of them would need to be requisitioned at some point, but that was a very visible process, and could only be done at the last possible moment.

The trick here was going to be not to spook the general population. Malcolm’s advice had been that they had to keep *them* doing whatever they normally do, for as long as possible. That was his job, the Prime Minister’s job, to keep everyone happy and calm for as long as he could. Malcolm had wryly quipped that Charles’ role now was to be nothing more than the string quartet on the promenade deck of the *Titanic*.

Just keep them happy with your reassuring smile, and words of encouragement.

In the meantime, for as long as the public could be fooled, they had to get as many of their boys as they could back from

Iraq and guarding key assets in the time they had. They had to get their hands on as much of the oil and food as was spread out there in warehouses and oil terminals.

It meant doing what he did best – bullshit the public for as long as possible.

Time was running out.

The travel lock-down was going to be explained as a 'large-scale unspecified threat' picked up by their secret services. That would also help to explain the higher than normal military traffic that people would undoubtedly have already noticed. There would be questions about the worsening situation in the Middle East, and whether that and the cessation of oil production from the region had anything to do with these 'security' measures.

And here he'd have to deliver the Big Lie, and he'd better do it convincingly.

'No,' muttered Charles aloud, staring at his reflection, knitting his dark eyebrows and narrowing his photogenic eyes; producing a very believable expression of sincere concern which he projected exclusively at the listener in the mirror. He backed it up with a reassuring nod as he continued.

'There's no link other than a general heightened security level. We have a healthy strategic reserve of crude oil to see us through this temporary upset. Potential choke points in oil supply, particularly from an unstable region like the Middle East, is something we have prepared for long in advance, and there is certainly no need for anyone to panic.'

His secretary was back, shuffling uncomfortably just outside the door once more. Charles could visualise him with his fist raised and knuckles hovering inches from the wooden door, agonising over whether to knock again, but knowing that he must.

'It's all right,' shouted Charles, loosening his tie ever so slightly and undoing the top button of his shirt to affect that tousled 'I've-just-been-dragged-away-from-my-desk-to-tell-you-how-I'm-fixing-things' look. He rolled up his sleeves for good measure. It was all about appearances. The right tone of voice, the right facial expression, the right look for the occasion. He'd learned a lot of that watching Tony Blair, a brilliant performer during moments of crisis.

Charles nodded at the reflection. He looked like a man who'd been working hard through the night but now had a firm handle on things.

'I'm ready.'

CHAPTER 27

3.42 p.m. local time

Al-Bayji, Iraq

Mike stared down at the corpse of the young man.

Amal had died quickly, only perhaps a minute or two after being dragged to safety behind the Land Cruiser. The bullet that had knocked him to the ground had also ripped a lung to shreds on its way through. Amal had died gurgling blood and struggling desperately for air in Mike's arms. His shirt, a Manchester United football shirt, was almost black with blood that was already congealing, drying in the heat of the afternoon.

Mike chugged a mouthful from his water bottle. The platoon medic had circulated some of the bottled water around the men half an hour earlier, and now that the situation outside had calmed down, he realised how dehydrated he'd become through the morning.

Farid squatted in the shade of the vehicle a few feet from him. He said nothing and stared at the body of the young lad, but Mike sensed the old man was actually studying him, wordlessly coming to some kind of conclusion about him. It felt uncomfortable being silently judged, appraised like that and he decided to break the silence.

'I dragged his ass back here because he had the goddamned car keys in his pocket,' Mike grunted coolly.

Farid nodded silently.

'He had the keys in his pocket, and I didn't want those fuckers outside getting hold of them,' he added for clarity.

Farid finally looked up at the Texan. 'But you have not take keys from Amal.'

Mike shrugged.

'Keys still in his pocket.'

'I'll get them when I'm good and ready.'

Farid's eyes narrowed as he looked at Mike. 'You not get him for the keys,' he said quietly.

Mike rolled his eyes tiredly. 'All right, you win, okay? I didn't get him because he had the keys. You happy now?'

Farid shook his head. 'Why?'

'Why did I go get him?'

The old man nodded in response.

Mike opened his mouth to speak before really knowing what sort of answer he was going to give. 'Shit, I don't know. Maybe because the kid had the balls to go out there and grab those guns, whilst the rest of us pussies were sitting back here sucking our thumbs.'

It took the Iraqi a moment to translate and understand what he'd said. 'You get him, because Amal was brave?'

Mike shrugged again. 'Yeah, so maybe I did, okay? That was a pretty fucking gutsy thing for the kid to do. And really shit luck that he didn't make it all the way back.'

Farid smiled and nodded. 'Allah smile upon you for your courage.'

Mike laughed. 'Yeah? If Allah sent me out to rescue the kid, why the hell did he allow him to die?'

The old man shrugged. 'His will. Is not for man to understand.'

'Yeah,' sniffed the American, 'that's what I figured, the usual religious rationale. Basically bullshit.'

'Not bullshit. But beyond our understanding.'

'Yeah see, though, that's the same old crap every goddamn fanatical imam or suicide bomber uses. *It is God's will* and who are we to question it, or try to understand it? Kind of open to a little abuse, isn't it?'

Farid nodded. 'Yes. Bad men do this. Imams who teach violence against others. That is bad, that is *haram*. As are those men who kill with terror bomb, or gun … or tank, and helicopter. To kill in Allah's name is *worst* sin of all.'

Mike looked up at the old man, surprised to hear him say that. 'That's the first time I've heard one of your lot say that.'

Farid shook his head wearily. 'There are many who say this. But, picture of brothers burning American flag, or firing gun in the air, and the sinful ones, calling for Jihad and war and death, those things are what is make the news on TV, uh?'

The American pursed his lips in consideration. 'Maybe.'

'The Qu'ran teaches peace above all.'

Andy squatted against the wall a dozen yards away and tried dialling Leona's number again, but the screen on his mobile winked out halfway through. That was it, the bloody thing was run flat. He pushed it back in his pocket and cursed to himself.

He had no idea if Leona had *really* understood not to go home. Yes, he'd told her that, but if they'd had a few more moments to talk, he could have explained why.

They were watching him. He had always half suspected that might be the case, but never fully convinced himself that they – whoever *they* were – would go to quite that much trouble.

And who the hell were they anyway? For a long time after that trip to New York, Andy had suspected he'd actually done business with some shady section of the CIA. He had read enough about them over the years to be more than a little spooked. And to know you don't mess them around.

Now he found himself wondering *did I really deal with the CIA?*

If not, who the fuck was it in that hotel room next door?

Andy cast his mind back to Saturday, just two days ago, sitting in his room in Haditha, using the PC there to log on and pick up his mail. He'd been pleasantly surprised at seeing one from Leona. It had been chatty but short, typical of her – Jenny got the long ones – no mention of any mysterious faces though. And Christ, he would have remembered *that* if he'd read it in her mail.

No doubt about it. The realisation had hit him as soon as she'd mentioned *who* she had seen during the earlier call this morning.

They're tapping my mail.

Leona's mail had been edited. Andy wished he could have quizzed Leona further over the phone, wished he'd asked her where she'd seen him, in whose company, in what setting?

What else had they intercepted? He looked down at his dead phone.

Oh shit.

Andy felt a surge of panic.

I said don't go home. I said go to Jill's. But I didn't say who Jill was, did I? I didn't say where Jill was, did I?

He was sure he hadn't. Of course not, because Leona knew Jill well.

Can they find out who she is? Is she in our phone book?

Probably not … no, definitely not. She was Jenny's mate. Jenny knew her number, it was in her head, in the quick-dial list on her phone. The phone book was for family, casual friends, people you sent the cheaper Christmas cards to.

Leona and Jake will be safe there for now. Jill will look after them.

As long as Leona did as she was told. As long as she stayed clear of their house, she and Jake would be safe, in theory. But, as far as he was concerned, the sooner he could get to them the better. Every hour, every minute that passed, with him stuck out here was an hour, a minute, too long.

Andy looked up at the situation around him. Smoke still billowing from the wreckage around the entrance, the British troops just a bunch of frightened young lads and Lieutenant Carter on his own, out of his depth and terrified.

I've got to find a way home, somehow.

He walked across the compound towards the young officer. Closer, he could see the young man was trembling, clearly shaken by the recent encounter. He looked up at Andy.

'They nearly h-had us. Fucking nearly broke in.'

Andy nodded, and squatted down. 'But you got us through it.'

He shook his head. 'Bolton got us through it.'

Andy looked around for the sergeant. Without the NCO, these men would be truly lost. He saw that Bolton was being treated by the platoon medic, Corporal Denwood. Bolton was smacking his fist on the ground angrily and cursing the medic loudly, as the wound was being dressed.

Somehow that seemed encouraging.

Andy saw that many of the lads in the platoon had noticed Carter slumped down; sensed the desperation in his body language.

'You know, they're watching you,' he said quietly.

Carter looked up at his men, grouped in weary, gasping clusters, sheltering behind the compound walls and several smouldering, tangled mounds that had not so long ago been vehicles. He could see the whites of eyes amidst soot-smudged faces, pairs of eyes that darted elsewhere as he met their gaze.

'You're right.'

'If you lose it, we're all dead.'

'We're all dead anyway. They're not going to send a relief force for us.'

'You managed to get through to your battalion again?' Andy asked.

Carter nodded. 'Through again to Henmarsh in the battalion ops room. They've already evacuated half the men holding position around K2. Their perimeter is beginning to get stretched thin. It sounds like they're getting a lot of contacts over there.' Carter stifled a grim, guttural laugh, 'The militia are smelling our blood. They know the army's leaving. It's party time for them. The best he said they could do was send a Chinook to wait for us outside the town.'

Andy grinned. 'Fuck, there we go then. That's our way home!'

'You're kidding me, right?' sighed Carter.

Andy looked up at the only way out of the compound. The entrance gate was twisted and welded into the carcass of the truck. There was no way they were going to shift that obstruction enough to drive out in the remaining vehicles.

‘We leave here, we’re doing it on foot,’ muttered Carter, ‘and they’ll cut us down before we get twenty yards from the wall.’

Andy leant forward, his face suddenly pulled back into a snarl. ‘There’s no way I’m bloody well sitting here like a lemon,’ he hissed.

Carter shook his head. ‘You want to go? Fine, take my gun if you want. There’s the exit. You’ll be dead inside thirty seconds.’

‘And we’re dead if we stay.’

Carter shrugged, ‘Pretty crappy deal, isn’t it?’

‘Shit! That isn’t fucking good enough, mate. I can’t afford to just give up like this. I’ve *got* to get home.’

‘We all want to go home, *mate*.’

Andy spat grime out of his mouth on to the ground, and then looked up at the walls for a moment. ‘So where will they send this Chinook if we want it?’

‘Anywhere outside the town.’

‘How about back over the Tigris, the way we came in this morning?’

Lieutenant Carter nodded wearily.

‘How much longer are they holding their position around K2?’

‘I don’t know. As long as it takes to complete the battalion’s evac.’

‘Tonight?’

Lieutenant Carter nodded. ‘Maybe.’

‘We’d stand half a chance at night at least, wouldn’t we? I mean,’ Andy picked up Carter’s SA80, ‘these have got those night-vision things, right?’

Carter looked at him and nodded. For the first time today Andy saw the faintest flicker of a smile spread across the young man’s mouth.

‘Yeah … and theirs haven’t.’

CHAPTER 28

12.57 p.m. GMT

Hammersmith, London

'Oh no we're going shopping? Why?' Jacob whined.

Leona led the way into the supermarket, pushing a trolley and dragging her brother along by the hand. Daniel obediently followed, trying to control two more trolleys simultaneously.

'Because we are, all right?' she snipped tersely. 'Mum and Dad want me to stock up our cupboards.' Jacob sagged.

'So we're doing a Big Shop?'

'Yes, Jake, we're doing a Big Shop. Now just shut up a moment and let me think.'

She looked around. It was busy with the sort of customers she'd expect to see midweek at lunchtime – people popping in for a sandwich, a snackpot, a pasty, and perhaps something convenient and microwave-able for this evening.

'So where do you want to start?' asked Daniel.

Leona pursed her lips as she decided.

She remembered a few years back when Dad had been momentarily distracted from his Peak Oil ramblings by the threat of bird flu. After the first case of human-contracted disease, he, like everyone else in the country, had hit the panic button and flocked to the supermarket to stock up on essentials.

He had returned home a few hours later with a car full of tinned pilchards in tomato sauce and, it seemed like, a hundred bottles of still water.

Tinned goods because they'll last longer. Pilchards because that's a very high protein meal.

That was how he explained only buying just the one type of

food. Of course it made sense, very practical. But when a month or so later, bird flu turned out like SARS to be yet another media-hyped non-event, they'd been stuck with their own little tin-can mountain of pilchards in ketchup to work their way through. After a couple of months of stepping round the damned tins of fish, and trying to conjure up some inventive family meals that could use a couple of tins, Mum finally had enough and donated the lot to a nearby hospice.

But that was then, a long time ago now. And now here she was, in the exact same situation as Dad had been, having to decide what to buy, and how much of it.

Daniel started up the first aisle: Fruit and Veg.

'Potatoes are good,' he said picking one up and inspecting it. 'I'm sure you could keep a small family going on one of these for weeks.'

Leona sighed, plucked it out of his hand and tossed it back onto the shelf. 'Dan ... are you making fun of me?'

Daniel instinctively shook his head, but a moment later the slightest smile leaked on to his face.

'I'm sorry ... this just seems, I dunno. It's just getting a little *intense*. So far this has turned out to be a really ... funny day.'

'Funny?'

'Wrong word, sorry. I guess I'm—'

'Shit Dan, I can't do this with you taking the piss out of me. I can't do this on my own. I know this time Dad's right; that we're in for a whole load of trouble. But I can't do this on my own.'

Jacob cocked his head. 'Who's in trouble?'

They both ignored him, staring at each other intently.

'I apologise for dragging you along, Dan. I really do. But I'm glad you're here with me. And if this goes the way Dad says it will then I think you'll be glad you came with me.'

He had no family to go home to, to worry about. He had a biological mother out there somewhere in Sheffield that he'd looked up once and who'd made it clear he wasn't that welcome. She had an all-new family, with all-new kids and a husband who was keeping her how she wanted to be kept. They had met just the once, and never would again, he had stoically assured her.

Daniel nodded silently. 'I … look, I'm sorry Lee, I guess that whole abduction scene at your brother's school has got me a bit, like, freaked. I sort of laugh and take the piss a bit, when I get nervous. It's just me being a dick, okay?'

She stood on tiptoes and kissed his cheek. 'You're no dick. And you were great back there. Thank you.'

Jacob curled his lips in disgust. 'Oh gross! That's puke-making.'

Leona rolled her eyes and let Daniel go. 'Come on,' she said patting his arm, 'work to do.'

'So where do we want to go?' he asked.

'Tinned stuff. I know just what to get.'

She led the way past aisles of chocolate treats and salty snacks, with Dan following, pushing one trolley, and Jake doing his best to steer the third one.

'What about stuff like rice and pasta?' called out Dan. 'That stuff keeps well doesn't it?'

Leona looked back at him. 'And how do you cook it when the power finally runs out?' she replied. 'We may only have a few more days of it.'

A woman passing by them with a trolley full of frozen pizzas and a variety of TV dinners overheard that and glanced curiously at them – she'd obviously heard her.

Leona smiled awkwardly back.

As they entered the tinned goods aisle, Leona was aware that it was noticeably busier than the other areas in the supermarket they had walked through; half-a-dozen shoppers, like herself, warily eyeing each other up, whilst filling their trolleys with canned goods. As she, Dan and Jacob wheeled their trolleys down towards them, there was a moment of shared communication, eyes meeting, and barely perceptible nods of acknowledgement.

My God, they're here for the same reason.

Somehow, the thought that there were other people out there who had begun to see beyond the news soundbites to something more disturbing, made the bizarre situation she was in right now feel that much more real.

They had that same look as Dad; a slightly rumpled, dishevelled appearance, unburdened with any fashion sense; a couple of them vaguely reminded her of lecturers she'd had back at UEA. They were unmistakably from the same … *tribe* as Dad; nerdish, the type that subscribed to obscure academic periodicals, took rock hammers on their holidays, the type who would never, in a month of Sundays, know who was still hanging in there on *Celebrity Big Brother.*

'So what are we getting?' Daniel asked quietly. She could tell he sensed it too, that they were amongst that tiny minority of *those who know.* Leona could see that these few people alone had already cleared the shelves of several ranges of product in this aisle.

My God. There's only six of them at it, and already the shelves in this aisle are beginning to empty.

She shuddered at the thought of what it was going to be like in this supermarket, and every other one around the country, when the penny finally dropped for everyone else.

'I know what we need,' she muttered in response, scanning the stock that was left in the aisle for tins of pilchards.

She looked at her watch. It was nearly half past one. She knew the Prime Minister was due to make some sort of big announcement around about now. Obviously it was to do with the strife her Dad was caught up in abroad – God, she hoped he was all right – and the impact it was going to have over here. She just hoped they were all done here in the supermarket before the hordes inevitably descended.

'Let's get a move on,' she said out of the side of her mouth.

CHAPTER 29

1.30 p.m. GMT

Whitehall, London

Jesus, you better make this good.

Charles walked briskly into the press room, accompanied by the Deputy Prime Minister, and Malcolm. The room was full, as it often was, but today there were so many people crammed into it that they were standing along the back wall and on either side of the rows of seats arranged in front of the small podium. It was stuffy and hot. The air conditioning in the room was struggling with both the increasing warmth of the day and such a high body count.

The small, well-lit auditorium flickered with camera flash-lights going off as Malcolm and the Deputy took seats to one side of the podium and Charles stepped on to it. He felt uncomfortably like a condemned man climbing a scaffold. He placed the small deck of index cards on the stand before him, each one with a simple bullet-point he wanted to get across.

A deep breath. A moment to shoo away the butterflies.

Make this good, Charlie.

He also remembered Malcolm's last words of advice, muttered quietly and accompanied by a friendly pat on his back.

Keep the focus away from oil.

'Okay,' he began. 'Good afternoon, and thanks for attending at such short notice. There's a lot to get through, so I'll just get started,' he said, and then cleared his throat before continuing. 'I'm sure you're all aware that we've got some problems to deal with. I'm going to start off by telling you what we know about the situation in Saudi Arabia, and the various other hot spots.

Yesterday morning, during morning prayers in Riyadh, the first of many bombs exploded in the Holy Mosques of Mecca and Medina, and in several more mosques in Riyadh. A radical Shi'ite group, shortly after, sent a message to Al Jazeera that they were responsible for the devices. This inevitably triggered a response among the Sunni majority in Saudi Arabia. At the same time, or very shortly afterwards, similar explosions occurred in several other cities in Saudi Arabia, Kuwait, Oman and Iraq. Each one of these incidents has added to the problem. Throughout yesterday, a state of, well – not to put too fine a point on it – civil war has erupted across most of the Arabian peninsula. The situation has continued to escalate today, and because of the potential danger this poses to our remaining troops in Iraq, after consultation with Arab leaders, a decision was taken last night to pull them out of the region until this particular problem has corrected itself.'

Good start.

'Because of the highly charged nature of this *sectarian* problem, there are security implications for virtually every country in the world. We are aware that, over here, emotions will be running high amongst various communities. And that there will be a tiny minority amongst them who will feel compelled to bring this civil war to our streets. For this reason, and lessons have been learned as a result of the appalling number of people who lost their lives on the seventh of July 2005, I have decided to act swiftly and concisely on this matter. Because the threat level has risen, all air and rail traffic has been temporarily suspended. Other potentially vulnerable terror targets around the country, such as our nuclear power stations and natural gas storage facilities, are now being guarded by members of the armed forces. And finally, because of the instability and uncertainty this situation is causing amongst the markets, I have also decided to close the stock exchange for today. Now, these are all temporary measures which will be reviewed throughout the rest of today. These are short-term measures … let me stress that … *short-term* … measures to ensure that we aren't caught out.

'It's my firm belief that the dreadful situation in the Middle

East will blow itself out in a matter of days, that common sense will prevail amongst these troubled people. I ask that you,' Charles gestured towards the gathered members of the press and the media, 'help me by not sensationalising current events.'

He aimed a reproachful gaze towards a row of seats in the middle, reserved for journalists from the various popular red-tops.

'One thing I really don't want to see are racial and religious differences being stirred up with inflammatory headlines. We're a responsible, liberal, tolerant nation, which is why we will *not* see the sort of things we've seen on the news in the last twenty-four hours occurring on the streets of Bradford or London or Birmingham.'

He paused for effect.

'Okay, I'll take one or two questions, no more.'

The press room was instantly a chaotic stew of noise and movement, as hands and voices were raised across the auditorium.

Charles looked for, and found, the face of *News Stand*'s correspondent, Desmond Hamlin. Desmond was one of the good guys. Malcolm and Desmond had some sort of history together. Malcolm had made sure the journalist had got a seat near the front, where his voice would be easily picked up by the boom and podium mics.

'Yes?'

Come on Desmond, give me one I can put in the back of the net.

'Desmond Hamlin, political correspondent for *News Stand*.'

Charles nodded and smiled.

'Prime Minister, the withdrawal of the remaining brigades in Iraq – our rapid reaction force – will, I'm sure, be applauded by our readers. We want those boys back home, and it's good to see you've acted quickly there. My question is about the troops we have stationed out in Afghanistan. We've heard they're being mobilised to come home as well. Can you comment on this?'

Charles nodded. 'Yes, of course.'

This was one he needed to handle deftly. Yes, the 20,000 troops they had committed to that country were coming home as fast as they could be shuttled out. It was the *why* he was going to have to be careful about. On the surface, an *unreasonable risk* to our armed forces came across as a weak but well-intentioned motive. In truth, Charles had been briefed that they were facing the very real prospect of several months of instability at home. Malcolm's comment that the riots in Paris not so long ago were going to be what they could be looking at, or worse, had had a sobering effect on the Prime Minister. They were going to need the manpower to enforce some sort of martial law.

'What's happening in Saudi Arabia, Iraq and the other states in the region, has already started to spread to Afghanistan. Military assessment on the ground is that it could ...' *a deep breath, inject some heartfelt remorse*, '... regrettably, become as bad there. Make no mistake ladies and gentlemen. The bombs that went off yesterday, damaging the Holy Mosque in Mecca, killing over three hundred and fifty Muslim pilgrims, have stirred some very powerful emotions throughout the Islamic world. The anguish, the rage is, I think, very difficult for us in the west to truly quantify. It would be prudent to pull our boys out for now, until this situation calms down, which is why I'm asking for you all to be measured in how you report this.'

Charles was happy with that. He had put the issue of a global religious schism right in front of these people, centre stage, and carefully shunted to one side the question of whether all our armed forces really needed to be brought back home quite so quickly. It was a good opening question.

Well placed, Malcolm.

The other good guy Malcolm had told him to pick out was also close to the front and centre, the correspondent for *News 24*. He couldn't remember her name, but the face was familiar. As he nodded towards her he wondered what question Malcolm had primed her with. It was Malcolm's suggestion that he keep the exact wording from him, otherwise the answer he came back with might sound too rehearsed. It didn't matter. Malcolm was good at playing this game.

Charles trusted him.

'Janet Corby, *News 24*,' she announced loudly and clearly. 'The unfolding riots in Saudi Arabia and Iraq seem to have eclipsed several other events in the last thirty-six hours, Prime Minister. I'm referring, of course, to the tanker that was damaged in the Straits of Hormuz. I believe the ship shed most of its full load, it's still burning and will do for some time. There are rumours that the ship was damaged by a mine placed in the middle of the shipping lane.'

Charles felt his cheeks flush ever so slightly.

'Effectively that closes down the world's busiest shipping choke point,' said Janet Corby. 'Then there was the explosion at the refinery in Venezuela, the Paraguaná refinery. And several other pipeline explosions in and around the refineries based in Baku, Kazakhstan ...'

Oh Christ, I can see where this is going.

'All these things within a few hours of each other—'

'Yes, we're aware of these other isolated events, and the details are hazy on what's happened there,' Charles cut in, 'but I think the unrest spreading across the Middle East deserves our focus right now. This is where we—'

Ms Corby wasn't going to let it rest. 'Prime Minister, these *isolated* events, as well as the spreading unrest, are all going to be part of the same overriding issue for us here.'

Shit shit shit, she's pulling this where we don't want to go.

'The overriding issue right now, is ensuring that the fear and anger and rage that is ripping the Middle East apart doesn't spread to the Muslim community in *our* country. There are over two million—'

'Prime Minister, the *big* issue has nothing to do with religion, or what British Muslims will or won't do ...'

Cut her off and move along.

'I'm sorry, I'll have to give someone else a go,' he said, smiling apologetically at her. He turned from her to survey the other journalists, most with their hands raised, and made a big gesture of deciding who to point to next. He settled on a familiar face, Louis Sergeant, political correspondent for *News Review*, BBC2.

'Louis?' he said.

'Thank you, Prime Minister. I'd like to echo the line of questioning my colleague from *News 24* was pursuing.'

Oh fuck.

'These events don't actually feel like isolated incidents. In fact, it feels like a concerted attempt at disrupting the global oil supply chain. My question is what is our exposure here?'

Charles stared at the BBC journalist, realising he was utterly trapped by the question, realising it wasn't one he could dodge by looking for someone else to pick. They were all of them, smelling something. If he tried to dodge it, it was going to look bad, very bad. Still, he needed a few more seconds to think how best to answer the man.

'I'm sorry,' he said, 'could you repeat your question?'

'Prime Minister, there's a real prospect of our oil supply being cut off. What's our exposure to this?'

CHAPTER 30

1.37 p.m. GMT

Whitehall, London

'What's our exposure?' The Prime Minister asked, repeating the question and buying himself another few seconds to pull together an answer.

He shook his head wearily, hoping that he looked like a man who was becoming tired of having to deal with a complete non-issue. The first prickling beads of sweat were starting to dampen his forehead.

Jesus, it's so hot in here.

'Listen,' replied Charles, 'of course there's a knock-on effect with what's going on. Of course there is. Which is why, for example, trading in the City has been suspended. The unnatural spike in the price per barrel that this is causing could be very damaging to the economic—'

'I'm not talking about the price of the stuff. I'm talking about the availability,' the journalist pressed him.

'Well naturally, whilst this problem is playing itself out, supply of oil from the region is going to be reduced. That is, of course, entirely predictable, and whilst the big Middle East suppliers are dealing with their problems, we are simply sourcing our needs from other places.'

A voice from the back of the room broke into the pause that Charles had deployed for effect.

'And what other places are these?'

Watch it. You're losing control of this.

The journalist continued, 'Caspian oil has been cut off with the bomb blasts in and around Baku. The remaining east-flowing pipelines are going to be contested by Russian, Chinese and Indian interests. Are you also aware of several minor explosions in Nigeria effectively disabling the refineries at Alesa-Eleme, Warri and Kaduna?'

Charles nodded, he was. He'd been hoping that the big Middle East story would have eclipsed a detail like that. There'd been few reported casualties, the explosions had been minor; but of course, they'd been large enough to ensure all three refinery complexes were effectively neutralised.

'My question is this; where exactly is the oil we need *tomorrow* coming from, Prime Minister?'

'Well yes, you're right, there's not a lot coming into the UK at this moment in time …'

Here we go.

Charles shot another glance at Malcolm, who calmly nodded, again, almost imperceptibly.

'But we have reserves in this country that will see us through this … blip.'

Inside he cringed at using the word 'blip'. He wondered if that was a soundbite that was going to come back and bite him somewhere down the line.

'And how long is this *blip* going to last?' called out another journalist in the audience.

'How long will our *reserves* last?' called out yet another.

It was obvious to Charles, the whole religious war spin was being pushed roughly aside. The bastards were smelling blood, and like a pack of hunting dogs they were going for the kill. The room became suddenly silent, everyone leaning forward, keenly interested in an answer to the last shouted-out question. Charles realised a point had been reached. He could bullshit them and have a go at trying to pull this press conference back on script, or he could take on the question and actually answer it.

They'll find out it's all about oil by the end of today … if not in the next few hours.

All of a sudden, Charles realised the best tactical move was an outburst of honesty. At the very least, he might buy himself the tiniest bit of political kudos; best-case scenario – an impassioned, heartfelt plea for calm and co-operation aimed squarely at the general public, might just mean the emergency measures they were putting into effect would keep this crisis manageable.

He took a deep breath. 'We have reserves that'll last us some months. But obviously, we will have to deploy some good old-fashioned common sense in how we use what we have.'

Janet Corby from *News 24*, stood up. 'Are the airport closures and the shutdown of railway lines linked to the oil issue?'

Before he could answer, another question was shouted from the back of the small room. 'Prime Minister, there are rumours that several large oil distribution points have been taken over by the army. Is this the first step towards controlled distribution? Petrol rationing?'

'Uhh, well, there will have to be some degree of rationing, of course,' he replied quickly. 'It's only common sense at this stage that we—'

'What about power supplies?' shouted another. 'Can we expect blackouts?'

Charles shook his head, 'It's too early for us to worry about shortages in power, food—'

Oh shit.

Several in the audience jumped on that.

'Will there be an effect on the supply of food?'

'What about the transportation of food supplies? Imports?'

He knew that he had to nail this down quickly. He raised his hands to quieten them down, before speaking. The chorus of voices in the room amongst the assembled journalists took a long while to settle down to a rustling hubbub that he could be heard clearly over.

'There is no need for anyone to panic here. *No one* needs to panic. There has been a lot of planning, a lot of forward thinking about a scenario like this, a scenario in which there's a temporary log-jam in the global distribution of crude oil—'

'Is the army being brought back from Iraq to keep order?' someone shouted out.

That comment left the room in near silence; a silence that Charles quickly realised he'd allowed to last one or two seconds too long.

They know that keep-the-boys-safe shtick was bullshit.

'Yes,' he replied, 'we will require the army to help keep order.'

'Does this mean we will be facing some form of martial law in Britain?'

He realised now that too much of the truth was out there. They had done as much as they could during the last eighteen hours under the veil of misdirection and various cover stories but, frankly, they were lucky not to have been vigorously challenged before. Perhaps this was the only opportunity, possibly the last opportunity, he would have to call upon the general public to keep calm, to pull together and not lose their heads.

There was a gesture he had once seen in a film, he couldn't remember which film it was, but it had starred someone like Morgan Freeman playing the President of the United States. He remembered it being a powerful gesture, something, during the last three troublesome years in office, he had fantasised about doing himself. Well, here was the best opportunity he was ever going to get to do it. And at an instinctive level, he knew it was the right thing to do.

It was what the people of this country needed to see right now; something visual, something strong, something powerful – not just another politician puffing more hot air. Charles picked up the index cards from the speaker's stand in front of him and silently ripped them up, tossing the shreds of card over his shoulder.

'Okay, that's probably enough crap for one day. You people deserve better than that.'

Once more the room was brought to an instant standstill. A droplet of sweat rolled down the side of his face.

'Yes,' he continued, 'all right, the truth is we *are* in a bit of trouble. Whilst this mess is sorting itself out, we're going to have to make do on the resources we have. We do have enough oil and we do have enough food to last us until normality returns. All right, it's not stockpiled in some giant, secret government warehouse, but spread out across every city, every town, every street. Our corner shops, our supermarkets, our local grocers, our nearest petrol stations … all these places contain the reserves we're going to need to draw upon to ride this thing out. I am asking all of you to work together with me. We are going to need to ration the food we have, restrict the sale of petrol and diesel to key personnel, in short, pull together, like we did once before, sixty years ago during the Second World War.'

And that was it. Charles realised he'd dried up. That was all he had to offer. The silence that followed was truly terrifying.

Oh God, what the fuck have I done?

In that moment he realised he'd been too bloody candid. Instead of inspiring the nation to dig deep and find within it some inner reserve of Dunkirk spirit, to pull together as once they had, and ride this thing out, he had effectively incited every person in the country to make a mad dash to the nearest shop before it was too late.

The press room once more erupted with a deafening chorus of voices. Charles found himself staring in shock at the sea of cameras and faces. Everyone was on their feet now, hands raised. He turned away from the lectern a little too quickly, realising what that would look like on this evening's news.

Running away.

He shot a glance at Malcolm as he strode towards the door. He expected him to be shaking his head grimly, realising too that Charles had really screwed things up, but instead, there was the slightest hint of a smile on the man's face.

CHAPTER 31

2.15 p.m. GMT

Hammersmith, London

Wheeling the trolleys out across the supermarket car-park towards Daniel's van, Leona noticed the first of many, many cars turning into the parking area from the high street. One after another, a steady procession, stopped only when a pedestrian light further up the street turned red.

Dan noticed too. 'It's getting busy.'

'Yeah.'

'Are we going home now?' asked Jacob. 'Or are you taking me back to school?'

'Home,' she replied, distracted as she watched a woman slew her car carelessly into a parking slot, scramble out quickly and run across the tarmac towards the supermarket's entrance. She watched as another driver did the same, this time coming in too quickly, and bumping another parked car, which set off its alarm. The driver climbed out oblivious to this, hastily zapping his car with the key-lock, and sprinted away from it towards a trolley station.

There were more and more cars coming in.

'Let's hurry up,' she said to Daniel.

He nodded, unlocked the back door of his van and started hastily shovelling in the mountain of tinned goods and bottled water they'd managed to buy, emptying Leona's bank account in the process. Leona joined him, tossing in what she had in her trolley.

I think they're beginning to realise.

She had hoped they would make it home safe and sound, triple-lock the front door, and be able to heave a sigh of relief before things started to get panicky. But it looked like it was starting already.

Maybe someone's made an announcement?

Yes, there was the Prime Minister. He was due to be on the telly at lunchtime, wasn't he?

A hefty 4x4 swung around into their row in the car-park and with a screech of tyres lurched forward towards the empty slot next to them. The woman behind the wheel spun it around into the parking space at the last moment, clipping one of their trolleys and knocking it over, spraying the last few dozen cans across the ground.

She climbed out quickly, locking the vehicle after her husband had emerged from the passenger side, and stepping over the scattered cans. 'Go get a trolley, Billy!' she shouted, as she began to make her way past, Daniel and Jacob staring at her in dismayed silence.

Leona stood in her way. 'Look what you just did,' she said icily.

The woman, a hard-faced bottle-blonde with an orange tan, barely registered her. 'Out of the way, love.'

'Hey, you just sent our stuff flying!'

The woman didn't respond, and simply pushed Leona back against the van, and stepped past.

Leona grabbed her wrist. 'Excuse me?'

The woman acknowledged her presence now, of course. 'Fuck off!' she snarled.

'But you just—'

'Let go or I'll fucking break your nose.'

Leona recoiled instantly, and released her grip. At which point Daniel stepped in.

'Hey! That's out of order,' he said walking around the other two, nearly empty, trolleys to join Leona.

The woman glanced at him with undisguised contempt. And then called out to her husband. 'Billy!'

The man, thickset with middle-age flab beginning to cover a muscular frame beneath, and equally orange in colour, stained with the blue of fading tattoos on each forearm, turned round and immediately began striding towards them.

'You better get out of my fucking way, you little prick,' said the woman.

Daniel stayed where he was, but Leona could see he was trembling like a yappy dog left tethered outside a pub.

'Just let her pass, Dan. It's not worth it. We need to just go.'

Daniel took another look at Billy, and then reluctantly stepped back out of the woman's way, allowing her to get past.

The woman hurried towards her husband, not even bothering to look back at them; jabbing her fingers towards the trolley station. The man, however, aimed one long menacing glare towards them, before turning around to go grab one of the few trolleys left. Leona figured if they weren't in such a big rush, ol' Billy-Boy would quite happily have slapped Daniel enough times to leave a spattered blood and snot trail down the side of his scruffy little van.

Daniel wheezed with relief. 'Shit, I thought he was going to have me. I really did.'

'Oh God, so did I.'

She surveyed the car-park. Whereas thirty minutes ago it was half full, now it was jam-packed, with cars, and people on foot, flooding in. She could see several minor altercations occurring in different places, as people squabbled over shopping trolleys, or jostled in the entrance to get inside against the flow of shoppers coming out.

'Let's get out of here as quickly as we can.'

'Okay,' said Dan, scooping up the last of the cans off the floor.

This is just the start of it. What are people going to be like tomorrow? Or in a week's time?

'This is how Dad said it was going to be,' muttered Leona anxiously, as she resumed loading the last of their cans into the back of the van.

Dan wasn't sure he understood what she meant by that. 'What are you talking about?'

She nodded towards the 4x4 couple, now jogging with a trolley towards the entrance of the supermarket and finally shouldering their way through the customers surging out with groceries piled high.

'Law of the jungle.'

Goldhawk Road, leading away from the bustling green at the centre of Shepherd's Bush towards the quieter, more suburban end, was normally quite sedate in the middle of the afternoon on a weekday. Right now it was as busy as Leona had ever seen it. The pavements on either side were packed with people laden with plastic grocery bags, pushing trolleys and wheelie baskets. Traffic along the road was crawling, log-jammed with vehicles. Occasionally it got this bad during the morning rush-hour, or when there was a match on at the nearby White City football ground.

She looked at her watch, it was only three in the afternoon.

'Everyone's going home early,' said Dan, 'to get what they need from the shops.'

She noticed a news-stand outside a convenience store that had so many customers, a queue was beginning to form outside on the street. She saw a headline hastily scrawled across it, beneath the *Evening Standard* banner, '"Please Don't Panic" – PM'.

Another stand next to it had another early edition headline, 'Oil and Food Will Run Out!'

Leona pointed them out to Daniel. 'That's it then. Everyone knows now.'

Daniel looked at her. 'Is it really going to get as bad as you say?'

'I'm just telling you what my dad's been telling me these last few years.'

She studied the desperate faces on the pavements either side of them. Most of the pedestrians were heading towards the Green or towards Hammersmith where the big supermarkets were. She wondered if there was still food on the shelves, or if they'd already been emptied.

‘Look at all these people Dan. How many of them do you think know how to do something as simple as grow a tomato plant?’

‘What?’

‘When they’ve finished stripping the shops clean, and they’ve eaten what they took home, they’re all going to starve.’

Daniel shook his head. ‘It’s not going to get that bad Leona, trust me.’

‘Yeah? So where’s all the food going to come from then, if the oil problem continues?’

Jacob leaned through the front seats. ‘Leona,’ he said, ‘is the world going to end?’

‘No, don’t be silly Jake,’ she replied, ‘but things are going to be a little difficult for a while.’

She hated the dismissive way she’d said that, because, in truth, it was going to be a lot worse than just ‘difficult for a while’. However, right now, she couldn’t face the twenty or thirty million questions she was going to be bombarded with if she’d answered him more truthfully.

Just then they heard a police siren, and a moment later a police van nudged its way through the traffic, the cars on the road obediently pulling over. As the van passed by she looked up, through the rear windows, and saw the grim faces of the officers inside. She could see the thin black stalks of what looked to her like gun barrels poking up from below. She suspected they were attempting to keep the guns out of sight as best they could. But failing … or maybe that was deliberate.

‘The police have got guns,’ she said quietly, as the van whisked by.

Jacob piped up cheerfully. ‘Oh cool!’

CHAPTER 32

2.45 p.m. GMT

M6 motorway, north of Birmingham

The roadblock was only a dozen or so vehicles ahead of them; a row of orange cones placed evenly across all three lanes and the hard shoulder. Behind this meagre barrier, three traffic police Rovers were parked end to end. The six officers that had arrived in them to set up the roadblock were now having to deal with a growing crowd of drivers who had climbed out of their vehicles to find out why the hell the motorway was being closed like this.

Jenny turned round to look out of the rear window of the taxi. Behind them, the traffic had backed up very quickly. They were wedged in a river of inert trucks, vans and cars that stretched into the distance as far as she could see.

'We're going nowhere,' said Paul Davies, the man Jenny had met only hours ago, and who she was sharing the taxi with.

'It looks like that, doesn't it?' she replied.

Paul looked up at a driver who passed by them on foot to join the gathering crowd up ahead. 'I'm going to find out what's up.' He opened the door and stepped onto the road.

'I'm coming too,' said Jenny, equally anxious to find out.

Jenny walked single file behind Paul as he made his way forward, weaving through the parked cars and trucks, finally reaching a knot of bewildered drivers remonstrating with the policemen.

'Can't fucking well block it like this!' a truck driver was shouting, 'I've got a fucking load I need to deliver this afternoon.'

A traffic cop standing opposite him, behind the thin line of cones, shook his head sympathetically. 'Sorry mate, the way's closed until further notice. There's nothing we can do about it.'

'This is to do with that lunchtime press conference,' a man standing beside Jenny said.

She turned to him. 'What's that?'

'Did you not hear it?' he replied with a look of surprise.

'No, what happened?'

'The PM? You don't know about that?'

She shook her head.

'It looks like we're going to be totally screwed. He said they're going to ration petrol and everything else.'

Jenny could see the people around her were beginning to catch on to how serious the situation was getting. These weren't just angry people, she could actually sense an undercurrent of growing panic, like a low charge of static electricity floating amongst them. Not good.

'I got a feeling this is going to get pretty nasty,' the man added in a hushed voice looking at her. 'Somebody on the telly was saying we could all be starving by the end of the week.'

One of the policemen pulled out a dash-mounted radio handset from inside one of the Rovers. 'Everyone, please return to your vehicles!' he said, his voice crackling over the loudspeakers on the roof of his car. 'This motorway will not be re-opened. You will all need to go back the way you came!'

A burly man at the front lost his temper and angrily kicked one of the cones aside. He stepped towards the policemen. 'You have got to be fucking kidding!' he said throwing a hand back to point at the jam behind him, 'I've got eighteen wheels of articulated back there with a full fucking load. How the fuck do I turn that around, you stupid—'

'Step back behind the barrier!' shouted one of the policemen.

'Or what?' he shouted, his face inches away from the nearest officer. 'This is bullshit!'

Several other drivers advanced behind the trucker through the gap in the cones, as if that was an open door.

'Everyone please step back!' shouted the policeman on the microphone. 'This is an official police line!'

Jenny could see the truck driver continuing to shout, his words lost in the growing cacophony of angry voices. He raised a hand, balled into a fist and shook it near the officer's face. It seemed the traffic cop decided that that was enough to be interpreted as a threatening gesture. He reached out for it and began twisting the truck driver's arm into an arrest hold. The trucker's other hand swung around, clasped into another fist and smashed into the officer's chin, dropping him effortlessly. Jenny watched with growing alarm, as three of the other policemen rushed to the aid of their fallen colleague, whilst the vanguard of angry people that had surged through the gap in the cones increased in number.

Paul turned to her. 'Jesus, this is getting out of hand!'

People surged past Jenny as she watched the policemen wrestle with the truck driver on the ground. A young woman started picking the traffic cones up and moving them to the central aisle, whilst a portly middle-aged man wearing an expensive-looking suit decided that someone needed to take the initiative and back the police Rovers out of the way so they could all pass. He opened the driver-side door of the nearest one and climbed in, started the engine and began reversing it slowly across the motorway to the hard shoulder to clear the way forward.

The policeman holding the microphone barked an order, 'Stop the vehicle immediately and get out!'

What happened next seemed to occur too quickly; all in a matter of seconds.

One of the traffic police, pulled out of the struggling scrum of bodies, stepped smartly to the back of his Land Rover, opened a door and swiftly produced what appeared to be a firearm. For the briefest moment she thought, assumed, hoped, that everyone had seen the weapon; the brawl would instantly break up, and the person behind the wheel of the police car would stop, and sheepishly step out.

He has a gun . . . a traffic copper with a gun. Jenny thought that should be enough to bring everyone to their senses, instantly.

But that didn't happen.

The policeman levelled the gun at the moving police car and fired. One of the headlights exploded. The sound of the gunshot stopped everyone in their tracks; the squirming trucker on the ground, the three policemen holding him down, the young woman collecting cones, and everyone else milling around nearby – they all froze as if someone had just hit a magic *pause* button.

The man with the smart suit inside the police Rover raised his hands.

'Get out of the vehicle!' shouted the traffic cop on the microphone.

He stepped out of the Rover, his hands timidly raised above his head.

And that really should have been the conclusion to the little drama. But it wasn't.

The gun went off a second time.

The man in the expensive-looking suit staggered backwards as his nice, smart, crisp, white business shirt exploded with a shower of dark crimson. For a moment Jenny couldn't believe what she was seeing, for a moment thinking someone in the crowd had inexplicably decided to shoot the man with a paintball gun.

He slumped back against the car and then slid down to the ground.

The traffic cop holding the gun looked like he had gone into shock, his jaw hung open, his face ashen. Jenny could see this wasn't meant to have happened. It was an accident; he'd been holding the gun in a way he shouldn't – finger resting too heavily on the trigger, the weapon not aimed down at the ground as it should have been. These men weren't trained to use firearms, that was obvious, they were out of their depth, these guys were panicking.

'Shit. I didn't mean to …' the policeman with the gun cried loudly, staring at the body in disbelief.

One of the crowd of drivers standing near to him, a big man, recovered his senses and broke the static tableau; he reached for the gun and snatched it out of the policeman's hand.

Replaying this in her mind later, Jenny suspected this big man, was removing the gun from the policeman in shock, not to use it on anyone, merely to take a dangerous element out of the equation.

But in the highly charged atmosphere of the moment, the gesture was misinterpreted.

The policeman with the microphone, whipped a second gun out of his car and aimed it at the man. Amidst the noise of people crying out and shouting, Jenny wasn't sure whether a warning was called out before the traffic cop fired. His shot clipped the man, who dropped to his knees clutching his upper arm.

The crowd that had been surging forward began to scatter in all directions. Paul grabbed Jenny by the arm and led her back towards their taxi, the driver standing beside the vehicle craning his neck to see what was going on.

'Come on!' he said. 'This is going to get worse.'

Jenny looked back at the blockade. The other traffic police had pulled back to their vehicles and produced their guns and were, thankfully, firing shots in the air to scatter the crowd, and not aiming at them instead.

This is Britain still, right? Not apartheid-era South Africa, or Tiananmen Square? Jenny's racing mind asked in disbelief as she and Paul hastily made their way back from the police line.

They're just trying to disperse the crowd, that's all.

But then she heard the loud growl of a diesel engine beside her, and a large container truck lurched forward, effortlessly shunting aside the cars in front of it. As the truck pushed forwards towards the blockade, the traffic cops trained their weapons towards it, and they all fired.

'Fuck this!' said Paul changing direction and heading towards the metal barrier beyond the hard shoulder. She watched him go and then, as the truck crashed into the blockade of police cars, she turned back to watch as the policemen peppered the truck with shots as it rolled past.

'Are you coming or what?' said Paul, swinging his other leg over and dropping down on his haunches on the other side of the barrier. She heard another burst of gunfire behind her.

Oh shit.

She followed him across the hard shoulder, lifted her light cotton skirt up and swung her legs over the barrier. On the other side, a grass verge descended down towards a field. She dropped down to a crouch beside him, and together, stooping low to keep their heads below the corrugated aluminium barrier they stumbled down the verge, away from the motorway, towards the lumpy, uneven field of waist-high luminous yellow rapeseed.

Behind her, she heard the rumble of several other trucks starting up, and the crunch of other vehicles being pushed forward. The sound of gunfire intensified.

She wondered if any of this would have happened if properly trained armed response units had been manning the roadblock. Maybe, maybe not. It was all so sudden, the escalation from an unintended shot to this.

'Where are we going?' she gasped.

'I don't know, but I don't want to stumble across any more highly strung, untrained cops carrying guns they can't handle. Do you?'

'No.'

They staggered across the uneven, muddy field of rapeseed, Jenny stopping once or twice to look back with disbelief at the roadblock behind them, wondering if that really did happen, or whether she was going mad.

CHAPTER 33

10 p.m. local time

Al-Bayji, Iraq

Andy watched as Lieutenant Carter put a hand to his ear and silently listened to the communication coming in on his headset. Eventually he whispered an acknowledgement and then turned to the fourteen men left of his platoon, gathered in a silent group in front of him. He had a man up on the front wall keeping an eye on the street, and three more were outside the compound, scanning the route they were going to have to take – they'd gone over the wall a few minutes earlier. The route they were planning to take back out of town was the one they had taken that morning. Andy suspected that in the dark, the twists and turns of these little streets could lose some of them.

'And try and remember the way we came this morning,' whispered Carter.

'If you get lost lads, just keep heading north-east,' added Andy quickly. 'You'll hit the river eventually.'

Carter nodded. 'S'right. And hopefully you'll be able to see the bridge from wherever you emerge.'

The young officer took a few deep breaths, looking around at the men in front of him.

Andy looked at his watch anxiously. 'We've got less than an hour.'

Carter nodded, 'Yeah you're right. No point messing around then. We've got an hour to make it a mile across town and over that bridge. Our ride's arriving at eleven, and they won't be hanging around for us for long.'

The men nodded.

'Okay, you all know what groups you're in. You all know where we're headed, and how long you've got. Five minutes between each group. If you lose your way, like he says,' said Carter, nodding towards Andy, 'just keep heading north-east, you'll hit the edge of town.'

The young squaddies nodded.

'Right then. First group ready?'

The platoon medic, Corporal Denwood, stood up, and marshalled the men that would be with him; five soldiers, the Ukrainian engineer, Ustov, and the young Iraqi driver, Salim.

'We'll dispense with this platoon's usual call-sign protocol, Corporal, since we're all mixed up with civvies. For the next hour, you're call-sign Zulu, understand?'

'Yes, sir.'

'Okay then, off you go. We'll see you on the other side of the bridge.'

Denwood beckoned for Ustov and Salim to join his men. Ustov clasped hands with Erich, Mike and Andy muttering a farewell, whilst Farid patted the young Iraqi lad on the back.

Denwood climbed up on to the wall, swung his legs over and was gone. The other men followed suit and within a minute call-sign Zulu had departed.

Carter started his stopwatch. 'Five minutes, then your group are up next, Private Tajican.'

The Fijian acknowledged that and gathered the men in his group to him.

To Andy it seemed the next five minutes passed unbearably slowly. And then with a nod from Lieutenant Carter, the next group, call-sign Yankee, which consisted of Tajican, five other soldiers and Erich, went quietly over the wall.

Carter once more started timing.

The next few minutes seemed to take an eternity, and then the young officer nodded at Lance Corporal Westley, to take his group over.

'You're X-ray. I'll see you at the bridge,' he said slapping Westley on the back.

'Aye, sir,' he replied.

Mike turned to Andy and held out a hand. 'Good luck.'

Andy grabbed his hand. 'See you in an hour.'

Westley waited until the two soldiers in his group along with Mike and Farid had climbed over the wall, before following them. His call-sign were going to pick up the other three men already waiting quietly in the dark outside the compound.

And now there was Andy, Sergeant Bolton, Lieutenant Carter, two more men, both bandaged from minor wounds, and another man on watch up on the wall, whom Carter quietly ordered over the radio, to join them.

Andy looked at Sergeant Bolton, holding one hand protectively against his dressed wound, and in the other, a cigarette. 'You know those things'll kill you,' he said.

Bolton's face creased with a wry smile. 'Ha bloody ha.'

Carter looked at his Sergeant. 'You going to be okay?'

Bolton grunted as he pulled himself up on to his haunches and stubbed out the cigarette. 'Just fine, sir.'

'Okay, good. Mind your footing. Denwood said that dressing can only take so much.'

The man who had been up on the wall, keeping watch over the boulevard, loped across the compound, the equipment on his webbing jangling in the silence. He squatted down beside Lieutenant Carter, and made a quick report.

'Nothing going on out there, sir. It's like a ghost-town. No lights, no noise. Nothing'

'All right, time to go.'

Carter went over the top first, and then with Andy and one of the other men helping from within the compound, they got Sergeant Bolton over and down on to the pavement on the other side managing, so far, not to unravel his field dressing, loosen the clamp and open the wound. He knelt down in silence, struggling with his breath, clearly in a lot of pain, and holding both of his hands over the wound.

Crouching at the base of the wall, Carter looked through the scope on his SA80; a bulky attachment on the top of the rifle, above the magazine – called the SUSAT – that allowed limited night vision. He swept it around, quickly scanning the cluster of narrow street openings ahead. He squinted at the grainy green image he was seeing through the small circular lens.

'You men see anything?' he whispered.

The other two soldiers, hunched over their weapons, staring keenly through their scopes and panning hastily left and right, were quick to answer that they could see no immediate threat.

'All right, then. We're heading up that street ahead of us. You see the one with the big old-style satellite dish sticking out on the first floor?'

'Yeah,' grunted one of the soldiers.

'That's the one we came down this morning. Let's go.'

Mike studied the grainy, glowing forms of the men in his group, through his weapon's night scope. Lance Corporal Westley was squatting against the corner of the wall looking out on to the junction. This was the wide road they had entered Al-Bayji on. Right would take them *into* town, left would take them to the *outskirts* of town, through the market-place and to the single lane bridge over the Tigris.

The other men were scanning the rooftops and both sides of the road, left and right, for activity.

He could see Farid resting against the wall, staring up at the sky, the scope making his eyes glow a devilish lurid green, flickering every now and then as he blinked.

Westley had put Mike in charge of the Iraqi man. The Lance Corporal didn't trust the translator, but didn't want to waste one of his men on the task of watching him.

Westley rose to his feet, and with a beckoning gesture, led them out into the wider road, turning left, heading roughly north-east towards their rendezvous. In the distance Mike could see the taller buildings giving way to single storey, and the opening out that signalled the market area.

And then there was a flicker of light up ahead.

He saw Lance Corporal Westley stop and suddenly place a

hand to his ear, an instinctive reaction. There was radio traffic coming in. He heard the young man's rasping whisper.

'Shit!'

Westley listened to some more, and then turned round to his men.

'There's a search-party up ahead coming down this road. Big mob, torches, guns. They're almost upon Zulu.'

They heard the sound of gunfire – a distant rattling and popping. Mike pulled the gun scope to his eye and aimed up the road. He could see sporadic flickerings of light, and a tracer lancing upwards into the sky. Then he spotted an amorphous glowing blob of light in the middle of the road that undulated like some cellular life form growing and dividing, growing and dividing.

'Bollocks!' hissed Westley. 'There's the bastards comin' down this way!'

Dropping his gun down, and looking with his bare eyes, Mike could see a large group cautiously advancing down the road towards them, a dozen beams of torchlight dancing from one side of the road to the other ahead of them. Meanwhile, beyond them in the market area, the fire-fight seemed to have intensified. It looked like the mob had found Zulu, and the poor bastards were having to fight their way out of it.

'Shit. What now?' whispered one of the other soldiers.

Westley looked anxiously around. They were walking alongside a long tall, flat wall with no places to hide nearby. Further up ahead of them on the left was another side-street. But that would take them closer to those advancing torch beams, and they were bound to be spotted making a run forward towards it. Opposite, across the wide road, was a garden wall, chest high.

Westley gestured with one gloved hand towards it. 'Over that wall, now!'

The five British soldiers sprinted desperately across the four lanes of open street, with Mike grabbing Farid's arm and leading the old man after them. As they stumbled across, he prayed that the approaching torch beams dancing from one side of the thoroughfare to the other, hadn't picked out the movement.

Mike thudded against the garden wall, catching his breath for a moment before turning to the old man.

'Get over the wall,' he said to Farid.

Farid didn't hesitate, pulling himself up and over. And Mike swiftly followed, dropping down inside the garden where Westley and his four comrades were waiting.

The veil of cloud in the sky was beginning to break, and a full moon shone down between the fleeting gaps.

'Shit, that doesn't help matters,' muttered Westley.

In the undulating moonlight Mike could see them hunched down in a semi-circle; he could hear their chorus of laboured and ragged breathing during the sporadic pauses between distant bursts of gunfire.

CHAPTER 34

7.23 p.m. GMT

Between Manchester and Birmingham

Jenny walked silently beside Paul for several hours, trying to digest what she'd recently witnessed on the motorway. They steered away from the main roads, spotting on several occasions in the distance convoys of army trucks and police wagons rumbling along the deserted tarmac, unhindered by traffic.

She found her shoes, with only a modest heel, were impractical for the fields they crossed, and the tufted grass verges they were keeping to. She was beginning to wish she'd packed more practical clothing in her overnight bag. But then yesterday morning, she couldn't have imagined she'd be travelling cross-country with a man she knew nothing about.

She tried her phone several times as they made their way, roughly heading south she guessed by the position of the waning sun. There was no signal on several attempts, and when she did pick up a signal, she received a message that the service was experiencing difficulties dealing with an abnormally large volume of traffic.

As the warm evening sun was beginning to dip below the tops of the trees ahead of them, Paul steered them towards a small wood.

'This way,' he said staring down at the glowing screen of his palm pilot. 'We'll be able to rejoin the M6 on the other side of it.' He had some sort of GPS functionality built into the gadget.

She looked at the woods; densely grouped mature trees that cast an impenetrable shadow on the undergrowth below. She had never been a big fan of that kind of thing – quiet, spooky woods and forests. It was always in places like that, certainly in fairy-tales, that nasty things happened to the carefree and innocent. It didn't help that Andy had taken her along to see *The Blair Witch Project* many years ago.

'Do we have to go through?' she said. 'I'm not exactly kitted out for this kind of off-road rambling.'

'It's half a mile through it, according to this. Or about five to ten miles to skirt around it. Look, I can see you're a little spooked, but trust me okay? We'll be quickly through it.'

Jenny looked at him.

'I'm knackered, okay?' he smiled apologetically, 'I just want to hit some flat, sturdy road as quickly as possible. Just half a mile through this and we're back to civilisation.'

She looked up at the trees, and the orange sun, bleeding through the leaves at the top, and the shadows lengthening across the field they had just crossed in long forbidding purple strips.

'The longer we leave it, the darker it'll get in there.'

'All right,' she said unhappily, 'let's go through as quickly as we can, okay?'

He smiled, 'Of course.'

He led the way, stooping through a barbed wire fence. He held the wire up for her as she doubled down and squeezed through the gap. Her blouse caught on the back, somewhere between her shoulder blades.

'Ouch,' she whimpered.

'I've got it,' said Paul, unhooking her deftly.

'Thanks,' she muttered.

The ground was overgrown with nettles and brambles, and fallen branches, all apparently competing to snag her skirt, scratch her calves or sting her ankles.

They made very slow progress. Half a mile began to seem like a lot more than she remembered it being. They spent almost as much time fighting through the undergrowth as they did traversing any noticeable distance.

Paul stopped. 'I need a rest. How about you?'

I'd rather get the hell out of here.

'No, I'm good,' she replied.

He sat down on a log anyway. 'Sorry, need to just catch my breath. We've been walking for hours.'

'Okay.' She looked around for somewhere else to sit – there was nowhere, so she squatted down against the base of a tree.

They sat in silence for a couple of minutes, he scowling down at his palm pilot, she trying her phone again and again. She was getting a signal, but the service was giving her that damned message. The mobile networks had to be overloaded with anxious people trying to get in touch with loved ones.

It was Paul that broke the silence. 'So, crazy fucking day or what, eh?'

She nodded. It was that all right.

'I can't believe that traffic policeman shot a guy dead,' he said, shaking his head.

'No, neither can I.'

'You just don't expect that kind of thing, you know, here in good ol' Britain.'

'No ... I suppose not.'

He turned his palm pilot off. 'I can't get the GPS signal in here. And the charge is running down.'

Jenny looked up at him urgently. 'We're not lost are we?'

He grinned. 'Nope, I know where we are. Don't need it now. Like I say, it's just a little way through the woods, and then we're right on the M6 again.'

'Oh, thank God for that. I don't think I could cope being stuck in here after dark.'

'You ever camped out in a wood at night?'

'Never. I don't ever plan to either.'

'I did a paintball weekend with my work mates last year. Night-time sessions with those cool night sights and everything. Very hardcore, very intense. As much fun as you can possibly have in a wood at night.'

Jenny nodded unenthusiastically.

'So, did you say you got kids or something?' he asked.

She nodded. 'They're at home in London, on their own. I just want to get back to them as quickly as possible.'

'No dad to look after them then?'

Why is he fishing for details?

Jenny felt uncomfortable with that, stuck out here, alone with him. She sure as hell wasn't going to tell this guy that she had recently split from her husband of eighteen years. He'd probably take that as some sort of encouragement.

That's not fair. Has he given you any reason to think of him like that?

She looked at him – he hadn't.

To be honest, there were many other blokes she'd worked alongside in the past, whom she would not trust for a moment in a situation like this. This guy, Paul, so far had kept his eyes, his hands and any sexually charged innuendoes to himself. He'd shown his little gadget more interest than her.

But you never know, do you?

Oh come on, she countered herself, if he was *that* kind of bloke, right here ... right now would be the moment he'd start getting just a little bit too familiar, probing the lay of the land, so to speak and ... and asking questions like 'no dad to look after them', perhaps?

Maybe he's just making conversation?

Yeah? And maybe the next thing he'll ask is, 'you got a fella out there worried about you?', or how about, 'you're looking a bit cold, it is getting a little fresh. Come on, why don't you sit over here next—'

'Come on,' said Paul, getting up off the log. 'I can see this place is giving you the heebie-jeebies. Let's press on and hit the road whilst we've still light to see.'

She smiled gratefully. 'Yeah, good idea.'

They managed to beat a path through undergrowth that seemed intent on preventing them getting any closer to the motorway. As the sun began to merge with the horizon, dipping behind a row of distant wind-turbines on the brow of a hill, they emerged from the wood and descended down a steep grass bank on to the motorway.

They both surveyed the six empty lanes, stretching as far as the eye could see in both directions, without a single vehicle to be seen.

'That's just such a weird sight,' said Paul.

They turned right, heading southbound, enjoying the firm flat surface beneath their feet.

'I'm really thirsty,' said Jenny.

'Yeah, me too. I bet we'll find somewhere along here soon. This part of the M6 is loaded with service stations and stop-overs.'

'You sure? I don't fancy walking all through the night without something to drink.'

'Christ, I've driven this section enough times to know. Got to admit though, I don't believe I've ever walked it.'

She smiled.

'If we get really desperate I might even consider going into a Little Chef.'

She managed a small laugh.

It felt good to do that. It wasn't exactly a funny joke, wasn't exactly a joke, but it was good to hear a little levity, especially after everything she'd seen and heard today.

'We'd have to be really desperate though,' she quipped. 'I mean, really desperate, and I'm still some way from that yet.'

Paul chuckled and nodded.

CHAPTER 35

10.24 p.m. local time

Al-Bayji, Iraq

'Shit, they're heading our way,' hissed Carter.

Andy looked up and down the narrow street. There was nowhere for them to hide, it was no more than four or five feet wide, and cluttered with a few small boxes and bins; nothing large enough to hide behind. Any second now the large group of militia the lieutenant had just spotted would be turning into it, and their flashlights would pick them out in a heartbeat.

Andy spotted a small side-door recessed in the flaking plaster of the wall to their left. 'Try the door,' he muttered to Derry, the young soldier next to him.

Lieutenant Carter nodded. 'Go on.'

The soldier tried the handle of the door and twisted it. It was locked, or stuck. It rattled as he pulled and pushed desperately on it.

'For fuck's sake Derry, you girl's blouse, kick it in!' growled Sergeant Bolton, leaning waxen-faced against the wall beside it.

Private Derry, took a step back, raised a booted foot, and kicked hard at the rusting metal door. A shower of rusty flakes fell to the ground and it clanged and rattled noisily in its frame, but the lock held. Behind them, out on the main thoroughfare they heard raised voices, and several beams of torchlight fell on the mouth of their side-street, dancing and bobbing as they began to run towards it. They'd heard the noise and were coming to investigate.

Private Derry swung his foot at the door right next to the lock the second time, and on impact, it swung in, with a clattering sound of a lock shattering inside.

'In, in, in!' shouted Carter desperately. Derry led the way and Andy followed in his wake. One of the other two privates and Carter hauled Sergeant Bolton up on to his feet and carried him through, whilst the last man fired off a dozen shots of covering fire, then dived in after them.

Inside, the darkness was complete, and once more Andy found himself having to fumble his way whilst the others picked out at least some detail through their weapon scopes. There were concrete stairs leading upwards, and walls that felt like rough breeze-blocks, scraping the skin from his fingertips as he held his hand out for guidance.

They had turned a corner, for a second flight of concrete steps, when it sounded like someone had taken a jackhammer to the rusty metal door. The dark stairwell below, suddenly strobed with sparks as a dozen or so rounds punched jagged holes through the door.

'Fuck, move it!' Andy heard one of the squaddies shout behind him.

They sprinted up the second flight of stairs in darkness, and then a door opened up ahead. Andy could see the glow of moon-light through the opening.

Down below, the metal door was kicked open again. He could hear footsteps and see the dancing flash of torchlight coming up the stairwell after them. The soldier behind him, gave Andy a hefty shove forward towards the open door, then turned round to face down the stairs.

The gunfire was deafening in the contained area, piercing, sharp, painful and punctuated by a cry from below as at least one shot found a target.

Andy tumbled forwards up the last few steps and out through the open door, his ears ringing. They were on a long balcony that overlooked a wide road. Andy recognised it as the road they had driven into town on this morning.

Beneath them, only fifteen or twenty feet below, Andy could see several dozen armed men and boys in loose clusters across the broad thoroughfare, torch beams arcing up and down the street, desperately trying to find them.

Oh shit. Please don't look up.

Ahead, Carter, Bolton, Derry and the other squaddie had dropped down low as they made their way along the balcony – a waist-high wall of breeze-blocks, crumbling, pitted and scarred, was keeping them from being seen. Behind him, through the open door to the stairwell, Andy could hear a concentrated barrage of fire as the last man in their group endeavoured to hold the mob back on the stairs.

Andy kept pace with the others, desperately trying to avoid the clutter of wicker chairs, children's toys, potted shrubs that were parked in front of a succession of front doors. Small windows looked out on to the balcony, and through several he passed by, grimy and fogged with dust, he could see the frightened faces of women and children cowering inside.

The gunfire in the stairwell suddenly stopped. Andy turned to look back along the balcony, hoping to see their man emerge from the doorway.

A single shot rung out from the stairwell.

One to the head to be certain. Our lad's down.

They'd be emerging through that doorway in the next few seconds. 'Fuckin' move it,' Andy found himself shouting at the men up ahead, slowed down by trying to drag Bolton along with them. 'They're right behind us!'

A second later he heard the door to the balcony swing open and a burst of gunfire behind him. Half-a-dozen shots whistled past him as he dived to the floor, tangling his legs with a discarded wicker chair.

'Down here!' Carter shouted back at them.

Andy got to his feet, and sprinted forward to join them. He caught up with Derry, kneeling and firing spurts of two and three rounds back at the doorway, and Carter struggling to manoeuvre Bolton down a narrow flight of stairs.

‘Gimme a gun,’ said Andy to Lieutenant Carter, ‘I can help Derry slow them down.’

Carter unslung Bolton’s SA80 and chucked it up at Andy. ‘Know how to use it?’

Andy shrugged, ‘Got a vague idea.’

‘God ’elp us,’ drawled Bolton.

Andy shouldered the weapon, feeling its reassuring weight in his hands. He swung the barrel around with his finger on the trigger; both Bolton and Carter cringed.

‘Safety’s off by the way,’ Bolton grunted, pointing at the weapon, as Carter pulled him clumsily down the stairs.

Andy grinned sheepishly. ‘Shit, sorry.’

He turned round, took half-a-dozen steps up to join Derry on the balcony.

Derry fired then ducked, as a long volley chipped, then shattered a large earthen pot beside him. ‘Fucking fuck!’ he yelled as he sprawled to the ground beside Andy. He looked up at him, surprised to see an assault rifle cradled in his hands.

‘Yeah, I get to have one now,’ Andy muttered. He then leaned out and fired a long burst down the length of the balcony, that had the pursuing militia picking their way forwards, needlessly diving for cover as the volley pulled the barrel up and his shots peppered the floor of the balcony above.

Derry used the bought seconds to squeeze past Andy, off the balcony and down on to the stairs. ‘Short bursts,’ he shouted.

‘Right.’

Andy jabbed again at the trigger and fired a short burst, more accurately this time.

‘I’m completely out,’ said Derry, ‘not exactly the world’s greatest fucking rearguard action.’

‘Go then,’ said Andy, ‘I’ll hold here a few more seconds.’

Derry nodded, slapped Andy on the back and staggered down the stairs.

Oh Jesus, what the hell am I doing?

He wondered what Jenny would make of this if she could see him now, doing his best Bruce Willis impersonation.

He fired a few shots into the open doorway, whilst Derry made it down to the bottom. Almost immediately two heads popped out from the darkness, and a couple of AKs fired a volley in response. He felt the puff of displaced air on his cheek as a shot whistled past his head only an inch away, whilst another glanced off the wall just behind his head.

'Okay, screw this,' he muttered, getting to his feet and scrambling down the stairwell after Derry. He fired another un-aimed burst into the air to deter them from following too closely, hopefully buying them a few more precious seconds.

Call-sign Whisky were reunited at the bottom of the stairs, in a small, rubbish-filled opening that led out on to a three-foot wide rat-run, strewn with a *mélange* of discarded furniture and bric-à-brac, rotting vegetation and a central sewage gully down which a clotted stream of faeces flowed.

'This way, I think,' said Carter pointing upwards.

'Yeah,' Andy replied, gasping and breathless, 'right or wrong though, we had better fucking run.'

CHAPTER 36

7.40 p.m. GMT

Shepherd's Bush, London

'This is it,' said Leona, 'turn left here.'

Dan swung his van out of the almost static river of traffic on Uxbridge Road into St Stephen's Avenue, a narrow tree-lined road, flanked on either side by a row of comfortable-looking Edwardian terraced houses.

'Home!' cheered Jacob from the back of the van.

Leona twisted in her seat. 'Jake, we're going to be staying at Jill's place.'

'Uh?'

Dan looked at her, 'Yeah ... *uh?* I thought I was taking you home?'

'She lives three doors down from our place, she's a good friend of the family.'

'Why aren't we going home?' asked Jacob

To be entirely honest she had no idea why, only that Dad had been really insistent that they go to Jill's and not home. There had been the sound of fear in his voice, implied danger. And deep down, she knew it had something to do with the man she saw. None of this was going to make sense to Dan or Jacob, nor to Jill of course.

'Dad said for us to go there, so Jill can mind us until Mum or he can get home.'

'Aren't you a bit big for a babysitter?' said Dan.

'You saw what it was like in Hammersmith.'

Dan nodded. 'Yeah, I see what you mean.'

They drove slowly down the narrow avenue, squeezing around

the large family vehicles parked half on, half off the pavement. Passing number twenty-five on their left, Leona looked out at their home. None of the lights were on. It looked lifeless.

'We live there,' Jacob informed Dan as they drove slowly past.

Leona pointed to a house ahead of them, on the right. 'Number thirty. That's Jill's house.'

Her car, a Lexus RX, was parked on the pavement outside, but there were no lights on. Dan parked up next to her car, and Leona quickly climbed out. She opened the garden gate and headed up the short path through her front yard – little more than a few square yards of shrivelled potted plants embedded in gravel – to the front door. She could see junk mail was piling up in the post-box, and knew that Jill must be abroad on one of her conferences.

'Damn!'

'What's up?' said Dan, joining her with several shopping bags in each hand.

'She's gone away.'

'Ah.'

Jacob staggered up the path with a solitary bag full of tins. 'Heavy,' he grunted like a martyr.

'So, back to yours then?' said Dan.

Leona looked over her shoulder at their house, thirty yards away on the other side of the avenue. 'I suppose we've got no choice, if Jill's gone on one of her visits.'

Dan nodded, 'Okay.' He turned and headed down the path.

Do NOT go home ... it's not safe.

There was no mistaking the urgency in Dad's voice. There was something he knew – didn't have time to tell her. The limited time he had on the phone was taken up with one thing; making sure she understood not to go home. That was it, explanations would no doubt come later.

'Wait!' she called out. Dan and Jacob stopped.

She looked around uncomfortably before picking up a stone from the front yard and quickly smashing the frosted narrow glass panel in the middle of the front door. The glass clattered down inside, as she reached through and fumbled with the latch.

'Oh boy,' said Jacob, 'that's against the law.'

Jill never double-locked her front door, even when she was going away. Instead she relied on the timed lights in her house, and the always-on radio in the kitchen to convince would-be burglars that elsewhere would be a better prospect. She was a little ditzy that way.

The door cracked open and she pushed it wide, spreading the junk mail across the wooden floor in the hallway.

Dan looked at her. 'Uh, Leona, you're breaking and entering.'

'She's a friend. She wouldn't press charges. Now let's get our stuff inside as quickly as possible.'

She headed out to the van to grab a load when she spotted the DiMarcios', two doors down, on the other side of the avenue. Mum was on pretty good terms with them, particularly Mrs DiMarcio.

'Leona!' she called across to her.

'Hi, Mrs DiMarcio,' she said offering a little wave.

The woman was slim and elegant, in her early forties – yet, as Mum often said of her, she could easily pass as someone ten years younger.

'Leona! What you do home?' she asked, her English clipped with a Portuguese accent.

'I … er … my mum and dad said I had to,' she replied.

'This thing? This thing we see on the news?' she asked.

'Yeah.'

'Pffft … this is terrible, hmm? This Mr Smith, your Prime Minister, he say we will have rations?'

'Rationing, that's right. That's what Dad was saying too. This could be quite bad.'

She looked over Leona's shoulder at Dan and Jacob carrying another load of shopping bags between them. 'You buy rations?'

She nodded. 'We went to Tesco, bought in some tinned goods and bottled water.'

Mrs DiMarcio looked at her with eyes that slowly widened. She knew about Dad's preoccupation with Peak Oil; he'd bored both her and Mr DiMarcio with it over dinner one night, after he'd had a couple of glasses of red.

'Your father? He tell you this could be bad?'

'Yeah.'

'Is this the thing, what he call it, Peak thing?'

'Peak Oil?'

'Yuh, that's it. Is this ...?'

'I don't know. But Dad said I had to come back, collect Jake, get some supplies in and stay over at Jill's house.'

Her hand covered her mouth. '*Oh, meu Deus, o teu pai estava certo!*'

'You know, you should hurry if you want to get some things,' said Leona. 'When we left, people were going mad in the supermarket, it was really quite scary.'

'I wonder, we maybe leave?' Mrs DiMarcio said, more to herself than Leona. She was thinking aloud. 'Is city,' she said gesturing with her hands at the avenue, 'this is a city ... I remember your father he say city is a bad place to be in a ... a ...'

'In a crisis?'

The woman nodded.

Leona was surprised at how much they'd taken in. Perhaps they had been listening after all when Dad had gone off on his anti-oil diatribe.

'I will talk with my husband when he comes in.'

'Maybe it's a good idea to leave if you can,' said Leona. 'Find somewhere out of town to stay.'

'We take you and Jacob with us, if we go?' she offered. 'We have spaces in car.'

Leona shook her head. 'Thanks, but I've got my orders to sit tight inside,' she said nodding at her home. 'And wait for Mum and Dad to get home.'

Mrs DiMarcio nodded. 'I understand. I talk with my husband. We stay? We go? We will talk about this.'

'Okay. Look, I better help with the shopping,' said Leona.

She reached out with her hands, grasped Leona's shoulders and smiled. 'You are good girl, very sensible girl. Jenny and Andy I think very proud of you.'

Leona shrugged awkwardly.

'I go. Maybe I ring Eduardo on his mobile,' she said, thinking aloud. With that she turned and headed hastily back to her house.

Up and down the normally quiet, leafy avenue, Leona noticed more activity than normal; a man was busy unloading bags of goods from his car, whilst talking animatedly on his phone. A few houses up, a woman emerged from her home, running; she hopped into her people carrier and started it up. Leona stepped out of the road to allow her to pass, as she drove down St Stephen's Avenue, at a guess heading towards the busy end of Shepherd's Bush to do some panic-buying.

You're probably too late, already.

The thought sent a chill down her spine.

She heard a car door slam, and another car engine start up with a throaty cough; it felt like the whole avenue was beginning to stir to life.

Leona reached into the van and grabbed an armful of bags and began to help the two boys get their supplies inside.

CHAPTER 37

10.41 p.m. local time

Al-Bayji, Iraq

They stumbled noisily down the back-street, picking their way through small stacks of rubbish, wooden crates of rotting vegetables, trying to avoid stepping in the sewage gully running down the middle.

Andy and the others were no longer worrying about keeping quiet. They scrambled through the mess and the crap as quickly as they could, doing their best not to lose their footing or tangle with the obstacles in their way.

Behind them, Andy could see the bouncing and flickering of torches as they were being chased, their pursuers having an equally difficult time with the terrain. Sergeant Bolton, however, was slowing them down, enough that the militia-men were closing the gap on them.

Lieutenant Carter and Private Peters, still carrying Bolton, stumbled and fell to the ground, splashing into the sewage gully; a tangle of shit-soaked limbs.

'Ah fucking hell!' Bolton cursed angrily. 'The bloody dressing's come off!'

'Hold still!' hissed Carter. In the dark the officer fumbled to find the surgical band amongst the river of faeces.

'It's bloody pouring out,' said Bolton.

Andy turned to look back down the narrow passage. The flashlights were getting closer. He aimed the Sergeant's assault rifle towards them spraying a long burst that had the torches lancing wildly around as they dived for cover.

'Short bursts, you twat,' cursed Bolton, 'it's not a bloody water pistol!'

Andy waited a moment before letting loose another three-round volley. This was only going to buy them time whilst the gun had rounds in the clip.

'All right, sod this for a laugh. Give me the friggin' gun and piss off.'

'No,' snapped Carter. 'We're not leaving you behind.'

'Yes you are. Because I'm bleeding like a bastard.'

Derry leant over, and placed a hand on Bolton's arm. 'You're a shithead if you think we're leaving you, sir.'

'Shut up Derry,' Bolton wheezed painfully, 'you'll all be dead if you carry on dragging me. Just give me a bloody gun and fuck off, all right?'

Andy looked at Carter, Peters and Derry. They were all thinking the same thing – Sergeant Bolton was right – but none of them wanted to be the one to say it.

There's no time for this macho crap.

'He's right,' said Andy. 'He can buy us the time we're going to need.' He pointed up the rat-run. There was a flickering glow in the distance, perhaps a couple of hundred yards away. 'That's the market-place up there.'

Carter struggled with the decision for a while, whilst back along the way they had come, the torches were on the move again, cautiously drawing nearer.

'All right Bolton,' said Carter, wearily resigned. 'Your way then. Give him a rifle.'

'Sir, we can't leave!' protested Derry.

'Shut it! And do as the officer says!' grunted Bolton.

Derry reluctantly handed him his rifle. 'It's out sir.'

Bolton took the gun, pulled a clip out from a pouch on his webbing and slammed it home with a grunt of pain. 'Good to go.'

Andy checked his watch. 'It's quarter to eleven. We have to go.'

'Bolton,' said Carter, 'keep those bastards off our tail.'

'Uh-huh,' he groaned, shifting painfully into a prone position behind a pile of rotting household rubbish.

Andy reached out for the Sergeant's leg holster and pulled out his service pistol. He placed it on the ground beside Bolton. 'Don't let them take you alive,' he said quietly. 'Understand?'

Bolton nodded. 'No fucking chance. Now you lot better piss off.'

The men shared a glance, there was no room for any words. Bolton racked the gun and stared down the barrel, through the scope at the flickering shapes moving swiftly up the side-street towards them.

They started off towards the flickering glow in the distance.

Sergeant Bolton watched the torch beams slowly approaching him. They were taking their time, cautiously sweeping the way ahead before advancing.

Very sensible. This little alleyway was a jumble of rubbish and boxes, discarded furniture and tufts of weeds. Nightmare terrain to be advancing through, especially at night.

Just a little closer and then he'd pop off a few rounds at the nearest git holding a flashlight. Sooner would be better than later. He could feel himself slipping. In fact, it felt a little like being pissed. Like having a pint mid-morning after a heavy session the night before – hair of the dog.

Slipping, and it was happening quite quickly.

He'd been leaking blood slowly for twenty minutes, and now he'd lost enough that things were beginning to shut down on him.

Bollocks.

He wanted to drop a few of them before he went under. Just a couple would do.

'Come on you fuckers!' he shouted out, realising with some amusement that he sounded like some drunken bastard at closing time brazenly taking on half-a-dozen coppers.

There was a flicker of reaction. The torch beams swept up the alley towards him, and then across the mound of detritus he was nicely hidden behind.

Yeah, yeah, yeah … can't see me, fuckers.

Slipping.

He decided it was time. He squeezed the trigger, aiming at one of the torches.

It spun into the air and dropped.

Score one.

Slipping further. He'd felt this pissed a couple of times before; once at his wedding, once when England caned the Aussies at Twickenham.

Fuckin' all right.

Vision was blurring, spinning. But he was lying down already. Good. He'd look a right twat if he was trying to stay on his feet.

The torches all winked out instantly, and half a second later he saw three or four muzzle flashes picking out the alley in stark relief. And the stinking pile of rubbish in front of him began to dance with the impact of bullets, and the air either side of his head was humming.

He felt his shoulder being punched. Just like a hearty pinch and a punch, first of the month.

Didn't bloody well hurt, so fuck you.

He fired again at the swirling, flickering muzzle flashes, pretty certain he was probably aiming at phantoms now.

Another punch, and another. Neither hurt.

Struggling to make sense now of the swirling light-show, he squeezed the trigger and held, firing until the magazine emptied.

Jesus, that was fun. Surely hit something down there.

And then with some effort he reached out for the pistol Andy had placed on the ground beside him. His arm seemed to have no strength in it, like pins and needles. He found the pistol's butt, fumbled at it with useless fingers, and then managed to get some semblance of a grip on it.

The rubbish was dancing again, the air humming … and he felt another punch in one of his legs.

Big … fucking … deal.

He fumbled for the pistol on the ground beside him.

But then another of those flailing, wimpy, pussy-punches landed home.

CHAPTER 38

7.46 p.m. GMT

Shepherd's Bush, London

You can tell so much about a family from their kitchen cork-board, or the mementoes, Post-it Notes and silly clutter that they'll stick to their fridge with little fruit-shaped magnets. Ash had a theory, one of many little theories he'd accumulated over the years, observing as he did, life – normal life, that is – from afar. This one went along the lines of, 'the more cluttered the family fridge, the happier they are', and it was a theory he'd just come up with.

The Sutherland fridge was bare. No photos, memos, notes or shopping lists.

And it was as clear as anything that this was a home in which things had pretty much come to a dismal conclusion. In the kitchen boxes were stacked in the corner, full of crockery and utensils, in the lounge there were boxes of CDs, DVDs and books; in the hallway, lined against one wall, boxes containing wellingtons, scarves and anoraks – on all of these boxes, scrawled with a Magic Marker, was written either 'Jenny' or 'Andy'.

The Sutherlands, as a family unit, were disintegrating.

Ash had hoped to find Mrs Sutherland home, in the hope that she might be able to help him find out who exactly 'Jill' was, and more importantly, where she lived. But alas, an empty house.

The study, Dr A. Sutherland's study, he'd hoped might yield something. Turning the PC on, he checked through the email addresses in Outlook Express's contact book, to no avail. There was no Rolodex, or equivalent, on the desk either.

In the lounge though, he found a tiny black phone book. It listed a small number of people, some friends, some family; not a huge number of friends, which was convenient. Ash could see no one called 'Jill' here either, nor anyone with 'J' as an initial.

But there was a sister not so far away. A sister, as opposed to a friend, because it was on the same page as 'Mum and Dad', written in the unmistakably round handwriting of a woman. Beside the tidy entry was scrawled 'Auntie'; the carefree scrawl of a child. Mrs Sutherland's sister, and obviously they were quite close, because as well as an address and a home phone number, there was a mobile number.

Sisters, he suspected, who probably get together quite often, who share the banal little details of everyday life. He looked down at the page.

Kate.

Yes, he was pretty sure Kate Marsh (née Marsh?) might have an idea who 'Jill' was. Obviously it was someone close enough to the family that Dad would entrust his kids to them during this period of crisis; someone who must have, at one time or another, been casually mentioned by Jenny whilst nattering with Kate over coffee and biscuits.

That was all he had to go on. Not brilliant.

He combed through the rest of the house, finally ending up in Leona's room.

Although there were still posters of boy bands on the wall, and a small mountain of soft toys piled on a chair by the window, it was clearly on its way to becoming a guest room. The child that had grown up in this space was gone now; *flown the coop*, to use a tired aphorism.

Standing well back from the window, away from the warm glow of the evening sun, he gazed out at the cosy suburban street below. In every house opposite he could see the flickering blue glow of television screens; most people, it seemed, glued to the news and no doubt beginning to wonder how an across-the-board fuck up like this could have been allowed to happen.

He watched as several more cars started up and weaved their

way down to the end of the avenue – no doubt in a last-minute bid to see what they could still pick up at their local supermarket – and outside, several houses up, he could see a young couple and their little boy, busily unloading bags of shopping from the boot of their white van.

Ash shook his head, feeling something almost akin to pity for all these people so unprepared for what was lying ahead of them.

CHAPTER 39

10.50 p.m. Local time

Al-Bayji, Iraq

Andy, Carter and the other men looked out at the market-place from the darkness of the rat-run.

'That's it, they've blocked us off,' Carter groaned.

In the middle of the market-place was a large bonfire; an oil drum, piled with broken-up wooden pallets that illuminated the whole area with a flickering amber glow. Surrounding it, enjoying the warmth and chattering animatedly were at least thirty militia. Beyond them, beyond the market-place, was the road out of town, and just visible, the bridge over the Tigris.

'What do you think?' asked Andy.

Carter was silent for a moment before replying. Andy noticed the young officer biting down on his bottom lip, a nervous gesture he'd been aware of back in the compound. But now it seemed a little more pronounced; the young man's head shook a little too, just the slightest tic that suggested to Andy that Carter was beginning to fracture inside.

'I d-don't know. There's a lot of those bastards out there, and a lot of distance for us to run across. Maybe if it wasn't for that bloody bonfire, we might have been able to sneak across to the bridge. But this, this isn't so good.'

Andy looked down at his watch. 'Shit, we've only got nine minutes left. We have to do something!'

Carter shook his head. 'We … we won't make it through.'

'Fuck it!' Andy hissed at him. 'We can't stay here either. They'll be coming up behind us in a minute. We've got to go—'

They heard the throaty rumble of a vehicle approaching – it

sounded like it was coming down the main road, from the centre of town, and fast, very fast.

A moment later, Andy noticed the men out in the market-place reacting, turning towards the source of the approaching noise. They weren't readying their guns yet, perhaps thinking the approaching vehicle was bringing more militia up to help them block off this end of town.

And then the truck rolled into view, rumbling down the main road, flanked on either side by the rows of empty market stalls. Without warning, it slewed to a halt. And from the back of the truck Andy saw several dark forms sitting up.

Carter's hand went up to his earpiece. 'Those are our boys … their PRR just came into range. They're chattering like a bunch of fishwives.'

'Who is it?' asked Andy, 'Westley's lot?'

'That might be Corporal Westley's lot,' whispered Carter, 'or the Fijian bloke's.'

Andy counted the heads on the back of the truck. 'Or maybe both.'

The truck came to a halt, on the edge of the perimeter clearly illuminated by the bonfire. The militia-men gathered round the fire, turned to look at the truck. From their casual demeanour, Andy guessed they assumed the men on the back of the truck were theirs.

'I think they're waiting for us,' he whispered to Carter. 'They've slowed down for us, but they can't stay for long.'

Lieutenant Carter nodded. 'Maybe.'

Carter studied the edge of the market-place.

'No sign of Zulu then.'

Andy shook his head. 'None.'

Carter cursed under his breath.

Andy looked out at the market-place. 'We've got to go!'

'They'll see us the moment we step out.'

Andy looked back down the rat-run. Bolton's gun had stopped chattering a minute ago, and he could see the flashlight beams bobbing towards them. 'We can't bloody stay!'

Derry and Peters looked uncertainly at their CO. 'Sir?'

Carter shook his head. 'It's too open, too far.'

Andy grabbed the officer's arm. 'Fuck it. This is it. This is our last chance. I'm going.'

He pulled himself to his feet, crouched low, ready to sprint out into the open.

'All right,' said Carter, 'we all go. Fire and manoeuvre in twos. Okay?'

Westley spotted them as soon as they emerged from the shadowy mouth of a small alleyway – four of them moving in pairs into the open. The first two dropped to the ground and started firing into the crowd of militia gathered around the fire, the second two taking advantage of the confusion and sprinting towards the truck.

'Friendlies coming in from our left lads! Give the bastards some covering fire!'

Almost immediately the dozen men on the back of the truck let rip, firing into the scattering shapes of the militia. The short volley took down about a dozen men and was initially uncontested as they scrambled for positions, but very quickly return fire forced the men on the truck to duck back down.

Westley waited a few seconds before sticking his head up to scan the situation. All the militia had gone to ground. There was a paucity of cover for them; the meagre planks and rusty tube-metal frames of the empty market stalls weren't going to stop anything. Some were firing back towards the truck, and the occasional rattle and spark against the thick side of the truck's bed was a testament to the fact that some of them had recovered from the surprise opening volley to be aiming their shots well.

'… we go. Got to move now!' Tajican's voice crackled over the radio, half the sentence lost amidst white noise and a whining, piercing feedback.

The incoming fire was intensifying now that the militia had recovered their senses. Not for the first time, Westley acknowledged that amongst the mob, there were definitely men who knew how to fight.

'Okay, but slow … we've got friendlies coming in!'

The truck began to roll forward with a roar of complaint from the diesel engine and a cloud of acrid smoke that burst out of the exhaust pipe and billowed around the back of the truck.

Westley watched as the four men came in closer, racing recklessly past the prone militia towards the truck – the fire and manoeuvre routine now already abandoned. They sprinted the last fifty yards towards the truck like children chasing desperately after an ice-cream van on a hot day.

'Come on move it, you wankers!' he shouted getting up and climbing over the back of the truck, leaning out and standing precariously on the rear bumper.

The truck was moving along a little too quickly.

'Taj, you got to slow down for 'em.'

There was no answer, just a popping and hissing. Maybe Tajican had heard and was replying, maybe he hadn't. The PRR was playing up on them.

The men were successfully closing the distance to thirty … twenty yards. But the truck was beginning to pick up speed and he could see they were beginning to flag.

'For fuck's sake Taj … slow down!' he shouted into his radio.

Shit. Taj isn't hearing me.

Westley tossed his SA80 up into the truck and then leant out towards the running men, stretching his arm out towards them. It was then that, catching a glimpse of their faces he registered *who* the four were.

Lieutenant Carter, Derry, Peters … and that civilian … Andy.

Sergeant Bolton's gone then. Shit.

'Come on!' he shouted.

The nearest was Peters. He grabbed Westley's hand, then quickly got a hold of the tailgate and pulled himself up. Derry was next, with the truck beginning to find some pace after grinding into second gear. Westley had to give his arm a viciously hard tug to pull him close enough that he could make a grab for the back of the truck. With a grunt of complete exhaustion he managed to get himself up and roll over the lip on to the rough bed, where he gasped like an asthmatic.

It was just Lieutenant Carter now and Andy, the Kiwi bloke. He could see both of them had blown whatever strength they had left in them whilst sprinting the last thirty yards, and were just about managing to keep pace, but that wasn't going to last for much longer. It was sheer terror that was keeping these two poor bastards swinging their spent legs now, nothing less.

Westley leant out as far as he could, stretching his hand so that his gloved fingers almost seemed to brush their faces.

Grab it! For fuck's sake, grab it!

He heard the truck clatter and complain loudly as Tajican slammed it up another gear. He turned round and shouted to one of the men near the back of the truck to go forward, bang on the roof of the cab and get Tajican's attention … and slow the fuck down. But his hoarse shout was lost against the rumble of the truck, and the staccato of the final retaliatory shots being fired out the back towards the militia in the market-place, who had now got to their feet and were pursuing *en masse*.

And then he felt his hand being grabbed.

One of them had done it; found enough left over to make a final lunge for his hand. The other? The other just wasn't going to make it. The truck was now picking up speed.

He spun round to see who it was – who was probably going to be the last man up.

CHAPTER 40

7.52 p.m. GMT

Shepherd's Bush, London

Leona looked out of the lounge window at St Stephen's Avenue. Diagonally opposite, one house up, was the DiMarcios' house. She could see the silhouette of their heads through the lounge window, both staring at their TV. In the house directly opposite, was another couple with a baby; she could see activity in their lounge, the woman striding up and down, feeding her baby, the man standing, watching TV as well.

Leona craned her neck, looking through the venetian blind to see her house, number 25. She could just about see it through the foliage of the stunted birch tree opposite.

Dark, still, lifeless.

Like Jacob, she'd much rather be settled in over there, amongst familiar surroundings, amongst her things.

She looked up at her bedroom window – and thought she saw something tall and dark against the back wall of her room. Motionless, like her, studying the gathering madness outside … the shape of a person.

'What …?' she mouthed silently.

A gentle breeze caused the birch to sway slightly and she lost sight of her bedroom window amidst the swirling of leaves. A few seconds passed, the breeze lapsed, the tree settled once more. For a long minute she struggled to peer into the gathering gloom of her bedroom, but it was made difficult with the fading evening light and the sheen of a reflected golden sun balancing on the rooftops.

She could see nothing now.

Don't go home.

Leona shuddered and turned away from the window to join Daniel sitting on the sofa in front of Jill's luxurious plasma screen TV, like everyone else in the world, watching the news. They sat in silence, whilst Jacob lay on the floor in front of them, sorting meticulously through his Yu-Gi-Oh cards.

'... spreading across the country, in every city. In most cases the flash point of each riot has been centred around the big supermarkets, the larger petrol stations. In many of the bigger cities, there simply isn't any sense of order or control. The police have been armed, and the armed forces have been mobilised and stationed around key government installations and supply depots, but beyond that, there simply are no uniforms to be seen ...'

The reporter on screen had a face that Leona recognised; he usually reported on business things, from the City. But now here he was on the rooftop or balcony of some building looking down on a street thick with black smoke from a burning car, and people running erratically. His usually well-groomed appearance, the smartly side-parted hair, the navy-blue suit and tie had been replaced with the look of someone who had been roused from sleep after an all-night vigil.

'Law and order has apparently vanished from the streets of this country in the last six hours, since the Prime Minister's disastrous lunchtime press conference. Amongst the chaos down there, below us, we have distinctly heard the sound of gunfire several times in the last few minutes,' the reporter continued, gazing down on the smoky scene below.

Leona, shuddered anxiously.

My God, he's really frightened.

'There have been unconfirmed reports of military personnel guarding key locations, using live rounds on civilians. There have been hundreds of eye-witness reports describing fights over food, killings in many cases. This is a truly horrifying scenario, Sean, being played out on every street in every major town and city in the country ...'

The image cut back to the studio.

'Diarmid, is there no sign at all of the police or the army out there? I mean, we're looking at Oxford Street right now, aren't we?'

'That's right, Sean. Wholly unrecognisable right now, but yes, this is Oxford Street. This particular disturbance began at about three in the afternoon around a Metro-Stop supermarket, when the staff attempted to close the store and pull down the shutters. This triggered a riot, which quickly led to the store being rushed and the stock completely looted. I saw people emerging from it hours ago pushing trolleys full of food, and then several fights breaking out on the street as other people attempted to lift goods from these trolleys. This particular riot then spread to the other stores up and down the street, with people, quite unbelievably, storming a sports clothes retailer nearby, and next to that, an electrical goods store. Looking down on this now Sean, one is reminded of some of the scenes we saw during the LA riots in 1992, and also in the aftermath of Katrina in New Orleans. But to answer your question Sean, I have seen absolutely no police or army since we arrived here.'

The image on screen cut back to the studio.

'Thank you for that report, Diarmid,' Sean said, looking down at a sheaf of papers in his hands. 'Those scenes of the rioting currently going on in central London.'

Sean Tillman took a long steadying breath, and then looked up again to camera; the trademark early morning smile that Leona found irritating, but frankly would have loved to have seen now, replaced with a chilling portrayal of grim resignation.

'There has still been no further comment from the Government since the lunchtime press conference. We have been informed though that the emergency committee, code-named "Cobra", with full legal authority, is in effect now governing the country. Whether the Prime Minister is steering that committee, or some other minister is, as yet, unclear.'

Leona turned to Daniel. 'Oh God, Dan, this is so scary,' she whispered.

Daniel nodded silently.

'Reports have been coming in from foreign correspondents throughout the afternoon. A similar pattern of events seems to be occurring in many other countries. In Paris, unrest that started in the suburb of Clichy-sous-Bois, has spread across the city, with many buildings now on fire, and reports of many hundreds of deaths amongst the rioters. In New York, the announcement of a city-wide emergency food rationing ordinance was met with demonstrations on the streets that quickly escalated to a full-scale riot.'

Daniel got up. 'Can I use your phone? I want to try my foster parents again.'

Leona nodded. 'Sure.'

As he headed out of the lounge to the hall phone table, Jacob stirred. 'Lee, are we having a big war?' he asked casually.

'What? No, of course not!' she snapped at him irritably. And then noticed from the worried scowl on his small face that even Jake was aware that all was not well with the world. 'No Jake, we're not having a war. But things have gone … wrong, and people are getting a bit panicky.'

Jacob nodded as he digested that, and then looked up at her again. 'I want Mum. Where is she?'

Leona smiled, she hoped reassuringly.

I want Mum too.

Daniel returned. 'There's no tone on the telephone line. It's, like, dead.'

'Dead?'

'Not a thing.'

'Who's dead?' asked Jake, his lips were beginning to quiver unhappily.

Leona could do without him whimpering right now. 'No one Jake. No one's dead. Just play with your cards right now, okay?'

Jacob nodded, but instead of returning to his cards and continuing to sort them into monster and spell decks, he looked up at the TV and watched the flickering montage of flaming cars, and smoke-smudged skylines. He listened to the words, with cocked head, not entirely understanding what was being said, but instinctively knowing that none of it was good.

'You want to use my mobile?' asked Leona.

'Yeah, please,' replied Daniel.

'... in Saudi Arabia, Iraq and Afghanistan particularly. From what we know, the evacuation of troops from the region is continuing apace, with a steady procession of Hercules transport planes depositing troops at several RAF bases, including ...'

On the TV screen Sean Tillman suddenly disappeared. The only thing left on screen was the *News 24* logo in the top left corner and the scrolling news feed along the bottom.

'It appears,' his voice announced, 'we have lost some lighting in the studio. I'm sure this will be rectified short—'

And then there was a chaotic blizzard of snow on the TV and a hiss.

'What happened to the TV man?' asked Jake.

Daniel, holding Leona's phone in his hand, looked up at her. 'Oh shit. What's going on now?'

She shook her head.

And then the lights in the lounge went out and the TV winked off.

'Whuh—?'

The amber-hued streetlights outside along the avenue, which had only minutes ago flickered on, went out.

'The power's gone,' she whispered in the dark.

Jacob began to panic. 'It's all dark! Can't see!' he whimpered.

'Relax Jake, you can see. It's not dark, it's just gloomy,' she said as calmly as she could manage, feeling the leading edge of a growing wave of panic preparing to steal up on her too.

Jacob started crying.

'Shhh Jake. Come up here and sit with us.'

He got up from the floor and squeezed on to Jill's leather Chesterfield sofa between Leona and Dan. 'There,' she said, 'nothing scary's going to happen, we're just going to sit here and—'

Then her phone rang and all three of them jumped.

CHAPTER 41

7.53 p.m. GMT

Between Manchester and Birmingham

'Leona?' cried Jenny with relief, 'Is that you?'

'Mum?'

'Yes. I've been trying to get hold of you all day. Are you all right love?' she replied quickly, not daring to waste a second of precious phone time. God knew how much longer the mobile phone system was going to last. 'Did you pick up Jacob?'

'Yes, he's here.'

'Are you at home?'

She heard Leona pause, a moment's hesitation was all.

'Mum,' Leona started, 'Dad told me to go to Jill's house.'

'Jill's place? Why?'

Another, even longer, pause. 'Dad just thought we'd be safer here in Jill's house.'

Jenny wondered what the hell Andy was thinking about. She'd be much happier knowing they were settled in safely at home. Anyway, she remembered Jill was away this week, on one of her sales team's get-togethers abroad.

'How did you get in to—?'

She could hear Leona crying.

'Doesn't matter, I'm sure Jill won't mind. Do you two have food?'

The question prompted a gasp from her daughter. 'Oh my God, it was horrible Mum. It was just ...'

Jenny could hear the tears tumbling in the timbre of her daughter's voice.

'... at the supermarket, as we came out, things began to go

really bad. We were nearly in a fight. And we've been watching the news, and it's …'

Jenny interrupted. 'I know love, I know.'

Oh Christ do I know.

Jenny had seen things in the last few hours that she never imagined she would see in a country like this; a civilised, prosperous country, with the exception of the odd gang of youths on the roughest of estates, it was a place where one largely felt safe.

'I know,' she replied falteringly. She could hear her own voice beginning to wobble too.

Be strong for her.

'Oh God, Mum. It's just how Dad said it would be, isn't it? It's all falling apart.'

Jenny wondered what was best for her children now. Denial? A blank-minded reassurance that everything was going to be as right as rain in a day or two? Was that what Leona needed to hear from her? Because that *wasn't* the truth, was it? If she now, finally, had come round to trusting Andy's prophetic wisdom; if her worn-down tolerance and weary cynicism was to be a thing of the past and she was now ready to fully take onboard his warnings … then she had to concede this wasn't going to sort itself out in a couple of days.

Things were going to get a lot worse. Andy had foreseen that. Andy had warned her, Christ, Andy had bored her to death with it, and now, finally, here it was.

'Leona, my love. Have you got food?' Jenny asked, swiftly wiping away the first tear to roll down her cheek as if somehow her daughter might catch sight of it.

'Y-yes, Mum. We got a load of tinned things from the supermarket.'

'Good girl Leona. Can I speak to Jacob?'

Jenny heard a muffled exchange in the background, and then her son was on the phone.

'Mummy?'

'Jake,' she replied, the trembling in her voice becoming too difficult to hide.

'Mum? Are you okay?'

'Oh I'm just fine, love.'

'You sound sad.'

'I'm not sad.'

'When are you coming home?'

'As soon as I can get home. I'm trying … really,' replied Jenny looking across at the face of the man she'd been walking beside for the last four hours. Paul. She didn't know him from Adam really. As much a stranger as the other dozen or so people sitting on the orange, plastic chairs around the burger van on the lay-by.

'Okay. Leona and Daniel are looking after me until you come home.'

'Who's Daniel?'

'He's a man. He's Leona's friend.'

A man?

'Jacob, let me speak to Leona.'

Jenny heard the rustle of the phone changing hands again.

'Mum?'

'Who the *hell* is Daniel?' asked Jenny. 'Jacob said it's a *man*.'

'It's all right Mum, he's a mate from uni. He drove us home. He helped us get the food.'

Jenny puffed a sigh of relief. This Daniel was just another kid then, no doubt her current boyfriend. Jenny had lost track of who was who on the list of names Leona casually ran through when she got her daughter's weekly social update over the phone. Jenny found that comforting, there was a lad there looking out for her, and Jake.

'Okay.'

'Have you heard from Dad?' asked Leona. 'I've not spoken to him since early this morning.'

'No love, that was when I last spoke to him.'

'Oh God, I hope he's okay.'

Jenny realised how much she hoped that as well. In the space of a day, she had found herself rewriting recent personal history;

the last five years of seeing him as a tiresome mole digging his own little lonely, paranoid tunnel to nowhere. That was all different now. Andy had been seeing *this* … she looked around at the frightened people beside her, the empty motorway, the dark night sky no longer stained a muted orange by light pollution from the cities beneath it … he had actually been seeing this with his own eyes. All he'd been trying to do was warn them, that's all.

'He'll be fine Leona, I'm sure he's doing okay.'

Leona started crying.

'Listen sweetheart, you have to be strong now—'

There was shrill warbling on the line, followed by crackling and static.

'Leona!'

The crackling continued.

'Leona!' Jenny cried again desperately.

'Mum?'

'Oh God, I thought the phone system had gone down.'

'Mum, please get home as quick as you can. The power went just before you called. It's getting dark now and we're all scared, and there's these noises outside in the stree—'

Then the line went dead.

'Leona!'

This time there was nothing, not even the crackling. Jenny looked across at Paul, who was hungrily devouring some of the stale buns the small group had managed to find inside the locked-up burger van parked in the lay-by.

'The phones aren't working now,' she whispered, feeling her scalp run cold and realising that this was it; her children were on their own just as things in London – as no doubt they were in every other city in the country, perhaps the world – were about to go to hell.

Paul took a swig from a can of Tango. Several twenty-four packs of fizzy sugary drinks and a dozen large catering packs of buns were all the small gathering of people, travelling on foot, had been able to liberate from the burger van. Some of these people, sitting silently on the bucket chairs outside the van, had been among the mob that had pushed past the police blockade. One or two others had joined them, emerging from the flat, featureless farmlands and drab industrial estates beyond the motorway, down the grass bankings lined with stunted, monoxide-withered saplings, as the light of the afternoon had slipped away.

'You better eat something,' Paul said quietly, handing her half-a-dozen buns.

Jenny stared down at the food in front of her.

'I can't eat. I'm not hungry.'

'You should. There's no knowing where we'll find our next meal.'

She tore a bun off from the rest and took a bite out of it, chewing the stale bread with little enthusiasm.

The children are home, they have food. They're safe inside.

That was all that mattered. Jenny knew it might take three or four days walking down the empty motorways on foot before she could be there for them. But they had food.

Andy's warning, his advance warning ... the one they should have heeded a little earlier than this, had sort of paid off, kind of. Of course, if she'd listened to him four or five years ago, they'd be living in some secluded valley in Wales, with an established vegetable garden, a water well, some chickens maybe, a generator and a turbine. Sitting pretty.

Instead, it seemed her kids had only *just* managed to beat the rest of the population, *the blinkered masses* – that used to be one of Andy's pet phrases – to the draw.

Sitting pretty.

Maybe not. They might have had their secluded, self-sufficient smallholding, but, she wondered, how long would they have been able to keep hold of it? Especially once the looted supermarket food ran out and hunger began to bite. Those people, the blinkered masses, would come looking, foraging.

Jenny shook her head.

Andy wasn't the kind of guy who could defend himself, his

family. He was a pacifist. She struggled to imagine him guarding their little survival fortress, with an assault rifle slung over one shoulder and his face dappled with that camouflage make-up the boys liked so much.

He could plan, but he wasn't a fighter.

CHAPTER 42

10.53 p.m. local time

Al-Bayji, Iraq

Westley yanked Andy forward with a savage jerk of his arm, almost pulling him off his feet. With his other hand, Andy managed to grab hold of the truck's tailgate, and together with the Lance Corporal grabbing hold of his sweat-soaked shirt, pulling him up, he found himself lying in the back of the truck, looking up at the flitting moonlit clouds.

With a crunch and a loose rattle of worn metal, the truck finally found third gear, and lurched forward.

Westley was screaming at Lieutenant Carter to get a move on. This truck was *not* going to slow down for him.

Andy sat up and looked over the rim at the back of the truck's bed to see the young officer falling behind them. Beyond, a hundred yards back, the mob were furiously pursuing.

'Come on, fuckin' move it, sir!' he shouted.

Lieutenant Carter ditched his webbing and his gun, and pounded the ground hard with his boots, his face a snarl of effort. His arms pumped hard, and to Andy's amazement, his pace had picked up enough that he began to close the gap. Andy climbed over the rim and joined Westley leaning out of the back of the truck, one arm fully extended. Carter was so exhausted he would need both of them to pull him up, there was no way he was going to have anything left over to get himself up. Once they grabbed hold of him he was going to be dead weight.

'That's it!' shouted Andy. 'Come on!'

Carter increased his pace, and raised one arm out towards the back of the truck, his fingers brushed Andy's.

A puff of crimson suddenly erupted from his torso; the young man lurched and fell forward.

'No!'

Carter shrank as the truck rumbled on and left him behind. He'd taken a hit. Andy could see him scrambling drunkenly to his feet again, clutching at his chest. It was over for him. He could see that on the young man's face. The gunshot wound looked bad.

'Oh shit! Oh shit! He's fucking dead.'

Carter collapsed to his knees, but stayed upright. Andy could see clearly the mob were going to get to him long before the wound did its job.

'Oh this is fucked up,' groaned Westley.

Andy quickly pulled himself back up and reached out for one of the SA80s in the truck. He steadied himself as best he could in the lurching rear of the vehicle as it rattled on to the bridge.

'What are you—?' Westley had time to say before Andy emptied the magazine.

The dirt around Carter danced. Most of Andy's shots missed, but mercifully, a couple landed home, knocking Carter to the ground, where, to Andy's relief, he appeared to lay still.

One of the soldiers up at the front of the truck shouted, 'Hang on! Blockade!' A moment later the truck careered into the flimsy burned-out shell of a small car, knocking it effortlessly aside amidst a shower of sparks and a cloud of soot, smoke and baked flecks of paint.

The truck roared past a dozen or so more militia, most of them diving out of the way of the truck and the tumbling chassis of the car. The truck rattled noisily across the bridge and Andy watched as the blockade, the dark, lifeless town and the enraged mob of people, dwindled behind them. The last he could vaguely pick out through the night-sight was the darkening mass of people, silhouetted against the distant bonfire, gathering around the body of Lieutenant Carter.

Already his mind was ready with the slow-motion playback.

He felt a slap on his shoulder, and turned to see Mike sitting behind. He nodded. 'You did good,' he said.

Andy looked at his watch. It was half past eleven and there was nothing at all to be seen, or, more importantly, heard, in the night sky.

Andy nodded. 'I guess they're not coming then.'

'Are you sure Lieutenant Carter said they were coming here?' asked Mike. 'At eleven?'

'I'm sure.'

There were any number of reasons why the Chinook hadn't turned up; perhaps it had tried to make the rendezvous but had been beaten back, or even brought down, by a surface-to-air missile? Or perhaps they'd simply been considered too high a risk and left to it? It didn't matter now. They were royally screwed.

'Those boys back there are wondering what the hell we're going to do next,' said Mike, 'they've lost both their commanding officers and they're scared shitless.'

Mike was right. The lads gathered in the back of the truck were just that, boys; nineteen, twenty, twenty-one … most of them. Andy was thirty-nine, old enough to be a dad to some. They were looking at him right now, two rows of eyes staring at him from the back of the truck, wanting to know what happens now.

Mike spoke to him quietly. 'They're looking to *you*, you know that don't you?'

Andy nodded. 'Yeah,' he said reluctantly.

'So we need to think what we're going to do now.'

'No shit. We can't drive south-west to the K-2 airstrip. We'd have to go back through Al-Bayji,' he muttered, thinking aloud. He looked once more at the night sky, clear now, and sparkling with stars. There was only one thing they could do. He looked toward the north. 'How far do you reckon?' asked Andy.

'How far to where?' Mike replied.

'Turkey.'

Mike's eyes widened, his thick eyebrows arching above them. 'Excuse me?'

'If we go north, we can drive out of Iraq and make our way home via Syria or Turkey.'

'You plan to drive all the way home?'

Andy turned to look at him. 'I've got two kids and a wife who need me. I want to go home, whatever it takes.'

'Hmmm. I guess there's not much we can do.'

'No. It's not like we got a shit-load of choice here,' said Andy. 'Anyway, we might get lucky and run into some troops … yours or ours. Who knows?'

Mike nodded. 'I guess it's about 150 miles to the border with Turkey.'

Andy pursed his lips. 'As the crow flies. More like 200 if we want to avoid any more big towns and stay off the main northbound road.'

'Then what?'

Andy shrugged. 'Then we drive through Turkey I guess.'

'That's the plan?'

'That's the plan.'

Mike grinned, his white teeth framed by his dark beard. 'You're a fucking tenacious hard-ass bastard Andy, I think I like that about you.'

Andy shrugged. 'If we make it home and you meet my wife, you tell her what a big *hard-ass* I am, okay Mike? Right now she thinks I'm just a dick.'

He slapped Andy's back. 'It's a deal.'

Andy smiled weakly in response.

'You got a family to get home to,' added Mike.

Andy's smile faded. 'Every minute that ticks by that I'm out here is another minute my kids are all alone.'

Mike nodded and looked back at the truck. 'So you better go tell those boys then,' he said, 'I get the feeling they've put you in charge.'

'Ah bollocks, I'm not sure I'm up to it. I can't even bloody well fire a gun straight.'

Mike shook his head and laughed. 'There you see, you ruined it. For a moment, you were almost sounding like a true alpha-male.'

Wednesday

CHAPTER 43

5 a.m. GMT

Between Manchester and Birmingham

Jenny stirred, and realised that she had actually managed to fall asleep in the plastic bucket seat for at least a couple of hours. The first light of dawn had penetrated the surreal, complete darkness of night, and as the steel-grey early morning hours passed, she studied the empty motorway across the narrow grass verge that separated it from the lay-by.

An empty motorway.

Such a strange and unsettling sight, she decided. At least, it was in this country. An empty motorway with weeds pushing up between the cracks in the tarmac – that was one of those iconic images of a long-dead society, a post-apocalyptic world. Well, they were halfway there, the weeds would come soon enough.

Looking around, she could see that five or six of the dozen or so people that had converged last night on the burger van, had set off during the night. There was nothing left to plunder here; the fizzy drinks and burger buns were all gone. She decided they should make a move too.

Paul stirred not long after Jenny.

He stretched a little, nodded silently at her and then with a discreet jerk of his head towards the M6, he suggested they might as well make a start whilst the going was good.

As she picked up her overnight bag, buttoned her jacket and turned up the collar against the cool morning breeze, one of the other travellers slumbering in the plastic chairs stirred.

'Is it okay if I come along with you?' she asked quietly.

Jenny could see why the woman was keen to come along. The

other people, still sleeping, were all men of varying ages. They stared at each other silently, both sharing the same thought.

Today, and tomorrow, and for God knows how long … you don't want to be a woman on your own.

'Sure,' muttered Jenny, pleased to make their number three.

The woman, dark haired, in her early thirties Jenny guessed, wore a navy-blue business trouser-suit that was doing a reasonable job of hiding forty or fifty pounds of surplus weight. She picked up her handbag and weaved her way through the occupied plastic chairs careful not to bump the snoring, wheezing occupants.

She put a hand out towards Jenny, 'I'm Ruth,' she muttered with a broad, no nonsense, tell-it-how-it-is Brummie accent.

'Jenny,' she replied, 'and this is Paul.'

'Hi,' he grunted, with a perfunctory glance towards her.

Jenny shook Ruth's extended hand with a tired smile.

'Let's go then,' said Paul, turning to go along the lay-by leading on to the motorway, heading south.

'So where are you two trying to get to?' Ruth asked Jenny, as they started after him.

'London.'

'I want to get to Coventry.'

'Okay, well that's on the way then.'

They walked down the fast lane alongside the central barrier most of the time, subconsciously keeping a wary distance from the hard shoulder, and the occasional clusters of bushes and exhaust-poisoned and atrophied trees that grew along the motorway banking. The sky was clear and the morning soon warmed up as the sun breached the horizon.

They walked in silence, each of them lost in their own thoughts and worries, but also aware of how strangely silent it was. No planes, no distant rumble of traffic, nothing at all on the motorway, not even military traffic, something Jenny had thought they might see a lot of. Eventually, it was Ruth who broke the silence.

'Are you two married or something?'

Jenny stepped in quickly, 'Oh God no! We just sort of ended up sharing a taxi that got caught up in a blockade on the M6. We're both heading for London, made sense to travel together,' she replied. And then added, 'I've got family in London, children I have to get to.'

'And I had a meeting,' said Paul, 'an important bloody meeting to close a deal. I had a lot of money riding on that one. I suppose that's all fucking history now,' he muttered. 'Now I just want to get back to my flat before some snotty little bastards see it's empty, break in and clear me out.'

'What about you?' Jenny asked, looking at Ruth.

'I'm an account manager. I was doing my rounds when this … thing started. I want to get home to my hubby. He's useless without me.'

'Not so far for you then.'

'Far enough on foot. This is ridiculous – closing the motorways like this. I mean what the hell was the bloody government thinking?'

Reduce population migration from the cities. That's what Andy would have dryly answered, thought Jenny. It was the first step in disaster management – you have to control the movement of people as quickly as possible.

'I can't believe what's happened in the last day,' continued Ruth. 'You just don't expect this sort of thing in this country. Do you know what I mean?'

'That's what I thought,' said Paul. 'I think this isn't as bad as it seems.'

Jenny looked at him. 'What do you mean?'

'Well, I think what's happened is that the government panicked, they overdid the measures, and *that's* what's caused all the rioting and disorder – classic fucking overkill cock-up. I mean blocking the motorways? Stopping the trains and coaches? What the hell was that all about? Of course, doing that, it's made everyone think the end of the world is nigh. So what does that make them do? They start panic-buying, you end up with food running out in the shops, people getting even more worked up. Christ, they couldn't have screwed this up more if they'd tried.'

'There's been a whole load of riots, I heard that on the news earlier,' said Ruth.

'And this is going to easily last another couple of days before everyone wakes up and realises we're not in as bad a state as we thought we were. Until then though, I'd rather get home and off the street.'

Ruth look appalled. 'This is England for God's sake! Surely we can look after ourselves for a week without acting like a bunch of savages going mad?'

'Who says this is going to all be over in a week?' said Jenny.

The other two looked at her.

'I'm just saying.'

Paul shook his head. 'This'll be over in a few days, once the rioting calms down in the Middle East, and then we'll look back at our own riots in disgust. And guess what? There'll be a whole load of voyeuristic CCTV reality programmes showing the thuggish idiots that took part. And hopefully the bastards will be arrested.'

'And what happens if things don't calm down in the Middle East? What happens if we continue into a second week, or a third week without oil and regular shipments of food from all over the world?' said Jenny.

'Oh, Paul's right. It'll sort itself out before then, I'm sure,' said Ruth.

'But what if it *doesn't*? This is the third day. Already with my own eyes I've seen someone killed! What am I going to see on day five? Or day seven? Let alone in two or three weeks?'

'Calm down,' said Paul, 'things have a way of being anti-climactic in this country. Remember the SARS scare, the bird flu scare? There were experts all over the TV telling us how millions would die and the economy would spiral out of control. This'll pass.'

*

They walked along the motorway until mid-morning, spotting no one except one group of people on the opposite side of the motorway heading north. As they passed each other, there was no exchange of news, just a politely exchanged 'good morning'.

Shortly after they saw a sign advertising Beauford Motorway Services five miles ahead, and as it turned midday they veered off the motorway on to the slip-road leading up to it.

They were all very thirsty. Paul had a notion that the facilities would most probably be closed up and the staff sent home until this unrest had played itself out. They could help themselves to a few bottles of water and a few sandwiches; even if they did end up being recorded on CCTV. He said he was thirsty and hungry enough to accept the risk of getting a rap on the knuckles and a fine several months from now.

They walked across the car-park, which was empty except for a small area reserved for staff, where a solitary car was parked snugly beside a delivery truck. The service station consisted of a Chevco petrol station, a glass-fronted pavilion with a billboard announcing that inside they'd find a Burger King, a KFC, an amusement arcade, a TQ Sports outlet, a Dillon's Newsagent and toilets.

Jenny looked at the pavilion, and through the smoky-brown tinted glass she could see movement. There were people inside, looking warily out at them.

'It's not empty,' she said.

'I know, I see them too,' Paul replied. 'Well, I've got some money on me. I'll buy us some water and sandwiches.'

They crossed the car-park, and as they approached the wide revolving glass door at the entrance, a lean man in his mid-fifties, with a receding hairline and small metal-rimmed glasses emerged from the gloom inside. He pushed against a glass panel of the motionless, revolving door, heaving it sluggishly round until he stood outside, in front of them.

He planted his legs firmly apart, straightened up, and produced a child's cricket bat, which he swung casually from side to side. It looked like his best attempt to appear threatening. His slight, marathon runner's frame, narrow shoulders, and nerdy short-sleeved office shirt topped with a lawn-green tie and matching green plastic name-tag weren't helping him.

'We're closed,' he announced curtly, slapping the cricket bat into the palm of one bony hand for effect. 'We've had enough trouble already this morning.'

Jenny noticed some cracks for the first time, scrapes and scuff marks on the thick, reinforced glass at the front of the services pavilion, and scattered across the deserted parking lot; dislodged paving tiles, broken – presumably picked up and dropped – to produce handy fist-sized projectiles. Clearly there had been something going on.

'Bloody pack of yobs were here last night, trying to break in and help themselves,' the man continued.

'Look,' said Jenny, 'we've been walking since yesterday lunchtime. We're thirsty and hungry. We've got money. We just wanted to buy a bottle or two of water, and maybe a few sandwiches.'

The man shook his head disdainfully. 'Money? Money doesn't mean anything right now.'

Jenny could see he was nervous, twitchy.

'Are you in charge here?'

He nodded. 'I'm the shift manager,' he replied.

'And the others?'

He cast a glance over his shoulder at the people inside, looking warily out through the smoky glass to see how their boss was handling the situation.

'What's left of yesterday's shift,' he replied. 'They're the ones who get the bus in. Those who had cars buggered off, leaving these poor sods behind. They're mostly immigrants, speak very little English and they're frightened and confused by what's going on.' He shrugged. 'They're better off here with me, whilst things are like this. And anyway, we've got power here – an auxiliary generator.'

'That's good.'

'And they're helping guard the stock,' he added. 'We had

some little bastards tried to force their way in last night, before we'd managed to lock up the front entrance. They beat up Julia, my deputy shift manager, when she tried to stop them.'

'*Little bastards?* Do you mean kids?' asked Paul.

'Kids – no. Most of them were teenagers. You know the kind, townies, hoodies, chavs, pikies, neds … I'm sure you know the type I mean.'

Townies. Jenny knew what those were. That was the term Leona used to describe the sort of mouthy little buggers who gathered in surly, hooded groups on street corners.

Ruth craned her neck around the manager to look at his staff peering out through the glass. 'Is she okay?'

'Of course she's not. They broke her arm, and her face is a mess.'

'I'm a nurse, let me have a look at her,' said Ruth.

Jenny and Paul turned to look at her. 'You said you were a—'

'I was a nurse first.'

The manager looked at Ruth. 'Oh blimey, would you? I just don't know what to do for her. She's in a lot of pain. She's been screaming, crying all morning, disturbing the other members of staff.'

'Can we all come in?' asked Paul.

The manager looked them over quickly. 'Well I suppose so.'

CHAPTER 44

11.31 a.m. GMT

Shepherd's Bush, London

Leona looked out of the lounge window, across Jill's small front garden, on to the leafy avenue outside, lined with parked cars, mostly very nice ones. Last night she had sat up in bed, terrified, unable to sleep, listening to the noises outside.

Several groups of kids, mostly lads judging by their voices, had been up and down the street in their cars, the bass from their music systems pounding so loud the bedroom window had rattled. She heard them running around kicking over bins, having a lot of fun by the sound of it.

They were drunk. She heard the clinking of carrier-bags full of booty, and the shatter of empty bottles casually tossed on to the pavement. Leona guessed they had been to Ashid's Off-licence at the top of their road, and swept the shelves clean. They were making the most of it, celebrating the total black-out, and the total absence of police.

What she found most disturbing was the sense of ownership these lads – there'd been teenagers and young men among them too – had of the street. It was all *their* playground now that it was clear the police weren't likely to come calling any time soon.

Leona wondered how long the novelty of messing around up and down the narrow avenue would last, though. She wondered when they'd decide that the houses on either side of it were a part of their playground too. She shuddered at the thought that the only reason they hadn't broken into any of the houses along St Stephen's Avenue last night was that the idea simply hadn't occurred to them yet.

They'd been having too much fun drag-racing up and down, messing around with the wheelie bins, smashing up some of the sillier garden ornaments and uprooting someone's willow saplings.

They hadn't worked out yet that in fact they could do *anything* they wanted right now.

Anything.

Until, that is, the police got a grip on things again – whenever that was likely to happen.

Leona noticed Daniel had managed to sleep beside her through most of it. But then he was a little more used to this kind of ruckus, coming as he had, from various foster homes in Southend, overlooking the sea, and the parking strip used most nights by joyriders showing off their PlayStation-honed driving skills.

Jake had somehow managed to get some sleep as well.

The noises had continued until the first grey rays of dawn had stained the sky, and then it had gradually quietened down, and the last thing she'd heard – as her watch showed half past five – was one of them, left behind by the others, heaving up his guts in someone's garden and groaning loudly, several dozen yards up the street.

At about nine, both Daniel and Jacob rose tiredly and padded barefoot downstairs to join her in the kitchen. Leona had found a wind-up radio in Jill's study, and had quickly found several stations still busily broadcasting.

'Is the power back on?' asked Daniel hopefully as he entered.

Leona shook her head and held up the radio for him to see. 'You wind it up for power.'

'Oh,' he replied, disappointed.

Jacob looked around. 'I want some cereal.'

'There's the BBC World Service still doing its thing. And Capital FM, and one or two others.'

Daniel offered her a hopeful shrug, 'So maybe it's not so bad out there then?'

She turned to look at him. 'Listen to it Dan, it's horrible … the things that are happening.'

'Can I have some cereal?' piped Jacob again.

Leona turned irritably on him. 'No!'

'Why not?'

'There's no milk in the fridge. If you want cereal, you'll just have to have it dry, without milk.'

'I want milk on it,' Jacob answered.

She turned the radio up. 'Just listen to it, Dan. God, we're in a real mess.'

'… burning across the city. It looks like Beirut, or no, more like Baghdad the day after the fall of Saddam's regime. I've never seen anything like this in Britain, the riots last night, the total lawlessness. I have heard there were isolated areas of order, and in some smaller towns we've heard the fire service was still functioning, and the police were seen, although largely unable to intervene. There has been no further comment from the Prime Minister or any senior government representatives; however, the provisional crisis authority, "Cobra", has continued to broadcast a general call for calm …'

'Can I have some toast then, Lee?'

'… amongst the population, reassuring everyone that measures have been taken to ensure order will be returned during the course of the day. Last night's widespread power-outs across the country, which helped fuel the panic and the riots, were described as a transitory event, with authority for the distribution and allocation of power being switched from the utility companies to regional emergency authorities. A spokesman for Cobra confirmed that, for the next few days, there was going to be a lot less power available with France no longer able to export a surplus, and Russia temporarily suspending exports of natural gas whilst the crisis is ongoing. A rationed system of distribution is being put into effect with most regions, we've been assured, receiving power for a short period every day. In addition, we're being told that supplies of food and bottled water have been secured and stockpiled and a rationing system will be announced shortly. Meanwhile, I've been hearing broadcasts from other countries in Europe and across the world. This has hit everyone equally badly it seems. In France, rioting in the southern . . .'

'Leona, can I have some toas—'

'Shut up!' snapped Leona. 'Can't you see I'm trying to listen?'

'But I'm hungry. I want some toast!'

'And how the fuck am I supposed to make you some toast, Jacob? Hmmm?'

Jacob's mouth hung open. 'You said the "F" word.'

'Yes I did, didn't I?' she replied. 'I'm sorry.'

Jacob shrugged, 'S'okay, I won't tell Mum or Dad, or anything.'

Leona felt a pang of guilt for lashing out at him like that. She knelt down beside him. 'No, I'm really sorry for shouting at you monkey-boy. It's just that things are . . . well, I just can't make any toast right now.'

'Because the power's all gone away?'

'That's right, Jakey. Because the power's gone away, and it might not come back again for a bit.'

Jacob nodded silently, his eyebrows knitted in concentration as he absorbed that concept for a moment.

'So,' he continued, 'if the power's gone away, how will Mum and Dad come home? They need power to come home.'

Leona suddenly felt tears fighting their way up; tears of panic and grief. They were both out there in this horrible mess, both of them alone. There was no way of knowing what sort of trouble they might be in, if they were hurt, or worse.

Jesus, don't even think like that.

'They'll find a way home, Jacob,' she said offering him a quick reassuring smile. 'They'll be home sometime soon. And all we've got to do is sit tight here and wait for them, okay?'

Jacob nodded. But he knew in some way that his big sister was telling him a white lie.

A good lie.

That's what Mum called white lies; the ones you tell to cheer people up.

'Okay,' he said, 'no toast then.'

Leona stood up, sniffed and wiped at her eyes. 'How do you fancy some baked beans for breakfast?'

Jacob nodded.

'Cold, like we have them in the summer sometimes?'

CHAPTER 45

12.15 p.m. GMT

Beauford Service Station

'We've got, let me see …' said the shift manager. He hadn't thought to introduce himself, instead Jenny had noticed the name on his plastic tag: Mr Stewart. She noticed all the other members of staff had only their first names printed on their tags; a privilege of rank she guessed, to be known by your surname.

'We've got a load of confectionery and snacks,' he repeated pointing towards the racks of chocolate bars, crisps, sweets and canned drinks in the newsagents, Dillon's. 'And then burgers, chicken, potato fries, we have in the freezers over there,' he said pointing towards the two fast food counters sitting side by side. 'We've got an auxiliary generator that kicks in if there's a power failure, and that'll keep going for about a week at most, and then of course the frozen stuff will start to go off. So we'll munch our way through that stock first. That's my plan.'

'So you're sorted for a while then?' said Paul.

Mr Stewart nodded eagerly. 'We'll be just fine here until things right themselves once more.'

Jenny looked out at the scuffed and damaged glass wall at the front of the pavilion. It had taken a pounding. It didn't look pretty any more, but it wasn't going to give any time soon.

'How did they manage to get in and assault your assistant manager?' Jenny asked.

'That was unlocked,' said Stewart pointing to the large revolving door in the middle of the front wall. 'I'd just sent Julia to bring in the ice-cream signs and other bits and pieces we have outside, when they turned up.'

He turned to face them with a confident smile. 'It's locked now, that's for bloody sure.'

'You think they'll be back?' asked Jenny.

'They might,' he answered quickly, 'and they can prat around out there and hurl as much abuse as they like, those little bastards won't be able to get in. Just you see.'

They heard the sound of someone moaning in pain.

'Ah, that's poor Julia. I better go and see how your friend is getting on with her.'

Mr Stewart turned smartly away and walked with an echoing click of heels across the foyer towards the manager's office. He passed by a huddle of his staff sat amongst the tables in the open-plan eating area and offered them a way-too-cheery smile.

'Cheer up!' he called out as he breezed past.

His staff, a worried and weary-looking group of eastern European women and a couple of young lads, nodded mutely and then returned to whispering quietly amongst themselves.

'I can't stay here any longer, Paul,' she said quietly. 'Every minute I'm sitting here, is another minute away from my kids. I've got to go.'

Paul looked at her. 'Listen to me. The smart thing to do, the clever thing to do, is to sit tight. Just for another day, and see how things are.'

'What?' she whispered. 'I can't stay! I have to get home!'

He nodded, thinking about that. 'I'd like to get home too. But you know … look, yesterday afternoon, at that roadblock was pretty scary, wasn't it?'

She nodded.

'Well, I think it's going to be even worse out there today and worse still tomorrow. You don't want to be out there walking the roads whilst things are so unstable.'

'My kids, I have to get home to them.'

'You said your kids were tucked up safely at your friend's home? And they got in a whole load of food? That's the last thing you heard right?'

Jenny nodded.

'Then, right now, they're probably a lot better off than everyone else.'

Jenny thought about that for a moment, and realised that Paul might well be right. Sitting tight in Jill's modest terraced house; one anonymous house amongst many identical houses in a sedate suburban back road, riding this thing out quietly, not drawing anybody's attention … Leona and Jacob were doing exactly the right thing.

'You won't be doing them any favours heading out there today,' said Paul. 'Not whilst it's one big lawless playtime for the kiddies. Hang on a day or two, let the worst of it pass. The police *will* get a grip on things later on today or tomorrow, mark my words. Then, shit, I'll come with you. I want to get home too.'

Jenny decided that he might have a point. On her own, today or tomorrow, out there on the road, anything could happen.

Oh bugger, Andy, what do I do? Our kids … are they really okay? Are they really safe at home?

Jenny would have happily sold her soul for five minutes on a mobile phone that worked right now. Just to know the kids were still okay, just to know that Andy was okay, and perhaps tell him that – you know what? – maybe she'd been a little hasty. Maybe she did still love him after all.

'You go wandering out there today, and well … your kids'll fare a lot better *with* a mum than *without*.'

Jenny looked uncertainly through the scuffed plastic.

'Hang on for today, okay? I promise you, we'll see police cars out there tomorrow.'

Jenny nodded. 'Okay, just today then.'

They heard the door to the manager's office open. Ruth and Stewart emerged and walked over towards Jenny and Paul.

'They broke her nose and dislocated her shoulder, and her jaw's swollen. I'm going to pop her shoulder back, but it's going to really hurt her. I've given her a load of painkillers,' she looked at her watch, 'which should kick-in in about ten minutes.'

Mr Stewart muttered angrily. 'Those vicious little bastards.

What I wouldn't give to catch one of them and give him a damn good hiding.'

'Is there anything I can do to help?' asked Jenny.

Ruth nodded. 'Yeah, thanks. You may need to hold her for me. It won't be nice.'

Jenny grimaced, 'I can handle it.'

Ruth looked at Mr Stewart. 'Is there any booze in this place?'

'Uh ... yes,' he answered awkwardly, 'there's ahh ... a bottle of brandy in my office.'

'Good, I need a nip, you might want to have one too,' she said to Jenny, 'and I'm sure poor old Julia might want a slurp too.'

Mr Stewart nodded, a tad reluctantly. 'Help yourselves.'

'Ta. Come on.'

Jenny looked at Paul, 'You going to give us a hand?'

But Paul was studying the glass front to the pavilion; his mind was elsewhere. 'So, you think those lads will be coming back?'

The shift manager nodded and smiled grimly. 'Oh yes. They said they'd be back sometime soon. And promised me that once they got in they would ... what was the phrase? Oh yes, "happy slap me till I were a shit-stain on the floor".'

'Nice.'

'Oh, I'm not worried. In fact I think I'd like it if they *did* come back. It'll be fun to watch those violent little shits getting hungry outside our nice big window. They can watch me serve up burgers and fries to my staff.'

'Yeah, that'll be great fun, better than TV,' he smiled uncertainly back at Mr Stewart.

CHAPTER 46

2 p.m. GMT

Shepherd's Bush, London

'Come on, let's see how things are,' said Dan. 'Maybe we'll find some policemen out there. There's gotta be someone cleaning things up, sorting things out.'

Leona said nothing.

'Come on, just to get some fresh air.'

'Not too far, okay? Just a quick look around.'

'Sure,' Dan nodded.

'All right.' She turned to Jacob. 'You stay inside Jake, okay?'

'Can't I come?'

'No. You stay inside and … I don't know, play with your toys. We won't be long.'

Leona decided Dan was right. They needed to find out, after yesterday's sudden and violent release of chaos, if the worst was now over. And finding a policeman, or a fireman, in fact anybody in uniform, out on the street making a start on clearing things up, was the sort of reassurance she needed right now.

She headed down the hallway to the front door, Dan beside her, unbolted and opened it. She turned back round to Jacob.

'You stay inside. Do you understand me?'

Jake nodded.

They stepped out on to the short path that led up Jill's scruffy, rarely tended front garden to the gate, and the avenue beyond. It was sunny, pleasant, T-shirt 'n' shorts warm.

'It's quiet,' said Dan. They could hear some birds in a nearby tree, but there was no hum of traffic coming from Uxbridge

Road; no car woofers pounding out a thudding bass line, or the distant warble of a police siren wafting over the rooftops.

Leona looked up and down. The kids last night had left something of a mess. Many of the parked cars, SUVs, 4x4s, had had one or more of their windows smashed. Glass granules littered the pavement all the way up and down on both sides. It looked like there'd been a hailstorm. She noticed discarded cans and bottles, dropped on the pavement and tossed into the front gardens.

'What a mess they made.'

Dan shrugged, 'Looks just like my mum's street.'

They walked up the avenue towards the junction with Uxbridge Road. As they passed by her home, Leona fought an urge to glance up at her bedroom, worried that she might again see the outline of someone staring out of the window. She had convinced herself since that the fleeting dark form she thought she'd seen had been nothing more than a trick of the evening light and an over-active imagination.

Uxbridge Road was the main thoroughfare for Shepherd's Bush. If there were going to be any police out, they'd be up there, where all the shops were; where the police station was.

As they reached the top, she looked up and down the main road.

'Oh ... my ... God,' she muttered.

On either side, every shop window was gone, and the goods spilled out on to the street; washing machines, TVs, clothes, newspapers and magazines, spread across from pavement to pavement. It seemed most of the damage and mess was focused around the many grocers, Halal mini-markets and takeaways. A hundred yards down, she could see the pale squat block that was the police station for Shepherd's Bush.

'You know, I haven't seen anyone yet,' said Dan. 'Where'd they all go?'

He was right – she'd not seen a single soul either.

'I don't know,' she replied, 'maybe everyone's too scared to come out.'

They picked their way down the street, stepping past the sooty carcass of a car that was still smouldering, and past puddles of mushed food that could have been something stolen from a takeaway nearby, or perhaps was merely someone's vomit.

'Let's try the police station,' said Leona, 'somebody's got to be there.'

The police station was set back from the road, up three steps from the mess on the street that was already beginning to smell, heated to a tepid stew by the midday sun.

The double frosted-glass doorway leading to the front desk swung easily inwards. Inside it was dimly lit by a single strip light fizzing and humming above the counter that normally would have had a desk sergeant manning it.

'Well *they've* got some electric,' snorted Dan, 'it's all right for some.'

'They probably have one of those back-up generators.'

Leona leaned against the desk. 'Hello?'

Her voice echoed ominously around inside.

'Is anyone on duty?' she called again. But there was no answer.

She turned to look at him. 'There must be someone manning this place, even if they're down to a skeleton crew. Surely?'

Dan shrugged. 'Dunno, it looks kind of deserted to me. I'll have a look.'

He lifted up a foldable section of the front counter, stepped through and looked around the office space on the far side of the counter. 'Shit, it's a bit of a mess back here, papers and stuff all over the place.'

He wandered through towards the rear of the area, towards a frosted-glass door, beside which was a keypad that kept it locked.

Leona could see from where she was standing that the frosted glass was cracked, and the door had been forced. 'Looks like someone's already been through this place and trashed it,' she called out after him.

Danny nodded. 'Yeah.'

'Just be careful.'

'Okay.' He pushed the door inwards and Leona heard his feet crunch on broken glass.

'Anyone around?' he called out as he poked his head into the room beyond. 'Any police?'

Leona watched as he stepped inside the room, the frosted-glass door swung to behind him, and all she could see was the foggy outline of his form moving beyond.

'Don't go too far Dan!' she called out, and she heard his muted voice beyond say, 'Okay'.

It was so eerily quiet. She looked back out at the street through the double doors they came in through. Uxbridge Road should have been humming with traffic, the pavements thick with pedestrians and groceries, fruit 'n' veg, laid out on benches and tables, alongside cheap mobile phone covers and dodgy SIM cards. But instead it was like some western ghost-town. She half expected tumbleweed to come rolling past.

Dad had once told her about a hurricane that hit London in '87, and emerging early for work to find the streets deserted and covered in flotsam and jetsam. She imagined it must have looked something like this, but surely not quite as bad.

So quiet.

She hadn't heard any movement from Dan for a while. 'Dan?'

No answer.

'Dan? You okay in there?' she called out again.

Nothing, for a moment, then the sound of something scraping in there.

'Dan?'

She saw something through the frosted glass, a dark outline, swaying slightly.

'Dan, is that you?'

It hesitated for a moment, froze. And then she saw it moving again, a hand reaching out for the door.

The door swung open and she saw Dan, his face expressionless, pale.

'Oh my God, are you all right?' she asked.

Dan nodded slowly, as he made his way back across the office towards the counter. 'Let's go,' he said quietly. 'Now. Let's just get out of here.'

'What's up? Did you see something?'

He joined her on the far side of the counter and grabbed her hand. 'Let's just go.'

'Any sign of the police?'

He nodded again and swallowed uncomfortably. 'Yeah, I saw one.'

They headed outside, screwing up their eyes against the bright sunlight as they stepped through the double doors. 'I think we should head back,' said Dan, 'I've seen enough for now.'

Leona pointed to her left. 'There's a supermarket just there, do you see? Maybe we'll find police guarding it?'

'Maybe, but why don't we just go home, Lee?'

Leona grabbed his arm and looked at him. 'I really want to find a policeman, Dan. I just want to hear from someone in charge what we're supposed to do.'

'Okay, okay,' he said, 'the supermarket then home.'

CHAPTER 47

2.01 p.m. GMT
Hammersmith, London

The motorbike across the road from him would be ideal, Ash decided. The man sitting on it was merely an inconvenience he would quickly dispense with. He picked his way across the junction, cluttered with some shopping baskets and about a million sheets of printer paper spread out across the silent road like snow, fluttering in the light afternoon breeze.

The man on the bike was a policeman, and he was busy surveying the junction. On any other day at this time, it would be locked to a standstill with traffic. Today it was deserted. Ash noticed a few dozen other people in the vicinity, picking through the fall-out of last night.

The policeman quickly became aware of Ash approaching in a direct line.

'Can you stay back please, sir,' he said in an even tone.

Ash slowed down, but didn't stop. 'I need some help,' he replied. 'I need an ambulance,' he added, in his mind quickly throwing together some story that needed to only hold together for another twenty seconds, another ten yards.

'What's the problem?' the policeman asked.

Ash continued forward. 'My wife, she needs a hospital, badly.'

The policeman held out an arm, 'Please stay where you are, sir. What's wrong with her?'

Ash slowed his pace right down, but kept closing the gap. His face crumpled with anguish. 'Oh God, I think she's dying! I can't . . . I can't . . .'

The policeman's hand drifted to the saddlebag where Ash could see the butt of a firearm sticking out of it. 'I said, stay where you are!'

He almost stopped.

Five yards ... just a little bit closer.

The policeman studied Ash, sobbing uncontrollably in front of him. 'There's nothing I can do right now, sir. I can call it in, but the service is stretched as it is. What's wrong with her?'

Ash took another tentative step forward.

Good enough.

'Stay where you are!'

Ash produced his thin blade and lunged forward, sliding into the policeman's stomach as he fumbled for his gun. He tugged it upwards with a sawing action the way you'd fillet a fish, knowing the catastrophic damage the blade was doing inside. With his other hand he grabbed one of the policeman's wrists and held it firmly. The policeman's unrestrained hand reached around to where the blade had gone in, fumbling and slapping ineffectually at it, trying to pull it out.

'Shhhh,' said Ash. 'Easy does it,' he whispered, his face close to the man's, almost intimate. 'It'll all be over in a second my friend.' Ash lifted him off the motorbike and laid him gently down on the pavement, his mouth flapping open and closed, producing only an unhappy gurgling sound.

Ash climbed on to the bike. A few of the people nearby seemed to have noticed and stared slack-jawed at him as he kick-started the bike.

Guildford.

He'd spent last night by candle-light, studying the Sutherlands' *London A to Z*. Provided the roads were clear and there weren't any roadblocks, he estimated he could find his way there sometime this afternoon. And hopefully find this sister, Kate, was in.

He spun the bike round, heading around the Hammersmith circular, and turning south, down Fulham Palace Road. Most of the shop windows were gone along this road as well.

He was surprised at how little it had taken to rip apart the veneer of law and order; at least within central London. No one was starving yet, probably not even hungry. But the mere *mention* of food rationing by that moronic Prime Minister had driven them all into a state of panic, further exacerbated by the hysterical way the media had responded and then the nationwide power-out last night – sudden, without any warning.

He smiled.

They had handled that very well over here, perfectly in fact; orchestrated complete disintegration within a couple of days.

CHAPTER 48

2.05 p.m. GMT

Shepherd's Bush, London

Leona led the way another hundred yards up Uxbridge Road. It was only as they crossed the debris-strewn road that they noticed someone else, the first sign of life so far. She could see about five people, an Asian family, picking through the mess of a jewellery shop, making a tentative start at clearing the mess up. She felt encouraged by that. It seemed like a good sign.

Ahead of them was a small shopping precinct, above it a multi-storey car-park. Normally, night and day, the precinct was awash with neon lights, backlit billboards, and thousands of little shopping mall spotlights embedded in the precinct's relatively low ceiling. Right now, despite being a sunny afternoon, it looked quite dark inside.

'The supermarket's just a little way inside,' said Leona. She might have turned back at this point, but seeing that family not so far away, making a start on fixing up their shop, there was a pervading sense that the worst of this might actually be over.

'Can't see any police down there,' said Dan.

'Let's take a quick look. And if there's no police inside, we might be able to pick up a few extra supplies in the supermarket.'

Dan didn't look so keen.

'A quick look, then we'll come out again.'

She led the way, heading into the precinct.

Out of the sunlight it felt cooler. Their footfall against the smooth, well-polished floor, echoed loudly inside. She was taken aback at how lifeless it looked, so used to the place always being busy and noisy with the sound of shopping muzak, squealing packs of teeny-boppers, and the clatter of heels and shopping trolleys and mums pushing baby buggies.

Every store-front window had been smashed.

At the far end of the precinct she could see the long and wide windows of the supermarket. From where they were, it was clear it had been looted; windows were smashed, shopping trolleys and hand baskets were tangled everywhere and the ground was covered with discarded packaging, cardboard boxes, spilled, crushed and spoiled food.

They approached a smashed window and looked inside. It was dark. No power. The shelves were uniformly empty, the floor space between littered with more debris from the orgy of looting that must have happened here yesterday afternoon and evening.

'It's been totally cleared out,' said Dan quietly. 'This is so-o-o like that New Orleans Katrina thing. I remember that on the news. It just … just looked like this.'

Leona nodded. 'I know. You just don't think that would happen here, you know, until it does.'

'We should head back now,' he said, 'we've left Jake long enough.'

Leona smiled and reached for his hand, 'You'd make a good older brother.'

They heard the scrape of a foot on glass shards behind them and both spun round.

'You got a fag, mate?'

CHAPTER 49

5 p.m. local time

Northern Iraq

Andy watched Tajican, Westley and Derry as they busily worked on siphoning the fuel from the damaged vehicles across the road – three Humvees and a truck. The small convoy had quite clearly been halted by an explosive device by the side of the road; the first Hummer was little more than a blackened and twisted carcass. Behind it, the other three vehicles were pockmarked with bullet-holes. Clearly, the halted convoy had subsequently been ambushed by gunmen from the cover of the sand berms either side of the road. Brass bullet-cases littered the ground around the vehicles, there had obviously been a sustained fire-fight, and from the dark smudges in the sand, and on the seared tarmac of the road, it was clear there had been a number of casualties.

There were bodies, barely recognisable as such, in the first vehicle, and a dozen more to be found in a ditch several dozen yards away from the road. The bodies were all those of American soldiers. To Andy it looked as if they had made their last stand here; fire coming from all sides, their vehicles providing inadequate cover, they must have bailed out and beat a retreat across the road towards the ditch, and the fight had finished there.

Whilst they were siphoning fuel out of the vehicles, Andy had asked Westley to post some look-outs. Four of the platoon, with Peters in charge, were a hundred yards up the road keeping a look-out, another four men under Benford, were back down the road keeping tabs on the other direction. It was another two or three hours before sundown and as far as Andy was concerned the cover of darkness couldn't come soon enough.

Mike studied the bodies in the ditch. 'Those boys were engineers, not frontline combat,' his voice rumbled angrily.

'Looks like this went down sometime on Monday,' said Andy, 'you know … judging by the state of the bodies.'

Mike nodded. 'Poor bastards.' He turned to Farid. 'These boys were probably on their way to repair or build something for *your* people, when this shit happened.'

Farid met his gaze. 'It is unfortunate.'

Mike laughed dryly and shook his head. 'Yeah see, I just don't get you people. Why? I mean why the fuck do you people not want your bridges fixed, your water treatment plants repaired? Why the hell don't you want this friggin' country repaired?'

Farid shrugged. 'Iraqi people want water, want bridges, Mike. We just not want America made here in this country.'

'We're not trying to rebuild America here, we're just trying to fix up your goddamn infrastructure—'

'Which I believe was intact and working just fine before we arrived,' said Andy. 'I think it's probably worth mentioning that.'

Mike stopped, and then to his credit nodded. 'Just pisses me off though. We get rid of your dictator, who I'm sure your people all agree, was a nasty piece of shit, and then give you the chance to create a fair and democratic nation here—'

'We not want that,' said Farid calmly. 'We tell you this, many times. But America not listens. We not want this democracy, it is rule of man by man. We want for rule of man by Allah.'

'I don't get that,' replied Mike.

'I've got to say I don't get that either, Farid,' said Andy. 'At least with the ability to vote, to decide who gets to run things, you can kick out the guys at the top if they turn out to be bad. What's so wrong with that?'

Farid shook his head. 'This put man in charge. It mean man decide things. Look what happen in your country when it is men in charge. They steal money, they make huge wars, they lie to people. And then, you have vote … yes? Then you have new man in your … White House, and then *he* steal money too, and make the same wars. No difference. Shari'ah law is God's law. It not be changed or … inter—'

'Interpreted?'

Farid nodded. 'Because man always will change things to suit his need. Always this happen.'

'You're saying Shari'ah law is incorruptible,' prompted Andy.

'Yes, that is what I try and say. Is *incorruptible*. Never change.'

'That's a load of crap,' muttered Mike. 'The men at the top, the imams, they play fast and loose with Islam. They make it say whatever they damn well want.'

'Those who do this are not good Muslims,' cautioned the old man. 'Saddam say he was a good Muslim. He was not.'

Andy could see his point. Perhaps, in theory, the simple laws of God, as defined in the Qur'an were a viable way for a society to live. Like communism, it worked on paper, but once you introduced a few self-serving bastards into the equation, it began to come unravelled. Perhaps though, there was something to be said for the simple code of Islam; the egalitarianism, the strong emphasis on charity, on family. If they could strip out the God bit, and the lopsided take on the woman's role in life, he wondered if it was something he could possibly embrace.

'Answer me this Farid,' said Mike, 'and I want you to be honest.'

The old man looked at him.

'What is it that you guys really want?'

Farid smiled disarmingly. 'You know what every good Muslim want?'

'What?'

'Islamic world. All of us, brothers together.'

Mike shook his head. 'See that's what I always suspected. There's no room for infidels like me, like Andy, like Israel. Secretly – and most of the time you guys are real careful what you say in public – secretly, you want us gone, you want us wiped—'

'No!' Farid cut in angrily. 'No! I want world of Islam with *all my heart*. But, I would not agree to the death of even *one* person, one *infidel* to do this.'

Mike studied him silently.

'Jihad not mean war, Mike. Jihad mean … *struggle*. I wish for you to accept Allah into heart. You as well, Andy. That is my struggle, my *Jihad*. But Allah can only be *accepted* … you understand? Not with gun, or bomb, or fear. He can only be *accepted*.'

Andy turned to the old man. 'You know something Farid, I'm never going to believe in a God. You know that, don't you? I consider religion, all of it, to be little more than mindless superstition.'

Mike shrugged. 'Me neither. Christian, Jewish or Islamic, ain't gonna happen. And I'll probably burn in hell for saying that.'

Farid offered them a broad smile. 'God accept in Heaven, believer and non-believer. If you are good man, there is room.'

'It's only the real assholes he doesn't let in?' said Andy.

Farid laughed and nodded. 'That is right.'

Mike nodded. 'I guess I can go with that.'

CHAPTER 50

2.30 p.m. GMT

Cabinet Office Briefing Room A (COBRA), London

The Prime Minister had buckled under pressure as Malcolm thought he might. Charles was exhibiting the signs of an approaching nervous breakdown. Which was understandable really. His appalling naivety yesterday, in attempting to appeal to some nebulous notion of a nascent Dunkirk spirit, had successfully thrown the country into a premature state of chaos. Making the job of mobilising the army and police to secure key assets around the country a hell of a lot easier.

Charles' well-intentioned gamble to try and get everyone on-side and pulling together had, in fact, worked wonderfully well for *them*. Certainly in Britain, it was all going to schedule. Social collapse had occurred far more quickly than they had predicted – all credit to Charles' contribution. Now, with all the key assets under guard, and a steady flow of troops coming back home to bolster their hold on things, the situation was pretty much manageable, and measurable.

Malcolm and his colleagues had firm control of COBRA, the civil contingencies authority. There were eight in this ruling committee, five of them were insiders – members of the One Hundred and Sixty. And now as it appeared that all the little pieces were sliding into the right places, it was time to carefully apply the pressure – to nudge the process along, little by little.

And they needed to do this very carefully.

Nearly a decade ago, when the need for an event like this was first discussed, there were those who had cautioned that it could spiral out of their control. Malcolm had been amongst them. Which was why this thing needed to be handled here in this country, and everywhere else, with surgical precision.

One foot on the accelerator … and one foot hovering just above the brakes.

There was a target, a goal to aim for. The danger would be in *overshooting* that, letting this whole process build up its own uncontrollable momentum and run away from them.

Malcolm looked down at the executive orders he had drafted ready to put in front of his fellow COBRA attendees. Four of the committee would pass these orders without even a murmur. They knew exactly why these things had to be done. The other three would no doubt blanch with horror and ask why the distribution of power was being so ruthlessly limited, why water supplies to large areas of the country were to be turned off.

And Malcolm would calmly justify it to them. Something along the lines of: *'This crisis could last for months, gentlemen. We have entered into an unknown, unpredictable and dangerously unstable period. The free flow of oil is the one thing, the ONE thing that sustains this interconnected, interdependent world. It's the scaffolding that holds this global house of cards up, and somebody, somewhere, God knows why, decided to pull it away. We're an island of sixty-five million people and very limited resources. It's our duty to ensure we preserve a pool of supplies that will sustain, if not the entire population, then at least a significant portion of it, through this period, through the aftershock, and through the recovery. Power, water and food are the three things we must now take complete responsibility for controlling, rationing and distributing …'*

And if those three members didn't go along with that line of hogwash, so be it, it really didn't matter. Five votes to three would sideline their opinion anyway.

Malcolm sighed. How tempting it would be to just come right out into the open and explain what he and his colleagues were up to. They would see the sense of it, he was sure. They would see the bigger picture. They would see that this needed to be done for *everyone's* benefit. They would see what would one day happen, the frightening future scenarios, if something as unpleasant as this wasn't orchestrated now.

But to do that, to talk openly of the *goal* to these three uninitiated committee members, would mean to hint at the controlling hand behind these events, the One Hundred and Sixty and the Twelve.

And, knowing of these things, they would, of course, have to die.

CHAPTER 51

3 p.m. GMT

Shepherd's Bush, London

Leona turned round to see three of them standing right behind them. She was surprised that they had managed to get so close without making a sound.

Unless they were trying to, of course.

'You got a fag mate?' said the one in the middle, who was black, shorter than the other two; a scrawnier version of 50 Cent. He was flanked on either side by two taller lads, both lean, white, wearing baggy tracksuit trousers that hung like full nappies. They called students that dressed like that 'wiggers' at uni – morons who pretended they were gangsters, homeboys; white kids who desperately yearned to be black, and did their faltering best to sound like they'd been brought up on the bad streets of LA She hated the term, almost as much as the one it was derived from, but it did a good job of summing them up.

'Uh, I don't smoke, mate,' replied Dan with a friendly but uncertain smile. 'Well I sort of do a little stuff, at parties and … and … but no, right now I don't have any smokes on me.'

The kid who looked like 50 Cent turned to address Leona. 'What about you, love?'

Leona already knew this wasn't about scrounging a cigarette. 'I don't smoke either. But I bet you'll find hundreds of cartons inside there,' she replied, pointing through the broken window behind them.

'Shit, yeah … maybe looksee,' replied 50 Cent, shooting a glance at the window, then back to her. 'You wanna go flicc with us, girl?'

Leona shook her head. She was pretty sure 'flicc' meant 'hang around' and not something worse, but she could guess that might be where this was headed, what he was thinking about.

'No thanks, I'm going home now with my boyfriend.'

Dan nodded. 'Yeah, we're all done here ... just ... just heading back home now.'

'It's jungle time now, not *urban* jungle no more,' said 50 Cent. 'Police are gone away. It's fuckin' mad out here.'

One of his two wingmen, his wigger homeboys, laughed and nodded. Leona guessed he must have been about seventeen, his baby-smooth skin pockmarked with spots around his eyebrows – one of which was shaved into little dashes.

'Yeah, we noticed,' said Dan. 'So, we're gonna make tracks—'

'Yo, man. Ain't talkin' to you,' said the kid with the dashed eyebrow. 'Fuckin' twat,' he added.

Leona squeezed Dan's hand gently to shut him up. There was probably a way for them to excuse themselves and be about their business, but only coming from *her* mouth; something clever, laddish, funny might just do it, make 'em laugh and move on. Anything coming from him was going to be considered a challenge.

'It's mad all right,' said Leona. 'Yeah ... really fuckin' buzzin' man. Buff ain't it?'

The three youths nodded and smiled. She guessed they liked her saying that, or maybe they were just laughing at her unconvincing *sister*-talk.

Dan took a step to the left, his feet noisily shuffling glass and clutter across the concrete.

'Fuck you goin'?' said 50 Cent.

'We're just going, okay?' said Dan. 'We don't want any trouble, we're just going to—'

'You goin' nowhere.'

Dan nodded obediently. 'Sure, okay. I'll just sit down or something,' he mumbled submissively stooping down with his hands reaching out for the ground. Leona knew, then and there, he was going to do something.

With a flick of both hands he flung a cloud of dust and shards of glass up at the three youths standing in front of them.

They flinched, covering their faces. Leona took the opportunity to scoop up a crushed and twisted can of pineapple segments and throw it at the nearest of them. It bounced off the forehead of the kid with the dashy-eyebrow just as he'd dropped his hands from protecting his face. Leona was about to grab another can when Dan turned to her and hissed, 'run!'

She turned to her left, and started to sprint, hoping he was following, hoping Dan was right behind her. She ran for twenty or thirty yards along the front of the supermarket, weaving through the discarded shopping trolleys, before she dared to turn round and check that that was the case.

But he wasn't right there as she hoped, expected … behind her. She couldn't see him anywhere.

She could see two of the three youths sprinting up the concourse she and Dan had been walking down a minute or so earlier. It led outside on to Uxbridge Road. Dan must have shot off that way – attempting to draw them away from her. Two of them had gone after him, but the white youth who'd called Dan a 'twat', 'Dasher', was chasing after her, kicking the trolleys out of his way as he hurtled towards her. In the split second that she looked at him, she could see a splash of crimson on his pale spotty forehead.

He was the one she'd got with the tin.

Leona turned back round, continuing to run another twenty yards, until she remembered this section of the precinct was a dead end – it went nowhere. There was a Boots chemist at the end of it, a newsagent and a Woolworths, but no access back on to the street.

She pushed past the last of the trolleys, swinging it round behind her to be sure it would lie in her wake and hopefully slow down the bastard behind her as he kicked it out of the way. Up ahead, emerging out of the gloom, Leona saw the dead end. Her only hope of avoiding him was through one of the stores on either side; a choice between Boots and Woolworths. Both of them were big outlets, large enough that she stood a chance of losing him inside, and big enough, she knew, that they had other street entrances – both of them opening on to Uxbridge Road and Goldhawk Road.

She swung towards Woolworths, she could see one of the automatic doors had either powered-down in the open position, or been yanked open by somebody; either way it decided the matter for her.

She could hear his trainers smacking against the ground, and the clatter and rattle as the last of the trolleys was kicked out of the way.

'Come 'ere you cu-u-u-n-n-t!' she heard him shout, his voice reverberating around the concourse behind her.

She ran in through the open door, not prepared for how dark it was going to be inside with the power gone. Although it was a sunny day outside, the light filtering in from the doorway, and the long tall windows along the front of the store either side of the entrance, did little to illuminate the low-ceilinged floor space ahead of her, criss-crossed with aisles and counters.

Here, as everywhere else, looters had been in and made a mess. Around the Pick 'n' Mix sweet stand, and the shelves near the tills, where twenty-four hours earlier Mars Bars, Twixes and KitKats had been stacked, was where most of the desperate scrabbling for things had occurred.

As she squeezed past a till-aisle, half-blocked by a trolley on its side, chocolate bars spilled from it across the floor and trampled to a sticky brown sludge, she turned to check his progress again.

Dasher hesitated for just a few moments in the open automatic doorway, either, smartly, allowing a few seconds for his eyes to adjust, or briefly intimidated by the gloomy labyrinth ahead of him.

'You bitch,' she heard his cold adolescent voice snarl. 'I'm going to fuckin' bitch-slap you, then I'll shag you senseless!'

Leona ducked down on the other side of the trolley, and crawled on all fours across the scuffed linoleum floor towards the nearest of the product aisles. She placed one of her feet on a packet of crisps, and the foil packet crinkled noisily in the silence.

It was enough of an invitation for him. She heard movement, a clatter of things falling to the floor, and then the slap-slap of his trainers.

'Where are you?' he called out, striding swiftly along the top of the aisles, just beyond the tills, looking down each one in turn, trying to find her.

She got to her feet, but still crouching low, began to jog as quietly as she could down the aisle she was in, before he could get to hers.

But she was too slow. Just as she reached the end of the aisle – still stocked with soft toys, untouched by yesterday's chaos – she heard him.

'I see you!'

Oh fuck.

She turned at the end, headed right, taking her towards the Music, DVDs and Games section. She skidded on her heels and dived in between two large racks of PlayStation games. Behind her, the sound of those bloody trainers slapping the floor, and now … she could hear his breathing. He was gaining on her.

She didn't stop. He was way too close to have been thrown off by that little manoeuvre. She needed somewhere in the shop she could really lose herself, somewhere—

'Fuckin' stop,' he called out again. 'I just want to talk!' he added breathlessly twenty yards behind.

Yeah right.

She reached the end of the games racks. Ahead she could make out a centre store lay-out of tables stacked with jumpers and fleeces, and jackets on garment rails; the children's clothing section.

She leapt forward, throwing herself almost immediately to the ground beneath a four-sided, rotating garment rail, from which long winter school coats were dangling.

Only three or four seconds later, she heard his slapping

trainers, that suddenly hushed as his feet passed on to the plain, cord carpet that marked this section, Clothing, from the rest of the store. In the dark she could only see the pale grey of daylight filtering across the low tiled ceiling, everything else now was black and formless.

She listened intently as he moved around, the only sound now the swishing of clothes, and jangling of plastic coat-hangers as he passed impatiently.

'Come on,' he hissed with frustration. 'I just want to fucking talk … I just …'

Dasher was struggling to keep the rage out of his voice … and the excitement. Leona shuddered at what awful fantasies were running through that shaved little bullet-head of his.

'Come on!' he pleaded, sounding for a moment like a child begging his mum for a tenner. 'I just want to …' his voice tailed off.

I know what you 'just want to'. You dirty shit.

Even though it was stifling, hidden as she was amongst the dangling winter coats, she shuddered violently as she imagined what he and his two buddies would do if they got hold of her.

Oh God, he's just a kid.

He was, really, just a snotty seventeen year old, surely no older than that, all bullet-head and big ears beneath that stupid baseball cap. But he was certainly strong enough to do what he wanted to do. And this was surely a game to him, just a game.

Find her – slap her – shag her – leave her, heh heh.

That's how his little game was going to be wrapped up. And he'd walk away from it, pulling up his pants and his baggy trousers, with a cocky 'I got mine' grin on his face, whilst she would be left on the floor, bruised and bleeding, and struggling to find the ragged remains of the clothes he'd torn off her.

'Come on, I thought you was after some fun!' he said again, this time terrifyingly close to her. 'Shit, it's like fuckin' Disneyland out there.'

He had to be only a dozen feet away. Leona held her breath.

'Everythin' for the takin'. It's fuckin' mad, man.'

He's getting closer.

'And no fuckin' pigs either. All gone, fucked off somewhere. Apart from that one we found, stupid tosser. It's playtime now. Playtime for the kiddies, yeah.'

She felt the gentlest breeze of displaced air waft over her skin as he walked by, only feet away from her.

'So come on,' he said in that whiny voice again, 'I'm beggin' you love. I won't hurt you or nuffing, we'll just have a bit of a laugh.'

Leona felt the stiff wire of a coat-hanger beneath her hand. She followed the curved hook with her fingers. It descended into a plastic base; the shoulders were plastic, but the hook was wire.

He was quiet for a moment, but she could hear him breathing as he stood there, above her, almost on top of her. He was breathing loudly, noisily, the run had winded him. On the other hand, she was still holding her breath and wasn't going to be able to hold it for much longer.

Please, please move away.

She needed to breathe, but knew the breath she let out would be deafening in the silence. Her hands worked on the metal wire of the coat-hanger, pulling the hook out into a straightened spike. A lousy weapon to be sure, but it was something she could lash out with.

'Oh fuck this,' Dasher growled angrily, 'I can fuckin' hear you anyway. You're round here somewhere, I can hear you fiddling about.'

All of a sudden, the coats above her moved, with a *swish* from the rail above. His hands groped through the layers of thick cloth.

'I'm gonna fuckin' have you!' he whispered, knowing she was right there, 'Then so are me mates, and then we're really gonna—'

Leona, grabbing the plastic shoulders of the coat-hanger with both hands, wire facing outwards, shoved it up hard, roughly where she guessed his face would be.

It jolted as it came into contact with something, the plastic shoulders broke off in her hands as it did so. She briefly heard something wet and viscous give before she heard him scream.

CHAPTER 52

3.47 p.m. GMT

Shepherd's Bush, London

Leona scrambled out from beneath the school coats, as the young man's shrill and protracted scream filled her ears. In the gloom she could see him staggering clumsily around with both of his hands to his face.

'My fuckin' eye! My fuckin' eye! You've popped it!'

She got to her feet and started for the glow of daylight on the far side of the shop. It would have been tempting to hang around, find something long, hard and heavy and beat him with it, but she was frightened his screams would attract the other two.

Best to quit whilst she was ahead.

She made her way out of the clothing section, her heels clacking on linoleum once more as she headed out past aisles of greeting cards, undisturbed, like the soft toys and the PlayStation games, by yesterday's looting spree, and towards the wide shop windows and the automatic glass doors leading out on to Goldhawk Road. All the while, the tall gangly youth behind her, Dasher, continued to scream in agony.

The automatic doors were closed. She tried to prise them open with her hands, but they weren't going to budge any time soon.

'Shit,' she whispered to herself.

Someone had had a go at one of the display windows to the right of the doors, the glass was cracked in several places. She decided to finish the job. Pulling a fire extinguisher from the wall nearby she hefted it in both hands and threw it towards the cracked glass. The window shattered easily and noisily and exploded out on to the pavement, all the while that idiot chav was wailing like a banshee in the background.

She stepped out on to the pavement, warily looking up and down Goldhawk Road for the two other lads that had been with him and given chase after Dan. There was no sign of them.

More importantly, she looked around for Dan. There was no sign of him either. She hoped he would have headed home, rather than come looking for her. She was now getting worried about Jacob, and was having visions of him wandering around Shepherd's Bush trying to find her.

Jake was dumb enough to do that.

Leona noticed a few more people. The Asian family were still trying to make a start on tidying up their shop, she noted several other storekeepers picking over the debris of their business, strewn outside on the pavement. They had stared at her and Dan earlier, suspiciously, no doubt wondering if they were out trawling for something to loot. She noticed one or two other *explorers*, like Dan and her, wandering about with a dazed expression on their faces. But nobody in uniform. No police, firemen, paramedics.

No one in authority.

No Dan.

Though there were a few people around, and that made her feel a little safer, she wondered if she were accosted right now, pulled to the ground by 50 Cent or Dasher or the other kid, in plain sight of them, whether *anyone* would dare come to her aid.

She decided to head back home the way they had come earlier, along Uxbridge Road, jogging back most of the way, looking from side to side for a sign of Dan. She counted about three dozen people in total, milling around on the streets, or rifling through the interiors of shops, but no Dan.

Walking down their avenue, she passed several neighbours she recognised by sight and nodded to them. They were in their small front gardens, tidying away the discarded beer cans and broken bottles.

They think this is all over.

Clearly that's what they were thinking, that this was now the clear-up phase, that the hurricane had been and gone. She guessed that they and those shopkeepers were expecting the power to come back on sometime this afternoon, the police and the army to arrive shortly after to supervise the clearing up. And to be honest, Leona allowed herself to hope that might be the case too.

She picked up the pace down towards their end of St Stephen's Avenue, guessing that Dan was already back at Jill's with Jacob and no doubt fretting about her. As she approached their house, she noticed the people opposite – she didn't know them by name – were out in their front garden nailing sheets of plywood over their downstairs windows.

She walked up the path to Jill's home and knocked on the front door, expecting it to open almost immediately. But it didn't.

'Dan? Jake?' she called through the letterbox.

She heard shuffling coming from inside, then a pair of legs came warily into view. A moment later she heard the bolt slide and the door opened. Jacob stood there, hugging a soft fluffy spotty dog he must have found lying around Jill's place. His eyes were puffy from crying, his bottom lip quivered.

'I thought you left me for ever,' he managed to whimper.

'Did Dan not come back?'

He shook his head silently.

CHAPTER 53

8.51 p.m. GMT

South of London

Ash made slow progress south, out of London; the roads were cluttered with abandoned vehicles and the mess left by last night's rioting. On several occasions he'd had to make an off-road diversion to avoid police and army roadblocks, knowing that driving a police motorbike, he was asking for trouble if he got too close.

Leaving the city behind and driving through into the suburbs he noticed that conditions seemed to fluctuate; some areas had been hit badly by last night's rampaging, others looked largely untouched. He drove down a high street in a well-to-do area, not noticing a single broken shop window. It was quiet of course, everyone tucked inside their homes – and he spotted many a curtain twitching as he passed through – but to all intents and purposes it could have been tea time on any given weekday evening.

He also noticed that the power-outage, which had swept across the country last night, was not as complete as he had thought it would be. He drove through a dozen or so areas that demonstrated at least an intermittent supply of electricity; neon shop-signs still steadfastly glowing, and street lights – their timing mechanisms knocked out of sync by the chaos of the last twenty-four hours – casting down unnecessary pools of flickering amber light during the daylight hours.

Ash had assumed the emergency authority would have cut *all* power, *everywhere*. But then, he wasn't privy to how the *details* were being handled in this country – that was for others to know. Each had their own responsibility, their own way of doing things. The bigger picture … that was the thing.

He finally managed to emerge from the extended suburban carpet around London, as the evening light began to falter.

Along the A road, heading south-west out of London, he came across clusters of pedestrians walking along the hard shoulder, most of them heading away from London. Ash presumed they were people who commuted into London to work and had been caught out by the suddenness of events, now wearily trying to make their way home. There were also a few who seemed to be heading into the capital.

I wouldn't recommend that folks.

But then, they too were probably making for home – where else would they be going?

That's where you long to be in a time of crisis, isn't it? Home.

He found himself wondering again about the whereabouts of the Sutherland girl. This family friend 'Jill', this good family friend, a friend who could be trusted to look after Mr and Mrs Sutherland's children, would she not live close by? Close enough to drop in regularly?

Probably.

But unless he had an address …

What if the girl decides to go home to get something? What if this 'Jill' decides she'll quickly drop in to pick up some changes of clothes for the kids … a favourite toy for the younger one?

Ash was momentarily unsettled with doubt. Perhaps he should have just stayed put there and waited?

No. He could be waiting there indefinitely. Time was everything. He had an address. His hunter's instinct told him this Kate would know who Jill was. Better to follow his nose, than sit in the dark at 25 St Stephen's Avenue doing nothing.

Along the road, he found a cluster of abandoned cars, left in an orderly bonnet-to-bumper queue along a slip-road leading into a petrol station. He presumed, sometime yesterday, the petrol station had run dry, or more likely the army had swept in to appropriate what was below ground in the storage tanks. The fuel gauge on his bike told him he was running low. With some effort, a little cursing, and too much wasted time, he managed to siphon off what was left in the discarded cars. He winced at the thought of the bottom of the barrel sludge he was putting through the bike's engine.

It was gone ten o'clock as his bike entered a place called Guildford. It was dark and quiet.

He found the address quickly enough.

The woman lived in one of a row of apartments overlooking a busy high street. One of those yuppie developments that young professional singles and couples like so much.

No kids then. Pity. They were so handy as leverage in a getting-some-information type scenario.

Ash didn't bother with the buzzer. It probably wasn't working anyway. He kicked in the front door of the apartment complex and entered the plush, carpeted foyer and took the steps up to the first floor.

He found her apartment door with no trouble. A swift kick near the handle and the door swung inwards. He stepped quickly inside.

'Kate?' he called out.

There was no answer. No one home. She lived alone, that much was obvious, there was no sign of the live-in presence of a man. The apartment was tidy, no one had been in and rifled through this place. For a few moments he had a concern that maybe this Kate had gone away, perhaps abroad this week. But then on the answerphone, he picked up a message from someone called Ron, presumably a boyfriend.

'Kate? You there? Pick up … pick up … oh shit. You must be caught up at work in London still. Give me a call when you get back home, okay? I'm worried.'

Ash winced with frustration. So Kate had gone to work as normal on Tuesday morning, and then found herself marooned in the capital. He had passed by many people walking out on foot, along the hard shoulder of the A roads he had been on – most probably driving right past her.

So, he would imagine a single woman like Kate would hole up at her place of work, probably with dozens of other colleagues, and wait for the worst of the rioting to subside, and the police to promptly reclaim the streets before considering a return home.

But how long would she wait?

A day? Two?

There was no way of guessing that. Ash decided he could give it a day. He found some food in the kitchen, and a well-stocked fridge that was still cool inside despite the power being off. He could eat, get some rest and take a view tomorrow. There were, after all, other people in the Sutherlands' address book he could go calling on. But that said, his gut reaction was to hang on at least for one night for this Kate.

CHAPTER 54

11.57 p.m. local time

Northern Iraq

Andy Sutherland sat at the front of the truck's open bed leaning against the roof of the driver's cab and studying the flat moonlit terrain ahead. The truck rumbled along the north road, a steady drone in the night. The others, as far as he could see, were asleep, rocking and bumping limply as the truck found the occasional pot-hole.

He could only think of one thing, now that there was time enough to spare a thought that was anything other than the basic next step to survive. Last night's desperate scramble through that town, the fire-fight, and watching that young lieutenant dying on the road leading out of town ... all of that had, through necessity, sucked his thoughts away from those he cared about.

God, I hope she did as I told her. I hope Jill's looking after them for me.

He'd tried his phone several dozen times since then, in the vain hope that the mobile system out in Iraq was still up and running. Not a thing, no signal. And the local radio stations still running in the country were no longer broadcasting news that could be considered reliable; instead it was a mishmash of religious sermons, calls to arms and incitement to sectarian violence.

They had managed to pick up some moments of the BBC World Service earlier in the day, and it made for grim listening; riots and looting in every city in the country, an emergency ruling authority, and nothing from the Prime Minister or government now for a while.

It was all as Andy thought it would be – a fucking mess.

But somehow, he'd retained a residual hope that things might have held together in the UK just a little longer. They were Brits right? The blitz spirit an' all that? Whilst the rest of the world might have descended to looting and pillaging, he'd hoped the Brits would have at least resorted to some sort of vigorous queuing for a while.

With more time to think, and having heard even more snippets of news, Andy was certain now that in some contributory way, his work of eight years ago had led to this. In that report he had focused on eleven specific nodes in the global oil distribution web; nodes that were vulnerable to the sort of hit-and-run tactics favoured by terrorist groups. So far he'd heard news of seven of those nodes being hit. That alone was suspicious, but the fact that they'd been hit within twenty-four hours of each other ... that was the clincher. Because that was the very point he had made near the end of the report ...

If all eleven of these highest risk distribution chokepoints were to be hit within a twenty-four hour period, the global distribution of oil would be completely shut off.

Recalling those words – he shuddered.

This is my report being actually fucking realised by someone.

It meant that once upon a time he had briefly dealt directly with the people who were responsible. But far worse – Leona had seen them. She could identify one or more of them. He wondered whose face she had recognised on the TV. Someone in the public eye, someone newsworthy? His mind paraded possibilities – a politician, a national leader? A pivotal member of Al-Qaeda? The spokesperson of some kind of hardcore eco-pressure group? An industrialist or an oil baron? Some eccentric billionaire?

Who the fuck would actually want something like this to happen? Who the hell benefits?

He had a fleeting vision of some stereotypical Bond bad guy, complete with an evil chuckle and a long-haired Persian cat perched on his lap. He was reminded of all the weird and wonderful 9/11 conspiracy theories he'd allowed himself to get sucked into for a while after the event. The kookiest one he'd heard was that an alien craft had crashed into the Pentagon and the US authorities had smothered it with the terrorist cover story so they could research all the lovely alien technology at their leisure.

He shook his head and laughed quietly to himself. People will believe any old crap if you show 'em a fuzzy photograph, or some shaky CCTV footage.

'What is make you laugh?'

Andy looked across the truck at Farid who seemed to be awake, studying him intently.

'Oh nothing, just a little wool-gathering.'

'Wool-gath …?'

Andy shook his head, 'Never mind. It's a saying. Look I wanted to talk to you … we'll be over the northern border into Turkey soon.'

Farid nodded, still gazing out at the desert. 'Yes.'

'So, what do you want to do?'

Farid turned to look at him. 'What you mean?'

'I mean, do you want us to put you down some place inside Iraq, before we go over the border line?'

Andy saw the Iraqi's tired half-smile by the silvery light of the stars and the moon. 'You drop me up here? Amongst the Kurds? I last only five minutes.'

'I'm sorry Farid. This whole fucking mess has screwed everyone up, left a lot of people hopelessly stranded.'

'Yes. Anyway,' the old man replied, 'borders no longer, it all gone for now.'

Andy nodded, he wasn't wrong. It was unlikely there would be anyone manning the roadside barrier, on either side of the border. The Turkish police, just like civil law enforcement in every other country in the world, would no doubt be fighting a losing battle to maintain order amongst their own people.

'Now there nothing left in Iraq for me,' added Farid, after a while.

'No family?'

'No. Not any more.'

He sensed the tone in the old man's voice revealed more than those few words.

'I lose son to militia and wife to American bomb.'

Andy studied the man and realised, at an instinctive or a subconscious level, that he had known that the old man carried a burden of sadness with him. He was a quiet man, not like the two younger drivers. He was reflective, thoughtful, the grief he carried with him so carefully locked away.

He wondered if the old man would open up to him.

'What happened to your family, Farid. Do you want to tell me?'

He nodded. 'I not talk about it much. It is my sadness alone.'

'I understand. I'm sorry for asking.'

'Is okay. I tell,' replied Farid, shuffling a little closer to Andy so as to be able to talk more quietly against the rattling drone of the engine. 'My son work for IPS … police. One day he and other men in station surrounded by militia. They take away police at gunpoint. His mother know he is dead, but I say he will be return. A good Muslim boy, they will let him go. He join police not for money, but for to … ahhh … rec … con …'

'Reconstruction?'

Farid nodded, 'Yes help recon … ah … rebuild Iraq.' The old man remained silent for a good few moments. Andy sensed he wanted to continue, but was composing himself, working hard to keep something painful inside carefully boxed up where he clearly wanted it to remain, and only let out the little bit he was prepared to share.

'We hearing three day later, they find bodies outside police building. My son was one of them. He was *officer* in IPS, the other men … below him, not officer. My son was in charge. So they make special example of him.'

Farid paused again.

'They cut throat of all the men. But my son, they torture for two day, then cut his eyes out. Then cut his throat.'

Andy stopped himself from blurting out something useless and inadequate. Instead he reached across and placed a hand on the old man's arm.

'My son's eyes they send to me in package later with message from leader that say, "Your son's eyes have seen the work of God". I know these men not doing Allah's will. I know these men evil. They film what they do with camera, and I know it is seen by many like them on Internet, and they cheer as my son scream.'

Andy nodded, wishing he could think of something, anything to say, that wouldn't sound blithe and clichéd. To lose a child is the end of things, to lose a child like that is beyond comprehension.

'My wife, she die a week later when American bomb is drop on our town to kill this leader of these militia. They drop bomb they know will destroy many house in street. My wife visiting with her sister, they living in house nearby, all dead. They did not kill this leader, but they kill my wife, and twenty other people. The Americans find out this, they take away all the bodies and they say only two or three die. They took my wife body six month ago, I never see her again I know. She is gone. I will never see body.'

'That's a pretty shit deal,' grunted Mike.

Andy thought the American had been asleep. Farid turned to look at him, and for a moment he thought the Iraqi would take Mike's comment the wrong way. He wouldn't blame him if he did, it was a clumsy intrusion on their private conversation.

'Pretty shit deal,' didn't even come close.

'*Both* your people and my people take from me all that I love. I have nothing left here.'

They rode in silence for a while, the rumble of the truck's diesel engine producing a steady, reassuring drone.

'Between us all we really fucked over this country pretty bad, didn't we?' said Mike.

Andy nodded. 'It probably could have been handled better.'

'Stupid, careless American soldiers and evil men who say

they fight for Allah, but they are *haram*, outside of God … they *all* fuck my country.'

Mike sat forward. 'Tell me Farid, how the hell do you still believe in God after all this shit has happened to you? And this stuff that's happening now, Muslims killing Muslims … all of this crap in the name of God. How the hell do you make sense of all of that?'

'I have the Qur'an. It is complete, it is correct. It is God's word. What is happen now, what we see … is bad work of man, not of Allah.'

'Maybe you're right,' Mike sighed. 'Us humans seem pretty good at screwing most things up.'

Andy turned to look at the American. That seemed like an interesting step for someone like him to take.

'So Farid,' said Andy, 'where do you want to go?'

'I have brother who go to Great Britain many year back. He is all my family now. I join him.'

Andy reached over again and rested a hand on his arm. 'We'll get you there old man, I promise you that.'

He looked around the truck. The lads were all asleep. And there was Erich, watching quietly. He nodded courteously.

CHAPTER 55

10.03 p.m. GMT

Shepherd's Bush, London

It was dark.

Oh God, where the hell are you Danny?

She'd put Jacob to bed as early as she could, after sharing another unappetising meal of cold pilchards in tomato sauce and a slice of buttered bread. When she had tried to pour them each a glass of water, nothing had come out of the tap. It rattled and gurgled noisily, and produced nothing but a few drips. She realised that from now on they would have to start using their bottled water.

It was another hot evening, stuffy inside again. She opened some of the upstairs windows whilst keeping all of the ones downstairs firmly closed and locked. She patiently reassured Jacob that all was going to turn out well, that Dan, whom it seemed Jacob quite openly hero-worshipped, would be back soon and then by torchlight, she found a Harry Potter book on Jill's bedside table and began to read that to him.

But it was all done in a distracted, worried stupor, one ear constantly cocked and listening out for Dan, whom she expected at any time to come rapping on the front door to be let in. Even though she had, in effect, taken charge of things since they'd left university in Dan's van, she hadn't realised how much she had been relying on him for support.

Just me and Jake now?

Already, she could feel herself beginning to come apart, sitting downstairs in the lounge, in the dark, waiting and listening. She knew she couldn't do this on her own for much longer.

*

The noises started just before eleven.

The gang of youths were back again. She watched them from the lounge window, concealed as she was, behind the blind. There were twenty, maybe thirty of them, some looked as young as fourteen or fifteen, others somewhere in their mid-twenties. There were one or two girls amongst them. Leona thought they looked a couple of years younger than her. The gang arrived in small groups, gradually amassing in the narrow street outside, over an hour, as if it had been some loosely agreed rendezvous made the night before.

A car turned up, bathing St Stephen's Avenue with the glare of its headlights, and the sound of a pummelling bass that had the lounge windows vibrating in sympathy. They were drinking again, presumably more of their haul taken from the nearby off-licence. Their voices grew louder as the evening advanced, and by midnight she could hear and see that most of them were pissed out of their skulls. One of them staggered into the front garden, tripped over a paving stone and fell on to Jill's small, poorly tended flower-bed. He lay there, quite content to look up at the stars for a while before turning to his side and retching.

There was a fight between two of the lads. She watched it brewing, it was over one of the girls; one of the 'smurfettes', as she'd decided to call them. She couldn't hear exactly what was being said, but from the gestures she could guess that the older-looking one wanted some squeeze-time with one of the girls, and the younger one wasn't too happy about it. The girl in question, of course, wasn't exactly being consulted about this. Leona had seen countless fights like this brewing outside the pubs and clubs she'd been used to frequenting in Norwich. Always the same pattern to them, a lot of shouting, chest beating, finally pushing and shoving and then the first punch is thrown.

This fight, though, seemed to escalate far more quickly. She watched in horror as it progressed from punches being exchanged, to a knife being produced by the younger-looking lad. It was hard to make out what was going on amidst the frantic movements of both of them, but caught in the glare of the headlight, she soon saw a bright crimson stain on the crisp white T-shirt of the older boy. They thrashed around together some more, until, suddenly, she saw the younger lad spasm violently. Some of the youths gathered round the fighting emitted a drunken howl of support. She noticed a lot of the others were silent, as they watched the younger one shuddering on the ground in front of the car.

One of the girls screamed.

Leona pulled back from the window, shaking as she sat in an armchair and stared instead at the undulating light from outside flickering across the lounge ceiling, as the gang gathered around in front of the car's headlights to study the body.

The party didn't break up though. It continued. The drinking went on, the music got louder. The party migrated up the avenue a little way and at about a quarter to midnight, she heard someone hammering on something repeatedly. She knew it was the door to one of the houses when she heard the splintering of wood, the sound of it rattling on its hinges and a roar of approval from the mob of lads gathered outside.

Then what she heard shortly after made her blood run cold, and her scalp tingle.

The house being ransacked, many things breaking, glass shattering … and the screams of a woman.

Oh shit, oh shit, oh shit.

Leona raced to the window again and peeped out through the blind. She could only see at an oblique angle what was going on; a lot of movement, the pale flash of many white trainers and baseball caps picked out by those headlights and the less distinct muddy colours of T-shirts and bare torsos. They were milling around the front of the house, in and out the front door. On any other, normal night, it could have passed, at this distance anyway, as some kid's house-party getting out of control.

But Leona looked at the body of the teenager, now dead for a half hour or so, lying forgotten in front of the car.

This is how it goes, like Dad said … like a jungle now.

Thursday

CHAPTER 56

[illegible]

The Turkey–Iraq Border

[illegible]

[illegible] as they [illegible] north through the [illegible], passing at one point within only a few miles of the Syrian border as they swung east, crossing the [illegible] river and heading towards the border with Turkey.

[illegible] At first they had [illegible] nearly 200 miles [illegible] roads. The truck, despite the [illegible], was making [illegible] hour down [illegible] had [illegible], but [illegible] they [illegible] across a second country.

They passed [illegible] the border [illegible] post into Turkey [illegible]

[illegible]

Private Tajeda was on driving duty; he shouted out of the driver-side window to Andy, who was leaning across the roof of the cab.

'We could take one of those for our new ride, chief?'

CHAPTER 56

7 a.m. local time

The Turkey/Iraq border

Driving north-west took them well clear of Mosul. They drove across the Ninawa region, a desolate and empty portion of northern Iraq. They passed between Sinjar and Tall Afar, two smaller rural towns, again managing to skirt them widely and avoid any unwanted contact. The arid desert swiftly gave way to irrigated farmland as they swung north through the second night, passing at one point within only a few miles of the Syrian border as they swung north-east crossing the Bachuk river and heading towards the border with Turkey.

From Al-Bayji they had traversed nearly 200 miles over two successive nights, and three siphoned refills. The truck, despite the dreadful noises it was making, hadn't let them down as Andy had feared it might, but he suspected they were asking too much to expect it to get them across a second country.

They passed through the border control point into Turkey without incident. The barriers were unmanned and left open. The truck rolled over a fading red paint line across the tarmac and they were now officially in Turkey.

To one side of a cluster of low concrete buildings was a fenced compound containing a collection of various parked vehicles; trucks, a couple of coaches, some small vans, impounded for various reasons.

Private Tajican was on driving duty; he shouted out of the driver-side window to Andy, who was leaning across the roof of the cab.

'We could take one of those for our new ride, chief.'

Andy looked across at the vehicles. This was probably the best opportunity they were going to get for a while to change their vehicle and perhaps scavenge for extra fuel, water, food; particularly water. In this heat they had quickly gone through the little water they'd brought with them.

'Okay, pull into the compound,' he shouted down.

Tajican steered the truck off the road and through a gap in the wire fencing on to the forecourt where the vehicles were parked up.

They dismounted quickly.

Lance Corporal Westley came over to Andy looking to him for orders he could parcel out to his men.

'Right then,' said Andy looking around, conscious of the fact their eyes were all on him, hoping he had some clear and concise instructions for them to carry out. 'We need someone to check over those vehicles for petrol we can siphon off, and which one we should take. Taj is right, we can't rely on that crappy old truck getting us much further, so we'll need a new ride. And whilst we're here, we should take a look inside those buildings, see if we can pick up some water and food. Westley?'

'Sir?'

'Whilst we're checking this place out, let's have some men on look-out duty too, okay?'

'Right-o,' said Westley and turned smartly around to bellow some orders to the eleven other soldiers of the platoon.

Andy smiled. *I sounded pretty convincing just then.*

He caught Mike's eye. The American grinned and nodded.

Westley put Tajican in charge of checking over the vehicles and sent six men off to help with that. He sent three of them out on the road to set up an improvised vehicle control point and keep an eye open for anyone approaching in either direction.

'You want to take a butcher's inside then?' asked Westley nodding towards the building nearby.

Andy nodded. 'Yeah. Let's see if there's anything inside we can grab.'

The young Lance Corporal turned to the two remaining men,

Derry and Peters, who had both put down their rifles and were preparing to unstrap their webbing. 'Come on, off your arses you fuckin' numpties. This isn't a bloody sit-down tea-party. We're going to sweep the buildings.'

'Hey Wes, go easy mate,' muttered Derry.

Westley cuffed the back of Derry's head as he sauntered past them. 'Any more shit from you Dezza, and I'll rip yer fucking cock off. Come on, get off your crap-'oles and follow me.'

They both groaned wearily as they got to their feet and headed dutifully after Westley. Mike, following in their wake, nudged Andy as he passed. 'You just need to pick up a little of that colourful language Andy, and you'll fit right in.'

Andy shrugged. Jenny might get a little buzz of excitement if she could see her nerdy husband playing – quite convincingly actually – at being a big tough soldier. He wasn't too sure she'd be thrilled if he brought the locker-room language home though.

CHAPTER 57

10 a.m. GMT

Beauford Service Station

A bump woke Jenny up; somebody had squeezed past the two plastic chairs she'd been lying across in the eating area, but accidentally knocked heavily against them. She was awake in an instant and sat up.

The staff at the service station were being served a cooked breakfast; quarter-pounder burgers, fried chicken, fried eggs, milk – basically all the refrigerated items … made sense.

Mr Stewart was overseeing the distribution of this, carefully pouring the milk and counting out the helpings to ensure everyone was getting their fair share.

He spotted Jenny sitting up.

'Good morning. We're serving up breakfast,' he called out cheerfully. 'Join the queue.'

She had to admit it smelled pretty good. She dutifully stood at the back of the short, shuffling line, and very soon was receiving her rations from Mr Stewart, who beamed with what he must have supposed was a morale-boosting smile.

Or maybe he just gets off on this sort of thing. She wondered if, outside of office hours, he was a Cub Scout leader or something.

'Thanks,' she said and wandered over to a table at which Paul and Ruth were sitting.

'Load of bollocks, that really is,' Paul was saying as Jenny sat down beside Ruth.

'What is?'

'Oh, according to this *Mirror*-reading moron here,' he said jerking a thumb at Ruth, 'this whole oil mess is the work of the Americans.'

Ruth shook her head and tutted, 'I didn't say that. I just said the whole thing seems to have been co-ordinated somehow. And surely the only country with enough clout across the world is America?'

Jenny thought about that. 'But what do they gain by disrupting the oil like this? Surely they need it more than anyone?'

'Maybe they have enough stockpiled to ride this out?'

'I heard they had riots in New York, just like we had in London,' said Jenny. 'It sounds like they're having just as tough a time of it.'

'Exactly,' scoffed Paul, 'what a load of crap. I suppose you're one of those nutters that think Bush and his cronies were behind the Trade Towers thing.'

'Well, there's a lot of stuff that didn't add up there. I always thought the whole thing was very fishy,' said Ruth. 'It was all very convenient, wasn't it?'

'Oh you'd get on well with my husband then,' murmured Jenny.

'Lemme guess, they knocked the Towers down just so's they'd have an excuse to go in and steal Saddam's oil … is that what you were going to say?'

Ruth nodded. 'Yup.'

'You know that just really fucking irritates me, that. That stupid conspiracy crap. You can't just accept that something happened the way it appeared, can you? There's always some gullible idiots, that being you by the way,' Paul smiled at Ruth, 'who have to think there's some big evil bogeyman behind it. Well yeah, okay, in this case there was … that Bin Laden bloke. But oh no! That's not interesting enough is it?. No. Of course it would be far more interesting if say … the President is behind it.'

'Well he was.'

'Let me guess … you think Princess Diana was assassinated by MI5 too, love?'

Ruth's face hardened, and her lips tightened. 'You're taking the piss out of me, aren't you?'

Paul sighed. 'I think the truth is a bunch of bloody Arabs got a little too excited with the idea of knocking seven shades of shit out of each other. It's incapacitated the world's biggest supplier at a time when we could have really done with their oil, and we've allowed ourselves to, rather stupidly, become so reliant on it, that we've all been caught with our pants down. Add to that a bloody government that couldn't organise a shit in a bucket, and didn't plan for anything like this. I don't see any conspiracy there, I see a lot of stupidity is all.'

Jenny nodded in agreement with some of that – the stupidity. 'We've been very short-sighted.' She took a bite out of a burger, savouring the juicy fatty flavour, but instinctively begrudging the calories. 'Really stupid,' she continued, 'for allowing ourselves to rely so much on stuff that comes through just half-a-dozen pipelines from around the world.'

'How long do you reckon this'll last?' asked Ruth.

'I'd say a few more days,' said Paul. 'Our dickhead of a Prime Minister was caught off guard and put the fear of God into everyone on Tuesday. It's no wonder there were riots in every bloody town. But the police will get a grip on things soon enough.'

Ruth shook her head. 'Where are the police though? I haven't seen one since Tuesday.'

Paul shrugged.

'See that's what worries me so much,' said Ruth, 'not having the police around. And how long is it going to be before we see another? Meantime,' Ruth pointed towards the two fast food counters, 'places like this, where there's still food and drink, pumping out nice yummy smells are going to become a target when everyone's tummies start rumbling.'

Paul flashed an uncomfortable glance at the wide, empty car-park outside.

Jenny followed his gaze. It was empty now, but she imagined it full and a crowd of starving people surging forward, their faces and hands pressed against the perspex front wall, begging for a handout.

Only they probably won't be begging.

CHAPTER 58

9.12 p.m. local time

Southern Turkey

In the darkness of the coach he could study Andy Sutherland more discreetly. It was an old tour coach; thirty rows of threadbare seats and air conditioning that didn't work. The men were spread out, legs and arms draped over neighbouring seats, and arm-rests that wouldn't budge.

He sat diagonally opposite Andy. The engineer was staring out at the evening sky, whilst everyone else, exhausted from the frantic activity of the last few days, slept.

What's on your mind, Dr Sutherland?

He wondered if this man from New Zealand was thinking about global events. Having been with him since the weekend, one thing was for certain. He was not on the inside. He was not one of them. This had genuinely taken him by surprise. In any case, Sutherland wouldn't have been stupid enough to be stuck out in the middle of Iraq if he'd known what was going to happen this week.

The big question, the really big one, was – *just how much does he know about them?*

They had used him years ago; falsely recruited his expertise to help them hard-focus their plans. If Sutherland had known *who* he was dealing with, if Sutherland had *any* way of identifying them, he would have been dealt with years before now.

So, unfortunately, it would seem … because he was still alive, he knew nothing about them; certainly nothing that *they* would consider dangerously revealing.

And he certainly wasn't one of *them*.

I could always take the direct approach. Pull him to one side, come right out with it and tell him who I am, who I work for, and pump him for any details that could help us.

It was an idea. If he could only get through to his people, that's what he'd suggest; to confront this man, but there was no way to do that right now.

Sutherland could be the key. He had dealt with them directly, he might have *seen* one of them, might even be able to identify one of them. This might be a golden opportunity to glimpse through that almost impenetrable veil of secrecy around them.

They had scraped together some scant details about them over the years; just enough to realise how little they knew. There was a larger group who referred to themselves as the One Hundred and Sixty, and a much smaller group referred to as the Twelve. A classic power pyramid – the Twelve decided policy, the One Hundred and Sixty enacted it. The secrecy surrounding them was complete ... truly impressive. In the many years his people had devoted entirely to unearthing the truth, there had only been one of them prepared to talk.

And he had, but only briefly. Two meetings, held in absolute darkness, in a basement of an abandoned building, in a nondescript industrial town in the middle of Germany. Two meetings that lasted only a few minutes, with the man's voice trembling like that of a condemned man on the scaffold. He revealed about himself that he was a banking man ... and that he was merely one of the One Hundred and Sixty.

A week after the second meeting, a man who was the largest private shareholder of one of the bigger merchant banks based in Frankfurt, a member of the ECB Advisory Committee, and a senior director of the Deutsche Bundesbank, apparently committed suicide by hurling himself from the rooftop of his penthouse apartment. The man was merely one of their foot soldiers.

By comparison, the Twelve, whose true identities were unknown even to the One Hundred and Sixty, were untouchable. And yet eight years ago, this man, Dr Sutherland – if the rumours they had unearthed were to be trusted – might have actually met one of them. That was why they had begun tapping his phone twelve months ago. He wondered, however, whether Dr Sutherland should just be directly approached now, and debriefed by his people.

Until then, the potential goldmine of what Sutherland might be able to remember of his dealings with them … was invaluable. He needed to stay alive.

CHAPTER 59

6 p.m. GMT

Beauford Service Station

Jenny was walking the perimeter at the back of the service station where it was slightly cooler, darker, away from the glare of the evening sun shining in through the front. It was like sitting in a greenhouse up at the front in the eating area.

She'd pulled out her phone, turned it on and tried once more to see if there was a signal. Of course there wasn't, and there was precious little charge left on her phone. She turned it off quickly to conserve what juice was left.

She self-consciously looked around to check that she was alone and not being observed before clasping her hands together.

'Oh God, please, please be looking after my kids,' she whispered, 'I know I'm not a believer or anything, but please … if you, you know, exist, please keep them safe.'

What the hell am I doing?

Jenny had never believed. *Never.* And that was something else she'd had in common with Andy: another proud atheist. They had even once gone into school together – Leona's primary school – to complain about the excessive religious content being rammed down the pupils' throats. An atheist household, they always had been, and now, here she was, praying, for Chrissakes.

I don't care. I'll bloody pray if I want to.

There was always an outside chance, a remote possibility, that there was a kernel of truth to all this God nonsense.

Anyway, when it comes to your kids, you'll do anything, right? You'd sell your soul to the Devil … if, of course, such a thing existed.

‘You didn’t strike me as the God-squad type.’

Jenny jerked her hands down, embarrassed. She looked around and saw Paul standing in a dark alcove lined with arcade machines.

‘I’m not,’ she replied defensively. ‘I’m just … you know, just desperate I suppose.’

‘Yeah, of course, you’ve got kids, haven’t you?’ said Paul, running his hands along the back of a plastic rally-car driver’s seat. ‘I don’t, so it makes things a little easier for me.’

Jenny nodded. ‘Yeah, it does. So what are you doing back here?’

He turned towards the arcade machine, stroking the padded vinyl of the seat. ‘I noticed they had a Toca Rally 2 machine. When I was a teenager I used to play that a lot. I put a lot of money in these over the years,’ he said wistfully. ‘Classic driving game. It’s old now. Booth like this is a bit of a collector’s item.’

Jenny nodded politely, listening, but not listening.

He sighed and patted it. ‘You know I can’t imagine a world without electricity … power. There’s so many things we take for granted, aren’t there? Losing it for a few days like this … and look at us.’ He smiled. ‘Living like cavemen. When things get back to normal, I’ll—’

‘Who says things *will* go back to normal?’

‘Of course they will,’ he replied, ‘things always right themselves.’

‘I think things will be different after this.’

‘Yeah? How do you mean?’

‘I don’t know … I just think … well, there’s something my husband Andy used to say.’

Paul cocked his head, interested. ‘Go on.’

‘He said oil was like the twentieth-century version of the Roman slave economy. We’ve grown used to having it. It does everything for us. It makes power, it’s used to fertilise crops, in pesticides, to make medicines, every kind of plastic … basically we use oil in absolutely everything. But I remember this one thing he said. He said some economist once calculated the ways in which oil helps us live and translated that into slave power. He compared the oil economy to the Roman slave economy.'

'Sorry, I don't understand.'

'Well, say you've come home from work and you want to wash your office shirt for tomorrow. You'd shove it in your washing machine, and then put it on a fast spin-dry afterwards, wouldn't you? And maybe you want a cup of tea whilst you're waiting, maybe put on the TV, and throw a frozen dinner in the microwave. Well in slave terms, that would have required a slave to take your shirt, chop wood to make a fire, to heat the water, to wash it. You'd probably need another slave to go hunt or gather the food for your dinner, another to chop wood and build a cooking fire, to boil the water for your tea, and cook the food that the hunter-slave brought in. Still more slaves to entertain you in place of a TV set. And let's not forget the four or five slaves that carried you home from work on their backs, instead of the car you drive home in. Anyway, you get the point right? So, this economist calculated that the average American or Western European would require ninety-six slaves tending to him night and day, to maintain this lifestyle we've all grown accustomed to.'

'Ninety-six slaves?'

'Ninety-six oil-slaves. Even the poorest person in this country, *the poorest*, has his own team of oil-slaves tending to him; a TV set, electric heating, hot water, a kettle, levels of luxury that only the richest aristocrats from the previous century could dream about.'

Jenny gestured towards Mr Stewart and his staff, sitting together in the sunlight. 'Look at them, look at us, everyone in fact ... we've just had our slaves taken away from us. We're all like those pampered aristocrats after the French Revolution, seeking refuge without their servants to tend them, incapable even of tying their own shoelaces.'

'Hardly,' Paul scoffed.

'Yeah? Who here knows how to do the basic things to

survive? How to grow their own food? Plan an allotment to provide enough sustenance all year round? How to locate drinkable water? How to sterilise a small cut so it doesn't become infected? How to make a loaf of bread?'

Paul smiled. 'You make it sound like some kind of on the edge of apocalypse thing. The oil will get flowing again. This is just a blip.'

'God, I hope you're right. But this little blip has only been going four days. Can you imagine what it's going to be like if it lasts a couple of weeks?'

Paul's smile faded a little.

'Or a month even?'

'What are you looking at?' asked Jenny.

Ruth stirred and pointed at the single car parked alongside the truck in the staff section on the other side of the car-park.

'Those,' she said.

'Why, what's up with them?'

Ruth turned to her. 'Mr Stewart's wonderful perspex wall might stand up to some bricks being thrown at it, but I'm not too sure how it would flippin' well cope with a car, or even that truck being driven into it.'

'Oh my God, you're right.'

'Where's that wally anyway?'

They both turned to look around, and saw the shift manager officiously overseeing the distribution of cups of tea, carefully pouring it from a large, steaming metal urn into Styrofoam cups. Ruth snorted, amused.

'What's so funny?' asked Jenny.

'You know who he reminds me of?'

Jenny shook her head.

'Remember *Dad's Army*? I used to love watching that. He reminds me of Captain Mainwaring – a real busybody who loves being the heroic little *organiser*.'

Jenny cocked her head slightly, not convinced.

'Remember that episode where they all end up marooned

on the end of the pier overnight?' Ruth persisted, 'And Captain Mainwaring takes charge of distributing their rations – a small bag of humbugs?'

Jenny managed a wan smile. 'Yeah, I see it now.'

'Don't you just get the feeling he's loving it? Loving the idea of leading his little *troops* through this crisis? Controlling the *rations*, and deciding how much everyone gets. A real flippin' power trip.'

Jenny could see how pompous and ridiculous he looked, but a small voice of reason inside her head chipped in.

Maybe, but he's doing the smart thing though, isn't he?

Carefully rationing from the very beginning … because …

That's right, because who knows how long this situation will last.

He was finished pouring for his staff and approached them holding his large steaming teapot and two cups.

'Tea?'

Ruth and Jenny nodded, and he poured them a cup each.

'Do you think those lads will be back again? The ones that beat up Julia?'

Mr Stewart nodded. 'Yes, I think they probably will.'

Ruth gestured towards the front of the pavilion. 'Your nice shiny perspex frontage may well hold out to another night of pelting with paving stones and rubble. But I'm not sure it'll stand up to a truck being driven into it.'

The manager looked out at the large vehicle parked out there in plain view … and blanched.

'Yup,' continued Ruth, 'I'm sure that'll occur to at least one of them nonces out there, eventually. And I'm also pretty sure at least one of the little buggers will know how to hotwire the car, or even that truck.'

Stewart nodded, his eyes widened anxiously. Some of the smug, irritating self-assurance he'd been coasting around on, had slipped away. 'Uh … m-maybe someone could go out there and immobilise them somehow?'

Ruth cocked an eyebrow, 'Yeah? Just *nip* out there and

quickly disable them both, huh? You going to volunteer?'

Mr Stewart replied, flustered. 'Of course I … I … but then, s-someone has to uh … look after my staff.'

'Uh-huh, pretty much what I thought you'd say,' sneered Ruth.

Jenny had an idea. 'We could drive that truck over here, and park it right before the front wall. I think the truck's probably just about as long as the wall is wide?'

Mr Stewart nodded. 'Yes … yes I think you're right.'

'And that'll be good enough to stop them using that car, or any others lying around.'

'Yes, a very good idea,' replied the shift manager, shaking his head vigorously. 'So … uh … who's going to go out there and drive it over though?'

'More importantly,' said Ruth, 'who knows how to drive a rig like that? I've never driven anything bigger than my little car.'

'And we don't have the keys anyway,' said Paul joining them in the middle of the foyer, 'unless someone here knows how to jack a truck. I'm sure there's a bit more to it than smashing the steering column and holding two wires together.'

'I have the keys,' said Mr Stewart. 'They're hanging up in my office. That's Big Ron's rig. He's one of our regulars. The night before last he'd had one too many drinks in the back of that cab of his and was planning to carry on with his run. I took the keys off him.'

'He's here?' asked Jenny.

'No, I don't know where he is. Probably took a room in the Lodge, a mile down the road. I've not seen him since this all started.'

Paul turned to look out at the front. 'Well, we should get on and do this now, before they turn up again for an evening of fun and games.'

Mr Stewart nodded. 'I'll go get the keys for you.'

'What?' said Paul shaking his head awkwardly. 'I've never driven a bloody truck before in my life.'

Ruth looked at Paul, her eyes narrowing suspiciously. 'I'd go do it if I knew how to flippin' well drive one. I'd probably flatten the building if I got behind the wheel.' She aimed her words at Paul. '*I'm* not afraid to go out there.'

'What? Neither am I.'

All eyes turned on Mr Stewart. His eyes widened. 'Well I would … but, someone has to look after—'

'The staff. Yeah, we know,' said Ruth flatly.

'I'll do it,' said Jenny reluctantly. 'I've got a tiny bit of experience with trucks.'

It took Mr Stewart a little while to find the keys, and ten minutes later Jenny was walking quickly across the tarmac, warmed by the evening sun, towards the truck, anxiously scanning the periphery of the car-park for signs of any gathering people. She swung the cricket bat Mr Stewart had given her in one hand, slapping it into the palm of the other, hoping the gesture was enough to deter any spotty young thug who might be lurking nearby from confronting her.

The sense of stillness outside was unsettling. The only sound she could hear was the chattering of some birds nestling in the stunted saplings along the edge of the car-park, and the caw of a crow, circling high up in the clear evening sky.

Idyllic … if it wasn't so damned unnatural – none of that ever-present rumble of passing traffic. It was just so strange, unsettling.

She quickened her pace, turning briefly to look back at the large window-wall at the front of the service station pavilion and seeing a row of pale ovals staring back out at her, waving her on.

Finally she reached the truck, unlocked the driver's door, yanked it open and then pulled herself up into the cab. Inside it was stifling. As the clouds had cleared throughout today, the sun had had ample opportunity this afternoon to flood in through the wide windscreen.

It smelled in here too. It reeked of body odour, cigarette

smoke and stale doner kebabs. In fact it smelled exactly as she imagined the inside of a long distance truck-driver's cab would smell.

It smelled of *bloke*.

She looked around the dashboard in front of her, completely unfamiliar with the lay-out. Jenny had driven a small truck once, a long, long time ago, some place in India in her backpacking days – but that experience wasn't going to help her a great deal. It had just meant that of those inside, she was marginally more qualified to try and give it a go at driving it over.

'Come on, where the hell's the ignition?' she muttered impatiently.

She finally located it.

She was about to insert the key when she heard a thud against the door beside her. It made her jump. She looked out of the window and saw below a group of about a dozen people; a random mixture of age and gender; they could well have been the first dozen pedestrians you passed on any pavement, in any city.

'Hello love? Open up, will ya?' a man called out.

Jenny wound the driver's window down, at the same time feeling a surge of nervous adrenalin welling up.

'Yeah? What d'ya want?' she grunted in a voice she hoped made her sound like she might just, plausibly be the legitimate driver of this truck.

'That your rig, love?' asked the man. He looked to be in his early thirties and graced with a fading tattoo on his upper left arm; one of those swirling Celtic patterns that Andy had once, almost, decided to have. Until, that is, he'd spotted David Beckham sporting one on a TV commercial that had him dressed, for whatever reason, as some sort of gladiator.

'Yeah, it's mine. I'm pissin' off,' she grunted, inwardly cringing at her lame impersonation of a tough bitch trucker.

'The roads are all blocked off, love,' said the man. 'The fuckin' army and police have blocked everything off. You're better just sittin' tight, love.'

Jenny shrugged. 'Yeah? Well I'm goin' to try me luck.

There's nothin' here. Just that bollocks service station over there, and they won't let me in.'

The man cast a glance towards it. 'Yeah. Selfish bastards inside won't open up. Water's stopped running now, and we're all getting fuckin' thirsty. Shit ... I mean some people, eh?'

Jenny nodded. 'Yeah. And there's no way in. It's all locked up tight. Pretty solid too. Bastards.'

'We came up night before last askin' for some food. There's no fuckin' food at all now on our estate. Just one corner shop selling fags and sweets, and that's all cleaned out now.'

She offered a grim supportive smile. 'Yeah. It's crazy. What's going on?'

The man nodded. 'Just fuckin' unbelievable. One minute it's all normal, the next minute everyone's going crazy. And now there's no fuckin' food anywhere, because the selfish bastards who got in first are hoardin' everything what they took.'

'I guess it's the same everywhere, not just here,' she replied.

'Yeah, s'pose. Anyway. We sort of formed a co-operative, over on the Runston housin' estate. There's old 'uns and a lot of mums and kids that're gettin' hungry over there,' said the man. He turned and pointed towards the pavilion. 'There's a shit-load of food in there they should be sharin' out with us. But the fuckin' manager of this place won't give us a thing.'

'Yeah, selfish bloody bastards,' Jenny said, shaking her head disdainfully. 'Look, good luck anyway mate. I hope you have better luck than I did.' She began to wind the window up.

'Hang on love,' said the man, placing his hand over the rising rim of glass.

She stopped winding it up. 'Yeah?'

'You can help us out.'

'I don't see how. They wouldn't let me in, so I guess I'll see if there's somewhere else—'

'Listen love. You could just smack their front wall in. It's only fuckin' plastic. We thought it was glass last time we was here, it wouldn't break. Things just kept fuckin' well bouncing off it.' The man pointed towards the pavilion. 'You could just run your truck into the front, beside the entrance. Wouldn't need to do it too hard neither, you could just reverse it in really. It wouldn't do your rig any damage.'

Jenny made a big show of giving it some thought as the man warily kept his hand over the rim of the window. Behind him, the other people looked up at her hopefully; a cluster of very normal and very worried people, very much at odds with Mr Stewart's description of the 'gang of yobbos that had terrorised us' earlier. Perhaps they had been kids that were passing through, or perhaps kids from the same housing estate as these people? Either way, *these* were just ordinary people trying to survive, no different to the lucky few inside who'd been working the evening shift here when things started to unravel.

Jenny wondered what right Mr Stewart had to decide who should receive and who shouldn't, and why he'd been willing to let her, Paul and Ruth in, and yet not prepared to help these people.

It was all down to our appearance, wasn't it? Ruth in her dark business trouser-suit, my smart interview clothes, Paul's tidy, expensive looking casuals. Not a single tattoo between us, no sportswear, no trouble.

That's what it boiled down to she supposed, at least to someone like Mr Stewart.

Those nice, smart-looking people can come in. But those bloody oiks from the estate? Let 'em starve.

Jenny looked up. She could see many, many more people emerging from the line of stunted saplings, coming down the slip-road and gathering in loose clusters and groups across the car-park. If there had been tattered piles of neatly ordered bric-à-brac on the ground and a row of sensibly parked Ford Escorts behind them, it would have looked like the early stages of a car-boot sale.

'What do you reckon?' prompted the man.

Jenny shifted uncomfortably. These people deserved to share what was in there, just as much as those inside. But, there were just too many of them – perhaps a hundred now, and, she suspected, there would be more to come. She could imagine the scale of this little siege growing quickly, as word spread to the various estates and villages around this nondescript piece of A road in the middle of nowhere.

Maybe Mr Stewart let us in simply because it was just the three of us, on our own?

Jenny looked around. In a matter of hours this car-park could be full of people pressed against the wall, hammering on it, pleading for food and water, and seeing them inside drinking tea and enjoying fried burgers … and that frustration quickly turning to anger, rage.

And if they found a way to smash in the front?

Jenny shook her head. 'Look, sorry mate.' She resumed winding up the window and stuck the key into the ignition.

'Fuckin' hell, love,' shouted the man through the glass, his matey, we're-in-this-together demeanour quickly replaced with a flash of aggression. 'Just askin' for a little fuckin' help!' he shouted over the throaty rumble of the truck's diesel engine, idling noisily. Jenny stabbed the accelerator and the truck growled deafeningly and belched smoke.

'Sorry!' she shouted apologetically back, and with an awkward backward lurch that almost pulled the man's tattooed arm out of its socket as he hung on to the driver's side door-handle, she reversed away from the knot of people that had gathered at the front.

The truck bunny-hopped manically, rocking alarmingly on its suspension as she struggled to get a feel for the pedals. The clusters of people that had gathered in the car-park had to quickly leap out of the way.

She guessed her crude bluff that she was the regular driver of this particular rig was well and truly blown now. Not that she had any illusions that the tattoo guy had been convinced in the first place.

Clear now of anything, or anyone, she might hit, she spun the large steering-wheel and swung the truck round towards the service station. Almost immediately, above the loud rattle of the engine, she heard a chorus of voices cheering her on.

They think I'm going to ram it for them.

The pavilion was only about seventy-five yards ahead of her. She drove slowly towards it, unsure how well she could control the vehicle – how quickly this monstrous bugger would come to a halt after she'd applied the brakes. It would be the definition of bloody irony if she *accidentally* rolled through that wall. Jenny needed to park it parallel to it, and as snugly close to it as she dared.

Thirty yards away she swung the truck to the right, taking it off course for a few moments, before turning it sharply left, back towards the entrance, swinging it round in a large loop so that now it was coming in at a tangent towards the front of the pavilion. Seconds later, the wheels beneath the cab rode the curb surrounding a stubby bush planted out front, then knocked aside an uninspiring children's little wooden climbing-frame and some picnic benches before riding up on to a small paved pedestrian area in front of the pavilion.

Jenny slowed the truck right down, gently rolling forward until the cab, and the trailer behind it – carrying a freight container – more or less covered the entire front wall of the pavilion. She then jabbed the brakes which spat and hissed loudly like a giant serpent. She swung open the driver-side door.

It thudded heavily against the front of the pavilion, scuffing the perspex and only half-opening – not quite enough to squeeze through.

Oh great.

She realised she'd done too bloody good a job of parking snugly against the front of the pavilion.

CHAPTER 60

6.11 p.m. GMT

Beauford Service Station

Jenny turned round to look over her shoulder, out through the passenger-side window at the car-park. Those people were coming this way; many of them walking swiftly, some jogging. She sensed there was some confusion amongst them over whether the truck had managed to knock a hole through, or was preparing to reverse and try again . . . or something else. Either way, people were gravitating towards it, curious to see what was going on.

They were going to be upon her in less than a minute, perhaps that tattoo man would be amongst the first to arrive, and she was sure he'd be mighty pissed off with her, when he sussed her intention had been to blockade the front with the articulated truck.

She guessed there was just about enough time to climb out of the passenger-side door, run around the front of the truck, squeeze into the narrow two or three foot gap between the side of the truck and the front wall, and hope to God the revolving door – which protruded a little – wasn't blocked, or obstructed by the truck in any way.

You've got to immobilise the truck.

Shit, yes she had to. It was a fair bet there was someone out there who'd know how to get this thing going without the need of the ignition key.

The approaching crowd was converging. Many of them now jogging towards her, perhaps hoping she'd broken through. She could see still more people emerging from the distant tree line around the edge of the car-park, and coming down the slip-road.

It was as if some jungle drums, playing on a frequency beyond her hearing, was summoning the thirsty and the hungry for miles around.

Oh Jesus … get a move on girl!

She grabbed the steering-wheel lock-bar off the passenger seat and fumbled with it, trying to work out how it fitted on to the steering-wheel. She looked up again.

They were running, sprinting towards her now – only forty or fifty yards away. She spotted the tattooed man leading the charge. Clearly he *had* twigged that she'd fooled him, that she was one of *those bastards inside* … one of the *selfish bastards.*

He was going to beat the crap out of her for sure.

'Oh shit! Come on!'

Jenny had used a locking-bar on her little Peugeot many years ago; a dinky little bar that, to be honest, could have been jimmied loose and opened with a two pence piece and a little patience. It looked nothing like this heavy-duty thing that looked like it belonged in a gym. But, she could see a groove cut into the thick side of the bar, where obviously it was designed to rest across the wheel. Placing the groove against the steering-wheel, everything quickly fell into place, and she could see how it closed and locked. With a reassuring click, the bar secured around it, and protruded two feet out, preventing the wheel turning more than halfway round. One might be able to turn the truck around with many backward and forward steps, with this lock still attached but it would have to do.

She clambered across both seats, cursing her calf-length cotton skirt as it caught momentarily on the gear stick, and then, pushed open the passenger-side door, just as the first of those people – the tattooed man amongst them – were bearing down on her, no more than a dozen yards away. His face was stony, rigid with anger, she thought she could hear him calling her all sorts. Jenny knew she was in big trouble if they got a hold of her.

She jumped down to the ground and immediately dropped to her hands and knees and began to crawl under the truck; it seemed the quickest way. Behind her she could hear the thud of trainers against tarmac, and the frustrated bellow of a winded voice.

'You fucking bitch!'

As she crawled on her belly beneath the lumpy grime and oil-encrusted chassis, she felt her ankle suddenly being squeezed by a vice. Looking back down, she could see a hand wrapped around it and the start of a tanned and muscular forearm. Then *his* face dipped down into view; tattoo-man.

'Fucking cow! You're with those bastards inside,' he snarled as he pulled hard on her leg. She felt the coarse pebbly paving slabs grate painfully against her stomach and chest as she was being dragged out roughly from beneath the truck.

'No!' she screamed. 'No please!'

Jenny wrapped her forearm around a support strut on the side of the chassis and held as tightly as she could. The man tightened his grip on her leg and redoubled his effort to pull her out.

'Come on out, bitch!'

Jenny could now see several pairs of legs had joined those of Mr Tattoo. She felt another pair of hands on her shin, and as they settled into a rhythmic jerking action, she felt her grip weakening with each successive pull.

'No, please!' she screamed pointlessly.

Another hard pull and Jenny found her armlock on the strut had been broken. She flailed around for something else to grab, once again feeling the rough paving slabs scrape away at her skin as her body was being pulled out into the open.

And then he was standing over her, flanked on one side by a short squat man who looked to be ten years older, and on the other, by a woman, perhaps the same age as Jenny, her platinum-blonde hair pulled back tightly away from a hard, lean, humourless face, into a ponytail.

Tattoo shook his head. 'Fuckin' selfish bastards like you always seem to do all right when things turn to shit,' he muttered angrily.

'Look, I'm sorry,' Jenny whimpered, 'I was just—'

'Yeah. I thought you was talking a load of *pony*. Bloody truck driver, my arse.'

Jenny tried again, 'I was just—'

'Yeah, we know what you was just doing, love,' said the woman. 'I've got three fuckin' kids and a baby at home all crying because I can't find anything to fuckin' feed them. And there's you, you stuck-up bitch, making sure you and those selfish bastards in there get to keep it all for yourselves.'

Oh God, they're really going to hurt me.

'Fuckin' do this bitch, Tom,' said the platinum blonde. 'I can't stand stuck-up cows like this – think they're better than everyone else.'

Tattoo looked down at her. 'I bet people like *you* are doin' all right. People like *you* who got the spare money to have extra food hidden away, to make sure you come out all right. Whilst us poor bastards are left on our own to fuckin' starve.'

'It's only been a couple of d-days,' Jenny muttered, her voice wobbling, 'n-nobody's s-starving yet.'

'Yeah? You think? My kids are!' screamed the blonde. 'There's nothin' where we live … nothin'. And no one's come to fuckin' help us.'

I've got to keep them talking.

'But they will,' replied Jenny. 'It's j-just like that New Orleans thing. Help will arrive. The p-police will be back.'

The woman leaned down and slapped Jenny across the face. 'Just shut up! SHUT UP!'

Tattoo shook his head. 'Police aren't fuckin' coming, 'cause they're too busy guarding important shit. It's just us. And we've got to look after ourselves.'

Jenny wiped the blood from her lip. 'You're right, we need to work tog—'

The blonde slapped her again. 'SHUT IT!' she screamed.

'Let's do her!' said the woman, 'Show those bastards inside that we mean business.'

Tattoo looked around at the growing pack of people. There was a knot of perhaps twenty or thirty gathered around Jenny looking down at her, and more were joining the crowd with every second. She could see they were all emotionally strung out – frightened, hungry, thirsty – desperate for someone to take the lead and point the way forward. She could see there were some who just wanted a share of what was inside – no violence please – just a fair share.

And there were some who wanted to rip her to shreds.

She knew it was those of the latter kind who tended to make the biggest noise, the *hidden sociopaths*, the ones who cried loudest and longest for a lynching when some paedophile, benefit-defrauding immigrant, or disgraced minor celebrity was being outed by the red-top press.

The witch burners.

'Pull her out where those shits inside can see her. Then let's do her!' goaded the blonde again. Voices in the crowd shouted approval at that.

Tattoo-man perhaps hadn't intended to take things that far, but Jenny could see him looking around at the crowd, the blonde bitch was baying for blood, and that was swaying the crowd.

'Okay!' he shouted above the noise. 'We'll do her where they can see!'

She saw a flicker of metal, a penknife in someone's hand.

Oh no, please no.

Jenny flushed cold, and her bladder loosened. She closed her eyes with shame.

She heard a younger man shout, 'Hey! She's pissed herself! Look!'

And then she felt hands all over her, on her arms and legs, and where they didn't need to be … pulling her roughly off the ground.

The fear of the knife she had seen pushed every other thought out of her mind.

Don't cut me, don't cut me, don't cut me.

CHAPTER 61

6.15 p.m. GMT

Beauford Service Station

'STOP RIGHT NOW!'

It was such a loud voice.

'WHAT THE *HELL* DO YOU THINK YOU'RE FLIPPIN' WELL DOING?'

A deafening, parade-ground loud voice that cut over the jeering and shouting of the crowd like a gunshot. Tattoo-man, the hard-faced platinum blonde and the dozen or so other people who were manhandling Jenny, stopped. They didn't put her down mind, but for the moment they hesitated.

'WHAT THE *HELL* IS GOING ON?'

It was Ruth's voice Jenny could hear; that no crap taken, tell it how I see it, call a spade a spade, Birmingham accent.

'IS THIS HOW GROWN-UPS ARE MEANT TO BEHAVE?' Ruth continued like a secondary school teacher chastising a classroom of unruly teenagers.

Jenny felt some of the hands that were holding her, begin to loosen, temporarily shamed. She was lowered back down to the ground. She looked up, squinting at the setting sun, melting against the horizon. Ruth stood beside the front of the truck, standing firmly with her legs planted apart, her hands held behind her back. In her dark business trouser-suit, she looked a little like a policewoman, a prison guard perhaps.

'That's right, put her down!' she barked again, a little less deafening, now the crowd had quietened down. 'What the bloody hell were you people thinking of?'

Tattoo-man was the first to regain his voice. 'Fuckin' bitch is with those bastards inside!'

Jenny looked across at Ruth, and realised.

They think Ruth's one of them?

Perhaps in the confusion they hadn't seen her emerge from behind the truck? Jenny made eye contact with her, and Ruth seemed to nod back, almost imperceptibly.

She's picked up on that too.

'Yeah? Well maybe she is, but this is no bloody way to behave! Absolutely disgraceful. We're not a bunch of flippin' savages are we?'

Ruth's chastising approach seemed to be working for now. Maybe somehow at an instinctive level she was tapping into that inner-child thing everyone has. The baying mob right now looked like a class of thirteen year olds being read the riot act by their deputy head.

'But those selfish bastards inside are sitting on all that food, and we're all fuckin' hungry!' replied the platinum blonde, still holding Jenny's arm in a tight, painful grip.

'We're thirsty too. There's no running water,' someone in the crowd called out.

Ruth took a few tentative steps forward towards Jenny. 'Well that's as maybe. I'll talk to them,' she announced. 'I'll make 'em see reason. But right now, let this poor young lady go,' she looked pointedly at the platinum blonde, 'there's a good girl.'

The mood of the crowd of people around Jenny seemed uncertain, wavering. She sensed even more than water or food, they wanted someone to step forward and be in charge, and this sturdy-looking lady with a foghorn voice and a reassuring line of common sense seemed to be filling that void.

Oh my God … she's going to get me out of this!

Tattoo-man loosened his grip on Jenny.

But platinum blonde still had one sinewy hand wrapped tightly around Jenny's upper arm, her long nails digging painfully into her skin.

Ruth now focused her stern gaze solely on the blonde.

'Listen love,' said Ruth taking another couple of steps forward until she was a mere yard away, and staring powerfully down at the whippet-thin woman. Ruth's generous figure, not inconsiderable height, and that dark business suit – all those subtle things were helping to sway the delicate situation in her favour.

'I'll talk to them, just as soon as you've let her go. We're Brits for Christ's sake! We are NOT going to behave like a bunch of flippin' Third-World savages. Do you understand, love?'

Ruth took another step forward and reached a hand out for Jenny, the other hand still tucked behind her back.

The blonde eyed her suspiciously, tightening her grasp on Jenny's arm. 'Yeah? And how you gonna get them to share out that food? Huh? And anyway, who fuckin' well put you in charge?'

Ruth's face hardened, she pursed her lips and her eyes narrowed. 'You re-e-e-ally don't want to tangle with someone like me darlin', you really don't. I eat little slappers like you for breakfast.'

Oh God, thought Jenny, sensing she was nearly home and dry *... she's truly terrifying.*

The blonde studied Ruth silently for a moment. 'Hang on, you're not from our fuckin' estate anyway. I know everyone's face. I don't know yours.'

Jenny's eyes flickered towards Ruth.

You've been rumbled.

'So flippin' what? I come from Burnside, fucking toughest estate in Birmingham. Doesn't mean shit really does it?'

Jenny heard it. That meant everyone else had heard it too; a slight wavering in Ruth's voice.

The blonde smiled, knowing the tide was swaying her way again.

'You're one of 'em wankers from inside aren't cha?' She turned to address the crowd. 'She's not from our estate, she's not one of us!'

There was a moment's lag. Clearly they would have preferred Ruth as a leader, but the unspoken agreement was that their neighbourhood was their *tribe*. They had to stick together, because it looked like no one else was going to come and help them out. When things turn to shit, you stick with your own.

Ruth took advantage of the moment.

With surprising speed for her size, she whipped her other hand out from behind her back and held it inches away from the face of the blonde. Jenny could see she was holding something small and blue, a can of something.

It hissed and sprayed something into her face.

The blonde screamed in agony and dropped to the floor where she clawed at her face with her hands. Ruth roughly jerked Jenny forward.

'RUN!' she bellowed, pointing towards the front of the truck. 'There's space to squeeze round!'

Jenny staggered forward, rushing past Ruth.

Ruth held her ground a moment longer, keeping her arm aloft.

'It's mace! Take a step closer and I'll flippin' well burn your face off with this stuff!' she yelled at the crowd of people in front of her.

As Jenny rounded the front of the truck, she spotted the squeeze-gap between the truck and the pavilion's perspex front. She shot a glance back at Ruth, who was now backing up one step at a time, with the can of mace held in front of her like a gun.

Some of the crowd were keeping pace with her, some more had spread out either side. Jenny could see Ruth's steady retreat was in danger of being cut off by some of these people. She needed to turn and run right now.

'Ruth!' she cried, 'Come on!'

'I'm coming!' Ruth called back, not daring to look away from the people in front of her. She took another couple of retreating steps, and then she began to turn.

But something lanced through the air towards her; a brick, a piece of loose paving … it hit her on the back of the head and she lost her footing and tumbled to the ground.

'Ruth!' Jenny screamed.

The crowd from the estate were upon her almost immediately and before the mob closed around Ruth's prone form, Jenny spotted the platinum blonde kneeling down over her, tears streaming from bloodshot eyes, punching Ruth's face repeatedly with a balled, bony fist.

'Oh my God!' she whispered, rooted to the spot.

'Jenny. For fuck's sake come inside!' hissed Paul, standing in the space between the truck and the pavilion.

She turned to look at him. 'We've got to help her! They'll kill her!'

Jenny turned back to look at the crowd. There seemed to be some amongst them who were reluctant to take part, there were even some who were desperately trying to pull others back off Ruth.

'Come on, inside!' Paul grabbed her by the arm and pulled her into the gap. 'There's nothing we can do for Ruth now.' He led her to the revolving door, pushed her ahead into the open segment and leant hard against the plastic door to turn it – looking anxiously over his shoulder, as the door slowly moved.

Without power turning it, he had to work hard to budge it.

Jenny emerged from the segment into the greenhouse heat of the foyer, just as Paul dived into the next open segment. She saw the first of the mob squeeze around the front of the truck, and along the pavilion wall towards the door, hammering their fists on the thick plastic to intimidate them.

'Come on Paul!' she screamed, and reached out to grab a panel as it swung round in front of her. She threw her weight against it, and the door turned a little faster.

Paul emerged just as the first of them entered an open segment. He quickly grabbed a bucket seat from nearby and wedged it into the closing gap. The door shuddered, and through the thick glass she could hear them outside jeering angrily.

Inside, she could hear a pin drop. Mr Stewart's staff, uncertain what was being shouted at them through the plastic, but clearly understanding the intent behind the jeering and taunting, stared in horrified silence at the pale, enraged faces outside.

One of Stewart's older ladies, a Nigerian, started crying, repeating something over and over.

A prayer?

Jenny's blood ran cold. 'They killed her,' she muttered to herself. 'They killed Ruth.'

And we're going to be next.

CHAPTER 62

9.51 p.m. GMT
Shepherd's Bush, London

If this had been a normal night, like, for example, this time last year, they would have been out in their tiny backyard. Perhaps Dad would have barbecued some kebabs, and Mum would have rustled up some salad and spoon-bread. She would almost certainly have invited over the neighbours from across the street, the DiMarcios, because they made Mum laugh. Dad probably would have kept to himself though, he just wasn't that good with Mum's crowd.

The point is, it being so warm now that the predictable early June clouds had gone away, they would have been outside, enjoying it – getting tipsy on sangria.

Instead she was trapped inside someone else's home, an unfamiliar environment, looking out at the last light of a warm summer evening.

Leona looked out of the front-room window – the blind drawn across to hide her – on to the avenue. She saw the net curtains twitch upstairs at the DiMarcios' house. They must still be there then; hiding like her and Jake, and hoping nothing about the outside of their hiding place would attract the attention of the gang tonight.

Last night had been truly terrifying, hearing the sounds of them breaking in to someone's home, just thirty or so yards up St Stephen's Avenue. Leona had heard a lot of voices; cheering, shouting, laughing. In and amongst that cacophony, she swore she heard someone screaming somewhere in that house.

She wished she hadn't.

'Are the Bad Boys back again?' asked Jacob anxiously, looking up from the deck of cards he had spread out on the lounge floor.

'Not yet, Jake. They won't come out until it's gone dark.'

Jacob nodded. It was still light now, light enough to be able to read the numbers on his Yu-Gi-Oh cards – just, and whilst there was daylight, they were safe.

Jacob wished Dan would come back. Leona said he'd decided to go home and look after his mum. Jake knew she was lying though. She lied bad, just like every other girl … lots of 'ummms' and 'ahhhs'. Jake on the other hand could tell huge porkers all day long without batting an eyelid.

Dan hadn't gone to look after his mum.

He'd dumped Leona. That's what he reckoned had happened. That's why she'd been doing that crying today when she thought he wasn't looking.

He'd teased her last time she'd split up with a boyfriend, Steve. Jacob hadn't liked him anyway. He was always looking in mirrors, and shiny surfaces, playing with his hair. And the one time he'd bothered to play with Jacob – whilst waiting for Leona to do *girl stuff* in the bathroom – he'd just been pretending, not re-e-eally playing with him … just trying to impress Leona, and look good in front of Mum and Dad.

Dan, on the other hand, was cool. Dan knew how to play. He missed Dan.

Leona did too.

And with him around, he'd felt a little safer too. He suspected the Bad Boys were scared of Dan, that's why they had been left alone, that's why they had stayed out in the street. But now he was gone, the Bad Boys might not be frightened any more.

He wondered if Dan had decided to be a Bad Boy too and make a nuisance outside long after bedtime. Maybe he'd got bored of sitting in the lounge, eating those gross tins of pilchards in that yucky ketchup – which tasted nothing like proper ketchup – bored of playing Yu-Gi-Oh with him?

Probably.

He looked up at the lounge window. The sky was getting dark now. *They* would be coming soon, coming out to play.

'Lee?'

Leona stirred, let the blind drop back into place and turned to him, wiping her cheek quickly. 'Yes Jake?'

'Can I sleep with you tonight?'

'I … I stay down here. I don't sleep in any of the upstairs rooms.'

'Can I stay down here with you then?'

Leona thought about it for a moment. 'Okay, go get a quilt and pillow and you can sleep on the sofa down here.'

Jacob got up and made for the stairs, and then had a thought. He came over and planted a clumsy kiss on her cheek. It was damp – she'd been doing some more of her secret crying.

'Nevermind,' he said hoping it was the right thing to say, 'I bet you'll have another boyfriend soon.'

She turned away to look out of the window again. 'Just get your things, there's a good boy.'

Jacob ran up the stairs quickly. It was too dark up here for his liking, so he made quick work of grabbing a quilt and pillow from the nearest bed. He entered the lounge to find Leona staring at him, a finger raised to her lips, the sadness that had been spread all over her face like chocolate after an éclair, was gone. She looked scared now.

'Shhh … they're back,' she whispered.

Jacob tiptoed quietly over to her, dropping his bedding on the floor, and then joined her by the window. Directly outside their house a car was parked, headlights lighting up the street, the doors open and the sound of bass-heavy music thumping from within. He saw movement inside the car.

The Bad Boys were back.

CHAPTER 63

11.43 p.m. GMT

Beauford Service Station

The truck parked hard up against the front of the pavilion obscured most of what was going on outside. But standing over on the right-hand side, Jenny could see round the front of the truck. There was a bonfire out in the middle of the car-park. They had amassed a pile of rubbish and set it alight. And now it was burning ferociously, bathing the place in a flickering amber glow.

Jenny stared out at it, and the mass of people that had gathered around it. It seemed in the last couple of hours, since …

... since I was nearly beaten to a pulp ... and Ruth was …

... since then the number of people out there had grown alarmingly. She guessed there must be a couple of hundred of them milling around outside.

Ruth.

She'd hardly got to know her really. They had spoken a bit this morning, and yesterday walking along the hard shoulder, but she knew very little about her. She'd perhaps learned more about her in those last moments outside, when Ruth had held a mob at bay for a couple of minutes with nothing but the force of her personality.

She was probably not the sort of person Jenny would have mixed with, done lunch with, back in normal times, but right now Jenny would have traded in every last one of her upwardly mobile friends, past and present, to have someone as Bolshie, loudmouthed and downright ballsy as Ruth, by her side.

She looked out at the Dante-esque scene before her. It looked like some sort of satanic cult gathering. She expected to see hooded and robed figures calling things to order, and some young virgin, raised on an inverted crucifix over the fire.

Of course, it was the dancing flames coming from the fire that lent the scene such a disturbing aura. She reminded herself they were normal people, just very frustrated and hungry normal people.

She looked around at Mr Stewart's staff. She could see they were frightened; staring at the scene outside and exchanging muted comments in Polish, Romanian, Cantonese. She realised that for them – unable to understand a lot of what had been going on over the last few days, and knowing they were so obviously *outsiders* – this must have been even more terrifying.

Paul wandered over to stand beside her. 'That doesn't look good,' said Paul. 'When you get the mob starting to light fires, it doesn't take long for buildings to start burning down.'

'They won't try and set this place on fire, surely? It would destroy all the food and water they're after.'

Paul shook his head. 'I don't know. Maybe they're too pissed off to care about that now. Maybe thirst is driving them a bit loopy.'

Yes, they had to be bloody thirsty out there.

It had been a very warm week since Monday; hot even, at times. And now, there was no longer any running tap-water. She had noticed earlier this afternoon when she'd tried to flush the toilet. They had to be getting thirsty outside, and other than tap-water, cans or bottles, what else could they drink? She'd not noticed any nearby rivers or reservoirs. And anyway, the state of most waterways these days, thick with foam and floating condoms – you'd need to be bloody desperate first.

Meanwhile, inside the pavilion, they had fridge-cold bottled water, hundreds of cans of Pepsi and Fanta glistening with dew-drops of condensation, cartons of fruit juice, even tubs of Ben and Jerry's ice-cream, for crying out loud.

'Yup,' said Paul quietly, 'thirst makes people do a whole load of crazy things.'

Jenny looked at him, wishing he hadn't said that. She looked back out again, at the milling crowd around the bonfire and then noticed that someone was standing on something, and addressing them. Jenny watched the person gesturing, shouting. Although she couldn't make out what was being said, she could guess.

She could just make out the raised voice drifting across the crowded car-park towards them. It had that unmistakable, shrill, humourless tone – it was the platinum-blonde woman. That skinny, hard-faced bitch, in her vest top and tracksuit bottoms, those long nails … and those thin lips stretched across those snarling teeth.

Platinum Blonde seemed to have won over the people out there. Not good. She was sure many of those people simply wanted to break in, grab some food and water and go home, that's all. But the blonde, she'd want to make an example of someone.

Me probably.

'They're going to get in here tonight. Aren't they?'

Paul looked out at the crowd. 'Yeah. I don't think they're going to be satisfied just throwing a few bricks and stones at this place. They need to get in tonight … they're getting desperate.'

'What if we throw some water out to them?'

A wry smile spread across his mouth. 'Yeah, I'm sure that'll placate them. And off they'll trot back home.'

Jenny ignored his sarcasm. 'So what do you suggest we do?'

He looked furtively over his shoulder before speaking. 'I suggest we leave before it all kicks off. As in, pretty bloody soon.'

She glanced at the staff, huddled together anxiously in the foyer, talking in hushed, frightened tones. Mr Stewart, meanwhile, was nowhere to be seen. He had retired to his office a couple of hours earlier. She hadn't seen him since.

'What? We can't abandon them. Look at the state of them.'

'And? They're not my responsibility, nor are they yours. I want to get home, and I don't particularly want to get caught up in this fucking mess.'

'It was your bloody idea to stay!'

'Yeah, well, guess what? I got that wrong. This is looking nasty and I suggest we sneak out whilst there's a chance.'

'And leave them?' she nodded towards the others.

'It sounds pretty shitty, but yeah.'

Jenny shook her head. 'I'm guessing you're a bit of a selfish bastard in normal life, aren't you?'

He shrugged. 'Call me selfish, but I just don't want to be lynched by the mob, all right?' he said. 'I just know we can't take on all these poor sods. They have to look after themselves. We have to put ourselves first. That's how things are now, I'm afraid. Who do you want to save? These strangers, these people who you've known for five minutes? Or your family?'

Jenny watched the silhouette of Platinum Blonde as she stirred up the crowd milling around the burning car.

'It all came undone so quickly. Just a few days,' she gestured towards those outside, 'and look at us.'

Paul nodded as he watched the people outside. 'I suppose, when the rules go, no matter which country you live in, we're all the same. We're just a few square meals, a power-cut, a sip of water away from doing things we never dreamed we would, from being a bunch of cavemen.'

Outside something was beginning to happen. Platinum Blonde had finished saying her piece and had stepped down off her box and merged with the milling crowd.

'Shit, I think they're about to do whatever it is they've been planning,' muttered Paul. 'We need to find a way out now.'

The thought of that woman breaking in to the service station and finding her sent a chill through Jenny. Paul was right, they had to think of themselves right now. Guilt, self-reproach, introspection – that could come later when there was time.

'Find a way out? Where? How?'

He turned away from the perspex wall, looking back at the dimly lit interior of the pavilion. The emergency generators still running the food freezers were also supplying power to a few muted emergency wall lamps towards the back of the area.

'My guess is there'll be a trade entrance at the rear somewhere, maybe we'll get lucky and no one's thought to watch the back of this place.'

The crowd outside began to approach them. Jenny noticed some were carrying containers; buckets, bottles. She backed away from the perspex wall as they came round the front of the truck and squeezed into the gap between the truck and the wall. They peered through the scuffed surface, shouting angrily as they made their way along the narrow space towards the locked revolving door. The first to get there was holding a two-litre plastic bottle of pop. There was a three or four inch gap between the revolving door's frame, and the door panel of one of the segments. He pushed his arm through the gap and poured something out of the bottle on to the floor inside.

The smell wafted through almost instantly.

'Petrol,' said Paul. 'They're going to burn the doorway down. That won't take long to melt. Let's stop dicking around and go.'

Jenny looked once more at the frightened huddle of staff. Paul grabbed her arm.

'No!' he said quietly. 'If you tell them we're going out the back, they'll all get up and follow us. Those people outside will see that and suss what's going on.'

He started towards the rear of the pavilion, pulling her arm. 'Come on.'

She reluctantly followed him, looking back over her shoulder at the doorway. Several more of the crowd had squeezed their arms through the gap and poured the contents of their containers into that segment. The reek of petrol was that much stronger.

Then she saw Platinum Blonde standing at the front of the truck holding a burning stick in one hand, and peering through the scuffed perspex wall, her face pushed up against it.

She's looking for me.

Jenny felt an even greater surge of fear take hold of her. For some reason, that woman had focused on her, as if Jenny personified somehow the desperate predicament they were all in.

I really ... really, don't want her to get hold of me.

She turned back to look at Paul. 'Okay, okay, let's go.'

CHAPTER 64

11.46 p.m. GMT

Beauford Service Station

Paul led her back into the dimly lit rear of the pavilion, past the amusement arcade, past the closed door to Mr Stewart's office. She wondered what he was doing in there. His staff, mostly older women, confused and frightened, needed him out there in the foyer, not hiding away like this.

There was a row of doors ahead of them. Three of them were toilets, the fourth was simply marked up as being for 'Staff Only'.

Paul pushed the door open to reveal a narrow passageway, lit by a red bulb dangling from a socket in the low ceiling. The passage was only about three or four feet wide and was cluttered with cardboard boxes and crates stacked untidily against the right-hand wall; stock and supplies for the shop and the non-perishables for the fast food counters. No food of course, just the useless crap you'd expect to pick up at a service station; *Rock Classics For The Road* – 48 x CD, 'Beauford Services Souvenir Mugs' – pack of 24, 'Celebrity Head Wobblers' – assorted characters, 24 units.

Paul led the way down the hallway, struggling in places to squeeze past the stacks of boxes.

'If this is where they've dumped their stock, I'd guess the delivery door is somewhere back here.'

She stopped beside a stack of boxes: Evian – 1 litre x 36. She tore open the top flap of the box and pulled out half-a-dozen bottles.

At the sound of the box being ripped open, Paul stopped and

turned round. 'Yeah, maybe a good idea.' He left her and carried on down the passage. Jenny cradled the bottles in her arms and followed on.

'Here we go,' he said pointing. 'That looks like a delivery gate.'

The passageway ended with a four-feet wide, floor to ceiling, corrugated metal shutter that looked like it slid from left to right. It was padlocked.

'Oh, there we go then, locked,' she muttered.

'It's okay,' replied Paul pulling out a bunch of keys from his trouser pocket. 'I lifted these off of Mr Stewart's desk a little earlier.'

'He didn't notice?'

'Not really. He was pissed, finished off that medicinal brandy of his.'

Paul sorted through the keys; inconveniently, none of them was marked or tagged.

Jenny sniffed the air. 'Oh shit! Can you smell that?'

Paul stopped what he was doing and inhaled. 'Burning plastic?'

'Yes. They've started on the front door already. You better hurry.'

'I'm going as fast as I can,' he muttered trying key after key in the padlock.

Jenny turned and looked up the narrow, dimly lit passageway, and listened intently to the muted noises that were coming down it. She could hear some of the staff in the main area of the pavilion crying and pleading to be left alone, either in pidgin English or their own tongue. Their voices sounded shrill, taut and wretched with panic and fear. Beyond that she could hear the distant taunting calls and jeers from the people trying to get in.

'Come on! Which one of you bastards is it?' Paul hissed with frustration, as he fumbled with the keys.

A thought occurred to Jenny. 'What if they're waiting for us just outside this door?'

Paul paused for a moment. 'Screw it, I don't know. They probably haven't thought that far ahead anyway. We'll just have to hope they're all around the front.'

Jenny nodded doubtfully; that wasn't the reassuring answer she'd been hoping for.

The smell of burning plastic was getting stronger and she could now hear some banging; it sounded like someone was kicking at the door panels, testing them to see if the perspex had softened enough to give.

'Oh Christ, please hurry!' she cried.

'I'm going as fast as I can.'

She heard him jangle the keys again and this time after a moment's frustrated jiggling around, she heard a *click*.

'That's it. Got it!'

He removed the padlock and tossed it aside, then reached for the handle of the sliding delivery door.

'Please open it quietly,' she whispered.

Paul nodded and then pulled gently on the handle. The door grated noisily, metal casters scraping in the runners along the top and bottom. He slid the door to the side by only an inch and Jenny saw a hairline vertical crack of deep blue light – a clear night's sky.

He waited a moment, hoping the scraping sound hadn't attracted any unwanted attention, and then slowly pushed the delivery door a little further to the side.

There was a thud and the corrugated door rattled, and then with a roar from the little metal castors, the door was yanked to the right, clattering noisily against the frame. Silhouetted against the evening sky, and dimly lit by the red emergency light back up the passageway, she saw about a dozen of them standing outside. From what she could make out they were mostly men, a couple of women, some young, some middle-aged; people from the estate.

'Please … don't hurt us!' she pleaded with them, feeling the cold grasp of fear suck the air from her lungs and the strength from her legs.

One of them stepped forward; a young man with a skinhead, his shirt tied around his waist, exposing a lean, taut and muscular torso, decorated down one side with those popular Celtic swirls. Jenny stared at him, his face hot and blotchy, aggressively thrust forward, close to hers. He looked hard, angry, ready to lash out at her.

He pointed at the bottles of water she held in her arms.

'Could I 'ave a drink of one of those? I'm fuckin' parched.'

Jenny was taken aback. 'Yeah ... uh ... sure,' she replied handing him a bottle. He took it and nodded.

'Thanks.'

'There's a load more back there,' said Paul. 'A stack of boxes on the right, go help yourself.'

The rest of the group of people surged quickly past the lad, some of them muttering a 'thank you' as they stepped by.

Jenny watched the lad gulping the Evian. He was desperately thirsty, his Adam's apple bobbing up and down as he made quick work of it. She turned and jerked her head toward the passageway. 'You better go after those others and get yourself some of that water before it's all gone.'

He nodded, handing back the nearly empty plastic bottle and wiping his mouth with the back of his hand.

'Yeah. Cheers for that,' he said and jogged down the narrow walkway after the others, weaving around the stacks of boxes.

Jenny turned to Paul. 'I thought he was going to tear me to pieces.'

Paul appeared equally surprised. 'A polite chav,' he replied shaking his head in disbelief. 'Come on, let's get out of here while the going's good.'

They both stepped outside.

The night was warm still. Under different circumstances, it would have been a lovely evening to sit out. Paul looked both ways up and down the back of the building. He saw the dark forms of another group of people jogging along the back of the building towards them, attracted by the red glow of light spilling out from the open delivery entrance.

Paul grabbed her arm and whispered. 'These ones might not be so polite. Pretend to be one of them.'

As the group approached them, Paul called out, 'The delivery door's open, there's loads of stuff inside.'

'Cheers mate,' a voice called out from the dark.

Another asked, 'Any water in there?'

'Yeah, but you want to get in there quick,' Paul replied.

The group passed by without further comment, and picked their pace up to a jog as they neared the delivery entrance.

Paul and Jenny rounded the corner of the pavilion, and from there they could see the car-park and the bonfire still burning, now all but deserted. Jenny assumed everyone who had been milling around it earlier on, must now be piling inside the service station at the front, helping themselves to whatever they could find. She could hear a lot of noise filtering out from inside; shouting, the clatter of goods being spilled and knocked over, but with an almost overwhelming sense of relief, she could hear no screaming – no sounds of violence, no pleas for mercy.

'What are we going to do now?' she whispered.

'That car,' he replied, 'it's Mr Stewart's. I grabbed his car keys as well.'

'Oh right. God I hope they haven't trashed it.'

'Come on.'

Paul started across the car-park, walking swiftly towards the staff-reserved area on the far side. Jenny set off after him, looking anxiously over her shoulder at the pavilion. The truck across the front was blocking most of the front to the building, but every now and then she could see the flickering beams of torches playing around the inside of the foyer and the amber glow of flames coming from the revolving door. The fire they'd used to weaken the entrance looked like it had begun to take hold and she was certain by morning the service station would be nothing more than a smouldering ruin.

Paul pulled out the bunch of keys from his pocket, and she heard them jangling again as he went through them.

'Ah, that feels like a car fob,' she heard him say in the dark, and a second later the car squawked and the hazard lights on it flashed a couple of times. They both headed for it. It looked like the vehicle had been untouched; no dents, scrapes, the tyres weren't flat. She allowed herself to hope they were going to get out of this mess.

They jumped in, anxious to take possession of the vehicle and be off before anyone else had noticed. Jenny dumped her armful of Evian bottles on the floor inside the car.

'Be nice if Mr Stewart thought to fill her up,' said Paul, jamming the key in the ignition. He turned it, and the lights on the dash came on.

'Thank fuck,' he sighed. 'Half a tank, fair enough. Better than nothing.'

'I thought you said you couldn't drive?'

Paul smiled sheepishly as he spun the car round. 'Okay, I lied – so shoot me.'

Jenny twisted in her seat and studied the pavilion anxiously, half-expecting a swarm of people to suddenly emerge from it and charge them down, hell-bent on pulling them out of the car and ripping their throats out.

My God, doesn't this feel just like that ... Like one of those crazy zombie movies?

This whole situation was like some post-apocalyptic scenario; the glimmering firelight from the bonfire, the debris and detritus strewn across the tarmac, the flickering torchlight and the frantically scrabbling crowd inside the building, the noise, the chaos.

Paul drove across the car-park towards the exit leading on to the slip-road that led out to the motorway and headed south once more.

She watched the service station in the wing mirror until it disappeared from view.

My God, this is how it is after only four days.

Friday

CHAPTER 65

3 a.m. local time

Southern Turkey

You've got to think they're all okay. You know they're okay … okay?

Andy fidgeted uncomfortably in the coach seat. It was an old coach and most of the seats were lumpy and uncomfortable, some with springs poking through the tattered and frayed covers. He'd tried sleeping, God knows he needed some. He had been awake since Monday morning; he had possibly managed to steal an hour of sleep here and there, but he wasn't aware of having been able to do that. During the events of the last few days, in the periods when things had been quiet enough to try for some rest, his mind wouldn't turn off, wouldn't stop thinking about the kids and Jenny.

You know they're okay.

Running the same things over and over; the last two or three telephone conversations … he'd given Leona and Jenny an early warning. They'd had time to get in the essentials and get home and lie low. That's all they had to do now, just lie low and let this thing play out.

Leona was a sensible, clever girl. Even though he'd not had time to put into crystal-clear words why she was in danger, why she couldn't go home, Andy was sure she'd do as she was told. But the possible pursuit of some shadowy men from God knows where was only *half* the equation.

He wondered how things were in London; a big city, a lot of people – it didn't take a genius to work out how nasty things could get if the British authorities had been caught on the hop by the oil cut-off. And knowing how useless the government in his adopted country could be at preparing for anything out of the ordinary – unseasonably heavy rain, too many leaves on the track, a drier than average summer – the prognosis wasn't great.

He conjured up an image of Jenny and the kids at Jill's house. Jill, a loudmouth with a big personality – a woman who quite honestly grated on his nerves, would be looking after them. He could visualise them huddled together in front of the radio, or her expensive plasma TV, hanging on every word from the newsreaders, eating tinned peaches and worrying ... maybe even about him.

They're fine Andy, ol' mate. Just you concentrate on getting home.

Private Peters, who was on driving duty, stirred.

'Headlights up ahead,' he called out over his shoulder to Andy, spread out across the row of seats behind.

That roused him instantly. His eyes snapped open. He shook away the muddy-headed drowsiness and once more swept thoughts and worries for his family to one side.

'Kill our lights and stop!'

Peters turned the coach's lights off, brought the vehicle to a standstill and quickly turned off the engine. It was then that Andy realised he'd made a really stupid call. He was reminded of the first time he and the other engineers had encountered Carter's platoon, stranded out in the desert – and how lucky they'd been that time, not to have been shot at.

Whoever those lights belonged to had almost certainly seen them as well.

The lights on the road up ahead winked off in response. That wasn't good.

Shit.

He saw half-a-dozen muzzle flashes, and a moment later the windshield of the coach exploded. Peters jerked violently in the driver's seat – a pale blizzard of seating foam blew out of the back of his seat and fluttered down like snowflakes. He flopped forward on to the steering-wheel.

He heard Westley's voice, bellowing coarsely from a seat two rows further back. 'This is a fuckin' kill box! Everyone out!'

The firing from up the road continued, shots whistling in through the exploded windshield, down the middle of the coach as the men squeezed out of their seats and converged in the central aisle. The soldier beside Andy, scrambling towards the steps beside the driver's seat, was thrown off his feet. He heard the exhaled 'oof' of the man, winded by the chest impact, the jangle of his equipment and webbing and the crumpled thud as he hit the floor.

'Shit! They're covering the exit!' yelled Westley.

Andy, squatting on his haunches behind the ineffectual cover of the seat in front of him, looked around. They were sitting ducks in the coach.

'Out of the windows!' he shouted hoarsely.

Westley picked up on that and echoed the order with a much louder bark as he smashed the nearest window to him with the butt of his rifle.

'Come on! Fuckin' move your arses!'

Windows all along the length of the coach shattered, and the men tumbled out of the coach and landed heavily on the road outside.

Andy, being right at the front, just behind the prone form of Peters was trapped. He needed to get to his feet in order to roll out over the open frame of the window beside him, but the shots were still whistling down the coach, every now and then thudding into the head-rest beside him, blasting away another chunk of his meagre cover.

He recognised the deeper chatter of a heavy machine-gun being fired from somewhere ahead, not dissimilar to the Minimi this platoon had used to suppress the mob back in Al-Bayji to great effect. He realised he might as well be cowering behind a wet paper bag. Those high calibre rounds were having no trouble shredding their way through the coach.

He just needed a second's pause in the firing to stand half a chance.

Outside on the road, he heard the lighter clatter of the platoon's SA80s, zeroing in on the muzzle flashes up the road.

And that bought him his pause.

Shit, here we go.

Andy stood up and hurled himself out of the open frame into the darkness of the night outside. He covered his head and neck with his arms, suspecting that if a single high calibre round didn't tear the top of his head off, he would undoubtedly smash his skull out on the concrete below.

He landed on his back, instantly winded, and stunned by the impact. The flickering lights, and tracer streaks in the air just above his face, were a blurred and beautiful kaleidoscope. If his lungs hadn't been struggling so desperately to get some air back in them, this would have been a beautiful moment. He felt a hand fumble clumsily across his face and chin until it found the collar of his jacket and began to pull on it, dragging him roughly across the pitted and jagged surface of the road. By the flickering light of the muzzle flashes coming from the lads, he looked up and saw the bearded face of Mike, grimacing with the exertion, and beside him, Lance Corporal Westley calmly squirting short bursts of covering fire.

In that dreamy, stoned moment he felt like drunkenly announcing to both of them they were his *bestest bloody mates ever … no really, you guys are just the best.*

Another of the lads tumbled out from the coach above him, almost landing right on top of him.

'For fuck's sake Warren, you fucking clumsy ape!' shouted Westley, still firing.

Mike continued to drag Andy, and as they rounded the back of the coach, he felt the fog of concussion beginning to clear.

Thud!

Mike's jacket exploded with a puff of cotton lining. Andy felt a light spray of warmth on his cheeks.

'Fucking bitch!' the Texan yelled as he dropped to his knees and clutched his side.

Andy, almost match fit again, scrambled to his feet, and

pushed Mike round the corner of the coach. 'Are you hit?' he shouted.

Mike looked at him with incredulity. 'Of course I'm fucking hit!'

Andy squatted down and pulled aside Mike's jacket, lifted up his 'Nobody Fucks with Texas' T-shirt, bloodied and tattered as if a chainsaw had been rammed through it. By the wan light of the moon, he could see nothing.

'Here, I have torch,' said Erich leaning against the rear of the coach beside them. He flicked on a penlight and handed it to him.

Andy studied the wound. There was no entry hole, just a deep gash along the side of his waist. The shot had glanced down his side.

'Ah, you're bloody lucky, it's nothing, Mike.'

Mike's eyes widened. 'Nothing? Try being on the goddamned receiving end of *nothing*.'

They heard Westley bellow an order from around the corner of the coach. 'Fuck this! Pull back lads! Round the back! Now!'

A moment later, the small area of shelter which Mike, Andy and the soldier all but filled, was inundated with the rest of the platoon, rolling, diving, flopping into the narrow space; a tangle of panting, adrenalin-fried bodies.

'Jesus-effing-Christ, those cunts up the road have got us cold,' one of the men grunted between gasps.

The deep rattle of the heavy machine-gun up ahead of them ceased, as did the lighter chatter of several assault rifles.

Silence, except for the sound of laboured breathing all around him.

'Hell this is fun. We should do it again sometime,' muttered Mike.

Andy looked at Westley. 'What will they do now?'

'Shit, I don't—'

'Well, what would *you* do?'

'Outflank,' the Lance Corporal replied quickly, automatically.

Andy nodded. 'Then that's why they've gone quiet.' He

looked around at them. 'We're all jammed together on top of each other. We're dead if we stay here. We've got to make a run for it. How are you fellas for ammo?'

'I'm out,' replied a voice in the dark.

'Me too,' said another, several more of them echoed that.

'Just what's in me clip,' Westley added.

'Couple of rounds left,' said Derry, 'after that, all I got is colourful language.'

'Great,' muttered Andy.

They heard a voice calling out. It was unclear, garbled by the distance and the echo bouncing back off distant rocky peaks either side of the road.

'Shhh, hear that?' muttered the Lance Corporal. 'Anyone hear that?'

Silence, except for a gentle breeze that rustled through the shrivelled, dried trees above them on the slopes. Then they heard the faint voice calling out again, a bit clearer this time.

'That sounded English,' said Derry.

There was another long silence that settled about them, broken only by the rasping sound of their breathing, fluttering with tension.

'Hey! You guys behind the coach! Hold up!'

Andy heard one of the boys whispering, 'Is that a Yank?'

The voice again. 'You guys! You American? You British?'

Westley turned to Andy, 'For fuck's sake. They're Yanks!'

Andy cupped his hands. 'We're British! Hold your fire!'

There was no reply for a few seconds, then they heard the same man shout, 'Come out in the open where we can see you, drop your guns!'

Westley turned to Andy. 'You reckon they're pukka?'

'I don't think we've got a choice anyway. I'll go first.'

Andy took a deep breath and stood up, then with hands raised, he walked out from behind the coach, his face screwed up in anticipation of a shot slamming home. But no one fired.

He heard Westley mutter behind him, 'The fight's over lads. Come on.'

The Lance Corporal and the others emerged reluctantly, one by one, their hands raised, and their empty weapons left behind.

To Andy it felt like an eternity, exposed like that, knowing that even in the dark, whoever was out there had their cross-hairs trained on them, fingers resting lightly on triggers and watching them silently.

After a few moments, he heard the unmistakable clump of army boots walking down the road towards him. A torch snapped on, into Andy's face.

'You're British, huh?' said a deep, gravelly American voice.

'Yes.'

'How many?'

'Fuck knows. There *were* fifteen of us, before you started firing, mate,' snapped Andy.

'Shit,' said the voice behind the torch. 'Real sorry about that.'

Peters had died instantly. The opening volley hit him in the head, the throat and the chest. He was dead even before he'd slid forward on to the wheel. Private Owen on the other hand, who had been hit in the aisle inside the coach, right next to Andy, had obviously lasted a few moments longer, having pulled himself up some way towards the front, leaving a snail-trail of already drying blood behind him.

Two others were killed on the road beside the coach, Private Craig and the platoon medic, Benford.

Westley saw to them, collecting their dog-tags after Benford's opposite number in the US platoon had briefly looked them over and pronounced all four of them dead. He and the other squaddies picked them up and laid them out side by side at the edge of the road.

Andy, meanwhile, realised Mike was nowhere to be seen. He finally found the American at the back of the coach, holding Farid. The old man had taken a hit in the stomach. His pale checked shirt was almost black with blood. On his belly, a small, perfectly round hole slowly oozed blood that looked as dark as oil by torchlight. But beneath him, the pooling blood, and shreds of expelled tissue, spoke of a much larger exit wound.

Mike looked up at Andy, silently shaking his head. 'Not good,' he said quietly.

Farid stared up at Mike with glassy eyes. He spoke, but in Arabic; private words, not for either of them. He spoke in short bursts, punctuated by painful spasms that caught his breath and made him screw up his eyes and grimace.

A US soldier approached down the aisle. He pointed his torch down on to the old man's face. 'Who's the—'

'Our translator,' interrupted Andy. He didn't want to know what euphemism the young American sergeant was about to use.

'Our friend,' added Mike, looking up pointedly at him.

The sergeant seemed to have the sense not to say anything, and nodded silently. He turned round and shouted up the aisle, 'Get the medic! We got a live one here!'

Mike stroked the old man's face. 'Hey, we got some help coming. You hang in there.'

Farid focused on him and managed a faint smile. 'I know you are good man. Good man inside.'

'Just a normal guy, that's all,' said Mike. 'Save it for later, okay?'

Farid placed a bloodied hand on his arm. 'God is open door to all good men.'

The medic squeezed past Andy and crouched down to look at the old man. His examination was brief, and after gently easing the old man over and inspecting the rear wound he looked up at his sergeant, barely shook his head before saying, 'I can hit him with morphine, but that's really all I can do.'

'Do it then,' said the sergeant.

The drug had an almost instant effect, and Farid sagged, no longer tensing and flexing with the pain. He smiled. 'I see my family soon. My son …' the rest he muttered in Arabic.

'You go see your son, and your wife,' said Mike quietly.

CHAPTER 66

3.25 a.m. Local time

Southern Turkey

'You're kidding? How far away from here?' asked Andy outside.

The sergeant nodded, 'No, I'm not kidding. It's not far, just a few miles. The landing strip's not big enough for the large transport planes, shit … nowhere near long enough. But we're getting a steady stream of C130s down on it okay.'

'You guys can get us out?'

'Fuck, I don't know. We got a lot of stragglers like you, American, British, some UN troops from all over. We got planes coming in and going out like a goddamn taxi rank. It's bedlam, man. Absolute fuckin' bedlam. And then we got all sorts crowding outside the strip, civilians – Turks, Kurds, Iraqis – all wanting us to fly 'em all over the place, thinking things ain't so bad elsewhere.'

'How *are* things elsewhere? We haven't heard anything much since Tuesday.'

The sergeant looked at him with incredulity. 'You don't know?'

Andy shook his head.

'The answer is … shit. We got food riots back home. My home state's under martial law. Fuckin' internment camps everywhere. And I'm pretty sure we're doin' better back home, than most places.'

'Hear anything about Britain?'

The sergeant shook his head. 'Not much, but I heard enough to know you guys have got it pretty bad over there. It's all very fucked up.'

‘Jesus.’

‘Anyway listen, you guys get back in your coach, and I’ll have one of my boys guide you there. You don’t want to waste any time. We’re holding that strip for just a while longer, maybe until tomorrow afternoon, then that’s it, we’re bailing out of here.’

Andy turned to head back inside the coach.

‘Listen fella,’ called out the American. ‘I’m sorry about the … we just. We’ve had hostiles taking pot-shots at us all week, you know? My boys’re all strung out.’

Andy nodded but didn’t say anything. ‘Sorry’ fixed nothing. It didn’t bring back to life the four young men lying beside the road, or an old Iraqi translator.

He turned back to the truck. Westley and Derry had lifted out Farid’s body from inside the coach and placed him alongside the four young squaddies, shoulder to shoulder with them. Maybe they’d not done that consciously, or maybe they had, but it said something about these boys that made Andy feel proud to have struggled out of Iraq alongside of them.

Well done lads.

He approached Westley. ‘You okay?’

Westley nodded. ‘Bad enough losin’ your mates in a contact with the enemy …’

He left that unfinished but Andy knew what he wanted to say.

But it really stinks when you lose them to friendly fire.

‘Get the boys back inside. The Yanks are going to lead us to an airstrip nearby.’

Westley looked up. ‘Seriously?’

Andy offered him a tired smile. ‘Yeah. It looks like we’re out of here.’

CHAPTER 67

4 a.m. local time

Southern Turkey

Half an hour later, they took a turning off the main road, down a smaller road – a single lane in both directions. As they approached the airstrip it became clogged with civilians, mostly on foot, many carrying a meagre bundle of possessions on their backs or dragging it behind them.

Tajican honked the coach's horn, and slowly the vehicle edged its way through the thickening river of people towards a hastily erected spool-wire perimeter lit every few hundred yards by powerful floodlights. Behind the curls of razor wire, US marines stood, evenly spaced, guns ready and coolly regarding the growing mass of people only a few yards away from them.

The American soldier sitting beside Private Tajican urged the Fijian to keep the vehicle moving and not let it come to a complete standstill.

'They'll overrun us in seconds,' he muttered warily eyeing the surging crowd ahead and either side of them.

Andy was impressed at how Tajican calmly kept a steady forward momentum, his face locked with concentration, whilst all around him palms and fists thumped noisily against the side and front of the coach.

Something suddenly flew into the coach through the open, glassless front; a stone, a rock ... whatever it was, it glanced off Tajican's head, and he clasped a hand to the gash it had caused. Blood rolled down the back of his hand, his arm and soaked into his sleeve.

But he continued calmly driving forward.

When another projectile arced through from the front into the coach, the American soldier sitting at Tajican's side decided he'd had enough. He swung his assault rifle down and fired a long burst over the heads of the people outside.

The effect was instant. The road ahead cleared.

'Hit the fuckin' gas!' the American shouted. Tajican did just that, and the coach sped up towards the perimeter fence ahead and the entrance gate – a Humvee, parked lengthways across a twelve-foot wide gap in the razor wire. The Humvee rolled out of the way at the very last moment, allowing the coach through, and then immediately rolled back to prevent the thick gathering of people surging through in its wake.

Andy was unprepared for the level of chaos he could see around him. He had seen the inside of several US and UK army bases since he'd started doing field-work in Iraq; always a hive of activity – chaos to the untrained eye. But the disarray he witnessed before him bore no resemblance to any military camp he had seen.

The sky was still dark, but showing the first pale stain of the coming dawn. The airfield was lit by dozens of floodlights erected on tripods and deployed along the main strip. From what he could see, it was an airfield that had been mothballed in recent years, but, in the space of the last forty-eight hours, had been hurriedly revived and adapted to meet immediate needs. There was a control tower to one side of the strip. Clearly the building had, at some point in the past, been gutted of all its electronic equipment, but was now being used in an *ad hoc* way. At its base a communications truck was parked, whilst several men stood up in the observation tower monitoring the steady stream of transport planes coming in and taking off; they were using laptops that trailed thick cables out through the tower's rusty old window-frames down to the truck below.

Along the airstrip Andy could see hundreds of men, clustered in groups, most of them lying down; a patchwork quilt of exhausted soldiers, each group awaiting its turn to board a plane.

On the strip, Andy watched a Hercules C130 coming in to

land at one end, whilst at the other, another plane was awaiting its chance to take off. Halfway along the strip, on a tarmac turn-off, a plane was being hurriedly loaded up with a group of men who had been roused from their slumber and herded at the double towards the boarding ramp.

The American soldier who had guided their coach in led Andy, Mike, Erich, Westley and his men towards a tent in the middle of the airfield. A flap was pulled to one side. The clinical blue glow of half-a-dozen halogen strip lights swinging from the tent support frame amidst drooping coils of electrical flex, spilled out through the opening into the pre-dawn gloom.

They entered the tent. Standing inside, looking harried, tired, and more than ready to grab some bunk time, was a Marine colonel; a short squat man with greying crew-cut hair and leathery skin pulled tight around a pair of narrowed eyes.

'Colonel Ellory, sir. We picked these guys up on the border road. They're Brits, sir.'

Ellory turned to look at them. His eyes ran quickly across Andy and the other two civilians, and then towards Westley, looking for rank insignia. 'Okay son, where's your CO?'

Westley saluted awkwardly. 'We lost him, also our senior platoon NCO. I'm highest rank here, sir. Lance Corporal Westley.'

Colonel Ellory frowned as he worked to make sense of Westley's Geordie accent. 'You're in charge, son?'

'Yessir.'

He turned to the others, 'And you are?'

'I'm a civilian contractor, Andy Sutherland.'

'Mike Kenrick, I'm a contractor too.'

'Erich Feillebois, engineer with Ceneco Oil.'

Ellory nodded. 'Okay guys. This is how it is. We're trying to get as many of our boys home as quickly as possible. There's a limited number of planes, a limited amount of fuel. Not everyone's getting home. Priority goes to military personnel, and amongst them, priority goes to *our* boys. That's the deal, I'm afraid. I know it sounds shitty, but … well, that's how we're doing it.'

'Have you got any other British troops?' asked Andy.

'Yeah, there's a few around. We've had some stragglers rolling in over the border road. A bunch of army vehicle retrieval engineers, quite a few independent security contractors, all goddamn nationalities. A mixed bunch out there. You'll just have to take your chances with them. The Brits and the other internationals are in two separate groups down the other end of the strip.'

Colonel Ellory looked like he was pretty much done with the conversation and ready to turn his attention elsewhere.

Andy stepped in quickly. 'How long are you planning on keeping this strip open?'

Ellory sighed. 'I'd like to say, as long as it takes. But we'll keep it going until I get orders to pull the plug and get out.'

'How bad is it out there?' asked Mike.

'Out where? You mean the Middle East? Or home?'

Mike shrugged. 'We've been out of the loop.'

Ellory ran a hand through his coarse grey crew-cut. 'The Middle East is a goddamn write-off. We sent our boys into Saudi to try and save what they could. The crazy Muslim sons of bitches made for the refineries first. Pretty much destroyed most of them before we could get in there.' Ellory looked at them. 'And that's pretty fucking smart if you ask me. There's multiple redundancy in those pipelines and the wells. Not the case with their refineries. Those sons of bitches targeted exactly the right things. And it's the same deal in Kuwait and the Emirates. You ask me, this wasn't a fucking spontaneous outbreak of religious civil war. It was a goddamned organised operation. Some serious military-level planning went into this shit. They hit Venezuela, they hit the refineries in Baku. These motherfuckers knew exactly what they were doing.'

'Who? Which motherfuckers?' asked Mike.

'Shit. You kidding me?'

'Don't tell me you think it was Al-Qaeda,' Mike laughed, 'because if you—'

'Do I look like a dumbass?' Ellory shook his head. 'Of

course I don't think it's Al-Qaeda. They couldn't organise a piss in a bucket. Fuck … they're just a bunch of phantoms anyway. No. I can make an educated guess as to who's behind this shit though,' said Ellory, placing his hands on the desk in front of him and arching a stiff and tired back. 'Those sons of bitches in Iran.'

Andy nodded. It was a possibility. Perhaps they were the ones behind all of this. They had the wherewithal to pull off something on this kind of scale. And motive too.

'Yeah, I could believe they're behind this,' said Mike. 'I mean, we stalled their nuclear programme. But this … this has worked better than God knows how many nukes would have done.'

'Exactly,' said Ellory. 'They know goddamn well they can hurt the world far more this way, by hitting the most vulnerable oil chokepoints. And shit, they got us all. But I'll say this. When we get this crap fixed-up again, and mark my words, we will, they'd better run for shelter in Tehran, because we are going to bomb those fuckers back to the Jurassic.'

Andy wondered whether plans were already being drawn up to deliver some payback, or whether the US government, like every other government, was focusing on damage limitation right now. If Iran really had been behind this, Andy reflected, they'd better bloody well hope the world wasn't going to recover enough to focus its attention on them and bring some retribution to bear. Proof of their involvement, or no proof.

'Shit, we should've seen this coming.' Ellory shook his head. 'Anyway, I haven't got time to talk this crap through with you guys.' He pointed towards Andy, Westley and his men standing just outside the tent. 'You guys'll have to take your chances with the other Brits assembled at the end of the strip.' He pointed to Erich, 'And you need to get yourself down and join the international group.'

He pointed to Mike. 'You, on the other hand, you'll need to make your way over to where we've put all our civilian contractors, US nationals, defence contractors.'

Mike looked across at Andy. 'These guys have been through a lot Colonel, they—'

'I do not have the fucking time to argue the point! If we have the time and the planes, we'll get them out, but American nationals and personnel are to go first. Now if you wouldn't mind getting your ass out of my tent, I've got a million and one things to attend to,' Colonel Ellory said, offering a formal nod and then turning towards a sergeant who had entered brandishing a clipboard.

Andy turned to Westley, 'Okay then, I guess we do as the man says, and go find the other Brits.'

They walked out of the tent into the half-light, towards Wesley's platoon gathered in a loose and weary-looking huddle beneath the glow of a floodlight several dozen yards away. Erich shook hands with Andy and Mike.

'I go now,' he said quietly. 'See if I find any other French here. You stay safe, eh?'

Andy nodded, 'Safe journey, mate.'

They watched him walk away along the edge of the airstrip, past silent islands of soldiers, sitting, resting, some smoking, some sleeping.

Lance Corporal Westley walked over towards his men and got them on their feet. He left Mike and Andy standing watching the planes come and go, listening to the roar of propeller engines turning, and the distant cries and chants of the civilians massing outside the perimeter of razor wire.

'Well I guess this is where we part company, Dr Sutherland,' said Mike.

'Yeah, we'll have to get together and do this again next year.'

Mike laughed.

Andy stuck out a hand. 'I'd give you my email address, but I'm not sure there'll be an Internet when we get back home.'

'No, you're probably right,' said Mike, grabbing the offered hand and shaking it.

'But look, if it turns out this isn't actually the end of the world,' Andy continued, 'you can always get me through my website – PeakOilWatch.co.uk.'

Mike nodded. 'I'll make a point of looking you up.' He watched Westley's men preparing to move off. 'You know, for a guy that's never handled a gun before,' he said pointing towards the remnants of the platoon, 'you did a good job leading those boys out of trouble.'

Andy shook his head. 'Not good enough. Telling Peters to turn off our lights—'

'Shit like that happens, Andy. But you got the rest of these boys through, that's what counts,' said Mike, a grin flashing from his dark beard. 'You did good.'

They shared an awkward silence, not really sure what came next, but knowing there was more to be said.

'We went through a lot of stuff, these last few days, didn't we?' said Mike.

'Yes. I'm sure we should be talking it out or something, Dr Phil style.'

'There never seems to be time enough to talk. It seems like all we've done in the last three days is fight, run and drive.'

'Yeah. Anyway,' said Andy, 'I'm not sure I want to revisit any of it right now. I've got a wife and two kids to get home to.'

Mike nodded. 'If they're half as resourceful as you, they'll be just fine, Andy. Trust me.'

He shrugged. 'What about you, Mike? You must have family you're worried about.'

'Nope,' said Mike shaking his head, 'it's just me. The job always seemed to come first.'

'I guess that makes things easier.'

'A lot.'

Andy caught sight of a smear of dry blood on the American's forearm. 'I'm sorry about Farid. I'd have liked him to have made it.'

'Yeah. He made some sense, didn't he?'

'I think he did.'

'And we lost some good men back there. Lieutenant Carter, Sergeant Bolton …'

Andy nodded.

'Good soldiers,' said Mike casting a glance at Westley and his men who were beginning to head wearily down towards the end of the strip, 'all of them, good men. You Brits can put up a good fight.'

Andy smiled, 'Ahh, except I'm not a Brit.'

'You Kiwis too,' Mike replied, slapping him on the shoulder.

'Take care Mike. I hope things aren't as fucked up for you back home as I suspect they are for us.'

'This mess will right itself eventually.'

'I'm not so confident.'

CHAPTER 68

4.05 a.m. GMT

Paul drove for several hours down the M6, bypassing Birmingham in the dark, marked not by city lights or the ever-present amber-tinged glow of urban light pollution bouncing off the night sky, but by the sporadic intervals of buildings on fire and the flickering movement of people around them.

Parts of Coventry, on the other hand, seemed to have power; they drove along a deserted section of dual carriageway that was fully lit by the arc sodium lights along the central island. To Jenny's eyes the distribution of power seemed almost haphazard, as if some central switchboard had been overrun by monkeys who were now randomly punching the shiny buttons in front of them. She'd thought there might have been an even-handed distribution of powered time-slots, or if not that, then certain 'safe' regions – a little unfairly maybe – which would be allocated a constant supply of power to the detriment of the lost-cause big cities.

But no. There seemed to be no discernible pattern at all to it.

South of Coventry, the lights along the motorway went out and they once again adjusted to the pitch-black of night. Paul spotted a sign for a Travelodge ahead and swung Mr Stewart's car down the slip-road as it came up.

'What are you doing?' asked Jenny.

'I need to sleep. I've not slept since Monday night. It would be stupid if having made our escape earlier, we end up wrapping ourselves around the central barrier on the motorway.'

Jenny nodded. It made sense.

'Let's give it a look. If it's surrounded by a baying mob, then we'll push on, all right?'

They drove off the slip-road into an empty car-park in front of the motel. There were tell-tale signs that similar things had happened here as at Beauford Service Station; bits and pieces scattered across the parking area, some broken windows in the lobby at the front of the building, but that was all. The Little Chef next door to it on the other hand, looked like it had been more thoroughly seen to, every window smashed and a trail of detritus and trampled goods strewn in front of it.

'Well, seems like whatever happened here has been and gone,' said Paul.

'I suppose everywhere that can be looted for food and drink has been emptied by now,' said Jenny. 'I wonder when all that's been gobbled up, what people will do for food?'

'I'm sure we'll start seeing troops or police on the streets sometime today. It's got to happen today,' he said with less conviction than the last time he'd bullishly asserted things would right themselves quickly. He swung the car round and parked it just outside the entrance to the motel.

'It seems okay to me.'

Jenny looked up at the two floors of dark little curtained windows. It would be nice to have a bed to sleep on, and the chance of stumbling across any wandering bands of thirst-maddened crazies here appeared to be acceptably remote.

There was no sign of anyone here and she wondered where exactly everyone was. Sixty-five million people on such a small island and since leaving Beauford Services, she'd seen hardly any.

They're all tucked away in their homes waiting this out. Only fools like us and those with bad intentions are outside, roaming around.

Paul climbed out of the car and led the way inside. It was dark, of course. Pitch-black inside, with no ambient light from any source at all coming in through the cracked smoked-glass at the front.

'Hang on,' she heard him murmur, and a moment later, a pale square of light lit the foyer up dimly.

'What's that?' she asked.

'My organiser.'

'Clever.'

In the absence of any other light, it was surprisingly bright.

'Okay … stairs,' said Paul. She watched the pale square of light float across in front of the reception desk towards a doorway, 'Over here,' she heard him say.

She followed him through, up one flight of stairs, through another door, and then they were standing in a corridor.

'You seem to know your way around this one,' she said.

'They're all very similar. And I use them quite a lot. Right then, first floor rooms. You choose.'

Jenny walked down the corridor, passing a door that was open. Jagged splinters of wood jutting out from the door-frame told her the door had been forced. She didn't want to sleep in a room that had been picked over by someone. That just somehow felt … *clammy*. The next door along had also been kicked in, and the next. Finally towards the end of the corridor, she found a door that remained intact, locked. 'I'll have this one,' she said.

'You're okay being alone? I spotted another locked one on the other side, up the far end. I can take that one.'

Jenny stopped to think about that. She wasn't entirely sure she wanted to spend the night sleeping in the same room as this guy, but then … being alone down one end of the corridor, in a deserted motel.

'Okay, maybe we should share this one.'

'I think that makes sense,' said Paul.

He lifted his organiser up towards the door to read the room number. 'How does Room 23 sound?'

With one well-aimed kick at the swipe-card door lock, the door swung in and banged off the wall inside; the noise echoed disturbingly down the empty corridor.

Inside, it was how she hoped she'd find it, undisturbed,

cleaned, bed made for the next customer. She opened the curtain and the blind behind it, then swung open the window. The room was hot, and a faint breeze wafted in.

In the sky the grey light of dawn was beginning to provide enough natural light for them to find their way around. Paul quickly turned his organiser off and pocketed it.

'Okay then, sleep,' said Jenny, sitting down on the bed; a double bed.

Paul pulled open a cabinet door to reveal a drinks fridge. 'A-hah. We're in luck.' Inside he found it decently stocked. 'There's several cans of Coke, ginger beer, tonic water, and a pleasing range of mini-liquors: vodka, gin, rum, whisky. Some beer even.'

Jenny smiled in the pale grey gloom of dawn. After the recent hours, the last few days, a single stiff rum and Coke would be absolutely what the doctor ordered, even if it was going to be warm and without ice.

'I'll have a rum and Coke, please.'

'Good choice, Ma'am,' said Paul. She heard the pop and hiss of the Coke can, the click of a lid being twisted off and the gurgle of the rum being poured.

'Here.'

The first one was a strong one. The second drink she asked for she wanted weak, but Paul's definition of 'weak' didn't seem to square with hers.

'So, you mentioned something a while back,' said Paul, 'about your hubby *predicting* this?'

'Well, sort of. He wrote a report a while back … lemme see, yeah it was back in 1999, because that was the year we did Christmas in New York. It was an academic paper really, he wrote most of it when he was at university in the States, but then when he got commissioned to write it again, he did some new research and updated chunks of it with new data he'd managed to track down.'

'And it was about this whole thing?'

'Well, sort of I suppose. Andy was very secretive about it,

client confidentiality kind of thing. But I know it had something to with Peak Oil, and our growing reliance on fewer and fewer major oil reserves, and how that made us much more vulnerable to someone needing only to disable a few places around the world to hold us all to ransom. He described how it could be done … which were the most vulnerable places … that sort of thing.'

And that's where Andy's obsession had truly began. Wasn't it?

The people who'd commissioned his work had paid him good money for that. Very good money – enough that they bought that house of theirs outright, and money left over that they were able to put both kids through fee-paying schools.

'But after doing that job, you know … he started changing. Became I guess … edgy, very serious. He spent too much time obsessing about the whole Peak Oil thing. And a little paranoid too. Just silly little things like worrying about viruses on his computer that might be spying on him, noises on the phone line. Daft really. I don't know, he used to be so much fun. Great company. And then, like I say, he changed after New York. And it's been a slow steady roll downhill ever since. So much so, in fact, I was actually in the middle of organising our big split-up when this happened.'

'That's too bad,' said Paul. 'So, where is he now?'

'Somewhere in Iraq. He's been getting regular assignments there for the last few years. He was over there when this started. And my kids are alone in London.'

Jenny's voice caught.

Shit, I should know by now drink does this to me.

'You okay?' Paul asked, placing a hand on her shoulder and squeezing gently.

'Of course I'm not. I just want to get home. They need me.'

His arm slid across one shoulder, across her neck to the other. 'Don't worry Jen, I'll get you home safe and sound. I've got you this far haven't I?'

She felt the tips of his fingers slide under her chin, lifting her face up to look at him, and it was then that she knew where this was going.

'Look, I … errr … I think I've had enough to drink.'

'You're kidding right? There's loads more, and Christ we deserve it after the shit we've been through together. What do you say?'

'I think we've probably both had too much. We need to keep our wits about us, right? Who knows what might happen tomorrow?'

Jenny swung her legs off the bed. 'And you know what? I might try one of the other rooms—'

A hand wrapped around her forearm. 'Why? What's up?'

It was a tight, urgent grip, and it hurt a little.

'Look, I just think it's a good idea, okay?'

'What? Come on. We're just talking here. No harm done.'

'Can you let go please?'

His grip remained firm. 'I've been looking out for you these last few days. It's not too much to bloody ask is it? A little … conversation?'

She could hear the slightest slur in his voice. He wasn't pissed as such, just a little tipsy. No worse than the couple of come-ons she'd fended off at the last office Christmas party she'd been to; harmless enough somewhere crowded, but a little disconcerting, alone like this.

'I've been looking out for you,' said Paul again. 'Not asking much, for Chrissakes.'

'I think Ruth looked out for me a little more than you did,' she replied, and almost immediately wished she hadn't.

'Fuck you,' he snarled.

'Would you mind letting go please?'

He let her go, and she headed for the door. 'I'll see you in a few hours, when you've sobered up.'

She stepped out into the corridor, and strode through the darkness of it, the only light, the faintest pre-dawn grey coming in through a window at the far end. She picked a doorway halfway down on the right. It was a door that had been forced by someone, and as she stepped in, she could see that the room had been hunted through and the drinks cabinet emptied.

Good, hopefully all the other cabinets in this place are empty too.

She'd hate to see what Paul was like when he was fully loaded.

Jenny pushed the door shut behind her. And as an after-thought, she pulled the armchair in the corner of the room across the doorway. Not that she thought it was entirely necessary. Paul was like the other office Romeos; emboldened a little by the booze, but still essentially a coward. A sharp 'no', or a 'piss off', did the trick for the likes of them … most of the time.

No … he'd probably drink himself into a stupor and fall asleep trying to whack himself off.

She lay down on the bed and then felt the tears coming – worried about Jacob and Leona, and Andy too, realising she'd been so wrong in the way she had treated him. She wished the robust, no-shit-taken Ruth was here with her right now, talking some good plain common sense, probably making her laugh too. If Ruth were here, they'd probably be raiding the drinks cabinet together right now and shamelessly taking the mickey out of Paul.

Jenny closed her eyes and was asleep within a minute.

CHAPTER 69

6.29 a.m. GMT

It was lighter when she opened her eyes again, fully daylight now. Jenny guessed she must have managed to get over an hour's sleep. A shard of sunlight streamed through the gap in the curtain, across the bed and on to the carpet.

Her head ached slightly, the mildest of hangovers, and more probably attributable to her general fatigue than the two generous rum and Cokes she'd had earlier. Paul would be feeling a lot worse this morning, deservedly. She was going to have to drive this morning instead.

The smell of alcohol on her breath seemed to be strong, very strong. There must have been a hell of a lot of rum in that drink for it to still be on her breath like that. She decided she was fit enough to get up and start rousing Paul. That was probably going to take a little time.

She started to sit up, and then saw him.

He was standing beside the bed, silently staring down at her.

'What the—'

'Took me ages to find you,' he said, his voice thick and slurred. He was swaying slightly. 'Thought you'd gone up a floor, didn't I? But here you were all along, just down the way from me.'

He was pissed out of his skull. He must have found another cabinet full of booze.

'What are you doing in here?'

He reached a hand out and grabbed her. 'For fuck's sake! Why d'you have to be such a stuffy bitch!'

Jenny pulled his hand off her shoulder, his fingernails raking across her skin. 'We were havin' a nice drink, we're both grown-up. There's no bloody law against you and me, you know ...'

'Paul. Look, I'm grateful for you finding a way out of that service station ... but it doesn't mean I want to sleep with you, okay?' said Jenny, shifting slowly past him towards the end of the bed.

Paul watched her moving, his head slowly turning, one hand reaching out for a wall to steady himself. 'Well what about what I *deserve*? I've been good ... looked after you. Could've jumped you anytime ... but I didn't. Been a perfect bloody gentleman, actch-erley.'

'Yes, you have,' Jenny replied slowly, beginning to rise from the bed. 'And you don't want to ruin that good behaviour now, do you?'

'Just want a shag ... that such a big fucking crime?' he announced loudly, angrily.

'It is a crime Paul, if the person you want to *shag*, doesn't want to shag *you*.'

He nodded and laughed. 'Oh ... see what you mean.' He took a couple of steps towards her, successfully blocking the doorway out of the room. 'So, what's so wrong with me? I'm what? Five or six years younger than you? I got all my hair,' he paused for a moment, gathering his thoughts, and reaching out again for a wall to steady him, 'not a fat bastard like most blokes ... wear nice clothes. Shit, I'm top salesman at Medi-Tech Supplies UK ... meaning I'm a rich bastard.' He looked at her, arching his eyebrows curiously. 'None of that good enough for you then?'

'No. Because right now, sex is the last thing on my mind.'

He recoiled, hurt, irritated. 'Guess you *are* ... a stuck-up bitch, then. Thought you were a sport ... stupid me,' he said, taking a step forward. 'You know, it's been a lo-o-o-ong time ... for me, a long time. My ex was a fuckin' tease, ripping me off, spending my money, never let me near her though. Bitch. I thought you were different. Not another fuckin' tease.'

Jenny pulled herself back on to the bed, there was no room to step past him. 'Rape's a crime, Paul,' she said, knowing full well she wasn't going to be able to reason with him. 'Even now, whilst everything's a mess out there, it's still a crime.'

Paul giggled. 'Oh, right ... well you know what? I think this week in particular ... maybe the *normal rules* don't apply. I think, that's what everyone else has figured out too. Know what I'm saying?'

Jenny shook her head.

'That's why everyone's behaving so *un-British*. Eh?' He giggled again. 'No rules this week, ladies and gents ... so you'll have to amuse yourselves till normal service can be resumed.'

'Come on. Let's forget about this. You go lie down and sleep it off. And then we'll get going down to London, when you're feeling fit enough to travel.'

He pursed his lips, thinking about that for a moment.

Jenny realised how silly she'd been to allow herself to wind up in this situation; alone with a man who was essentially a stranger, who was drunk, during a chaotic and lawless time like this. She should have guessed that at some point travelling with him, there would end up being a moment like this.

'Sorry love ... need a shag ... you'll fucking well do.'

He took another step towards her. Jenny kept her distance, retreating back across the bed, putting her feet on the floor on the far side.

'Think what you're doing,' she said. She hated the wavering, shrill sound creeping into her voice; it was a pleading, begging tone. To his ears that was going to sound like submission.

He smiled as he started to unbuckle his belt. 'Maybe a fucking crime, love, but who's going to know now, eh?'

He put a foot on the bed and stepped up on to it, wobbling precariously. 'Here's Jo-o-o-n-n-y!!' he announced excitedly peeling his shirt off.

Sod this.

Jenny leant forward and slapped him hard across the face. It was more a punch than a slap. Her hand had been balled up into a fist. He fell backwards, rolling off the bed on to the floor with a heavy thump.

Not waiting around to see if that was a KO, or merely going to buy her a few seconds, she ran around the end of the bed and out of the room into the corridor.

What now?

She had decked him. But now she could hear him struggling to his feet. 'You fucking bitch!' she heard him shouting inside the room. 'I'm going to bloody well get you!'

'Who's going to know now … eh?'

Those words chilled her. It meant the bastard had crossed a line. He was beginning to realise what every other potential rapist … bully … abuser … *murderer* … must be aware of. Here was a window of time in which he could do whatever he wanted, indulge *any* fantasy, certain in the knowledge that when – if – order was restored again, evidence of his deed would be untraceable; lost amidst the chaotic aftermath.

And I'd be that evidence …

She could imagine … her body stuffed in a cupboard somewhere in this motel, perhaps never to be discovered, or maybe chanced upon months from now when the clear-up operation began in earnest.

Paul? He'd do something like that?

Possibly. She didn't really know him at all.

She heard him stumbling across her room, into that armchair, cursing.

What now, come on … what now?

Jenny decided to go for the car and leave him behind. She really couldn't trust him now, not even if he got down on his knees this instant and pleaded for her forgiveness, and swore he'd never even look sideways at her again.

Up the corridor for the stairs down –

'Shit, the keys,' she whispered.

Paul had them in his room, and she knew exactly where they were; sitting on the little writing-desk, next to the television. She remembered seeing him tossing them on there when they entered the room, by the light of his palm pilot.

She ran down the corridor to the open door of his room, 23.

Behind her, he staggered out, calling after her every name he could drunkenly think of.

She stepped into the room, over to the writing-desk. They weren't there.

'No ... no,' she muttered, a desperate panic beginning to get a hold of her. She could hear him lurching up the corridor towards her, weaving from side to side, pissed out of his tiny little mind. Jenny decided she could probably take him on. He was all over the place, his judgement and reaction time shot to hell. But he had the ace card, as all men do over women – brute strength. If he got a good grip on her, it wouldn't matter how much faster she could move. It wouldn't matter one bit – brute strength was everything.

'Come on, come on!' she hissed. 'Where are they?'

She looked all over the desk, trying both of the drawers, before finally spotting them on the floor. He must have knocked them off during the last few hours, during his binge. She scooped the keys up into one hand and was turning to leave just as he appeared in the doorway.

'A-ha!' he grinned and wagged a finger at her. 'I got you!' he cheerfully announced in a sing-song voice as if they were playing a game of playground tag.

'Paul,' she tried a scolding tone, 'this is unacceptable.'

He laughed. 'What are you? ... My mum?'

He started towards her. Jenny realised this might be the last opportunity left to her, to catch him off guard. She ducked down low and charged towards him, crashing into him like a battering-ram, sending them both out through the doorway into the corridor, sprawling on to the floor together.

He was winded, but he still managed to grunt, 'Bitch, bitch, bitch', his hands scrabbling to get a firm hold of both of her arms, which she was frantically flailing, landing soft ineffectual blows on his face; slaps, scratches and punches that were achieving nothing.

He swung a leg over hers, instantly trapping them both in a vice-like grip on the floor.

Oh God, he's getting hold of me.

She kept her hands and arms moving, but he managed to grab one wrist, and then very quickly the other. He rolled over, moving his body weight on top of hers, his face – stinking of every different liquor that could be found in the cabinet – was close to hers; close enough that the tip of his nose was touching her cheek.

'Why the fuck … was this … such a big problem, eh?' he whispered.

She struggled. There was no answer she could give that he'd understand.

'Eh? I just wanted a one-night stand. You'd have … had a good time too. Now … look at us.'

Jenny realised she had one last chance.

She turned her head towards him, towards that breath, towards that face of his; a face at any other time, under different circumstances, from a distance, she might have even thought was vaguely attractive, but instead was now a vicious, snarling mask – one hundred per cent frustrated testosterone. Fighting to keep the sense of revulsion and anger inside; struggling to produce something that was almost impossible right now …

She managed to smile.

'All right then, let's do it,' she whispered.

As if she'd uttered a magic password, the effect was almost instant. The thigh-hold he had on her legs loosened.

'You sure about that?' he muttered, his voice suddenly changed, the anger gone and now, in its place the considerate tone of a gentleman seeking consent.

Jenny struggled to keep the solicitous smile on her face and nodded.

He let go of one of her wrists, his hand travelling down to the zip on his trousers.

Her loose hand could punch him right now, scratch him, jab at one of his eyes. But she decided that just wasn't going to be enough. She needed to really incapacitate him with something much more effective.

She head-butted him. Her forehead smacked hard against the bridge of his nose and she heard it crunch and crackle.

He rolled off her, both hands now on his face, blood instantly beginning to stream down over his lips on to his chin. Jenny was up on her feet and running before the shock of the blow had subsided enough for Paul to let loose the first enraged howl of pain.

Two-thirds of the way down the corridor was the entrance to the stairs. She flew down them, out into the foyer, through the doorway into the morning light and was heading towards Mr Stewart's car before she allowed herself to believe that she had actually managed to escape him.

The car fob made it easy to single out the key from the rest on the key-ring. The headlights flashed and the car squawked as she unlocked it and quickly hopped inside.

She wasn't going to scramble to insert the ignition key as danger raced towards her, as she'd seen in countless teen slasher movies. No. She sensibly locked the car first; all four doors responded simultaneously, securing themselves with a reassuring *thock!*

Through the windscreen she suddenly saw Paul, emerging from the foyer of the hotel, a crimson stream of blood down his nice, expensive shirt, one hand cradling his broken nose, the other waving frantically at her to stop.

She started the engine.

He rushed over to the car. If he'd had a bat or a brick in his hand, she would have thrown the car into reverse and got the hell out of there before he could even try and smash his way in. But he didn't. All he had were his two soft office-hands – good for tapping out emails on a Blackberry organiser, or shaking on a big deal – but not quite so good for smashing, bare-knuckled, through a windscreen.

He splayed his hand out on the driver-side window. 'Jesus! I'm sorry Jenny. I'm really, really sorry!' The thick slur was gone now, the adrenalin rush had instantly sobered him up. His snarling manner, now one of genuine regret.

She looked at him through the glass, and shook her head.

'Please! I … it was the drink,' he pleaded, 'I'm … I've worked it off now! I don't know what the hell came over me!'

His splayed hand was leaving blood smears on the window.

'Come on Jen … we've got to stick together … you and me. It's a … it's a jungle out there!'

That's right.

She felt a pang of guilt as she threw the car into reverse and pulled out of the parking slot. He stumbled after her. She could hear him calling, pleading, bleating, over the whine of the engine and the sound of her crunching the gears into first. But there was no way she could feel safe again with him – booze or no booze. She spun the steering-wheel round and headed towards a sign pointing towards the slip-road that led on to the M6, southbound.

CHAPTER 70

12.31 a.m. EST

New York, USA

The line connected. There was a solitary ring before it was answered by a male voice.

'Cornell and Watson Financial Services, how can I help you?'

'I want to book an appointment,' he replied quickly.

'I'm afraid we're booked up for the foreseeable future, sir.'

'How about Christmas Day?'

A pause. 'What time sir?'

He sighed. 'A minute past midnight.'

'One minute.'

It was a necessary ritual. They were as much at risk of being exposed and destroyed by *them*; more so in fact, since their resources were dwarfed by those of their quarry. The agency was small, tiny in fact … a staff of no more than about thirty agents operating out of the rear offices of a discreet back-street firm in New York. The firm, seemingly, offered walk-in financial services, but never quite seemed to be able to fit an appointment in to anyone who might actually walk in off the street.

He heard a male voice. 'Jesus! We thought you were dead! We've been trying to contact you since Tuesday!'

'If you must know, Jim, I've been through a shitting war zone. My—'

'No names remember.'

'My fucking sat' phone got blown to pieces on Tuesday, and I've been shot at God knows how many times since—'

'We've had a breakthrough. A huge goddamn solid gold breakthrough.'

'—this whole crazy thing … Breakthrough? What are you talking about?'

'Our target, the one you're with right now … he's not who we want.'

'Well I'm not with him right now, not any more. We got separated. I'm waiting for the military to find me space on a flight out of Turkey right now.'

'It's his *daughter*. It's the target's daughter.'

'What? What the hell are you talking about?'

'We think she could be able to identify one or more of *them*.'

He suddenly found his pulse racing. 'You're shitting me. What's happened?'

'She called him on his cell, Tuesday morning. Christ, you might have even seen him take the call.'

He tried to think back. Tuesday morning, they'd been fighting for their lives in that pink compound, all hell breaking loose. He couldn't specifically remember Sutherland taking any calls, but then that whole day was a jumble of blurred, panic-stricken memories.

'And listen, we think she saw *several* of *them*.'

'Several? Several of the One Hundred and Sixty?'

'No, better than that … several of the Twelve.'

'My God!' He looked anxiously around the communications tent. No one was close enough to hear him talking, no one was even watching. The soldiers were all too busy holding the razor-wire perimeter or hustling. He spoke more quietly all the same. 'We have to find her.'

'I know, we have to re-deploy very quickly. *They* may know what we know. They might even be closing in on her as we speak.'

'We've got to try.'

'Yes.'

'She's in England?'

'That's right, London.'

'I can try and swing the next plane out of here heading that way. I'll do it somehow. Can you get some more assets on the ground over there?'

'It'll be difficult under current circumstances. We might be able to fly a couple of men in to help you.'

'Do it. Do it now.'

'We will.'

Mike was about to hang up; the Marine colonel had said he had just a couple of minutes, no more.

'What's it like there?'

'Here? New York? It's shit. The place is falling apart, just like everywhere else. We get power for a couple of hours a day, and there are riots everywhere. Not good.'

CHAPTER 71

7.31 a.m. GMT
Guildford

Ash was awake with the first light of dawn. The thought of spending another twenty-four hours in Kate's apartment, waiting for her to show up, was an agonising prospect. He had the patience of a saint, if he was waiting on a certainty, but this was a long shot. This woman might never return.

But she would try, wouldn't she? It's the homing instinct. In a time of crisis, that's exactly where everyone tries to get – home.

And the delay could be quite legitimately rationalised. Tuesday afternoon things went pear-shaped. Kate would have decided after seeing the riots, and finding out the trains weren't running, to camp out at work overnight. Wednesday came – she'd have been hoping the police had restored order, and perhaps a limited train service had returned. But there'd been no sign of that. There's a canteen at work maybe? So another night camping there, basic food and drink laid on. Thursday, same thing again. Only by then the canteen would be running low on food, and everyone would be getting very anxious to return home. There'd still be no news on the radio, and no sign of police retaking the streets. Friday, it'd be obvious to her and her colleagues they couldn't stay there forever, the rioting must have died down once everything that could be looted, had been looted.

At some point today, Ash decided, she'll set off for home, walking with other wary pedestrians along the main arteries out of London. It'll take her seven, eight maybe nine hours on foot? Provided nothing stops or delays her.

She'll arrive sometime today.

That sounded very much like wishful thinking to Ash. But there was not a lot else he could consider doing. Perhaps, he could return to the Sutherlands' house and wait there? Pointless … Sutherland had warned her to stay well away. There were many other names in the phone book he could try, one by one. But most of the places – he'd looked them up on a road map he had found by Kate's telephone table – were a long way out of London.

He decided the best course of action would be to hang on until tomorrow. And then if she still hadn't turned up, he would camp out at the Sutherland home. Sutherland's daughter, or his wife, or even the man himself might come by, just to pick up one or two essentials … that ol' homing instinct was very, very strong.

Yes, that would do then. First thing tomorrow morning, Ash decided he'd head back up.

CHAPTER 72

7.51 a.m. GMT

Shepherd's Bush, London

'Please don't go outside Lee!' Jacob whimpered, putting down his knife and fork heavily. They clattered noisily against the plate, and on to the dining-table. He hopped off his chair, scurried round the table and held on to her arm. 'Please don't go!'

She looked down at her little brother, his face crumpled with worry.

'Look Jakey, it's safe right now. They only come out at night, the Bad Boys. We're perfectly safe in the daytime,' she said, not entirely convinced by her own assurance.

'But last time you went out, you were gone for ever. I thought … I thought you were … dead.'

'I'll be fine, Jake. I'm just going to check on our neighbours, that's all. You can watch me out of the window of Jill's bedroom, okay? Keep an eye on me as I do the rounds.'

Jacob stared at her silently. His face looked unhealthily pale and unnaturally older; skin rumpled with the bumps, grooves and lines of unceasing worry. She wondered if he had a suspicion of what had happened to Dan. If he'd guessed that he must be lying dead down some back-street …

Don't do this Leona, think about something, anything, else.

Now really wouldn't be a good time to fold and start sobbing, not whilst she was trying to settle down Jake's jangling nerves.

'I'll be fine. Now, let's both finish our pilchards, okay?'

She wanted to check on the DiMarcios' house, a few doors up. The DiMarcios' next-door neighbours had been broken into last night. Leona had heard the noises; very unsettling, chilling noises. It had all proved too much for her and she had scooped Jacob up and taken him into the back room to sleep, where the sounds of the house being ransacked were, at least, muted.

Shortly after they had finished their breakfast she stepped out of the front door, and her heart skipped a beat; she spotted gouge-marks in the green paint on the front door, around the lock. Someone had been working on it, trying to jimmy the door quietly. She wondered if it had been one or two of the gang members discreetly hoping to break into a house on their own, whilst their colleagues were busy elsewhere? Or someone else?

Either way, it suggested their turn was approaching, if not next, then soon. The thought of them, all of them, the bad boys, streaming into the house, raucous shouts, smashing, grabbing … and finding Jacob, and finding her …?

Time was running out.

She desperately wanted to locate some other people they could group together with. She'd be more than ready to share the tinned food and bottles of water they had left. It wouldn't last them quite so long, but she would happily trade a week's sustenance for some others that she could feel safe with; preferably adults, older adults.

Leona found herself remembering a childhood fantasy she'd once had: living in a world populated only by teenagers – the beautiful people, young, alive, energetic and fun. It was an essay she'd written at school. A world that was one long party, nobody to boss them around, no parents to tell them what time the party had to end, or to turn the music down, or how much they were allowed to drink, or getting them up early the next morning so they wouldn't be late for school or college.

She laughed weakly. Well, that was it, she'd witnessed that little fantasy of hers being played out in the avenue over the last few nights. But it was no fantasy – it was a nightmare, and it reminded her of a book on the required reading list for her English Literature A-level.

Lord of the Flies.

She headed down the short path, out through the gate and

on to St Stephen's Avenue. The casually discarded refuse was beginning to build up now. Not just discarded bottles and cans, but broken pieces of furniture, smashed crockery. A mattress lay in the middle of the street, stained with drink, some blood, and other things she didn't want to think about.

It was their sex-pit.

That's where they were doing it, with their gang girls, their Smurfettes.

The house to the right of the DiMarcios' had been 'done' by the gang; that much she knew already. She'd seen them breaking into it last night. But her heart sank as she approached the DiMarcios' home. They had been paid a visit as well. Leona had been hoping to hook up with them. She liked Mr and Mrs DiMarcio, trusted them even. Mr DiMarcio, Eduardo, was a cab-driver, a big round man originally from southern Portugal, whose laugh was loud and infectious. He was fun. But she also knew he could handle himself. Last year he'd caught a couple of lads trying to break into a car parked down this street; boys from the rough White City estate nearby who'd spotted this avenue as a soft target and started to prey on it. Mr DiMarcio had handed out a hiding to them both. She vaguely recalled the boys had tried to press assault charges, but she wasn't sure it had got anywhere close to going to court. By contrast, Mrs DiMarcio was slim, always well-groomed and came across as very cultured, well-educated. Leona wished she'd accepted their offer to take her and Jacob away from all this on Tuesday, even though it might have meant the chance of missing Mum or Dad coming home.

The DiMarcios' front door had been smashed open.

She knew they hadn't been away. Leona had seen the curtain twitching on Wednesday.

She wondered whether they had managed to escape; perhaps when the house next door was being ransacked they had decided the smart thing to do was to leave their house, to creep out, hopefully to find someone further up the street who would take them in. If they'd come knocking on her door, she would have opened it to them in a heartbeat.

She looked round, diagonally across the avenue back towards Jill's house. Upstairs she could see the little blonde tuft of Jacob's head looking out at her. He waved. She waved back and then stepped up the DiMarcios' path and in through the open front door.

The mess inside was horrendous. The floor was strewn with broken things; plates, dishes, expensive-looking crockery, Mrs DiMarcio's beloved china cats. The walls were gouged, scratched and scuffed, ragged strips of their lovely expensive wallpaper had been torn away, graffiti sprayed here and there.

In their kitchen, it was obvious the room had been stripped clean of anything remotely edible or drinkable. The Bad Boys had been through it like a horde of locusts.

Leona was relieved not to have found any signs of violence done to the family, so far. She quickly checked through their lounge and dining-room which opened on to a conservatory and a small area of decking beyond that. Everything was dislodged, moved, overturned or broken.

With a growing sense of relief that they had vacated before the Bad Boys had arrived, she decided she had to at least take a quick look upstairs. She needed to know that they'd got out okay. She took the stairs quickly, not wanting to spook herself by taking one at a time and cringing with each creak.

She jogged up to the top of the stairs. Only to find Mr DiMarcio's thick, rounded legs sticking out of the doorway to their bedroom.

'Oh God, no,' Leona whimpered. She took a few quick steps across the landing towards his body and saw the rest of him lying in the doorway. His head was battered and bruised. His face almost unrecognisable with swellings and bumps and abrasions. But he had probably died of blood loss from the stab wounds. There were several of them on his chest, his lower arms, his hands.

He was fighting them off with his fists.

She could imagine him doing that, throwing big hard punches at them, flailing at them furiously, shouting curses at them in

Portuguese. But they'd brought him down with their knives; slashing at him, like a pack of dogs bringing down a bear.

'Oh, Mr DiMarcio,' she whispered.

She knew he would have only fought like that to defend his wife. With a heavy heart she could guess what she was going to find in the bedroom if she stepped over his body and looked inside. She resolved not to go in, but looking up at the wall opposite the doorway, she caught sight of Mrs DiMarcio's bare legs in a cracked mirror on a chest of drawers. Her bare legs, scratched and bruised, and blood, dark and dried on the bed-sheet beneath.

She felt a momentary rush of nausea. It passed quickly, swept aside by an overpowering surge of rage.

'You fucking bastards!' she found herself hissing angrily. She knew if she had a gun in her hand now, and one of those evil little shits was cowering in front of her, she'd be able to pull the trigger.

'You fucking bastards!' she screamed angrily. Her voice bounced back at her off the walls, and then it was silent.

Except it wasn't.

She heard movement. Someone was upstairs with her, and, probably startled by her cry, had been thrown off balance and kicked something by accident that rolled noisily across the parquet floor in the next room and came to a rest.

Oh shit, oh God, oh fuck.

Run? Yes.

She turned quickly, stepping across Mr DiMarcio's feet and heading for the top of the stairs. She bounded down them, nearly losing her footing and taking a tumble. At the bottom of the stairs she chanced a look back up but saw nothing, and heard nothing either. She headed towards the open front door and out into the morning sunlight.

She sprinted across the street, weaving around the broken furniture towards Jill's house. As she reached the gate, she chanced another look back, and saw a curtain upstairs twitch ever so slightly.

Oh my God, someone was in there with me.

She hammered on the door with the palm of her hand, and a moment later heard the bolt slide and it creaked open.

'W-what happened Lee?' asked Jacob.

She looked at him and realised the time had come to start levelling with her little brother.

'We're going to have to defend ourselves Jake.'

He said nothing.

'Okay ... okay,' she gasped, her mind racing. 'You saw that film, *Home Alone*, right?'

He nodded.

'Well like that, booby traps and stuff, okay? Just like the film ... just in case the Bad Boys try coming in here.'

'They won't, will they?'

Leona found she was too tired and too frightened to even try putting an optimistic spin on this. If they were coming tonight, Jacob needed to know.

'Tonight they might.'

He didn't go into hysterics as she thought he might. He simply nodded and said quietly, 'Okay, let's get ready for them.'

CHAPTER 73

4.23 p.m. GMT

Outskirts of London

South of Coventry there had been a roadblock on the M1 which had forced Jenny to take a roundabout route along some A roads clogged with abandoned cars, coaches and container trucks, and one or two B roads – some plugged with discarded vehicles and utterly impassable. She'd got lost at least twice before eventually finding her way back on to the motorway heading into London. She had wasted most of the day, cursing and crying with frustration as time ticked by and she seemed not to be getting any closer to her children. The arrow on the fuel of Mr Stewart's car had been wobbling uncertainly over 'empty' for the last hour. Finding the M1 again cheered her up and seeing the distant sprawl of London ahead, lifted her spirits further … until she came across yet another roadblock.

Jenny slowed down as soon as she saw it; a barrier across the M1 and the slip-roads leading on to the M25. It was comprised of triangular blocks of concrete laid side by side, designed to prevent any kind of vehicle smashing through. Behind that was a barrier of barbed wire. And behind that, several dozen soldiers watched her approaching slowly.

She came to a halt in front of the concrete blocks, and climbed out.

'You can't come through. I'm sorry, love,' shouted one of the soldiers across the barricade.

Jenny felt her shoulders wilt with fatigue and despair. 'Why not?' she called out.

'Orders.'

‘Oh come on,’ she cried, ‘what orders?’

‘We’re not to let anyone through, either way, in or out of London,’ the soldier replied.

‘Why?’

The soldier shrugged. ‘Those are our orders, love.’

She felt anger welling up inside her. It erupted so quickly it caught her by surprise. ‘For fuck’s sake! You idiots are sitting here with your thumbs up your arses, and out there,’ she pointed back up the motorway, ‘people are killing each other for water and food.’

The soldier said nothing, his face impassive.

‘It’s like the end of the world out there! Women being raped, people fighting, killing. And you’re doing nothing! Just sitting here!’

The soldier continued to stare silently at her, but then finally, perhaps feeling she deserved some kind of response, he said, ‘I know it’s rough, love. My advice … just go back home, sit tight, and wait for this situation to work itself out.’

‘I’m trying to bloody well do that!’ She pointed to the city skyline behind them. ‘I live there! I just want to get home to my children. Please let me through … please,’ Jenny pleaded, her voice beginning to break.

She took a few steps forward, until she was almost upon the razor wire, only a yard away from the soldier who had bothered to reply.

‘Please,’ she whispered.

The soldier looked around, left and right, then spoke quietly. ‘Look love, we can’t let your car through, and don’t even think of trying any other roadways in. They’re all like this, blockaded.’ He lowered his voice still further, ‘But … there’s plenty of ways in on foot … all right?’

Jenny looked around. He was right. She could abandon the car somewhere on the hard shoulder, leave the motorway and walk in. The soldiers might have blocked all the roads, but of course London was a porous urban spread not just accessible by roads – there were cycle lanes, paths, kerbs, alleyways, unused scraps of rubbish-encrusted ground.

She nodded and thanked him quietly for the suggestion. She climbed into the car, turned it around and headed on back up the M1. She drove far enough away that she was sure they could no longer see her and then pulled over to the hard shoulder.

'So, I'm going to walk across north London then, no problem,' she spoke to herself. 'How far is that? A day's walking?'

A day, if nothing holds me up.

She had managed to come this far. Home was just fifteen or so miles away now. Not so far. She decided nothing was going to stop her now. She climbed out of the car and looked across the industrial estate beyond the hard shoulder. It was deserted. There was little sign that anything was amiss there …

Other than the fact that on any other Friday afternoon there would be half-a-dozen people outside the delivery bay of that sheet-metal works, having a mug of tea and a fag break; there would be smoke coming from the chimney of that ceramic tile factory; there'd be a lifter moving those pallets of goods outside that distribution warehouse …

Jenny surveyed the lifeless landscape. Beyond the industrial park, looking south-west towards central London, the direction she had to head, she could see scattered pillars of smoke here and there, not from factories though, but from the shells of cars, homes, shops, where rioting had occurred over the last week.

There was activity in there, people there.

My children are in there.

She picked up the last couple of bottles of water and put them in her shoulder-bag. She slammed the car door and walked across the hard shoulder, swinging a leg over the waist-high metal barrier and stepped on to the grass verge. It sloped down towards the back lot of the deserted industrial estate.

'Okay, then,' she muttered to herself.

On Tuesday, or Wednesday, she doubted she would have dared to head into this kind of landscape alone, unarmed. But today was Friday. The last two days in that service station and overnight in that Travelodge, had changed her. She realised if the need came, she could handle herself, she could do what was needed to survive.

She spotted a short length of metal piping lying outside the sheet-metal works. She bent down and picked it up, hefted it in one hand, then in both, and swung it a couple of times, feeling mildly comforted by the *swishing* sound it made through the air.

It'll do for now.

If she came across any young buck who fancied trying out his luck on her, she decided she would probably just swing first and ask questions later.

She checked her watch. It was just approaching half past; she guessed she had another four hours before the sun hit the horizon. That would be a good time to find some safe, dark corner to huddle up in, and let the crazies, the gangs – whoever it was at the top of the predatory food chain – have their night-time fun.

Nearly home.

Tomorrow, some time in the morning, she was finally going to get home.

And Leona and Jacob will be there, no doubt frightened, but alive, well.

She swished the metal pipe once more into the palm of her hand with a satisfying smack.

'Okay then,' she said loudly, her voice echoing back off the corrugated iron wall of the nearest industrial unit.

CHAPTER 74

10.27 p.m. local time
Over Europe

Andy looked out of the window of the 727. It was a civilian plane, one of the fleet belonging to GoJet; one of the bigger budget airlines flying the various European holiday runs. They were over Hungary right now, not far off Bucharest. Outside though, it was pitch-black. No faint strings of orange pinpricks to mark out major roadways, nor mini constellations of amber-coloured stars marking out a town or a village – just pitch-black.

The airliner was packed to capacity, every single seat taken, the vast majority of them filled with soldiers from various mixed, jumbled-up units, all of them stripped of their bulky kit, their webbing and weapons. Amongst them, a handful of civilians, contractors like Andy caught in the chaos, but lucky enough to have been scooped up in this hastily scrambled repatriation effort.

Westley was sitting beside him, the rest of the platoon – just six men – in the two three-seat rows behind them. They were all fast asleep.

'Can't believe we're on our way home, like,' said the Lance Corporal. He nodded towards the window. 'What've you seen outside?'

'Nothing, not a single thing,' Andy turned to look at him, 'I haven't seen a single light since we took off.'

'That's not so good then, is it?'

'No.'

'You think it'll be as bad back home, you know … as it was back *there*?' Westley cocked his head, gesturing behind them.

‘I don’t know. I think it’ll be pretty desperate. It’s been almost a week now without oil. I don’t know how they’ll be coping. I wish there was some news.’

‘A lad from one of the other units says there’s good bits and bad bits. Some places, like London, where it’s a fuckin’ mess, and other places, like, where it’s okay.’

Andy nodded. He could quite clearly imagine what London was like. It wouldn’t be an easy place to maintain order. It was too large, too many people. He would guess there would be many smaller towns, perhaps the dormitory towns of various military bases or barracks, and areas around key installations, resource depots and storage centres where some semblance of order had been maintained. But the rest of the country, particularly the large urban conglomerations, he surmised, was being left to its own devices. He could see farmers dusting off their old shotguns and changing the birdshot for something a little stronger, jealously guarding their modest crops, and cornershop owners – those that had yet to have their stores stripped bare – barricading themselves in, armed with baseball bats and butchers’ knives.

And how long would that state of affairs last?

His best guess was a month, perhaps two. That’s how long it might take to repair the damaged oil infrastructure; the sabotaged refineries, the blown pipelines.

And it might be some time after that before commercial freight ships and aeroplanes were flying once more, loaded up with oranges from South Africa, lamb from New Zealand, Brussels sprouts from Romania.

Oil companies ... big business interests ... they were the first culprits that had sprung to mind. But as far as Andy could see, this had devastated the oil market, irreparably. And when the world recovered ... *if* the world recovered, it would be hypersensitive to oil dependencies, and the dwindling reserves that were left. There was simply no economic motive – for anyone – that he could see behind what had been happening. There were no winners.

The only way one could work out who might have been behind it all would be to look back in a few months' time – or perhaps a few years' time – and see who got hurt the least, or who benefited the most from this chaos. All Andy could see now was that millions, perhaps hundreds of millions of people, billions even, were struggling to survive, simply because somebody had temporarily grabbed hold of the world's oil drip-feed, and squeezed tightly.

How fragile the world is, how very fragile.

There was that metaphor he had used in the report, one he'd been very proud of and thought quite clearly illustrated the tenuous situation of this interdependent modern world. Stopping the continual flow of oil, even for a very short time, was akin to an embolism or stroke a sick man might suffer. And that's exactly what this oil strangulation had turned out to be – a global, economic heart attack.

His eyes grew heavy. The soothing rumble and hiss of the jet engines, carrying them over an unlit Europe, was as good as any sedative. A week of stolen sleep finally caught up on him with a vengeance, and as his chin drooped to his chest, his last conscious thought was that Jenny and the kids had probably fared better than most this week.

CHAPTER 75

10.05 p.m. GMT

Shepherd's Bush, London

The Bad Boys turned up as they had on the previous three nights, appearing, as they did, in surly twos and threes, just after the last glow of dusk had gone from the sky, and the darkness of night was complete. They were not so boisterous tonight she noticed, no catcalling, no wolf-whistling amongst them.

She sensed, for them, tonight wasn't going to be about recreation. It was going to be about necessity; quenching their thirst and hunger. This little avenue was their *larder*. It had provided them with rich pickings since Tuesday. They were going to keep coming back until every last house had been plundered, and then, and only then, would they move on to somewhere else.

She had been in and out of the house this afternoon, using the few tools Jill kept in the cupboard under the sink to fashion the crudest and most basic of weapons and traps. Hopefully they would prove dissuasive enough to the gang tonight, that they might pick on someone else.

Just one more night.

Leona was certain Mum or Dad would come for them tomorrow. Instinct? Or wishful thinking? Or maybe the alternative, that they were gone for ever, was simply unthinkable.

After finding Mr and Mrs DiMarcio this morning, and worried about the chances of being broken into tonight, she had taken a count of the houses down St Stephen's Avenue, and how many had already been looted. There were just over fifty homes along the short leafy avenue. Fifteen had been done over by the gang, including their home. Leona had been tempted to wander inside, but remembered Dad's warning and steered clear of it. She was pretty sure six of the houses had been entered during the course of last night. It seemed like the gang of boys weren't rationing themselves at all; just breaking and entering until they'd had enough. All of the six homes hit last night had been roughly in the middle, too close for comfort. Jill's house and a couple of others, remained prominently untouched amidst the gutted shells of the other homes; they stuck out like a sore thumb.

She watched them as they gathered right outside the gate to Jill's garden.

Their behaviour was noticeably different from previous nights. Not quite so full of cocky attitude, not so noisy. She sensed the seriousness of the situation had finally become apparent to them. This was no longer about having a *larrrf* in the absence of the law; things were becoming serious for them now. It was about getting their hands on what they needed to survive; drink, food. The plunder of Tuesday night – what they'd taken from the off-licence – had obviously been consumed very quickly. The subsequent nights of ransacking had yielded barely enough to keep all of them going. Finding enough to keep them all fit and well was going to become increasingly hard for them. Soon she imagined, after the last house had been plundered, they would turn on each other, as the stakes for survival increased.

From what she could see through the slats of the blind, tonight they all looked sober, thirsty, hungry … and for the first time, a little frightened. Perhaps the hierarchy amongst their group was already beginning to fragment.

'They're back, already?' asked Jacob, seeing the look on her face.

'They're back.'

His face turned ashen.

Leona forced a smile. 'Don't worry Jake. We've got our special secret weapons. We'll be fine. Just remember how well that little boy in *Home Alone* did, eh? He showed them, didn't he?'

Jacob nodded, trying to match his sister's bravado.

Outside the pack of Bad Boys grew. She noticed the Smurfettes were no longer with them. What did that mean? That they had been left at what this gang considered their HQ to keep them safe? Because this was *men's* work – the hunting and gathering, and *their* job was simply to lay down and provide gratification for the boys?

Or worse, the novelty factor had been exhausted and they'd been *dispensed* with?

She spotted the older boy, the one who had stabbed to death the other lad the night before last. He stood in the middle of the street, wearing a vest top sporting the Nike swoosh. She could see him talking animatedly, his hands swooping and flickering around in front of him in that *street* way. He had clearly assumed the mantle of leadership; the others, younger, shorter and less self-assured, nodded with his every instruction.

And then she knew why he seemed so familiar. She had seen him up close before.

50 Cent.

One of the three who had accosted her and Dan on Wednesday. She leaned closer to the window, trying to get a better look.

Yes. It's him.

He and one of his Wigger protégés had chased after Dan and – she was almost certain now – killed him.

His wrist suddenly flicked towards Leona, and their heads all turned as one to look in her direction.

Shit.

She pulled back from the window, hoping they hadn't seen her staring out at them. 50 Cent then gestured towards the house opposite, and they looked that way in unison.

They're deciding which house to go for first. Eeny-meeny-miney-mo . . .

That's what they were doing.

She reached out for her weapon; a rounders bat, with several six-inch nails hammered through it. She had been too eager to cram the end of it with nails, and the wood at the end of the bat had begun to split. So she'd had to wrap sellotape around the end of it to stop the thing splintering and falling apart. She really wasn't sure whether it would disintegrate the first time she swung it at something, but it was all she had.

Jacob held a plastic Swingball bat in one hand. Leona had knocked a few short nails through the holes of the grid in the middle. She thought it looked like it could do some harm if Jacob managed to swat at someone's face with it. During the afternoon he had swished it around a few times, getting some practice. Although she was more worried the clumsy little sod would swat himself with it, and she'd end up having to bandage his face up.

They could have left this afternoon – just grabbed some bottles of water and run for it. But to where? No, she'd decided to stay. This is the only place Dad and Mum would know to come to. If they left, then the pair of them would be well and truly on their own.

He held it tightly in one hand now, and whether or not it was going to be an effective weapon, she could see it was giving him a little confidence – that *tooled-up* feeling. It was going to be his comfort blanket tonight.

50 Cent, the gang's unassailable leader, the one whom she'd seen stab that younger lad the night before, had stopped talking, and now in silence, looked towards Leona, then at the house opposite. He was the one making the decision.

Please no … no.

He nodded towards the other house and Leona let out a gasp of relief. The Bad Boys turned their backs on Jill's and headed *en masse* towards the front door of the house opposite. Leona saw a curtain twitch inside, and in that moment, the name of the family who lived there – the McAllisters, came to her. They had only recently moved in, six months ago. She remembered Mum briefly mentioning them, 'a nice young couple, with a toddler and a baby'.

She could imagine Mr McAllister inside, just behind the front door and ready with whatever household weapon he'd managed to crudely fashion, trembling so violently his heels would be tapping the floor, but driven by something deep down to fight to the very last for his young family, as Eduardo DiMarcio had done for his wife.

The gang began to smash against the front door, taking turns to kick at it around the handle.

She shot a glance towards their front door, buried behind a barricade of heavy furniture they had hauled across during the afternoon. The barricade would slow the gang down a little. It wasn't going to stop them though, not if they were determined to get in here tonight.

The McAllister's front door cracked with the next kick. The next blow caused it to splinter around the handle. A final blow sent it swinging inwards. Last night the Bad Boys had cheered when each front door had caved in, in the same way patrons of a crowded pub might raucously cheer at the sound of a pint-pot being accidentally dropped. Not so tonight. They were less rowdy. More single-minded, more determined.

She saw them stream into the dark interior.

'Cover your ears Jake,' she said. He did so obediently.

And then came the chilling, muted noises she had expected to hear – Mr McAllister's last stand.

It took them an hour to finish what they were doing inside the house. All two dozen of them had pushed their way in. This time there had been no spill out on to the street, no furniture being dragged out and smashed up. No sense of a house-party out of control. It had been much quieter … after the screaming coming from inside had stopped, that is.

The light was completely gone from the sky now. When she saw the flickering beams of several flashlights emerge from the front door, she knew it was now their turn.

'Jacob, go upstairs to our hiding place,' she whispered.

'I don't want to go alone.'

'Go! Now!'

She could hear his shuddering breath in the dark, or was it hers?

'Go!' she hissed.

Leona felt one of his arms reach out and fumble for her, wrapping itself around her waist. 'Please don't die.'

'Shit! I'm not going to … die, okay? Please … go.'

The arms unwrapped, and she heard his footfall towards the stairs.

Outside, the narrow street was filling up again, as the gang members emerged single file from the house opposite. 50 Cent and several others seemed to be nursing minor wounds. She could hear one or two of them crying out intermittently from the pain of their injuries.

A vague hope crossed her mind that the young father opposite, Mr McAllister, had knocked some of the fight out of them before going down. But after only a few moments, and a few words of discussion, she saw the gate to Jill's garden being pushed open and a party of half a dozen of them walking up the path towards the front door.

Her grasp tightened on the bat.

The first blow came quickly and sounded deafening, a heavy thud that made the barricade of furniture stacked against the inside of the front door rattle worryingly. She heard a sharp crack after the second blow.

If only Dan was here.

Several more hard and focused blows landed against the door, and all of a sudden she could see a shaft of torchlight piercing through the tangle of stacked furniture. They'd managed to knock a hole through the flimsy wood of the front door. She turned her torch on and shone it towards the door. She could see a face peering through a jagged hole in the bottom door-panel.

'Go away!' she screamed frantically.

The face, momentarily startled, disappeared. She heard voices outside, not whispering, just conferring quietly. Then one of them kneeled down and shouted through the hole. It was 50 Cent.

'Come on, open the door!'

'Please, go away!' she whimpered. 'We've got nothing in here. Nothing!'

'Yeah right,' he replied. 'Don't fuck with me. Just open up or we'll kick it in eventually.'

She said nothing.

The voice coming through the hole tried a different tack. 'Look, you open up, see, and share out what you got in there, and we let you go.'

She wanted to answer him, to ask if he really meant that. But she knew that he was making an empty promise.

His face appeared at the ragged hole in the front door again. She shone her torch on him and he squinted.

'What you lookin' like?' he said, and then produced his torch and aimed it through the hole at her. The light lingered on her face, and then travelled down her body and then up again. 'Oh … I know you. You the bitch I see up in the precinc', innit.' He laughed, a friendly, cheeky laugh, or at least it might have sounded friendly in another context.

'You *my* honey when we get in,' he grinned. He pushed his hand through the hole in the door, and then panned the torch he was holding around at the barricade stacked against the door. 'You think this is going to stop us?' he said laughing. His face disappeared from the hole and then she heard him talking quietly to the others.

They're going to try another way in.

The lounge windows were the obvious alternative.

She raced back into the lounge from the hall, just as the first brick flew in, sending a shower of jagged shards into the room.

The first of the gang was already pulling himself cautiously in through the window-frame, when his foot found the plank on the window-sill; the plank she had hammered a row of nails into earlier this afternoon.

'Ouch shit! Fuckin' something, fuckin' … shit!' he yelled, pulling his leg back out.

Another of them squeezed in through the window-frame, two hands feeling cautiously for the plank. They found it, and pulled the thing out and flung it across the garden.

'The tricky little bitch,' she heard one of them say outside.

The window-frame was full once more with the hunched-over form of another of them trying to climb in, and this time she realised she had to swing.

The bat came down on top of his head, several nails piercing the baseball hat perched on his head, and punching through the skull beneath with a sickening crunch. The boy jerked violently, one of his hands reaching up curiously fumbling to discover what was attached to his head.

Leona yanked hard on the rounders bat to pull it lose. It came out with a grating sound, and the boy flopped back out of the window on to the ground outside.

She heard several of them gasp. 'Fuck! Bitch killed Steve. She killed Steve.'

A second window smashed, beside the first. She waited with the bat raised, but nothing came through for a few seconds. Then she saw something large filling the second window-frame. It blocked the light coming from the torches outside. It squeezed in through the frame. She switched on her torch and saw it was the bulging form of a bed mattress being pushed through; a makeshift shield, behind which they would be waiting to surge through.

She swung her bat at it, hoping to dislodge it from the grip of those behind. The nails tore through the material exposing the white foamy stuffing inside.

'Go away, go away!' she screamed several times, her voice growing shrill and ragged.

'Here we co-ome!' someone outside called in a teasing singsong way.

Run to the hiding place. Now!

Leona had failed to pay attention to where she was standing as she'd swung ferociously at the bulging mattress. Her back was to the other open window. All of a sudden, she felt a pair of hands grab hold of her left wrist, and another hand snaked up her shoulder and tangled with her hair. She screamed in agony as the hand pulled hard, almost ripping her hair out by the roots.

Oh my God, they've got me!

Her head banged heavily against the window-frame as the hands struggled to pull her out over the jagged shards of glass still stuck in the frame into the front garden.

Then he appeared out of nowhere, out of the darkness in the lounge, an ice-white face, eyes wide like porcelain marbles behind the rim of his spectacles, his mouth a dark yawning oval of rage. She felt the swish of air, and saw a pale-blue plastic blur.

The Swingball bat smacked the forearm of the hand that had hold of her hair.

'Let go of my sister!' screamed Jacob like a banshee. He pulled the bat back off the arm, revealing half-a-dozen gouges, and then swung it down again on the forearm. The hand instantly let go and retreated taking the Swingball bat with it, still firmly attached.

Leona ducked down and sank her teeth into the hands around her wrist. They too swiftly let go.

The mattress was almost wholly inside the lounge now, and she sensed she and Jacob had already lost the initiative. They were coming in regardless.

She turned to Jacob, grabbing him by the hand, she turned on her heels, leading him out of the lounge, into the hall, and towards the bottom of the stairs.

CHAPTER 76

10.09 p.m. GMT

London

When the sky had started to darken she knew she had only a little daylight left to make use of. Jenny decided it was dangerous to be walking out in the streets on her own. The length of pipe she had picked up earlier today had felt like an all-powerful mace capable of dealing out death with one blow. But that had been back when it was in the middle of the afternoon. She'd felt a lot braver then. Now it was dark, and every shadow promised to be the poised form of some starving ghoul, waiting for her to get just a little bit closer before leaping out at her.

Her big metal pipe, right now, felt about as effective and menacing as one of those long twisty party balloons you can make a poodle out of.

Her feet were tired and blistered. She must have walked ten or fifteen miles from Watford.

Along the way she had counted the number of people she had spotted; 47, that was all. Most of them through windows, behind curtains and blinds, picking through piles of discarded plunder in the doorways of stores, or cowering in the dim shells of their homes.

As she had passed through the outskirts of north-west London, entering Kenton, and started seeing bodies, pushed to the kerbside, half-buried down rubbish-strewn alleyways, tucked behind wheelie bins, she'd decided to count them too.

She gave up at 100.

As she passed north-east of Wembley and spotted the unmistakable archway of the stadium in the distance, she entered

Edgware. It had gone ten in the evening when she decided the prudent thing would be to find somewhere discreet to curl up and hide until the morning, even though Shepherd's Bush was now only a few miles away. It would be the cruellest irony if only three or four miles from home she was jumped by someone.

She found a furniture store that had been broken into and some of the stock dragged out and carried away. She was bemused by that, that someone would decide *now* was a good time to get their hands on that lusted-after leather couch. She felt confident that no one would be lurking inside though. There was no food or water to be had here. That meant it was relatively safe.

She found a comfy couch near the front of the shop, where she could look out of the still intact display window on to the high street, yet she was shielded from view by the high back and the over-large cushions. Safe-ish, comfortable, a good enough place to quietly curl up, watch the sky darken and wait for dawn to come. She finished off her last bottle of water.

She awoke with a start. It was fully dark. The glow-hands on her watch showed it was 10.31 p.m. Something had prodded her awake. A sound? She could hear nothing right now.

It was pitch-black inside.

Outside, on the other hand, was faintly discernible, lit by the pallid glow from the moon. There was nothing she could see in detail, just the outlines of the buildings opposite. There was no movement of any kind. But something had awoken her from a very deep sleep. Something had jabbed her sharply to pull her out of that.

And then she sensed it wasn't anything outside on the high street. It wasn't anything inside the furniture shop either. It was within her. An alarm going off; a shrill, terrifying shriek warning her at an intuitive level, that something was happening *right now*, to her children.

'Oh no,' she whispered to herself.

Her adult mind chided her.

Just a nightmare, Jenny. God knows you're due one after everything you've been through this week.

Yes … a nightmare. That was it. But the sensation was strong; an overpowering sense of being hunted, chased, fleeing from certain death.

Classic nightmare material is all this is, Jen. This really isn't what you think it is.

Isn't what? Maternal instinct? Of course not. She reminded herself that that was the sort of nonsense that belonged in those silly agony aunt columns, or tales from the heart short stories you'd find somewhere in the middle of those glossy Moronic Mummy Mags, tales of mothers *sensing* their child calling out to them for help.

But it felt so intense, so real, that Jenny found herself sitting up, and clasping a hand to her chest. It hurt, something in her was hurting, like a stomach ulcer that had gravitated up into her chest.

'Please … please,' she cried, as huge rolling tears coursed down her face in the absolute darkness, her hand kneading her breastbone.

She desperately wanted to rush out into the street and start running towards home. She was maybe as little as what … five or six miles away? She could be home in the space of an hour. But it was dark out there, in which direction would she run? She might start running in the dark, and end up in the morning further away, lost amidst some anonymous suburban warren in Finchley.

Your kids need you to be smart, Jenny. Not stupid. It was a bloody nightmare. Lie down. Get some rest. Just a nightmare … just a nightmare. You'll see the kids tomorrow.

Jenny did as she was told. She lay down. She couldn't sleep though.

CHAPTER 77

10.11 p.m. GMT

Shepherd's Bush, London

Leona dragged Jacob up the stairs.

At the top, they crossed the small landing and dived into Jill's guest bedroom. In the corner of the room was a wash-basin. It wasn't plumbed in, that was something Jill had yet to arrange – '*you know how it is, you can never find a good plumber in London*'.

The basin had been built into a recess in the wall, and the space beneath it, where, one day, plumbing and pipes would descend to the floor, had been boxed in with plywood panels and a little access hatch to make it presentable and flush with the bedroom wall.

Leona knew there was space in there for both of them, they'd tried it out this afternoon. And, as an afterthought, Leona had pulled one of Jill's chintzy tea-towels out from beneath the kitchen sink, and with thumbtacks, attached it so that it draped down over the hatch. She hoped none of the Bad Boys would think to lift the tea-towel and pull on the small brass handle beneath.

Well at least that's what she hoped.

She lifted the corner of the towel up and opened the hatch. 'In you go.'

Jacob scrambled inside. She climbed in after him, curling up with her knees jammed under her chin and her arms wrapped tightly around them; curled up snugly, foetus-like, she just about managed to squeeze into the space beside him. She pulled the hatch to, hoping that the towel hadn't caught on the handle and had flopped down smoothly, concealing their hiding place.

'Are we safe Lee?' whispered Jacob.

'We're safe. But you have to be very quiet now, okay?'

She felt him trembling as he nodded silently.

The noises coming from downstairs indicated that several of them were inside the house now. She could hear the furniture barricade being pulled aside in the hallway, the clatter of furniture being yanked at angrily and thrown across the hall. She could hear footfalls along the hallway, kitchen unit doors being opened and slammed as the first of the gang to make it inside hunted for the most important thing … something to drink, alcoholic or not. Quenching the thirst came above all else.

She knew they were going to easily find all those two-litre bottles of water stacked in the broom cupboard and it would all be quickly consumed by the gang.

There seemed to be a lot of movement in the kitchen. She heard several voices raised angrily, the sound of a scuffle, a fight amongst them. It seemed that although 50 Cent might be nominally in charge, there was no firmly established pecking order or agreement on how the spoils were to be distributed amongst them. It was just a free-for-all.

The noises from the kitchen died down after a few minutes … thirsts had been quenched.

That's all our water gone.

Under any other circumstances that would have been a frightening realisation; to know the next drink they managed to find would probably come from the Thames, or the putrid, microbe-infested offerings of someone's roof storage-tank, festering in the heat of the last few days.

But her thoughts were on right now, her focus was on remaining undiscovered for the next ten, twenty, thirty minutes. That would surely be more than enough time for the Bad Boys to find all of their carefully stored rations of food and water; enough time to completely clean them out and then collectively decide who was the next lucky household to be paid a night-time visit.

But that's not everything they want, is it?

She shuddered at the thought, her arms and knees twitching violently.

'What's up?' Jacob whispered.

'Shhhh.'

It wasn't just food and water they were after, was it? They'd be looking for a replacement Smurfette, a gang sex-slave. If she was unlucky, she'd end up like Mrs DiMarcio.

We should have run.

Leona realised they had made a big mistake staying here. They should have run during the afternoon. Those boys downstairs – no, *boys* was the wrong word – Leona realised she had stopped thinking of them as such, some time over the last couple of days. She saw them as feral creatures now; wild things, ogres, trolls, hobgoblins. They reminded her of a pack of baboons she had once seen on a family trip to the zoo many years ago, simple-minded creatures with a basic set of overpowering drives: thirst, hunger, anger … rape.

Oh God, we should have gone this afternoon.

She heard footsteps coming up the stairs, so many of them, a dozen or more coming upstairs to hunt her down. Because they knew she was somewhere inside still. They knew it, and they were coming for their cookies.

Leona realised if she'd been smarter, she would have left the back door open, suggesting that they had bolted out into the night. But of course, she hadn't thought ahead, she hadn't been smart, and now they *knew* she was still here, somewhere inside. This was going to be another playground game for them to have fun with; hide and seek … with the special prize going to the first of them to find her and drag her out kicking and screaming.

The door to the guest bedroom swung in and she heard four or five of them enter. They were giggling. Now that the pressing need to quench their thirst had been dealt with, it was fun and games time. The anticipation, the excitement, the thrill of the hunt and the promise of the fun they'd have as soon as they found her, and raped her, was making them giggle like little boys sharing a guilty secret, an in-joke.

She could feel Jacob's little frog-like arms quivering against her in shuddering waves that ebbed and flowed. His breathing fluttered in and out. If those boys weren't making so much noise, they'd hear that so easily.

'Tch … tch … tch … Here pussy! Here pussy!' one of them called as if trying to coax out a household pet. The others laughed.

Leona flinched as a narrow shard of light swept across her hand. A flashlight was being panned about the room, a sliver of it had found a narrow crack or a seam in the panelling.

That giggling again … Beavis and Butt-head giggling. She used to find that cartoon funny. She used to find the sniggering they used to do hilarious, for some unfathomable reason. Right now, that sound was as terrifying as the metallic rasp of a blade sliding from its sheath.

Her throat constricted with fear, the breath she'd held for far too long, now had to come out. Exhaling, she let out the slightest strangled whimper.

'Hear that?'

'She's in here?'

'Shit, yeah.'

She heard them spreading out, pulling open the wardrobe doors, opening a closet … then the sound of a hand brushing aside the tea-towel and fumbling at the brass handle for the hatch.

Oh God this is it.

Leona leant over and kissed the top of Jacob's head, she knew this was going to be her very last opportunity to do that.

'Be brave Jakey,' she whispered into his ear.

A shout from downstairs.

Another frantic shout and then a scream.

'What's up?' she heard the voice just outside, beyond the panel, utter.

'Fuck, dunno.'

Leona could hear something crashing around downstairs, as

if a bull had somehow found its way inside and was struggling to find a way back out again.

A single gunshot!

The scream of one of the lads.

Then about a dozen more shots.

A voice downstairs screaming, 'Fuckin' Boomers! Wankers!'

More crashing and thumping.

The boys in the room were spooked. 'Shit, Boomers. They got fuckin' pieces!'

'Shit, we're dead if they catch us!'

Leona heard their feet on the bedroom floor, then the rumble of a dozen or so of them charging down the stairs. The noise coming from downstairs continued for about five minutes; shouting, screaming, the crash of young men throwing each other around, and the sporadic pop of a gun.

And then it diminished as the fighting migrated out of the house into the avenue.

She heard the fighting continue for another couple of minutes, diminishing still further as it moved up the street.

And then eventually, silence.

'Have the Bad Boys gone, Lee?' whispered Jacob.

'I think they have,' she replied.

'Should we get out now?'

Leona wasn't ready to climb out of their little hidey-hole just yet. It was uncomfortable, insufferably stuffy and she was getting terrible cramp in her legs, but right now, she'd rather be tucked in here than anywhere else on the planet.

'Why don't we stay in here for a while longer, okay?'

'Sure,' said Jacob.

CHAPTER 78

11.59 p.m. GMT

Guildford

His wishful thinking paid off. He heard the tentative shuffling of feet outside in the hallway, and a moment later he heard a key in the door. Ash moved quickly, from the first sound of footsteps outside to the door creaking open had only been a few seconds, but enough time for him to rouse himself and be ready to deal with any travelling companion she might have brought with her.

As it happened, she entered alone, and almost immediately sensed, even though it was pitch-black, that something was not quite right.

Before she could turn and go, he was upon her, an arm around her neck, his blade tickling her left cheek, and his mouth close to her ear.

'Kate, I've been waiting *ages* for you.'

She let out a scream, and his hand quickly stifled it.

'I thought you were never going to come home, Kate.'

She struggled in his firm grasp.

'Easy, let's not wiggle about too much. I might pop your eye out with this thing.'

Kate's eyes rolled down at the glinting object beside her face, and she stopped struggling.

'That's better. Now, I need to have a quick chat, Kate. So let's both sit down. We'll get a little candle-light going so I can see what I'm doing, okay?'

Five minutes later he had a scented candle from the kitchen glowing prettily in a saucer. Kate sat on the floor, her hands taped up behind her back and Ash squatted over her, swinging his blade like a pendulum in front of her.

And he realised he could have handled this a little more cleverly.

'Please! Please,' she whimpered, her eyes locked on to the blade of his knife, as it moved from side to side in front of her face.

Ash had screwed this up. It just goes to show, he mused; you think you're at the top of your game, and then you find you can still make mistakes.

His error was in letting Kate realise that he was after the Sutherland girl. He could have ... *should have* made out he was after Jill – Kate of course didn't care much about her sister's friend. She said she'd met her once or twice, had heard Jenny prattle on about Jill from time to time ... but she clearly wouldn't lay down her life to protect this woman.

It seemed though, she was prepared to go quite a long way toward protecting her sister's kids.

'I ... I d-don't know where she lives ... please ...'

'Does she live *close* to them?'

There was a flicker of reaction on her face. One of those involuntary micro-tics difficult to control, and the sort of thing a trained interrogator, a hostage negotiator ... or even a big business deal-closer looks out for; better, much better, than a blip on a polygraph.

'Ahh, so she *does* live nearby then?' he said smiling.

Kate shook her head.

'Too late, Kate. Your very expressive and very pretty face just told me, you know. Now, I suppose I could go look up all the *J. Harriotts* in the phone book, and pick out any that live nearby your sister's place. But that sounds to me like a bit of a chore. And you know what? I'm a little pressed for time. Far easier if you just tell me, hmm?'

Kate shook her head.

Ash sighed. 'Oh dear.' He gently prodded her left cheek, just below the eye, with the tip of his knife. 'How shall we do this?

Fingers? Or perhaps I could start on your face. What do you think?'

'P-please … please don't h-hurt me,' she whispered.

He stroked the bristles on his chin – a normally well-trimmed goatee, that after the last two days of neglect was just beginning to look the slightest bit untidy. 'You do have a very pretty face, Kate. It would be horrible, wouldn't it, to no longer have a nose? Or perhaps be missing a bottom lip?'

'Oh … G-god, no!' she gasped.

He smiled and looked at his knife. 'This little blade has seen plenty of action, Kate, over the years. I've actually popped this little sucker into some quite important people … you might even have heard of one or two of them, if you read around the Sunday papers enough. So you're going to be in good company.'

Kate stifled a whimper.

'It's a very sharp blade. I really wouldn't have to apply too much pressure for it to slide through the skin and gristle of that very nice nose of yours.'

She shuddered, and a tear rolled down her cheek. Ash tenderly brushed it away. 'I think you're ready to tell me now, aren't you?'

She nodded.

'Okay then, let's have it.'

'What w-will you d-do to my niece?' Kate whispered.

He decided a little white lie would keep things rolling along nicely. 'We just want to talk to her, Kate. That's all. It's something to do with her daddy's work.'

'Y-you won't h-hurt her?'

Ash shook his head. 'She's just a child. What sort of person—?' he snapped, scowling at her. 'Look, I have a sister her age, for Chrissakes. No, Kate, I won't hurt her. But I need to talk to her, quickly.'

Kate glanced again at the knife, still only a few inches away from her face.

'Who are you?' she asked.

Ash's eyes widened with surprise. 'Oh, *you're* asking the

questions now, are you?' He laughed. She smiled anxiously, hoping that was helping her somehow.

'Since you ask, I'm with the secret services, I can't tell you which branch of course. But I'm on very important government business.'

He knew that sounded hooky, but frightened and wanting to believe it, she might just.

She nodded. 'I … but you don't s-sound British,' she whispered sceptically.

Ah well, worth a try.

Ash smiled. 'You're right, I'm not. But believe me when I say I will mutilate you badly if you don't tell me what I need to know, right now.'

'Jill lives in the same street as them,' Kate blurted quickly.

Ash grimaced. *I knew it.*

'Where exactly?'

'A … a few doors d-down, on the o-other side.'

You saw her, you fucking idiot. You saw her, didn't you? Unloading that van … and then later on, looking out of the window of that house, looking straight at you.

He cursed under his breath. That could have been her. On both occasions he hadn't been close enough to get a clear look at her face, but yes, thinking back, it was the girl in the photo – a different hair colour, and maybe a little slimmer than the girl in the picture he had. He even recalled thinking there was a passing resemblance, but for crying out loud, who would be so stupid as to go into hiding a mere fifty yards from home?

Shit.

He could have had her already.

Kate looked intently at him, wary of the flickering signs of distraction and anger on his face. 'What are you g-going to do with m—?'

'Oh shut up!' he snapped irritably, swiping the blade quickly across her throat, and stepping smartly back as blood arced out in front of her and pitter-pattered on to the spotless cream carpet in front of her.

He wiped the blade clean as she recovered from the shock and realised what had just happened. She wriggled around on the floor, trying to work her hands free. Why exactly, Ash didn't know; holding her hands to her gaping neck wasn't going help her much now.

He looked down at her and offered her a smile. 'It's not personal, Kate. As a rule I prefer to leave bodies behind me, instead of yapping mouths.'

She tried to gurgle something to him and then slumped forward on to her knees, her forehead pressed against the carpet. The blood splattered out as the wound across her neck opened wider.

'That's a good girl, that'll speed things up for you.' He stepped towards her front door. 'I'll let myself out then.'

Saturday

CHAPTER [illegible]

[illegible]

[illegible]

[illegible]

[illegible]

[illegible]

[illegible] is your pilot speaking [illegible] Captain [illegible] And there [illegible] So we [illegible] Kingdom [illegible] the [illegible]

CHAPTER 79

4.21 a.m. GMT

Heathrow, London

They landed at Heathrow Airport at a few minutes after four a.m.

Andy had awoken from a deep sleep twenty minutes before they were due to land. He guessed his body had sensed the change in air pressure, or been awoken by the increase in chatter and excitement around him. Looking out of the window, as the plane made several stepped drops in altitude, he saw the same pitch-black nothing, the same absence of any sign of human activity that they'd seen earlier across Europe.

On the final approach to Heathrow he finally spotted a string of lights marking out the landing strip, and, in the sky, the strobing navigation lights of a dozen other planes that were either coming in to land, or had recently taken off.

There were no announcements from the airliner's captain. It had been an oddly silent trip. They landed heavily with a bump and a bounce, and taxied swiftly off the main runway, following the tail of a military truck instead of the usual CAA follow-me buggy.

At last, as the plane rolled towards its slot amidst a mixed assortment of military planes, C130 Hercules transports, Tristars and various passenger jets, Andy heard the pilot speak for the first time.

'Uh … this is your pilot speaking. My name's Captain Andrew Melton. And this is a GoJet plane flying under military jurisdiction right now. So, we're home again, back in the United Kingdom,' his tired voice announced over the cabin-speakers.

There was a muted cheer from some of the soldiers up and down the cabin.

'But … uh … as you may have guessed, things have changed a lot back here in the UK over the last week. I've just been told by air traffic control that Heathrow Airport is under military control at the moment, and has been for the last two days.'

Through the window Andy watched passengers emerge from a neighbouring plane, an EasyJet A320. They looked to be mostly military personnel, but he thought he spotted amongst them some civilians, a few women and one or two children.

Very, very lucky holidaymakers.

The order of priority for getting British nationals home had been military first. That's what this huge effort had been all about, not for civilians stranded abroad whilst on holiday, but to get troops back home. Given the state of things right now, Andy could see that made perfect sense.

'I've been told that all military passengers aboard are going to be processed off this plane first. Then the civilian passengers will be processed,' said the captain. 'I'm not really sure what they mean by "processed" folks, but that's the word they're asking me to use.'

Westley gave Andy a nod. 'Looks like this is where we part company, like.'

'Yeah.'

They both stared out of the window at the floodlit scene. They could see lines of people from recently arrived planes, snaking across the tarmac towards the terminal ahead. Watching over them, directing the disembarked passengers, were armed soldiers looking to all intents and purposes like prison guards overseeing a shuffling chain-gang.

The pilot came on again. 'I'm not sure how much you people are aware of. Since this crisis started on Monday an emergency authority has taken over control and we are effectively under some sort of martial law. I'm not sure what that means in terms of what we can and can't do, but obviously things are different … uh … one second.'

The cabin-speakers clicked as the pilot switched channels and now all they could hear was a hiss.

'Right,' the pilot's voice returned over the speakers. 'There's a stairway locking on now. When the doors open, can we have military personnel disembarking first please?'

Andy could hear the mobile stairs as they gently nudged the plane. A moment later the plane's hatches opened with a clunk. Immediately the noise from outside roared in; the whine of jet engines from the planes parked either side, the distant roar of a jet getting ready to take off, and the rumble of another touching down.

Westley unbuckled his belt and stood up in the central aisle between the rows of seats, stretching tiredly and looking down at the few remaining members of his platoon.

'Shake a leg lads,' he said. 'Hey, Derry, wake up you soft lad.'

The aisle filled with soldiers, most of them stripped down to their olive T-shirts, their desert camouflage shirts tied around their waists or slung over one arm. Andy looked around, there were about twenty people still seated – civilians, contractors like himself, mostly.

At the front of the plane an officer appeared in the aisle. 'All right lads, let's go. Down the stairs, there's a truck waiting for you,' he called out loudly.

Westley turned to Andy and held out a hand. 'This is it then,' he said.

Andy grabbed his hand. 'Yup. You look after yourself, okay? We've been through way too much shit for you to get knocked over by a baggage trolley now.'

Westley laughed. 'Right-o, sir.'

'You know what? I might even let you call me Andy instead of "Sir".'

The lance corporal smiled. 'Sorry, force of habit.'

'Take care of yourself Westley.'

He shrugged. 'Ahh, we've been through the worst of it, eh? Can't be any bloody worse here.'

Andy nodded. 'Yeah, you're right.'

'When things get better, we'll meet up, yeah?'

'Beers are on me; you and the platoon,' said Andy.

Westley laughed. 'You'll probably regret that.' He let go of his hand. 'Take care Sutherland.'

'You too.'

Westley nodded and smiled and then shuffled awkwardly. They'd said all that needed to be said. He then turned to face his men. 'Come on lads, let's do as the officer says, and get a move on!' he barked. The lads of the platoon shuffled past Westley, each nodding a goodbye towards Andy as they went.

'Good luck lads,' said Andy, watching them make their way down towards the front of the plane.

Westley was about to follow on after them but he stopped and turned round, and leant forward over the seat in front of Andy. 'Oh, by the way, I left you a pressie,' he whispered, 'you might need it.' He winked at Andy and then turned to join his men. Andy watched him go before looking down at the seat to his right; there was nothing he could see there. He then looked at the pouch on the back of the seat in front and saw that the sick-bag bulged with something.

Andy could guess what it was. He let the last of the soldiers squeeze past in the narrow aisle before pulling the paper bag out of the pouch and looking inside it.

Yup.

He took the service pistol and the two spare clips out and tucked them into the thigh pocket of his shorts.

CHAPTER 80

10.03 a.m. GMT

Shepherd's Bush, London

Leona stirred in the complete darkness. For a second she wondered where she was, and then remembered. She tried to move her arms and legs, but they were numb, and when she did finally manage to coax some movement out of them, she felt an explosion of pins and needles in all four limbs.

She pushed the hatch open, and a pale morning glow flooded into their hidey-hole. She realised she must have actually managed to fall asleep in there.

'C'mon Jakey,' she said to her little brother. He stirred quickly, his yawn no more than a tired squeak.

She climbed out, helped Jacob scramble out, and then, wary that there might still be members of the gang hanging around, they stepped lightly across the room to the hallway.

She glanced into each room. There was no one. The rooms had all been ransacked, of course.

They tiptoed down the stairs and quickly came across the results of last night's ruckus on the ground floor.

The lounge, the kitchen, Jill's study, were completely trashed. It looked like the entire house had been gently lifted a couple of yards off the ground, and then dropped. She noticed a row of shallow craters along the lounge wall, and realised they were bullet-holes. And she noticed a fair amount of blood splattered along the skirting-boards, and smeared across the smooth parquet floor of the entrance hall, as if a body had been dragged, or someone badly hurt had tried to drag himself away.

The barricade built from the stacked kitchen chairs, table,

and a couple of heavy chests had been pushed to one side and the front door was dangling from one last screw holding the top hinge to the door-frame. It swung with a gentle creak.

She found two bodies in the kitchen. They both looked younger than her, perhaps fifteen, sixteen; smooth, young, porcelain faces, eyes closed as if sleeping – they looked almost angelic lying side by side amidst a dark, almost black pool of blood that had spread during the night across most of the kitchen floor. Several of the MDF kitchen units sported jagged splintered bullet-holes. Under foot, shards of glass crackled and popped against the tile floor.

Jacob wandered in before she could stop him.

'Oh,' he said.

'Jake, out ... go on.'

Jacob didn't budge, fascinated by the two corpses, 'They're dead aren't they?' a hint of awe in his voice.

'Yes, Jake, they're dead.'

'Did someone shoot them?'

'Yup.' She counted a dozen jagged holes around the kitchen. Someone had fired off a lot of bullets in here. One of the dead boys was clutching a kitchen knife, beside the other one she spotted a baseball bat.

Hardly an even fight.

She recognised both of them as being members of the gang that had been preying on the avenue these last few nights. She had guessed that the fight last night must have been between the Bad Boys and some other group – perhaps a rival gang from White City.

But these other ones had guns.

She led Jacob out of the kitchen, literally dragging him away from the bodies, which he studied with an intense fascination.

And then she saw him, through the open front door, lying amongst the weeds in Jill's front garden; caught the slightest movement.

'Go into the lounge and stay there,' she commanded Jacob.

'Why?'

'I'm just going to take a peek outside.'

Jake nodded. 'Be careful, Lee,' he whispered as he padded across the hallway and sat down in front of the shattered screen of Jill's extravagant TV set and stared at it, willing it to come on.

She stepped out of the house, cautiously advancing on the body writhing slowly on the ground.

She recognised him.

50 Cent.

Closer now, she could see he'd been shot in the shoulder, his crisp white Nike shirt was almost entirely coloured a rich, dark sepia, and he lay on a bed of pebbles now glued together by a sticky bond of drying blood. He looked weak, he had lost too much blood during the night to last for very much longer. She would have thought the underlings in his gang would have returned for their leader.

Apparently not.

So much for the notion of gang loyalty – not so much this lifelong brotherly bond, as she'd heard many a rapper say of his homies – instead, more like a group of feral creatures, co-operating under the intimidating gaze of the pack alpha. When it came to it, they'd all scurried off, leaving the little shit bleeding out on the gravel.

In one hand he held a pistol, which he tried desperately to raise off the ground and aim at her, but he had only the strength to shuffle it around on the ground.

He looked up at her, recognised her face and smiled. 'My honey,' he grunted with some effort. 'Help me.'

Leona knelt down beside him and reached out for the gun. He hung on to it, but she managed to prise it loose from his fingers with little effort.

'I need help,' he said again, his voice was no more than a gummy rattle.

This was probably an opportune moment.

'You recognised me last night, didn't you? You were the one who asked me for a fag up at the mall.'

The boy said nothing.

'What did you do to my boyfriend?'

50 Cent shook his head almost imperceptibly. 'He ran.'

And then she noticed the ankh pendant nestling amongst the stained folds of his T-shirt.

Dan's pendant.

Leona knew right then that she didn't need to hear the lie in his voice to know what had happened to Dan. With a movement so swift that there was no room for any internal debate, she aimed the gun at his head, closed her eyes and pulled the trigger.

There was an overpowering stench that hung in the warm midday air; a mixture of rotting cabbage and burning rubber. She noticed several thin wispy columns of dark smoke on the horizon. London wasn't exactly ablaze, just smouldering in one or two far-off places. But that burning smell certainly carried. After a while, Leona decided she'd rather breathe just through her mouth.

They walked up Uxbridge Road, which was even more cluttered with detritus than it had been on Wednesday, the last time she had been out. She noticed one or two bundles of clothing amongst the piles of rubbish that turned out to be bodies. She made a point of distracting Jacob as they walked past the closest of them. He didn't need to see any more stuff like that, not so up-close anyway. They walked past Shepherd's Bush Green, over the large roundabout, which was normally surrounded by a moat of stationary cars, vans and trucks beeping, honking, getting nowhere fast, but was now just an isolated island of grass with a large, pointless, blue thermometer sculpture in the middle. On the top of it, a row of crows patiently sat and watched them.

Where did all the pigeons go?

She wondered whether the bird world mirrored the human world. The crows were the gangs, and the pigeons were nervously hiding away somewhere else.

'I'm scared,' muttered Jacob.

'Don't be, we've got this now,' she replied calmly, lifting

her shirt an inch or two to reveal the gun stuffed into the waist of her jeans.

'Can I fire it?'

'No.'

'You had a go,' he complained.

'It went off when I picked it up,' she lied, feeling the slightest unpleasant twinge; the thin end of something she knew was going to inhabit her dreams for years to come.

'Can I hold it then?'

'No.'

They walked over the roundabout towards Holland Park where the homes came with an extra zero to their price tag, and looked a good deal grander than their humble terraced house. Here, she noticed, there had been less rioting and looting. The road, although still cluttered with some debris, was a lot clearer than it was back over the roundabout in Shepherd's Bush. Leona guessed the people there had so much less need to loot. There'd be well-stocked larders in every home, and the chavs and hoodies who normally populated the corners round here, were probably up in those grand three-storey town houses helping mother and father work their way through the wine collection.

'I'm sure we'll find something to drink and eat round here,' she said. 'It looks much less messed up than back home.'

'This is where the really rich people live,' he said.

She nodded, 'Yeah, and they always seem to do all right when there's a problem.'

Five minutes later they spotted a small convenience store tucked down a cul-de-sac, lined with hanging baskets of flowers; very *villagey*, very pretty and largely untouched by the last week's chaos. Metal roller-shutters had come down, probably at the first sign of trouble, and apart from a couple of dents in them where someone had tried their luck smashing through, and one of the large windows behind had been cracked but not shattered, it looked like the store had yet to be looted.

'Is there food in there?' asked Jacob.

Leona nodded. 'I think as much as we need. Stand back.'

She aimed the pistol at a sturdy looking padlock at the bottom of the shutter, and grimaced as she slowly squeezed the trigger.

Jacob yelped with excitement, hopping up and down as the gun cracked loudly. The padlock fragmented into several jagged parts and the glass door behind the shutter shattered.

'Yeah!' shouted Jacob, as the smoke cleared and the glass finished falling. 'Wicked!'

'Stay out here,' she said.

She pushed the shutter up and stepped inside the shop, holding the gun up in front of her, shakily panning it around the gloomy interior.

'Okay,' she called out to Jacob. 'Looks clear.'

He joined her inside.

It was a small convenience store, a baker's and delicatessen. The meat was spoiled, she could smell that and a few blue spots of mould had blossomed on most of the bread. There was, however, a heartening array of tinned produce on the shelves, and two large fridges full of bottles and cans, all of them of course warm, but that didn't matter.

She pulled out a bottle of water and gulped it, then handed it to Jacob. He shook his head.

'Not thirsty?'

'Yeah, but I want Coke,' he replied, reaching into the fridge on tiptoes and pulling out a litre bottle.

'Mum would have a fit if she saw you drinking that. It's just sugar and chemicals.'

Jacob shrugged as he twisted the cap off and slurped from the bottle.

'I can't believe this,' she said, with a big grin spreading across her face. 'We've struck a gold-mine.'

'No more pilchards,' added Jacob, wiping his mouth with the back of his hand and belching.

Leona looked back at the open shutter. 'Let's grab what we need quickly. Other people may have heard the bang.'

*

They found a tartan wheelie bag nearby, one of those shabby things that only old blue-rinsed ladies seem to favour, and filled it with as many tins and bottles of drink as they could squeeze in. Leona found some wire hand-baskets and filled those with some more tins and bottles. She gave a couple of lighter basket-loads to Jacob to struggle home with, filled the wheelie bag, and stacked another couple of baskets full of supplies on top of it.

As they emerged out of the convenience store on to the cul-de-sac, they saw several people warily approaching the entrance, presumably lured by the sound of the padlock being shot off and the glass shattering. The nearest to them, an old couple, eyed the pair of them cautiously.

'Is the shop uh … open now?' the old man asked.

Jacob, grinning, piped up. 'Yup, open for business.'

The old couple nodded gratefully and quickly disappeared inside.

'We should go,' said Leona, 'it's going to get busy here.'

They headed out of the cul-de-sac and turned right on to Holland Park Avenue, towards the Shepherd's Bush roundabout. They passed a few people along the way, who eyed their plunder with interest, and hurried along swiftly in the direction they had come from.

'We need to be careful,' she said, 'when we get closer to home, there might be some who will try and take what we have.' She patted the bulge on her hip, the heavy, cold lump of metal there felt reassuring.

Heading back past the grand town houses, Leona saw dozens of people curiously emerging on to their balconies and the twitching of countless curtains and blinds. The streets might have been all but deserted, but there seemed to still be plenty of people around, hidden away in their homes. At least here there were.

They approached the roundabout, the crows still sitting atop the big blue thermometer in the middle, watching events with idle interest. Leona spotted someone in the middle of the road up ahead, walking around the central island briskly.

A woman in a white, cheesecloth skirt, holding her shoes in one hand, her back to them as she rounded the grassy island and began to disappear from view.

Her hair, her movement, it was all so very familiar.

'Mum?' she called out, but not loudly enough. The woman carried on, leaving them behind. Leona could only see her head bobbing around the far side of the roundabout's island.

'Mum!' she shouted, her voice breaking. The cry echoed off the tall buildings either side of the road and the woman on the far side of the roundabout stopped dead.

She turned round, and looked back.

Even 200 yards away, her face just a distant pale oval, Leona recognised her.

'MUM!'

The woman looked around, uncertain where the cry had come from. Leona let go of the wheelie bag and waved frantically. The movement caught the woman's eye, and a second later, Leona heard what sounded very much like her mother's voice; a mixture of surprise, shock, joy and tears.

'Leona?' she heard the woman ask more than say.

'Oh my God! … It *is* Mum, Jake! It's Mum.'

Jacob dropped his basket as well, some of the tins and bottles bounced out on to the road – unimportant to them now. She grabbed her brother's hand and ran forward down the road towards the roundabout, completely unaware that her face had crumpled up like a baby's and she was crying a river of tears, just like her little brother.

They collided into each other's arms a moment later, a three-way scrum of flailing arms and buried faces.

'Oh God, oh God!' sobbed Jenny, squeezing them both as hard as she could. 'Thank God you're all right!'

Leona struggled to reply, but her words were an unintelligible syrupy mewl.

'Mummy!' cried Jacob, 'I missed you, I missed you.'

'God, I missed you too, sweetheart. I was so frightened for both of you.'

'We've been in a battle,' said Jacob. 'It was frightening.'

Jenny looked into Leona's face, and her daughter nodded, her lips curled, tears streaming down her cheeks.

'Leona? Honey?'

She swept a sleeve across her face. 'Yeah, they attacked the house. We nearly … we nearly …'

'We nearly died Mum,' Jacob finished helpfully. 'But we've got a real gun now,' he added brightly.

CHAPTER 81

11.35 a.m. GMT

Heathrow, London

It could almost have been any normal midsummer's morning there in Terminal 3's departure lounge, thought Andy. It looked unchanged since last time he came through here two weeks ago, on his way out to Iraq to make that assessment on the northern pipeline and pumping stations. However, this time round, the shops and places to eat were closed, the metal shutters pulled down, and beyond the large floor-to-ceiling viewing windows, the tarmac was a hive of activity.

He could see soldiers streaming wearily out of military and civilian jets; a jumbled mess of units, some in desert khakis, some wearing the temperate green camo version. With so many men in uniform, looking lost, weary and confused, it was what the ports along the south coast of England must have looked like on the morning after Dunkirk.

In the departure lounge with him, Andy guessed there were about two hundred people; civilians – mostly men, a few women and a handful of children. They were mainly businessmen caught out by events and some holidaymakers; a mishmash of the lucky few British nationals abroad who had managed to stumble upon the various efforts being made to repatriate military personnel. Most of them looked exhausted, dehydrated, and many of them lay stretched out and sleeping on the long, blue couches.

They had been kept waiting in the lounge for several hours without any information. If they weren't all so exhausted, he suspected a ruckus would have been kicked up before now. They had been promised that someone would come and talk to them, and tell them what would happen next.

Finally some people arrived; a woman, accompanied by a couple of armed policemen, and a young man carrying a clipboard. She wore a radio on her belt, and had an official-looking badge pinned to her chest.

'Excuse me!' she called out. 'Excuse me!'

The people in the departure lounge, including Andy, quickly roused themselves and gathered round her.

'We're sorry for keeping you all waiting so long.' She looked harried, flustered and almost as exhausted as the anxious people surrounding her. 'We're going to be moving all of you to a safe zone where we can supply you with food and water rations whilst the current situation continues.'

'What's going on out there?' asked someone behind Andy.

The woman, he could see from her name badge, was an emergency manager with the Civil Emergency Response Agency. She shook her head. 'I'm afraid things are a bit of a mess out there, across the country. The emergency authorities have been establishing several safe zones where we can control things more easily and sensibly distribute rations. Outside of those, it's …' she shook her head again, '… well, it's not good.'

'Where are these "safe zones"? How many, how big?'

Her head spun round to face the direction from which the query had come. 'I don't know how many exactly. But in the capital, the Millennium Dome is being used as an emergency mustering point and supply centre. We have another major supply and distribution safety zone based in Battersea and another at Leatherhead. These zones are being guarded by the police and the army to ensure …'

'Guarded? From who?' Andy raised his voice from the back.

She turned to face him, and took a moment to think before answering. 'We have supplies in the safe zones to keep some of the population going for the foreseeable future. But I'm afraid not all.'

The crowd stirred, he heard voices murmuring, whispered concern amongst them.

'Are people dying out there?'

That's a stupid bloody question, thought Andy.

She nodded. 'There's a lot of instability, riots, chaos. The water system stopped functioning several days ago. People are drinking unclean water, they're becoming sick, and yes … some will eventually die. We're seeing what we've seen on the telly in the aftermath of disasters like the tsunami; infectious diseases, spoiled food and water … those sorts of things. Until the oil flows again, supplies of sterile water and food are the critical issues.'

'When will the oil flow again?' shouted another in the crowd.

She shrugged. 'I don't have the answer to that.' She put on a reassuring smile for them. 'But when it does … we'll be on our way out of this situation. And every effort will be made to distribute medicines and emergency supplies of food and water to those who need it most. In the meantime, we're working hard to ensure we can help as many people as possible ride this out in, like I say, these safe zones.'

She gestured towards the young man standing beside her with the clipboard. 'We need to take all of your names, a few particulars, look at your passports if you have them … and then when we're done, there's a couple of army trucks which will be taking you to either the Leatherhead or the Battersea safe zone. So if you can form an orderly line here, we'll get started.'

The crowd of people around her shuffled compliantly into a long queue, and the young man pulled up a seat to sit on and another stool to use as a makeshift desk. The two armed policemen, wearing Kevlar vests and casually cradling their machine-guns, took a step back, perhaps sensing this crowd was too beaten and tired to pose any sort of security risk.

The woman, meanwhile, disengaged from the process and found a quiet space between two large potted plastic plants and, ignoring the sign on the wall behind her, lit up a cigarette.

Andy wandered over towards her. Closer, he could see how tired and drawn she was; there were bags beneath her eyes, and a nervous tremor shook the hand that held the cigarette shakily to her lips.

Her eyes fixed on him as he closed the last few yards. She almost bothered to put her 'we've-got-it-all-under-control' smile back on for him … but clearly decided it was too much trouble.

'Help you?' she asked, blowing smoke out of her nose.

'Do I get a choice?'

'Sorry?'

'Do I get a choice? I mean, if I don't want to be taken into one of these safe zones?'

'You don't?' She was genuinely surprised. 'Why the hell would you not?' she said, and then took another long pull on her cigarette.

'I need to get home to my family.'

She shrugged, 'I can understand that.'

Andy turned round. 'These people,' he said gesturing at the queue that had formed in the middle of the departure lounge, 'are going to die in your safe zones. You know that, don't you?'

'Excuse me?'

'How many people have you rounded up at Battersea, Leatherhead, the Dome?'

'Look, I don't know off hand … I'm just a sub-regional co-ordinator.'

'Guess.'

'Shit, I don't know,' she shook her head, too tired and strung out to want to get sucked into this kind of conversation.

'A hundred thousand? A million?'

She nodded. 'Yeah, maybe half a million around London, and in other places too. Look, we're doing our best—'

'I don't doubt you are. But do you have enough food and water to feed them for six months? Nine months? Maybe even a year?'

'What?' she said, her eyebrows knotted with confusion. She blew out a veil of smoke. 'What the hell are you talking about?'

'Recovery.'

'Listen,' she said flicking ash into one of the pots beside her and glancing casually at the 'No Smoking' sign on a wall nearby, 'it's not going to take a year for the oil to get flowing again. Some pipelines got blown, some oil refineries got damaged, right? That's what happened.'

Andy nodded.

'So how long does it take to fix that? I'm sure there're people out there working on it right now. We'll have oil again in a couple of weeks, okay? So look, why don't you give me a break, join the queue and let me have a fag in peace?' She offered him an apologetic shrug. 'It's been a really long, fucking day.'

Andy took a step closer and lowered his voice. 'Somebody up there, in charge of things, is being very naive if they think it's all going to be hunky-dory again within a few weeks.'

'So … what? You want us to let you go?'

Andy nodded, 'Yup. I'll take my chances outside one of your safe zones.'

She stubbed her cigarette out and tossed it into one of the pots. 'Okay then, your funeral. I'll have one of our lads escort you out of the perimeter.' She pulled the radio off her belt and talked quickly and quietly into it. 'Somebody will be along shortly to take you out,' she said to him.

'Thanks,' said Andy and then turned to go and sit down again.

'Wait,' said the woman.

He turned back to face her.

'You really think this is going to go on that long? Six months?'

'Sure. The oil might start gushing again next week, but where's our food going to come from? The Brazilian farmer growing our coffee beans, the Ukrainian farmer growing our spuds, the Spanish farmer growing our apples … think about it. Is his little business still functioning? Is he still alive, or is he injured, or sick? Or how about this … has his crop spoiled in the ground, uncollected because he didn't have fuel to operate his tractor? And what about all those crop-buyers, packagers, processors, distributors … all the links in the chain that get food out of the soil around the world and into the supermarket up the road? Can those companies still function? Do they still exist, or are their factories looted, burned down? And what about their workforce? Are they alive still? Or lying in their homes puking their guts up because they've been drinking the same water that they're shitting into?'

The woman was silent.

'Just a few questions off the top of my head that somebody up the chain of command needs to be asking right now,' said Andy dryly. 'It's not just a case of handing out water bottles and high-energy protein bars for the next fortnight. The oil being stopped … even for just this week, has well and truly fucked everything up.'

'It can't be that bad,' she replied.

'System-wide failure. It's all stalled. The world was never designed to reboot after something like that.'

'And you'd rather take your chances out there? There's no food, nothing. Whatever there was to loot has been taken by now. Do you not think you're being a bit stupid?'

'Six months from now, the Millennium Dome and all those other safe zones? They'll be death camps.'

The woman looked at him incredulously. 'Oh come on.'

Andy noticed a couple of armed police officers enter the departure lounge and walk towards them.

'Ah,' she said, 'here they are.' She reached a hand out and placed it on his arm. 'Look, why don't you join the queue like the others? I can send them away. It's dangerous in London right now.'

He could see her plea was a genuine act of compassion. She meant well.

'Thanks, but right now I'd rather find my family and get as far as I can from *anyone* else. The last place I'd want to be in six months' time is crammed into a holding-pen with thousands of other people.'

The police escort arrived, and the woman instructed them to guide him out of the building and through the guarded security perimeter around the terminal.

She wished him good luck as they parted.

CHAPTER 82

2.32 p.m. GMT

Shepherd's Bush, London

'Why?' Jenny asked, looking at her daughter. 'Why is it so important that we don't go back to our house?'

Leona shook her head. 'It's what Dad said.'

'I know it's what he said, but he thought Jill was going to be here to look after you. I thought that's why he said to come here.'

Jenny stared at the two bodies in the kitchen, at the pool of blood and splatter streaks on the walls and cupboards. 'We can't stay here. I don't want Jacob having to see any more of this than he has alread—'

'We *have* to stay away, Mum,' said Leona. 'We can't go home.'

Jenny grabbed her shoulders and turned her round. 'Why?'

Leona shook her head. Jenny could see there was something she wanted to say.

'Come on. We can't talk in here,' said Jenny looking down at the corpses. She led her children through to the conservatory at the back of the house, where things were a little less topsy-turvy. She sat Leona down in a wicker chair, and pulled up another. Jacob climbed on to Jenny's lap, holding her tightly. She rocked him without even thinking about it.

'Come on Lee, this isn't making any sense.'

Leona was silent for a while, watching Jacob. His eyes quickly grew heavy, and after a couple of minutes the even sound of his breathing told them both that he was fast asleep.

'It's dangerous at ours,' said Leona, in a hushed voice.

'What?' Jenny shook her head, confused. 'It's no more dangerous than here.'

'Mum,' Leona looked up at her, 'I think Dad tried to tell me on the phone … tried to tell me someone's after me.'

'What?'

'A man, or men – I'm not sure.'

'What the hell are you talking about?'

Leona slumped in the chair. 'You remember our trip to New York?'

Jenny nodded. 'Of course, who could forget such an extravagant Christmas?'

'It was a business trip for Dad, as well as a treat for us, wasn't it?'

'Yes, of course.'

'Dad had written something important, and was giving it to someone very important.'

Jenny nodded. She'd known there was an issue of confidentiality surrounding the work, and that had definitely put Andy on edge throughout their trip. She remembered thinking that there was perhaps something about this business that was … somewhat *unusual.*

'I think it had something to do with *that*,' Leona said, gesturing with both hands, 'what's been going on.'

Jenny shook her head again. Jacob murmured, disturbed by the movement. She wanted to say that was crazy. But something stopped her. What Leona was suggesting sounded ridiculous … and yet, so many things over the last eight years began to make some sort of sense, if what she said was true. Andy's paranoia – if she thought about it, yes – it did really start with New York; his obsession with Peak Oil, with privacy, his gradual detachment from the world … it all began then.

And let's not forget his very special area of expertise, Jenny, it's always been specifically THIS – the choking of global oil … what's happening right now.

'Mum,' said Leona. 'Dad was never meant to *see* the

important men he was dealing with, it was that big a deal. That's what he told me.'

'*That's what he told you*? Why didn't he tell *me* any of this? Why the hell am I finding out about this now?'

'Because it wasn't Dad who saw them … it was me.'

'What?'

'In that really posh hotel? Remember I went up to get something? I walked into the wrong room, the one next door. I saw some men. And I knew even then they were important, like … running-countries kind of important.'

'Oh my God.'

'And now this whole oil thing is happening, I think they …' Leona's voice quivered, 'I think they might need me to be dead.'

CHAPTER 83

9 p.m. GMT

Cabinet Office Briefing Room A (COBRA), London

Malcolm looked at the other two members of the COBRA committee. 'I think we're in danger of losing control of this situation.'

The other two looked at him sternly.

'The longer this situation persists, the harder it's going to be to pick up the pieces afterwards.'

'This situation will persist Malcolm, for as long as they say it needs to,' said Sir Jeremy Bosworth. 'We don't have a choice on this.'

Malcolm sighed. 'I know, I understand that we're all in this together, but the level of attrition this situation is causing isn't evenly spread, gentlemen. It's hitting us much, much harder than others. I'm a little concerned that by the time the satisfactory conditions are met, there'll be nothing left to salvage in this country.'

'You're exaggerating Malcolm,' replied the other man, Howard Campbell. 'We all need to remain calm whilst this is going on.'

'Exaggerating? I wonder. You *are* aware of conditions out there aren't you?'

'Of course, it's not pretty,' said Sir Jeremy.

'The safe zones we established to concentrate resources and manpower, are not forming up as we'd hoped. We simply don't have enough manpower to maintain them; we don't have enough troops on the ground.'

'The troops are mostly back from our various commitments overseas, aren't they?'

'There are still significant numbers stranded abroad. And even if we had managed to get them all back home, we just wouldn't have the numbers we need to do this properly.'

'We have large numbers of territorials we can draw on don't we?'

Malcolm nodded, 'But hardly any have turned up for duty, and of the few thousand that have, many have already abandoned their posts. I might add, we're also losing a lot of police officers.'

'It's understandable,' said Jeremy. 'People want to be with their families.'

Malcolm looked at him 'Does that not concern you, though?'

Sir Jeremy nodded. 'It's a concern, of course it is. But we have to continue looking at the bigger picture. That's what this has always been about, the bigger picture.'

'Look, I'll be honest. I'm worried that once they are happy that the goal has been met, the time it will take to get things running again will be too long.'

'Now is not the time to start being squeamish, Malcolm,' said Howard.

'I'm not being bloody squeamish, Howard. I simply would like to have something left that's governable once we're done with this!'

'Come on, Malcolm, let's not squabble like politicians. We're better than that.'

Malcolm nodded, 'You're right.' He smiled at them. 'I'm merely suggesting that we need to start thinking about applying the brakes to this thing. It's picked up a lot more momentum than I think any of us really expected.'

Jeremy shrugged. 'I must admit, I was a little surprised at the riots on Tuesday. Your man, Charles, did a superb job frightening everyone.'

Howard looked from one to the other. 'You know we can't do that. We can't effect any sort of recovery until we receive word. You are *bound*.'

Malcolm sensed the veiled threat behind that one word. They did not readily forgive colleagues who acted alone.

'It's not starting a recovery procedure I'm talking about. I just believe we've perhaps been a little … over-zealous this week. We've achieved the required result far more quickly than our colleagues have elsewhere. I take the blame for that. I underestimated the fragility of this country.'

Howard leant forward and placed a gentle, supportive hand on Malcolm's arm. 'This was never going to be easy, we all accepted that. Future generations will no doubt judge us harsh, ruthless, cruel. But they will understand, Malcolm, they *will* understand.'

CHAPTER 84

9.15 p.m. GMT
London

Hammersmith without a single light? It was the proverbial ghost-town. On a normal Saturday evening, this place would be buzzing with people streaming out of the tube station, through the mall and out on to the pavement, ready to try and cross the busy ring road. The pubs would already be full and spilling merry twenty-somethings outside to discuss where they were going next.

It shouldn't be like this; the tall buildings dark and lifeless, the opening into the mall, a gloomy entrance to a forbidding chasm.

There was a constant smell too. A smell he'd started to register on his way north-east from Heathrow, passing through Hounslow. It was the smell of bin-bags ripped open by an urban fox and left to fester in the sun for a few too many days. Walking through Kew, he noticed there was more to the odour than that; the faintest whiff of decay – the first smells of the dead. Andy had spotted only a dozen bodies. That was, perhaps, encouraging. In anticipation of what London would be like in this exact scenario, he'd painted a mental image of the dead and dying filling the streets. He'd imagined the gutters awash with the jettisoned fluids of those who might have drunk, in desperation, from the Thames, from the drip trays of air-conditioning units, or worse.

By the time he'd made his way into Hammersmith, there was a suggestion of the smell of human shit, added to all the other odours.

Of course, there aren't any flushing toilets. There'll be several days of that lying around.

Nice.

Andy had seen about fifty people since leaving the guarded perimeter around Heathrow's Terminal 3. They had all looked very unwell, bearing the symptoms of food poisoning, having no doubt eaten things that had spoiled, or consumed tainted water.

The sun had gone down. And now only the day's afterglow dimly stained the cloudless sky.

His foot kicked a tin can that clattered across the empty road, startling him and a cluster of birds nearby that took off with an urgent flutter and rustle of flapping wings.

He pulled the gun out, the gift from Lance Corporal Westley. He had to admit, it felt bloody good in his hands. That was something he never thought he'd feel and so whole-heartedly appreciate – the righteous power of a loaded firearm.

'Thanks Westley,' he muttered quietly.

It was getting dark, but he was so nearly home now, just two or three miles away. He walked up Shepherd's Bush Road, towards the Green, passing a Tesco supermarket on his left. By the last of the light, he spotted about half-a-dozen people picking through a small mound of detritus in the supermarket's car-park, like seagulls on a landfill site.

A few minutes later he was looking out across the triangular area of Shepherd's Bush Green, and the dark row of shops bordering it. This was his neighbourhood, so nearly home now.

He had allowed himself to nurture a foolhardy hope that when he finally made it here, he'd discover an enclave in Greater London that had got its act together, blocked the roads in, and was sharing out the pooled essentials amongst the locals. After all, this area was home to the BBC. For every rough housing estate in the area, there were rows and rows of supposedly sensible middle-class, middle-management types and media-moppets – the *Guardian* sold just as well as the *Sunday Sport* round here.

But then, that was clearly a silly supposition; blue collar or white collar, if you're starving enough, you'll do anything to survive; middle-class, lower-class, tabloid or broadsheet reader. You scratch the surface and we're all the same underneath.

He walked up past the Green and turned left on to Uxbridge Road, seeing what he expected to see; the mess strewn across the road, every shop window broken … one or two bodies.

All of a sudden he found himself breaking into a run, the fatigue of walking the last fifteen miles forgotten now that he was less than five minutes from home. His heart was beginning to pound with a growing fear of what he'd find when he finally pushed open the front door of Jill's home.

'Oh God, please let them be okay,' he whispered.

His footsteps echoed down the empty street as his jog escalated in pace to a run, and he repeated that hypocritical, atheist's prayer under his breath.

Let them be okay, let them be okay, let them be okay …

As he turned left off Uxbridge Road into St Stephen's Avenue, his run was a sprint, and his heart was in his throat.

And that's when he saw them, standing ahead of him, blocking the road. Three people; three men, by the shape of their dark outlines. They were standing there, almost as if they'd been waiting all along for him, expecting him.

Andy whipped out his pistol and held it in front of him in both hands. 'I've got a gun, so back the fuck up and let me past!' he shouted at them.

There was no response. The three dark forms were motionless. The one in the middle then slowly moved towards him. Andy racked the pistol noisily and aimed it. 'Another fucking step and I'll blow your fucking brains out, mate.'

The dark form stopped in his tracks. 'Dr Andrew Sutherland?'

CHAPTER 85

9.51 p.m. GMT

Shepherd's Bush, London

Jenny sat at the top of the stairs, the gun that Leona had managed to get hold of resting in her lap. After some resistance from them both, she had convinced them to go and get some sleep upstairs. They were exhausted and needed some rest. Only when she had assured them that she would stand guard at the top of the stairs would either of them leave her side.

She was tired too, but there was much on her mind. There was no way she was going to sleep. Leona's confession earlier on was the problem.

On the one hand, it introduced a whole new level of fear to the equation – the thought that some shady characters might just be out there looking for her daughter, with one intention only. To kill her. On the other hand, she was angry that Andy's business affairs had jeopardised their daughter's life, their family. She was angry that he had never confided in her that their paths might have briefly crossed with those of some very dangerous people. She was angry that he'd sworn his daughter to secrecy.

And finally, she was sad that he'd been living with that kind of unsettling, nagging anxiety alone, for so long. It explained so much … it even put into context all those little tics Andy had developed in the last few years; his irritating habit of checking the tone on the house phone immediately after ending a call, the ritual tour of the downstairs windows and doors before bedtime. Jenny had even begun to suspect he was developing a minor case of obsessive compulsive disorder.

And now she knew why.

Christ.

It made her shudder. Rampaging chavs were one thing, Big Brother watching you, that was quite another.

'Dr Andrew Sutherland?' the dark form in front of him asked again in a quiet voice.

'I said stay where you are, or I'll put a bloody great hole in your head!'

Andy wished Westley had decided to leave him one of those SA80 night-scopes. Right now the edge of those silhouettes were fast merging with the darkening night sky and, for all he knew, they were watching him through scopes of their own and lining up cross-hairs on his forehead.

'Just take it easy, Andy.'

The voice was familiar – very familiar.

'Who's that? I know you.'

'Hi, Andy, it's me.'

Mike? It sounded like the American.

'Mike? Is that you?'

'It's me. How're you doing?'

'What … what are you doing here?' he asked, and then looked at the other two forms. 'And who's that you're with?'

The form in the middle, the one he guessed was Mike, took another step forward and Andy felt the weight of a hand rest on his gun, pushing it gently down until he was pointing it at the ground.

'We have to talk Andy, and we have to talk very quickly about your family.'

Those words chilled him to the core.

'Oh God. What is it? What's happened? Are they okay?'

Mike hesitated to reply. 'We don't know. It's your daughter Andy, Leona. That's who we're really worried about. That's who we need to talk to.'

Andy studied the dark form in front of him.

Oh God, he's with them!

Andy raised his gun. 'Stay back! Or I'll shoot. I mean it.'

Mike advanced slowly. 'Andy my friend, I'm sorry, but I've got a gun trained on your head right now. And,' Mike laughed, 'I also know how bloody awful your aim is. Lower your gun or I'm afraid I'm going to have to put most of your brains out on the road.'

Andy suspected the other two men were aiming at him as well. He lowered his gun.

Mike addressed the other two sharply. 'Get him inside.'

They disarmed him, grabbed him forcefully by the arms and dragged him across the narrow street, through the gate of a small front garden and into a house that had clearly been ransacked and looted by someone in the last few days. They dropped him unceremoniously into an armchair.

He could see nothing, it was so dark. He felt someone brush past his legs, and then a moment later a small lantern popped on – a handheld sodium arc strip light, that glowed a dim, pallid cyan. Mike was kneeling before him, his gun still held in one hand, not aimed at him, but not exactly put away either.

'Andy,' he said, 'you ever seen that film with Keanu Reeves and Laurence Fishburne … *The Matrix*?'

Andy nodded silently.

'You remember the blue pill?'

He nodded – the moment in the movie when one character, the one played by Keanu Reeves, was being asked to forget everything he knows and prepare himself for a new reality. The blue pill had been the visual metaphor.

'Yeah, okay … the blue pill, so?'

'Well, I guess this is going to be *your* blue pill moment.'

Jenny heard it distinctly; in the dark, somewhere downstairs in the hall, the unmistakable rasp of cloth against cloth, the faintest *whiff* of friction, someone or something moving.

She held her breath, and listened.

A moment later she heard another faint rasp, followed by the slightest creak of one of the parquet slats in the hallway.

She reached for the gun in her lap and aimed it down at the bottom of the stairs.

'I can hear you,' she said quietly, almost a whisper, yet sounding so loud in the absolute stillness of the night.

The creaking, the rasping, stopped instantly. Even more frightening for Jenny, it was confirmation that someone *was* down there, and not just a phantom of her imagination.

'I-I've got a gun, and I'm aiming it right now,' she whispered again.

That was met with silence, again.

Then she sensed something on the bottom step. 'Stop!' she hissed, 'or I'll shoot.'

'Mrs Sutherland?' a soft voice, a man's voice.

Hearing her name emerging from the darkness like that rattled her.

'Who's that? Who are you?'

'Who I am really doesn't matter,' the voice replied. 'I'm here for a reason. I'm here because a hundred yards away are men who have come to kill your daughter.'

'What?' she gasped.

'They're coming for her, you know, we've only got a few seconds before they arrive.'

'Who the fuck are you?'

'Like I've said, who I am doesn't matter. I have to get your daughter out of here before it's too late.'

'I think you suspect some of this already, Andy,' said Mike. 'The things that are going on in the world, hmm?'

Andy nodded. 'My work, it's based on my work.'

Mike smiled, 'Yes, your report. And you must have been wondering who it was you handed it over to all those years ago. You were doing a lot of thinking in the back of that truck in Iraq, Andy, weren't you?'

Andy stared at the gun, only a few inches away from him. Was he fast enough?

'Well, you gave that report to the right sort of people. What did they tell you when you were first approached? That they were security experts working for several anonymous clients in the oil industry?'

Andy nodded, 'Yes, pretty much those words.'

'It never occurred to you that they might have been terrorists? Or middle-men for some rogue foreign power?'

'I wouldn't have handed it over if I did.'

Mike nodded. 'No, I suspect you wouldn't, despite the money. It was quite a lot, wasn't it?'

Andy shrugged.

'These people value their anonymity. That's very important to them, particularly now that they've done this thing; brought the world to its knees. You know, millions will starve. There will be hundreds of small-scale wars in which many more will die. Old scores settled, old rivalries emerging, whilst the world deals with this temporary instability. Now is really not a good time for them to be publicly named. And here's the problem they have,' Mike said, 'your daughter could do just that.'

Andy looked at Mike. 'You're with *Them* aren't you?'

'Come on Mrs Sutherland, put the gun down. We don't have time for this.'

'So wh-who's out there?' she asked.

'People, bad people – those that are behind the disaster. It's all tied up you see, it's all one thing.'

'And what about you?' she asked the voice at the bottom of the stairs.

'Me? The less you know the better. Let's just say I'm a hired hand, hmm?'

'Hired to … what?'

'Find your daughter and protect her, of course. Look, now isn't the time for this,' he continued. 'You keep hold of your gun, just as long as you know how to slide the safety on. Let's get her out of here, let's get her safe and then you can slide the safety back off, turn your gun on me, and ask as many questions as you like.'

That sounded convincing. God knows, she wanted the voice down there to be that of a saviour, and not her daughter's executioner.

'Can I trust you?' she asked.

'What do you expect me to say, Mrs Sutherland? No? A stupid question given the situation, given we really don't have much time left.'

It was stupid.

'Mrs Sutherland? Can I come up and get your daughter now?'

She heard a stair creak under his weight. 'Stay where you are!' she hissed.

'Okay,' the voice replied. 'I'm right here, not going anywhere.'

Oh God she wanted to trust him.

He said I could keep hold of my gun, didn't he? He said that. If he meant to harm Leona, why would he allow me to keep hold of it?

She was about to lower her weapon and cautiously accept his help when a thought occurred to her.

'How did you know Leona was here, not at her home?'

Mike looked at Andy. 'You're kidding me, right?'

They heard three rounds being fired in quick succession.

Fuck it.

Andy reached out, grabbed the lamp and hurled it across the room against the wall. It smashed and the room was thrown into darkness. As the three men recoiled in surprise, Andy was already on his feet. He shoved hard against Mike, knocking him on to his back, and cannoned into another of the men on his way out of the room, into the hallway, and out through the open front door, on to the moonlit street.

His feet pounded the tarmac as he weaved around a mattress, the broken remains of chairs and a table, and other household bric-à-brac strewn across the avenue.

He shot a glance at their home on the left as he sprinted past it. It had been broken into like all the other houses, the front door wide open and their things smashed and discarded in the front garden.

Up ahead on his right, was Jill's house.

He kicked the gate aside, and raced up the garden path in a couple of seconds. The front door was shut. He could see that it had been damaged, a large ragged hole had been kicked through the wooden panelling. He charged the door with his shoulder without breaking stride. The last hinge gave way, and the door clattered loudly on to the hallway floor.

'JENNY!' he shouted, his voice echoed around inside. There was no response, just a silence that had his blood running cold and the dawning realisation that he had so nearly made it home in time to save his family.

He'd heard the executioner's shots; one for his wife, one for each of his children, and it was all over.

Then he heard it, faintly, the sound of sobbing coming from the top of the stairs. He could see absolutely nothing, but it grew louder and more distinct as it migrated down the stairs, and then it was beside him. In the wan glow of the moon, he saw two pale white hands reach out for him.

'Oh God, Andy!' Jenny cried, grasping him tightly and burying her head into his shoulder. 'Andy! Andy!' she sobbed uncontrollably.

'Jenny,' he had to ask, 'Jenny … the kids?'

She looked up at him, 'They're both all right.'

'I heard gunshots.'

She was about to answer, when a beam of torchlight fell across them, and they heard the sound of footsteps pounding down the avenue towards them.

'Oh God!' she gasped, breaking her hold on Andy and producing a gun.

'Give it to me,' he said. She handed it to him and he trained it on a space above the nearest bobbing torch.

'Who are they?' she whispered, as the torch's motion slowed to a halt and the sound of footfalls ceased.

'I don't know yet.'

'Andy!' Mike called out from the darkness just beyond the garden gate. 'Don't be stupid, there's three of us, and one of you. Lower the gun.'

Andy wasn't ready to surrender. In the last minute, he had gone from absolute certainty that his family had been murdered, to finding out they were unharmed and now, quite possibly, were about to fall victim to these men.

'Who the fuck are you, Mike?' his voice rasped.

'We're the good guys Andy, the good guys, trust me,' the American replied, sounding short of breath, recovering from the pursuit.

'He said there were men outside after our daughter,' said Jenny.

'He?' replied Mike. 'Who?'

Andy looked at her.

'He was here moments ago, on the stairs. He said he'd come to protect Leona. I told him to stay where he was …' Her voice faltered. '… But he didn't listen … I fired … and then he ran away.'

'Andy,' said Mike. '*They* are here, they know where she is. You've got to trust me now.'

Andy kept the gun levelled.

'Look, if we wanted your daughter dead, I wouldn't be talking with you right now – we'd already be stepping over your bodies and on our way inside. Think about it.'

From the top of the stairs, Andy heard Jacob calling out.

'Is Daddy home?'

CHAPTER 86

10.25 p.m. GMT

Shepherd's Bush, London

They sat together in the ransacked lounge, illuminated only by a couple of scented candles Jenny had found in a kitchen drawer. Andy and his family were gathered together on Jill's leather sofa, slashed and stained, and Mike sat opposite them on the one wooden kitchen chair that hadn't been smashed to pieces.

'There's some fresh blood at the bottom of the stairs. I think you hit something,' he said.

'He just kept coming closer,' whispered Jenny.

'You did the right thing,' Mike replied. 'If you had let him come another step closer you and your children would be …' He looked at Jacob's wide-eyed expression. 'Well, he would have acquired his target.'

'Me?' muttered Leona.

Mike nodded.

Andy shook his head. 'Look Mike, if that's really your name—'

The American smiled, 'Mike's my first name, yeah.'

'I really don't know who the hell you are now; I thought I did, back in Iraq … but I haven't got a clue now. All I know is that some very powerful bastards want my girl. Who are they Mike? And for that matter where do you,' he shot a glance at one of Mike's men standing guard in the hallway, 'and your sidekicks, fit into all of this?'

'I can tell you a lot more about us than I can about them,' he replied. 'Which is why your daughter is so important to us.'

'Let's start with you then.'

Mike shrugged. 'I work for an … let's call it an *agency*. A small operation, once upon a time part of the FBI, that was a long time ago. Now we're privately funded, which allows us to stay off the radar. We do one thing in this agency Andy, just one thing … we try to find *them*.' He stroked his beard as he considered how to continue.

'They … *they* … don't even have a name; they're that smart. They don't have a logo, or a motto, they don't have a headquarters, they don't reside in any particular country, they don't have any political allegiance, or ideology; they are just wealth and influence. They're a club. We … my little agency was set up forty years ago Andy, in 1963 to be precise, after this club decided they'd put the wrong man in the White House.'

'My God … Kennedy?'

Mike nodded. 'It was his brother, Robert, that put us together in the aftermath. And that's why the bastards nailed him too. And we've had to operate off the grid since then.'

'Shit,' Andy whispered.

'Yeah. Eight years ago you did some work for a bunch of very dangerous and powerful people. Breaking through the secrecy around them has been virtually impossible. In forty years we've learned little more than they number 160 members, and twelve who make the big decisions.'

'You must have an idea who these people are, right?'

'We can guess. That's pretty much all we've been able to do. We've only ever had one informant; if you're up on European politics you'd probably recognise the name … he talked to us twice, briefly, before they got to him.' He looked briefly from Andy to Leona.

'And then we come to you two,' he sighed. 'Andy, you did business with *Them* – you actually dealt directly with the Twelve. Did you have any idea what you were dealing with?'

Andy shrugged, 'I guessed they were oil execs.'

Mike chuckled. 'The world's a pyramid of power. Everyone makes the mistake of thinking the apex of the pyramid is government. That's the big mistake. *Governments* are merely a tool for them to use. You have corporations, and they're owned by bigger corporations, who in turn are owned by even bigger corporations. The bigger they get, the less familiar people are with the corporate names. Ultimately these huge corporations are owned by banks that in turn are controlled by bigger banks, again, with names that aren't commonly known … and ultimately these bigger banks are owned by shareholders; very rich, very reclusive shareholders. If I was to hazard a guess at who the Twelve members are, I'd start there.'

'But, it seems,' he smiled at Leona, 'you actually saw some of them. More importantly, you recognised one of their faces; someone who was on the television just before things went screwy, right?'

Leona nodded. 'I don't know who he is though, I don't know the name.'

'It doesn't matter. Because what we're going to do is get you out of here to somewhere safe, and then we'll show you a whole bunch of photographs, and all you've got to do is say which ones you saw.'

He turned back to Andy. 'Your daughter has in her head, right now, the most important nugget of information in the world. And that makes her very precious to us, and dangerous to them.'

'What about the man who was here?' asked Jenny. 'He was one of them then?'

Mike was cautious. 'He's gone, but maybe not too far. We'll sit tight until we've got daylight.'

'What if he comes back?' asked Andy.

'I've got my men covering the front and back doors. They're well-equipped and well-trained; they're packing night scopes and body armour, both very capable men.'

Jenny shook her head. 'You know I almost let him up. He was so believable.'

'And he's lethal too,' cut in Mike. 'I think he's someone we know of. Well, at least, we know of his work. He's their best field-operative, I'm certain they've used this same man many times before. He works on his own, completely autonomously.

I've never seen him but I've seen his handiwork.' He stopped himself. 'Not nice. I just wish we had more information on him.'

Jenny turned to Andy, 'We're safe aren't we? I mean the kids … you and me?'

Andy squeezed her hand, 'I think we are now,' he replied tiredly. 'We've survived the worst of it, Jen.'

Mike got up and patted Andy on the shoulder. 'Your husband turned out to be a real alpha-male back in Iraq, a sharp thinker – a good field-man,' he said. 'If you still don't think you can trust me, you can certainly trust him.'

Jenny nodded and looked up at her husband. 'I do,' she said. 'I'm so sorry that I didn't, you know, before this.'

'You guys might want to get some sleep, if you can. We're all leaving here at first light,' said Mike. 'We'll take you somewhere safe.'

'Okay. We'll sleep down here, if that's okay?'

'Fine. That's nice and close where I can keep an eye on you,' he said with a reassuring nod. 'Get some sleep. I'll go and check on my fellas.'

Mike stepped out of the room, and left them to snuggle down together on the sofa. There were a couple of sleepy questions from Jacob that neither Andy nor Jenny could answer adequately. Then they curled up together, and after a few more whispered words, and some more shared tears of relief, Jenny, Leona and Jacob were fast asleep.

Andy felt a week of fatigue creeping up on him quickly. The chorus of rustling, even, untroubled breathing of his family asleep, and the distant murmur of Mike conferring with his colleagues outside, was comforting enough that he finally allowed himself to join them.

CHAPTER 87

11.36 p.m. GMT

Shepherd's Bush, London

The lucky bitch had caught him with one of those three shots. It cracked his collarbone on the way in and tore a bloody exit wound from the rear of his shoulder on the way out.

He would have carried on up the stairs, finished her off with a quick swipe of his blade, and gutted the two children in two blinks of an eye. But he knew the sound of the gun would have those men outside running.

He would have been trapped upstairs with nowhere to go.

Ash beat a retreat out through the front door and crouched amongst the clutter on the avenue. The father, Sutherland, passed within a few feet of him and then those three men, seconds later. None of them saw him squatting down in the middle of the avenue, visible amongst the mess to anyone who bothered to look closely enough. He remained absolutely motionless, knowing movement would draw someone's eye, and watched them from the darkness.

When finally the big American man, *Mike*, had won over Mrs Sutherland, they went inside … and he could move. He let himself into the house opposite, pulled some clothing out of a wardrobe and ripped a length of material to use as a bandage. He bound it diagonally and tightly round his neck and down under his left armpit, grimacing with every movement of his left arm. It wasn't going to stop the bleeding, but the compression would slow it.

The bullet had sheered some nerves or tendons in his left shoulder, and he found his arm dangling uselessly by his side.

If it had been the other side, his knife arm, that might have presented a bit of a problem.

Sitting in the darkness of the house, he assessed the situation.

Three on one.

They were all packing guns with night scopes and wearing vests, whilst he had a knife.

Ash smiled; they didn't stand a chance.

He knew they were nervous, they'd be jumping at shadows. Ash's reputation had a habit of preceding him, and he knew these men were well aware of his work. That always worked in his favour; their nerves would get the better of them. He knew what they would do – they would stay there until daylight, rather than risk moving out into the dark. There'd be a man posted at the rear of the house in that sun lounge, watching the back garden, and another guarding the front door.

They know I'm wounded. There'd be fresh blood on the floor. That might make them a little more confident ... *a little foolhardy perhaps?*

He smiled. Even with the use of only one arm, they were going to be putty in his hands. He suspected that they – knowing he was wounded – might even be foolish enough to attempt to trap him, to capture him alive, if an opportunity presented itself.

That's how they'd come unstuck, he realised. These boys were jumpy and keen to bag him as quickly as possible, of that he had no doubt.

He knew what to do.

'It's got to be the same guy that they're using,' Mike murmured quietly to the man standing beside him in the doorway. 'I wish we had more on this sonofabitch.'

He scanned the street silently; the only noise the gentle murmur of a light breeze through the branches that arched over the avenue.

'You think this guy's coming back?' asked Blaine in a

hushed voice, sweeping the road outside through the scope on his pistol.

'Of course he will. Come on, you know who we're dealing with.'

'Yeah, I guess I was hoping maybe they'd used someone else this time.'

'Too much at stake, Blaine. They were only ever going to send this guy to clean up.'

Blaine nodded, and licked his lips nervously.

'Just relax. The bottom line is, no matter how good he is, he's only human.'

'Sometimes I wonder.'

'What?'

'If he *is* just human,' Blaine grinned sheepishly. 'I mean in our dossier, somebody nicknamed this guy "the ghost".'

'Whoever decided to come up with that was a moron. He's just a good freelancer who's managed to stay lucky so far. Well, up to now that is. Andy's wife got him at least once. My biggest worry is the bastard has scampered off and died somewhere out there. It would have been good to get a hold of him. God knows how much *he* knows about *them*.'

'Kind of embarrassing that, eh? In the end it's an untrained civilian, a woman at that, who finally nailed the ghost.'

'Blaine, you call him that again, and I'll shoot you dead,' whispered Mike, not entirely joking. 'Now shut up and concentrate.'

'Right.'

They stood in silence for a full minute before Blaine opened his mouth to ask another question.

'Shhh … less talk, more watching,' whispered Mike.

'Okay boss.'

It was then that Mike thought he saw a flicker of movement in the upstairs window of the house opposite. He tapped Blaine on the shoulder.

'Straight ahead, first floor window on the left.'

The man raised the line of his night scope. 'Shit, yeah … I saw something move.'

Mike had to evaluate quickly.

He's upstairs in that house. He's trapped, stairs the only way down – that or out the window with the chance of breaking a leg. He's already been wounded, perhaps two or three hits. We've got a good chance of nailing this cocksucker tonight. Catch him alive, we might even get him to talk. Bonus.

'We can trap him if we move right now.'

Blaine nodded, 'Fuck it, you're right.'

'Cover!' hissed Mike. He headed across the avenue, scooting through the rubbish, whilst Blaine kept his weapon trained on the window. Mike signalled for Blaine to join him against the wall beside the open front door. The man scrambled over quickly and quietly, and presently squatted down beside him.

'There's still movement up in that room. He's up to something in there.'

'Right, standard room-by-room procedure ... only we know downstairs is clear. I'll take point.'

Blaine nodded.

Mike entered first, his pistol and scope aimed up the narrow stairs to the first floor.

These houses are all built the same; small bathroom at the top, landing doubles round, three bedroom doors in a row on the left, boiler cupboard at the far end.

He took the first few steps and then paused, listening for any sound of movement from up above. It was silent, except for the occasional gust of wind coursing through the broken windows of the house, moaning gently. He waved to Blaine, who climbed the stairs quietly, squeezed past Mike and went another half a dozen beyond him – nearly to the top.

They waited to see if they'd been detected, for some sort of reaction. However, it remained silent, except for the rustling of paper and plastic bags being teased gently across the avenue.

Mike overtook his man. Reaching the top of the stairs he whipped his gun one way then the other, staring intently through the scope.

If this was the ghost ... then he was a very slippery sonofabitch.

They knew painfully little about him, except he favoured a long thin knife, and had been described by the few people who had encountered him – and lived – as looking Middle Eastern. He had no name, and a million names; using a new alias on every job. And he was used exclusively by *them*. Mike knew of three jobs that had his unique signature on them. There was the fireman from Ladder 57 who claimed to have discovered un-detonated demolition charges amidst the rubble at Ground Zero and had died as the result of a *supposed* street stabbing. The minister in Saddam Hussein's government who had a *world shattering* revelation to make, and then was supposed to have slit his own throat. And there was that Russian banker championing the sale of Tengiz oil in euros instead of dollars – all of them victims of a never-recovered, narrow-bladed knife. All of them victims, Mike was certain, of this guy.

He waved Blaine up and pointed to the bathroom at the top of the stairs. The man squeezed past him. And after silently counting to three, he lent deftly in to check the bathroom was clear.

'It's clear,' he whispered.

Mike decided playing quiet was pointless. This man undoubtedly knew they were inside the house with him.

'We know who you are,' said Mike. 'We know your work.'

There was no reply.

'You're *their* man, you only work for *them*. We've been watching you.'

Silence.

'We will take you, and that will probably mean killing you in the process. If you come out unarmed, then we can at least talk.'

The only sound was the flapping of a curtain coming from a front room.

Damn.

Mike had hoped they could bag this guy alive. He was too dangerous to fuck around with. If they were going to *take* him, then they'd have to go in hard, and go for a quick kill.

He signalled to Blaine that he would take the next room.

Again they counted down, he kicked the door, and stepped in, sweeping his gun frantically one way then the other. It was clear.

Blaine took the next, again nothing.

So by a process of elimination … the last room.

'I'll take this one,' whispered Mike. 'Watch my back, I want you right behind me as we go in.'

The man nodded. 'Got it, Mike.'

He took a deep breath, counted down from five silently, sticking his hand up so that Blaine, crouched behind him, could see the fingers folding down one after the other.

Three … two … one …

Mike kicked the door, and barged into the front bedroom, rolling to a stop against the opposite wall. He whipped his gun around, left then right – scoping the room with rapid jerking movements. His aim was drawn almost instantly towards something moving near the bedroom's window. It was a bed sheet, draped over what looked like a floor-standing lamp, the breeze was toying with it, fluttering the corners of cotton. That's what they'd seen through the window from the front door of the Sutherlands' house.

'Shit!' muttered Mike. 'It's clear,' he called out.

It was obvious they'd been played with. The bastard had lured them out.

'Blaine! Back to the fucking house! RUN!'

Mike turned on his heels to head out of the room. Out on the landing, at the top of the stairs he saw Blaine's body, stretched out like he was taking a nap.

And that's when he felt a vicious punch to his kidneys. There was an explosion of pain and his first thought was that the well-aimed punch had hit a vulnerable nerve-cluster. But reaching to grab his side, he felt a protruding shaft, and a wetness on his fingers.

'Oh fuck,' he grunted. Something had found the three-inch gap between the front and rear plates of his vest.

'Yes,' whispered a voice in his ear, 'it's fatal. You have no more than five minutes to live. If you lie still, maybe a minute or two longer.

Mike felt his legs buckle, and as he slumped down, he felt the knife come out, and a hand grabbed him under each armpit. He felt himself being gently lowered to the ground.

CHAPTER 88

11.54 p.m. GMT
Shepherd's Bush, London

Ash kneeled over him. He snapped on a torch and checked the man's wound. The blood was jetting out in rhythmic spurts.

'Understand,' said Ash gently, 'this will be a relatively easy death. The painful bit is over. Bleeding out will be relatively quick. I apologise for not making it instant,' he said with a hint of regret.

The dying man stared up at him, expressions of bewilderment and anger flickering across his face. Ash could empathise with the anger; to be caught off guard like that … lured out and skewered.

'You must be Mike, I'm guessing by deduction,' he said. 'Yes, just a silly trick. The sheet, over the lamp, and the help of a light breeze.'

'Fucking shit trick,' groaned Mike.

'Let me ask you. Do you believe in God?'

Mike laughed defiantly and winced. 'No I fucking don't.'

'Maybe now's a good a time as any to find some faith, eh? Hedge your bets.'

'You know … a friend of mine assured me … God accepts non-believers too … it's just assholes he doesn't let in.'

That was quite funny, he liked this American's defiance in the face of death. It was admirable.

Mike grunted something, his voice warbling and weakening.

'You're asking about your other colleague in the house? Yes, I'm afraid he's dead too. I did him first. You probably didn't hear him drop did you? Too busy chatting away at the front.'

Mike grasped one of his hands. 'Let the … family … go,' he struggled between gasps to get the words out.

'Sorry, they're on my "to do" list,' he replied and then smiled down at him, with a shred of sympathy it seemed, as the American struggled to draw air in. 'We know you've been out there watching us for a long time – your humble agency. The funny thing is, we've been trying to track you down as well.'

They … they had known of it, and hunted for this persistent nuisance, whilst this microdot of an agency, in turn, had been doing the same; two predators blindly stalking each other over four decades, their subtle tracks imprinted on recent history.

To be fair, the agency was no real match for the people Ash kept things tidy for. The resources of a couple of dozen field and desk agents and the black budget that kept them ticking over, versus the sort of wealth, power and influence that decided world leaders, initiated and concluded wars, timed and controlled global economic cycles. No real match there, a proverbial David and Goliath.

This man's agency though, had done well, identifying and homing in on the only weak link in their chain, the traitor … the son-in-law and heir-apparent to one of the highest echelon – one of the Twelve; the young man, a banker, a member of the lower order, who had suddenly got cold feet – he had given this agency just enough to zero in on Dr A. Sutherland.

Of course all of this unpleasantness now, chasing around this shitty little country, could have been avoided if they'd let him finish that girl in the hotel room, back in New York.

Hypocrites.

They were preparing to orchestrate events that were ultimately going to lead to the deaths of hundreds of millions, and yet they didn't have the stomach to witness the death firsthand of one solitary child. He realised, in some ways, he had more in common with this man before him, than the privileged and pampered elite that he worked for.

'You nearly exposed them. You nearly won, my friend. The girl could have identified three of the Twelve for you.'

Ash knew then that he alone had a unique status … knowing more than any of the members of the lower order; he had been entrusted with an almost sacred confidentiality because he was their personal watchdog. He knew these twelve men, and they were not brave men; they were weak.

Knowing the identity of just one of them would be enough for this determined, tenacious little agency. They'd find a way to get to an identified member, they'd find a way to get him to talk, that wouldn't be so hard.

'You came so close,' Ash said.

'Fuck you,' grunted Mike. 'We know all about you shitheads.'

Mike tried to move, to reach out towards his gun, dropped on the landing just a few feet away. Ash kicked it casually across the floor and out of reach.

'Stay still,' he cautioned Mike, 'or you'll bleed out faster. I want you to know my friend, because, well … because you've *earned* it.'

The American could do little but nod weakly.

'Know *all* about us?' Ash laughed. 'You don't know anything. What you know is just the little bit you've managed to scratch off the surface. You think a group of fat industrialists in expensive suits are behind this, don't you? It goes much higher. You can trace the reins of power up through banks that own banks that own banks to just a dozen names.'

Mike frowned, struggling through the growing fogginess to comprehend what he was hearing.

'The world is owned by a dozen families headed by a dozen men, some of whom have surnames that even the mindless sheep on the streets would recognise, and other names that have always remained hidden.

'And believe me when I say their influence, even before recent years, was pretty damn impressive.' He leant over Mike, moving closer to his face. It looked like the American's pupils were beginning to dilate, as he started his inevitable slide into unconsciousness.

'These people I work for … you can see their fingerprint everywhere in history, Mike, fingerprints smeared everywhere like a crime scene. Take the Second World War for instanc …'

Mike's breathing caught.

'Oh yeah,' Ash grinned, 'that was their ill-conceived attemp to stifle the further spread of communism. They've never like popular uprisings. They *made* Hitler, they paved the way for him … so long as he did what he was told, he was unassailable. Bu then, of course, he went *off script*, and the rest, as they say, i history.'

'The war …?'

'Yes, of course, it was orchestrated by them.'

Mike tried to gurgle something.

'Did you know the American Civil War was a power strug gle amongst members of the lower order? That war was just a squabble between two groups of business men. What about you War of Independence? That was *them* struggling to keep a hol of the colonies, via England. Of course, they lost that war. Bu then, instead, down the road they *bought* the country, throug investment.'

Ash laughed gently. 'Your history Mike, American history .. don't you see? It was written by a cartel of European families The wars, the hundreds of thousands of dead young America boys, the poverty and hardship, the great depression, two worl wars … ultimately nothing more than a boardroom struggl amongst the ruling elite; the growing pains, my friend, of thei influence.'

Mike struggled to talk. A small trickle of black-as-oil bloo trickled from the side of his mouth and ran down into his beard

'Why … this?'

'What's happening now?' Ash cut in. The dying man nodded but it was nothing but the weakest twitch of his head. Ash looke down at the blade in his hand, it needed cleaning. He wiped i along the length of Mike's shirt-sleeve.

'They decided it, Mike, it was something that needed t

be done; a correction, an adjustment, a little bit of house cleaning.'

Ash paused.

'It's running out, you know?' he said. 'There's a lot less of it than people think … oil. Yes, a lot less than the publicly stated reserves. They decided there were simply too many of us all expecting our oil-rich luxuries, all expecting our big cars, big homes, and an endless supply of power and oil to feed them. It wasn't going to last for much longer. They knew that fact long before anyone else. And they knew that there were going to be wars, horrific wars, most probably with a few nukes being thrown around … for the last of that oil. And you don't want that – nukes being thrown around. They knew economic necessity, oil-hunger, would drive us to destroy ourselves. And I suppose you can see it from their point of view, after struggling so hard for … well, one could say, since the Middle Ages, they didn't want to see it all thrown away. You can see how annoying that might be, can't you?'

He slid his blade back into his ankle sheath.

'So they made the decision at a gathering back in 1999. A decision to lance the boil, if you'll excuse such a crude euphemism. They chose to cull mankind, before we went too far down that road. You see Mike, these people I work for, they're like … I don't know … they're like caretakers, quietly steering things, balancing things, keeping those big old cogs turning. They did this for the sake of us all … because it needed to be done.'

He studied the face of the dying American. There still seemed to be life in those glazed eyes, Mike was still hearing this, he was sure.

'So, the decision was made back in '99, right at the end of that year,' Ash laughed gently, 'as the sheep all prepared to celebrate an exciting new century and got all worked up about that millennium bug, and had their big, big parties, and nursed sore heads the morning after. It was decided that things needed to be put in place for this; to get everything ready to turn the taps off.'

Ash nudged Mike. 'You see, that's the great thing about oil, it really *is* our oxygen, our life's blood … it's the *perfect controlling mechanism*. If you turn the tap up, the world gets really busy; you turn it down enough, things grind to a halt. It's like the throttle on a motorbike – a perfect device.'

The American let out a bubbling gasp of air, a noise Ash recognised as a man's final gasp.

'It's taken them some time to organise this, a very big project you see. And you know, everything since '99 …' he looked down at Mike. His pupils had completely dilated now and gazed sightlessly up at the ceiling. He wasn't hearing him any more.

'Everything, I mean, *everything* – all starting with two passenger jets crashing into New York – *everything* since then, my friend, has been about one thing; getting the world ready for this … the culling.'

The American was dead.

'Pity,' said Ash, and listened for a moment to the breeze, whistling along the landing and down the stairs. He'd wanted this dying man to hear it all, to understand why it had to happen, perhaps even to agree with him that it was a measure that had to be taken, for mankind's benefit. But most probably a good portion of what he'd said had made no sense in the man's dying mind.

'Pity.'

He closed the American's eyes and got to his feet, grunting with pain. Sutherland's wife had hit him in the collarbone, and even though he'd bound the wound up efficiently, he knew all was not well – he was bleeding internally.

He felt a little light-headed.

Not good.

There were still some loose ends to tidy up.

Sunday

CHAPTER 89

12.01 a.m. GMT

Shepherd's Bush, London

Andy awoke. Something had disturbed him; a noise, one of the kids stirring? His eyes opened and he let them adjust to the dark whilst he sat still, listening.

Just the breeze outside. Mike and his colleagues were silent; there was no quiet, wary murmuring as there had been earlier.

That's worrying.

He eased himself out of the tangle of limbs on the sofa and walked quietly across to the door that opened on to the hallway. He looked to his left and saw the weak light of the moon casting flickering half-shadows of branches and leaves through the open front door on to the smooth parquet floor.

Where's Mike?

He turned to the right. The hallway led to the rear of the house and Jill's sun lounge. He wondered if they were gathered back there. If they were he'd be bloody worried – leaving the front door unguarded like that?

A dozen light, soundless steps down the hall and he stood in the doorway. His eyes, now more accustomed to the dark, couldn't pick out any shape that might be someone standing guard.

'Hello?' he whispered. 'Anyone awake?'

There was no reply and, with a shudder of realisation, he knew something must have happened. His hand reached for the gun tucked into his trousers. He felt some small comfort sensing the rough carbon grip of the handle.

Then he sensed the draught of movement behind him.

He whipped round, the gun raised and ready to fire.

'Shit Dad! It's me!' Leona whimpered.

He exhaled. 'Christ, Lee, I nearly blew a hole in your head.'

She smiled and shrugged. 'Sorry,' she whispered. 'What are you doing up, anyway?'

'I can't find Mike and his guys.'

Her mouth dropped and her eyes widened. 'Oh God!' she cried a little too loudly.

He raised a finger to his mouth to hush her.

There can't have been a fight. Surely any shots fired would have awoken us all? They're out in the front garden, checking something out, maybe?

He took a step into the hall again and his foot slipped in something. He looked down and noticed a dark mat on the floor.

'You bring a torch?' he whispered.

Leona nodded.

'Shine it on the floor.'

She switched it on, and instantly recoiled at the bright red pool at their feet.

'Oh shit!' she hissed.

Andy grabbed the torch from her and panned it around the sun lounge. The beam picked out one of Mike's men curled in a foetal position behind the wicker armchair beside them.

They're here!

'Get behind me!' he whispered into her ear. He snapped off the torch, turned and headed up the hallway again, towards the lounge; slow, cautious steps, his gun arm extended, sweeping with quick jerks from one side to the other.

Andy knew there was only one course of action to take. Grab Jenny and Jacob, get out of the house, and run, and run … and keep running. He swung his aim up the stairs, a dark abyss that could be hiding anything.

They reached the open doorway to the lounge. He could hear Jacob stirring, no longer the even rasp of rest, but short tremulous gasps.

'Jenny we have to leave now,' he said, quietly snapping on the torch again.

The halo of light fell on Jacob, standing. A dark forearm was wrapped across his narrow shoulders, and above the tuft of blond hair he saw the dark face of a man, smiling mischievously. The tip of a long, thin-bladed knife was pressed into his son's pale neck, creating a dimple that threatened to burst blood if another gram of pressure was applied to it.

Jenny was on her knees, on the floor, rocking, too frightened to cry, too frightened even to breathe.

'Lose the gun, Andy Sutherland,' the man said calmly.

Andy kept the weapon trained on him.

You drop the gun and that's it for bargaining.

'I won't do that, mate,' Andy said.

Jenny turned to look at him. 'What? Andy! For fuck's sake! Drop the gun!'

He hushed her with a wave of his hand. 'I can't do that Jenny. If I do that, we die.'

The man smiled. 'Your husband's being quite sensible under the circumstances, Mrs Sutherland.'

He looked up at Andy. 'We can talk for a bit anyway. I think I'd like that. You can call me Ash, by the way.'

He's in no hurry. That means …

'The others?' Andy nodded towards the front door. 'They're out there somewhere … dead?'

Ash nodded. 'Just a little too keen to try and take me alive.'

'So, this is all about what my daughter thought she saw, right?'

'What we *know* she saw. You see, this lovely young lady,' he said gesturing with his knife-hand, a flick of the wrist that took the blade away from Jacob's throat for a moment, 'knows enough to be very dangerous. When things start sorting themselves out again—'

'You are mightily fucking mistaken,' Andy sneered, 'if you think things are going to sort themselves out.'

Ash cocked an eyebrow.

'What? You thought it would?' he asked, genuinely incredulous.

'They will ensure the oil flows again, when the time's right.'

Andy shook his head and sighed. 'It doesn't work that way. I thought I made that patently bloody clear in my report. It's a zero sum thing. You don't just bounce back from something like this. I don't know what fucking morons you work for, but they've seriously screwed things up.'

The blade returned to Jacob's neck. 'Whatever. You're the *big expert.*'

Andy nodded. 'Yeah … yeah, you got that right. I've spent enough time thinking about it over the years.'

'Nonetheless, I have my objective,' his blade-hand flicked away again from Jacob's neck, the tip pointing towards Leona, '… her.'

Leona sobbed. 'Oh, please …'

Ash shrugged, pouting a lip with sympathy. 'I'm afraid so, my dear. However we resolve this situation, I can't let you walk away. I can, however, make it quick and painless.'

'Oh Christ! Oh God! Andy, don't let him. DON'T LET HIM!' Jenny cried.

'I really don't see how you can stop me,' said Ash.

Andy noticed a blood-soaked bandage of material wrapped tightly around his shoulder.

Is he losing blood slowly? Can I stall him until he drops?

'Look, it's over. It's out of control. Whoever you're working for isn't going to be able to make things right again. They're screwed, we're screwed, even you … you're screwed too. It really doesn't matter what my daughter saw,' said Andy, 'not any more. Because once things shut down at the scale that they have done, there's no going back.'

'I think you're talking shit.'

'Am I? How long will it take for the Saudi refineries to come on tap? How long will it take to get the Baku refineries, the Paraguaná refinery? Months is my best guess. And that's plenty of time for things to get worse; for the likes of China and Russia to see an opportunity, for every simmering border dispute to flare up, for the US economy to drop into free fall. Don't forget, that's an economy that's remained afloat for the last thirty years on the value of trillions of petro-dollars. That's been wiped out.'

'And so I should just let your little girl walk away?'

Oh fuck, am I convincing him?

'You know, maybe the world needed something like this,' said Andy.

Ash eyed him warily.

'We're a planet that was only ever capable of supporting what? Two? Three billion? We were well on our way towards eight billion before this happened,' Andy continued. 'I don't know who's behind this, and I don't know why they've done this. But … maybe something like this needed to happen?'

Ash nodded. 'Of course it did,' he said, his voice sounded thick and lazy.

Make it sound good Andy.

'So, listen. Maybe I agree with the people you work for? Hmm? Okay it's not nice. But at least this has been a global sacrifice; everyone has paid the price, right? Not just … say, the Third World.'

Ash nodded again.

'I can see now, this needed to happen. Even if we knew, we're not about to go and tell the world *who* made it happen,' he turned to Leona, 'are we honey?'

Leona shook her head vigorously, 'No, n-no.'

'Please … she doesn't *need* to die.'

Ash swayed slightly. 'Almost convincing. But I have my contract.'

'Contract?' Andy shook his head. 'You do realise the money you're being paid, if it isn't already worthless, this time next week it will be.'

Ash frowned, irritated by that. 'It's not about fucking money,' he snapped.

Andy noticed he was beginning to slur his words.

'Well, what is it about, for Christ's sake? Why does my girl have to die?'

Ash sighed, his grip loosened and the point of his knife

dropped away again from the scored skin on Jacob's neck. He pursed his lips with thought. 'You see, it's about professional pride, I guess. It's about finishing the job.'

Oh Christ. This isn't about money, or conviction …

'There's a reason why I know their identities … The Twelve, the most powerful men in the world. It's because I'm reliable. It's because I *always* finish the job, I always come through. I'm the best freelancer. The best there is. That means something –'

This is about pride. I won't be able to reason with him …

'– to me. It's what I am. I've become the best there is. I've earned that. So you see, I really don't give a shit about her life. I've killed much younger, much more innocent victims, believe me. It's water off a duck's back.'

Ash swayed enough that he staggered slightly.

'I'm not that interested in hearing any more impassioned pleas for mercy, that's not going to help you one little bit. Oh fuck it … you know what?'

Ash was expecting him to answer.

'What?'

'I'm now getting a little bored with this.'

Shit, is he weakening? Is this the wound talking?

'So, here's how it goes. Drop your gun, and you can have Tiny Tim back unharmed, and in return, I'll have your daughter, please.'

'Oh God, no, don't … !' cried Jenny.

'Shut up!' Ash spat, his calm, softly spoken voice, raised for the first time. 'The alternative is – I'll finish him in a blink, and be upon you, Sutherland, gutting you before you know it. And then, of course, I'll be able to take all the time in the world with your wife and your daughter. So how's that sound to you?'

Ash swayed again, ever so slightly. 'Decision time. I'll give you, let me see … yeah, let's say, five seconds. Five …'

Leona grabbed hold of Andy, she began screaming. 'Dad! Please! Don't let him kill me!'

'Four …'

Jacob's eyes were swollen with fear.

‘Three …’

Jenny sobbed uncontrollably on the floor, and Leona collapsed to her knees.

‘Two …’

Andy realised he’d now run out of options.

CHAPTER 90

12.07 a.m. GMT

Shepherd's Bush, London

He fired.

The shot missed his son by inches and punched a hole in Ash's chest, knocking him back against the wall. He pulled Jacob back with him, tumbling with him to the floor, the blade still held to his son's throat. Andy charged across the lounge, knowing in the three long strides it would take to reach them, this man could sink the blade in with one convulsive twitch of his hand.

Somewhere across the small room, his hand let go of the torch and it dropped to the floor, the beam of light bouncing and flailing around.

He hurled himself at where the man had gone down, and landed heavily on top of Jacob's writhing body. In the dark, Andy's hands fumbled around, desperately seeking the knife before it was pushed home and extinguished his son's life.

Jenny could hear both men struggling in the dark and Jacob's muffled voice, crying, presumably tangled up with them, sandwiched in between them, that blade still, presumably, inches away from his throat or his face. She reached out for the torch on the floor and swung it around.

By the light of the torch, she could see the man's and Andy's legs kicking and swinging around. She could see one of Jacob's little arms emerging from between both men's writhing torsos, it flapped around raining small ineffectual un-aimed blows on both the man and Andy.

She could hear both men grunting with effort, and then she saw the glint of the knife amidst the confused tangle of limbs.

Andy had a hold of the man's long knife by the blade. It was lacerating his fingers, and dots and splatters of Andy's blood flew up against the lounge wall.

The man lurched to one side, pulling Andy over with him. And then Jenny saw Jacob manage to wriggle some way out. She stepped toward him, reached out and grabbed Jacob's extended hand and pulled as hard as she could. He tumbled on to the floor with her, freed from the two men.

'Shoot him Andy!' she screamed, now that Jacob was safely out of the way. 'SHOOT HIM!'

The men rolled across the floor, behind the sofa, and now all she could see in the dancing light of the torch, were two pairs of legs, kicking, scissoring, flailing … and more blood flicking up on to the wall.

'Oh God, Mum!' howled Leona. 'He's gonna kill Dad! He's going to KILL DAD!'

Jenny looked around the floor, hoping that the gun might have been dropped and kicked clear in the struggle.

And then the room flickered as if a firecracker had gone off, and simultaneously they heard the bang of the gun.

Both pairs of legs ceased moving. Jenny studied them for a moment, unable to move, not daring to look behind the back of the sofa.

'Andy?' she whispered.

Then the man's – Ash's – legs began to move, a short, jerking, twitching movement. Andy's legs remained still.

'Andy?' she cried.

Ash's legs stopped moving.

'Oh shit!'

Andy's voice.

'Oh, shit!' Andy grunted again.

'Dad, are you all right?' cried Leona, her voice trembling.

'Ah, jeeez, that's just bloody disgusting,' sighed Andy.

Jenny watched his legs kick at the body as he emerged from beneath it, and a moment later she saw his bloodied and torn hands on the back of the sofa.

'Don't let the kids come round the back, Jenny,' he muttered. 'I've got most of this guy's brains down the front of my shirt.'

His face appeared and he pulled himself up, wincing as he looked down at the thick dark slick across his chest.

'Daddy won,' whispered Jacob, the hint of awe in his voice unmistakable. 'He beat the baddie.'

'Oh my God, Andy,' Jenny uttered. And that was all she could say for the moment. The 'God I Love You's … were all going to have to come later. For now the only thing that Jenny could do was sob with relief.

Andy looked up from the splattered debris of Ash's head on his shirt and offered his family a goofy grin.

'Should've changed my bloody shirt first. I liked this one.'

Leona and Jenny both managed to push a smile through the tears. Jacob grinned proudly at his father, then studied with a mixture of revulsion and fascination, the bloody mess.

'What's that?' Jake asked, pointing at another rapidly expanding crimson stain lower down the shirt.

Andy looked down, and saw the small, slim handle jutting out from his lower abdomen.

'Oh, just great,' he managed to mutter before collapsing.

Epilogue

It's been a while now since the world collapsed.

I miss Andy. I miss him so much. And his children miss him.

I don't know how we've survived, how we managed to keep going. It's been a blur to me, just moving from one day into the next. I know we left London soon after that night. I remember Leona had to drag me out of our house, away from our bedroom, where we left Andy.

Leona's been a tower of strength. I was useless for a long time. She got us out of London, and then we finally found a community in the countryside willing to take us in.

Very kind people, very different – historical re-enactors; the sort of people you would see at those big English Heritage events where they replayed battles from the English Civil War. Normal people with jobs and mortgages (back before the collapse), but with this other parallel life, attempting to revive, to learn the everyday skills of a time long before we had oil doing everything for us. Very different people, unlike any I've met before; they had already mastered so many of those skills of survival, the basics like ... how to make soap, how to make bread from grain. You know? The simple things.

And there's so much to do, we're kept busy, which is just as well.

We have several wind-up radios in the community, and from time to time there are broadcasts from the BBC World Service. For a time, just after the first week, it looked like a recovery might be on the cards. Oil lines were being fixed and a trickle of oil was getting through. But things were too broken, too messed up. We heard horror stories coming from the two dozen or so 'safe areas' the government had established. The supplies ran out at the end of the second month, and the people crammed inside turned on each other. And the same thing, so we hear, has happened in other countries around the world. America, I think, has been hit particularly badly.

In the months that followed, there was a worrying time … there was a limited war between China, India and Russia over the Tengiz oilfields. It started with tanks and infantry, and escalated to a few nuclear bombs. Then very quickly it blew itself out. Perhaps some sanity broke out at the last moment, or perhaps their troops decided to stop fighting. Or maybe they simply ran out of the oil they needed to continue fighting.

Often, in the evenings, when the community gathers together, we discuss who was behind it all. Because, you see, it's obvious to everyone now that there was someone behind this. The theories are many and varied. The most-voiced opinions are that it was either a Muslim plot to destroy the decadent western lifestyle, or, alternatively, an attempt by America to destabilise all her economic rivals in one go … but somehow it went wrong for them too.

I'm not convinced by either theory, but I don't know enough about politics to offer a better suggestion. Andy would have known. He knew all about that kind of thing.

We're being kept very busy right now, as I was saying. There's a lot to do, crops to grow, tend, cultivate or pick. We're digging a well, down to the clean water-table below us, and we have animals that need looking after. Jake's landed the main role as chicken tender; feeding them, collecting the eggs. When he's a little older, he'll also have to cope with killing them on occasion, plucking them, gutting them.

Leona's struggling a bit now. She was strong for me when I needed her. Now, she's finding it hard to cope. I know she misses her father, and I know some of the things that happened before I got home really traumatised her. There's a lot of crying.

Jacob misses Andy terribly too. But he's also so proud of his dad, and tells anyone who'll listen that his dad was a superhero. I love that he thinks that about Andy.

Anyway, we're alive, and my kids will mend eventually. And things will eventually knit themselves back together again. All those empty cities, full of burned-out homes, and looted shops … one day people will migrate back to them. When it all eventually comes back together again, I think it's going to be very different.

To use one of Andy's pet phrases … the oil age is over.

Just like all those other ages; the Stone Age, the Bronze Age, the Steam Age … it's been and gone. Hopefully what replaces it will be a world less greedy, less obsessed with having things; trinkets and baubles, gadgets and bling. I wonder what my children's children will make of the weathered and faded mail order catalogues they'll undoubtedly come across, everything lavishly powered by electricity; giant American-style fridge freezers, those extravagant patio heaters, electric sonic-pulse hi-spin toothbrushes, automatic can-openers.

God, did we really get that lazy?

That's something Andy would have said, isn't it? Christ, I miss him.

I need to say something though, out loud.

I'm pretty sure you won't hear this Andy, you're gone. There's none of that looking down from heaven nonsense, is there? You're gone, that's it. But all the same, I need to say this even if it's just for my own ears …

I'm sorry. I did always love you, I just forgot that for a while. You came back for us, and you saved us. Our son and our daughter will always, always remember you as a hero.

And so will I.

Love you, Andy.

Author's Note

Last Light started out four years ago as a result of my stumbling across a phrase being repeated over and over by two posters for a forum. They were hotly debating a geological issue and this phrase kept cropping up: Peak Oil. Being capitalised like that suggested that this was some sort of technical term in common use by those in the know. Curious, I Googled it.

And so, to indulge in an appalling cliché, a journey of discovery followed. Out there in internet-land are hundreds, perhaps thousands, of websites devoted to Peak Oil. I should perhaps explain what the term means before going any further. Simply put, it refers to the point at which all the easy-to-extract oil has been sucked out of the ground leaving only the really hard to get to, very expensive to refine, stuff. Now, there is a great deal of debate amongst geologists and petro-industry experts about how much oil there is left in the ground. It ranges from either a doom 'n' gloom scenario that we've already 'peaked' and it's rapidly running out, to a naively optimistic view that we have another fifty or sixty years of untapped oil. I'm not going to make a call on that debate here. But what no one disagrees on is how utterly reliant we are on the stuff. If you're reading this, having read the book, you don't need me to reiterate here the warnings Andy offered his family. The fact is, with *globalism* having run its course, the world is now inextricably linked as one large, interlocked set of dependencies; we get our sausages from *this* far flung country, our trainers from *that* far flung country, our plasma TVs from yet another far flung country ... and so on.

Whether we're about to run out of oil, or whether the world is approaching a clash of religious ideologies or an economic – possibly military – showdown between the new economic superpowers and the old; whether the world's climate is on the cusp of a dramatic change that could imperil billions and lead to mass migration; whichever one of these scenarios lies ahead of us, to be so completely dependent – as we are here in the UK – on produce grown, packaged and manufactured on the other side of the world … well, that's simply asking for trouble.

Last Light is the book I've wanted to, no, *needed* to write since … well, since 9/11. It's not really a book about Peak Oil – that was merely the starting point for me. No, it's a book about how lazy and vulnerable we've allowed ourselves to become. How reliant on the system we are. How little responsibility we are prepared to take for our actions, for ourselves, for our children. Somewhere along the way, in the last two or three decades, we *broke* this society of ours; whether it was during Blair's tenure of power, or Thatcher's, I'm not sure. But somehow it got broken.

And here we are, the ghastly events of 7/7; the increasing prevalence of gang related gun crime in London; legions of disaffected kids packing blades to go to school; a media that night and day pumps out the message – *screw everyone else, just get what's yours*; reality TV that celebrates effortless transitory fame over something as old-fashioned as 'achievement'; corporations that rip off their employees' pension funds; a Prime Minister deceiving us into entering an ill-conceived war; and politicians of all flavours putting themselves and their benefits first. All these things, I suspect, are the visible hairline cracks of our broken society that hint at the deeper, very dangerous, fault lines beneath. And all it'll take is some event, some catalyst, for the whole thing to come tumbling down.

Damn … this has turned into something of a rant, hasn't it? That wasn't my intention. Ah well sod it, 'author's note' is my one opportunity to get things off my chest without having to worry about plot, character and pacing.

Anyway, I'd like to think that a whiff of *Last Light* will remain with you once you snap the cover shut. I'm hoping Andy Sutherland achieved something; that the world looks slightly different to you now – more fragile, more vulnerable. After all, to be aware is to be better prepared.

I dunno … is it just me? Or do you get that feeling too? That something's coming, something on the horizon … a *correction* of some sort?

Peak Oil – Do you want to know more?

I came across numerous websites on this subject whilst researching for the book; they range from being very dry, statistics-heavy pages for industry insiders to the more bizarre survivalist sites that feature banner ads for automatic weapons and nuclear shelters. But one of the best laid-out sites that I came across – a site that spells out the whole issue in a way that is easily digestible and appropriately sobering – is this one:

http://www.lifeaftertheoilcrash.net

If this book has piqued your interest, and you want to follow the trail yourself, you can do far worse than start right there.

Alex Scarrow 12.09.07